Review

"*Celia Martin's new novel Perfidious Brambles is a delight. In deft and nimble strokes, she has created an entire world for us to revel in, rich in history and detail, so skillfully rendered that we can see the bricks of the old towers and the stones of the ancient walls. Her characters are finely drawn, and we feel we would know them were we to meet them at tea, each unique and very real. Readers will love the plot with its high romance and touch of intrigue. If you are looking for a lovely novel in which to get lost, you have certainly found it here.*"

—**Riana Everly, (rianaeverly.com) two Jane Austen Readers Awards for** *The Assistant and Through a Different Lens*, **and also the** *Discovering Diamonds review for Teaching Eliza*

Perfidious Brambles

Celia Martin

KITSAP
PUBLISHING

KITSAP PUBLISHING

Perfidious Brambles
First edition, published 2020

By Celia Martin

Book Layout: Tim Meikle, Reprospace

Copyright ©2020, Celia Martin

ISBN-13 Softcover: 978-1-952685-20-0

Published by Kitsap Publishing
P.O. Box 572
Poulsbo, WA 98370
www.KitsapPublishing.com

Also by Celia Martin

To Challenge Destiny

"Exquisite passion and breath-taking action! A historical romance feast!"

—Curt Locklear, Laramie Award Winner

"Martin proves she has the vision and talent to make bygone times come alive for modern readers."

—Anne Hollister, Professional Book Reviews

A Bewitching Dilemma

"A willful heroine cornered by a relentless foe and a dashing sea captain tormented by his past cast their lots against the tides of a history dark with treachery. A compelling read cover to cover."

—Michael Donnelly, Author of False Harbor

With Every Breath I take

A love story laced with fun and surprises

Taking A Chance

"I've no hesitation to recommend this five-star read to new or old readers of historical fiction."

—Trisha J. Kelly, multi-genre award-winning author of children and middle school books, and of cozy mysteries and crime thrillers.

"Celia Martin captures the complex landscape of people dealing with Puritanism which squelches the fun out of life for ordinary people. A great backdrop for the heroine to shine as she strives to marry the man she loves"

—C.A. Asbrey - author of the 19th century murder mysteries, 'The Innocents' and of articles on history for magazines and periodicals.

Precarious Game of Hide and Seek

"Celia Martin's historical romance ranks as above average fare in the this genre.

—Jason Hillenburg, Reprospace Reviews™

Fate Takes a Hand

"Each character, lovingly written, pulls the reader into the story, contributing to the elegance of this beautiful work of fiction. Love stories like this are timeless. If you are looking for a wonderful historical romance with a truly satisfying conclusion, I highly recommend Fate Takes A Hand."

—Kristen Morgen, Author of Behind The Glass

"Celia Martin's Fate Takes a Hand provides a reading experience any devotee of historical romantic fiction will enjoy and holds up under multiple readings."

—Jason Hillenburg, Reprospace Reviews™

And The Ground Trembled

"Celia Martin is an engaging storyteller. I absolutely loved And the Ground Trembled. It is beautifully written, entertaining, and a lot of fun"

—Vonda Sinclair, USA Today Bestselling Author

"I see fans of the historical romance genre flocking to Celia Martin's And the Ground Trembled. Lush descriptive passages, a vivid rendering of the historical period, and strong characterizations highlight this novel. Martin feels a strong personal connection with this era in history. The book shows her familiarity with even the smallest of details about its fashion, a keen ear for human speech of the time, and more than a nodding acquaintance with its history."

—Mindy McCall, Reprospace Reviews™

---

cmartinbooks.kitsappublishing.com

To my husband Ken for his never failing love and support.

A Collection of Romantic Adventures

Follow the romantic adventures of the D'Arcy, Hayward, and Lotterby families and their captivating friends in seventeenth century England and the American colonies. In Perfidious Brambles, Lady Timandra Lotterby accompanies her friend, Eliza Tilbury, to Northumberland and meets the man of her dreams, Gavin Merritt. But while striving to win Gavin's love, she and he must contend with mysterious ghosts, a hidden staircase, and murder attempts on Eliza's two little brothers. Can Lady Timandra and Gavin solve the mystery before Gavin or the two boys are killed? Be sure to watch for An Unexpected Treasure when Lady Rotherby attempts to train Lady Selena D'Arcy to be a lady of quality. But Selena has other plans. She wants to marry Calder Grantham and be a farmer's wife. She could care less which earl is seated next to which baron at the dinner table. But will her station in life prevent her from marrying the man she has given her heart?

Excerpt from
And the Ground Trembled
At the end of the book.

Visit my web site at:
cmartinbooks.kitsappublishing.com

Chapter 1

Northumberland, England 1673

In the day's dying light, Lady Timandra Lotterby peered out the coach window at the dark and shuttered house and wished she had never offered to accompany her friend, Eliza Tilbury, to Perfidious Brambles. A cold shiver crept up her spine, and she squiggled uncomfortably on the padded seat cushion. Eliza's trembling hand slid over hers, and Timandra felt instant shame. She was here to support her friend, not give way to silly, baseless fears. Yes, the estate grounds appeared unkempt, and the house foreboding, but an old man living on his own might find little need to keep up appearances.

"Holy Mary, would you be looking at that house," Timandra's Irish maid said in breathless awe. "Nary a light peeping from nary a window. Be you after thinking anyone is to home, Lady Timandra?"

Timandra drew her lips into a thin line and spoke in a firm voice meant to chastise her outspoken maid. "Mind your tongue, Finola. Indeed, I do think someone is home. We are expected. We sent a message from our lodgings last night that we should be arriving today. I have no doubt all will be ready for us." She smiled at Eliza and patted her hand. "You will see, dear friend, all will be well. Your great Uncle Percival's steward wrote that your uncle was graciously giving you and your siblings a home. Tomorrow in the light of day, when we are not so tired, all will look brighter. There now, give me a smile."

Timandra had seen the letter Percival Seldon's steward had sent. There had actually been nothing gracious about it. It simply stated Eliza's uncle recognized and accepted his office of guardian to his nieces and nephews and would fulfill his duties. Their uncle expected them to make their own travel arrangements to Perfidious Brambles. Should further communications be necessary, they should apply to him, the steward, Mister Eustace Colyer. Their uncle had not bothered to address even a short note to his new wards. Of course, he was old, and mayhap had failing eyesight. Or he might have suffered an apoplexy and be debilitated. Still, he might have expressed some sympathy to the Tilburys for the loss of their father.

Eliza blinked her large brown eyes, and her soft pouty lips tried to muster a smile, but she failed so miserably, Timandra had to laugh. Her pretty friend with her perfect little nose and her perfect little white teeth, her naturally pink cheeks and glowing complexion, not to mention a sweetly curvaceous figure, was going to need a lot of reassuring. Until three months ago, Eliza's life had been that of a fairytale princess. Pretty and pampered, but with a sweet disposition, she had been betrothed to a handsome, charming prince. Overnight, all had changed.

Timandra was glad she had been with her friend when Eliza received word of her father's sudden death, and her world crashed down around her. They had been planning Eliza's wedding. Eliza's mother having died when Eliza was fifteen, Eliza had asked Timandra to help her with the wedding arrangements. 'Twas to be a Spring wedding. The invitations had been addressed. Plans for an opulent wedding breakfast were being organized. Eliza's gown of burgundy with a cream-colored petticoat with gold-embroidered roses had had its final fitting. Her thick golden hair was to be curled and interwoven with burgundy ribbons and gold roses. The third announcement of the wedding banns were set to be read in the village church the following Sunday. Then the messenger from London arrived.

Over the next few weeks, the initial shock turned to horror as first the details of Vincent Tilbury's death – he died in the arms of his mistress, a woman his family had no knowledge of – then the sad state of his financial affairs surfaced. After his wife's death five years earlier, Tilbury had turned to drink and took lodgings in London. He fell into the company of what his solicitor termed a scheming woman who introduced him to London's increasing number of gambling houses. What with his drinking, gambling, and numerous exorbitantly expensive gifts to said woman, along with his neglect of his estate, he fell deeply into debt. By the time all his obligations were settled, little was left for his children.

The Tilbury estate, Merrywic, was sold to pay off the mortgage Tilbury had taken out. Most of the house furnishings, as well as some of Eliza's mother's jewelry, needed to be sold to cover other debts. To Eliza's dismay, her mother's pearls, which she had planned to wear on her wedding day, were missing. Tilbury's solicitor, Andrew Kenelm, an older partner in the firm of Kenelm and Severin, had hemmed and hawed, then despite a frown from the younger partner, Bartley Severin, had said he believed they had been given as a gift to her father's mistress. He had seen the woman wearing a lovely string of pearls mere days before Eliza's father's death.

Later that evening, Timandra rocked a weeping Eliza in her arms. Hands over her face, Eliza squeaked, "I cannot believe Father would take Mother's pearls. He was home for such a short visit. I went over the wedding plans with him. He was so jovial. He went riding with Herman and Bennet, and he kidded Charissa and Delilah that they would soon be making their wedding plans. He seemed happier than I had seen him in years. He had not been so gay since before Mother died. He visited with Ralph's parents and finalized our nuptial contract." Eliza took several convulsive gulps, hiccupped, then wept, "And all the time he knew he could not honor the contract."

"Mayhap he had no knowledge his financial affairs were in such disarray." 'Twas possible, Timandra thought. Tilbury's excessive drinking could have fogged his brain. "As you say," she added, "he was so happy. He certainly never thought he would be dying so suddenly."

"But to take the pearls and give them to that woman! Oh, Timandra, how could he!"

To that question, Timandra had no answer. She could do naught but continue to rock and croon to her friend.

The coach coming to a stop nudged Timandra's thoughts back to the present. She noted the ragged, overgrown island in the rutted circular drive, then looked out at the house. It was huge, and ugly. It had been added on to a couple of times, but with no thought to art or symmetry. The main section of rough stone was old. She guessed it dated back to Henry IV or earlier. With its two projecting corner turrets, it must at one time have been a fortified keep. She wondered if a portion of the drive might once have been a moat. Though more rustic, the keep reminded her of her aunt and uncle's home where she had been fostered for ten of her twenty-two years. A wide stone staircase of some twenty steps led up to heavy oak doors. One of her footmen raced up the steps to knock while another opened the coach door and let down the steps. Descending onto the drive, Timandra looked up at the west wing of the house. H-shaped and timber-framed, with brick and plaster infill, and with its multitude of windows and spiral chimney stacks, it harkened back to the time of Queen Elizabeth

The east wing appeared more classical in design, mayhap dating to Charles I. It was similar in some ways to her own home. In 1630, her grandfather tore down the old Harp's Ridge fortified house dating from the days of Henry IV and built a beautiful new home for his family. Her father made few changes to the elegant house. Timandra looked forward to exploring the various sections of Perfidious Brambles. It would give them all something to do and would hopefully dispel some of the eeriness surrounding the house.

Eliza alighted, and Timandra reached for her hand. "Come, dear friend, let us mount these steps and have done with it. I am dead tired and can think not even an ogre of the worst sort can keep me from my supper and bed."

Not waiting for a footman to open the door to their coach, Eliza's two young brothers scrambled out the moment the coach drew to a stop. Eliza had to restrain them from racing up the steps. "Herman, Bennet, calm yourselves. You must need want to make a good impression on Uncle Percival. We cannot have him think he has invited two bully-huffs to move into his home."

"Eliza is right, boys. Wait for your sisters," Timandra said. Over the past three months, she had learned the youths paid more heed to her than to their older sister. She guessed her imperious visage gave her an advantage. Tall and stately, she had her mother's dark hair, high fore-head, and blue-green eyes, and her father's slim aquiline nose, wide, thin-lipped mouth, and strong jutting chin. To her mind, the combina-tion melded poorly, and despite her mother's assurances she had a regal appearance, she could not consider herself beautiful.

Emerging more slowly from the coach, Charissa and Delilah seemed far less eager to enter their new abode. Clutching each other's hands, they gazed wide eyed as the sound of a bolt being drawn aside echoed off the stone steps. Timandra looked back in time to see one of the heavy oak doors grate slowly open. The footman stepped aside to reveal a stooped, wizened old man standing in the doorway. Behind him a woman holding a candle peered over his shoulder.

"Be you the Tilburys?" rasped the old man.

Eliza at Timandra's urging stepped forward. "I am Eliza Tilbury," she reached back a hand, "and this is my friend, Lady Timandra Lotterby, who has accompanied us and provided us with a much needed second coach."

"I have no knowledge was the master expecting an extra person," wheezed the old man. "He made no mention to me, but no matter, you best all come in." He stepped aside and Timandra followed Eliza inside. The only light came from the flickering candle the woman held and the last rays of sunshine filtering in through the high windows above the doorway. Peeking around a beautifully carved, dark-wood screen, Timandra noted they had entered a grand old hall. She could tell at a glance few changes had been made to the hall. Not even the central hearth had been replaced by a wall hearth.

"I am Mistress Weston, housekeeper," the tall, lean woman with the candle said. "That is Old John Orvin. Used to be the house steward, now he just ..." She shrugged. "He does what he can." She turned to the old man, and speaking loudly said, "Old John, you show the footmen where to take the baggage and point the coachmen the way to the stables. Guess they will need a light. Best give them a candle from the entry so they can light a lantern."

Old John shuffled out and Mistress Weston looked back at Eliza. "We never use this section of the house, but Old John and I thought you might come knocking at this door, so we were on the alert." Turning, she said, "Follow me, and I will see you to your rooms. You are late you know. Mister Seldon has a'ready retired. We keep early hours here." She looked back over her shoulder. "Mind your step and make sure to close the door. Old John will see it is bolted when he has seen to your baggage."

Timandra waited to insure the door was closed properly, and to make certain Herman and Bennet's tutor regained control of his young charges. Ernest Knolles, barely out of school, had replaced the boy's older tutor who had not wished to continue in the Tilbury's employ at reduced wages. Nor had the former tutor wanted to travel from Warwickshire to Northumberland. For that, Timandra could not blame him. It had been a long, tedious trip. Over two weeks of bumping, bouncing, and jostling about in the coach, combined with poor food and poorer beds whenever they were forced to lodge at inns rather than stay with families of Timandra's father's and uncles' acquaintance, the trip could be considered naught but an ordeal. The nagging fear of highwaymen waylaying them, should they be delayed reaching their evening's stop-over, added a strain to the already stressful situation.

Grateful to her father for providing not only his coach and six as well as the postilion, extra footmen, and an outrider, Timandra could not help but wonder that her parents had acquiesced to her wish to accompany Eliza. She could but think her Aunt Venetia must have persuaded them to permit her to take the extensive journey. Next to her aunt's cousin, Delphine, Eliza's mother had been Aunt Venetia's dearest friend. Aunt Venetia would want to help her departed friend's children in any means she could.

With the door secured, and Eliza's brothers in an orderly line in front of Mister Knolles, her sisters in front of them, and Finola, and Eliza's young maid, Audrey, bringing up the rear, Timandra fell in behind Eliza. They passed from the great hall into a narrow corridor, then into a small chamber with a narrow staircase leading up into darkness. Mistress Weston paused before a large oak door, and handing her candle to Eliza, used both hands to lift a stiff iron latch and pull the door open. Taking the candle back, she said, "We will be entering the west wing where Mister Seldon lives, and where you will live. The west wing was built during the reign of good Queen Bess," she added, reverence in her voice.

"What of the east wing?" Timandra asked. "Is it not newer?"

"Aye, but Mister Seldon keeps it locked up. No one is allowed into the east wing."

Timandra found Mistress Weston's statement intriguing, but as the housekeeper failed to elaborate, she decided not to press for details at the moment. She was tired and hungry, and the mysteries of the house could wait.

Descending a stone staircase, Mistress Weston tossed back over her shoulder, "Be certain the door is closed." Timandra again waited to make sure all were in line and Mister Knolles had the door firmly shut behind them. The staircase ended at another door which Mistress Weston swept open with one hand, and they followed her into a well-appointed parlor. Large windows covered two walls, but heavy draperies were drawn over them, shutting out any lingering daylight. A large fireplace on the wall opposite the front windows showed no sign of use. Either Mistress Weston kept a very tidy house, or a fire was seldom lit. Timandra guessed the latter. Still, it could be a bright comfortable room that would catch the morning sun.

When they were all assembled in the parlor, Mistress Weston counted noses. "My, you are more than I was expecting. Three girls and two boys, that is what Mister Seldon told me to prepare rooms for. He said the boys were young so I was expecting a nanny, and I had the nursery made up for them."

"The nursery!" ten-year-old Herman yelped. "I will not stay in a nursery."

"Surely 'tis but for one night, Hermie," Eliza said.

"I will not stay in the nursery either," the seven-year-old Bennet stated, though he had been out of the nursery for less than a year. His lips in a pout and his arms folded across his small chest, he added a stomp of his foot.

"Now boys," Mister Knolles said, "if I can stay in the nanny's room for one night, you can manage the nursery. We cannot ask Mistress Weston to make up new beds at this hour."

The boys again started to complain, but Mistress Weston said, "Girl what does the beds is gone home. No one else here to make up new beds. 'Tis the nursery or nothing."

"You heard Mistress Weston," Timandra said. "Herman, Bennet, you may sleep in warm beds in the nursery for this one night, or you may make your own beds in a room you think more acceptable. And you may not think Mister Knolles will make the beds for you. He is tired like the rest of us, and after his supper, he plans to sleep in the nanny's room. 'Tis your choice."

Having an eight-year-old brother, Timandra was used to the vagaries of young boys. Herman and Bennet were tired and hungry, and that would make them cranky. Their world had been turned upside down. Orphaned, they had been forced to leave the only home they had ever known. They had no control over what was happening to their lives, and they needed to make a stand. Controlling a chuckle, she watched the emotions wash over Herman's face. Bennet was watching him, too. He would follow his older brother's lead.

Herman firmed his lips and ran a hand through his dark brown hair. "Oh, I suppose does Mister Knolles sleep in the nanny's bed, we can sleep in the nursery for one night." His brown eyes alight, he looked up and stated, "But 'tis for only one night."

"So be it," Timandra said. "Mistress Weston, the crisis is resolved. Do lead on."

"What of these two?" Mistress Weston indicted Finola and Eliza's maid. "We have made up no beds for them."

"Finola and Audrey are our personal maids. Do you give them linens, they will make up their cots in the closets next to our rooms or on trundle beds, whichever you may have for them."

"Got a cot in the closet off Mistress Tilbury's room, and one in the closet off the young misses' room," Mistress Weston said. "Should serve, I suppose. Master has not entertained for near on thirty years except when his sister used to visit, and she died ten years back. I fear, Lady Timandra, you will be needing to sleep with Mistress Tilbury. I had no knowledge the young mistress was bringing you, so I made no arrangements." She looked to Charissa and Delilah. "I put the two young misses together. We got but one girl does the cleaning. Only so much she can be expected to keep up with."

Timandra wondered that Eliza's great uncle had not informed his staff that she would be accompanying Eliza. She had seen the letter Eliza had written him giving the approximate date of their expected arrival. Mayhap they should have written the steward instead, but that would have seemed discourteous. Seldon's age must have made him forgetful.

"Sharing a bed with Eliza will be no hardship," she said, smiling at Eliza. "We have shared beds this entire trip. And when fostered at my aunt's, we shared a bed and many a secret."

Eliza returned her smile. "Indeed, 'tis no hardship to share a bed with my dearest friend."

Timandra expected sharing the bed was for the better. She doubted Eliza would want to be abed alone this first night in this strange house. And it was a strange house.

Chapter 2

Mistress Weston led the way from the parlor into the west wing's great hall. As with the parlor, the drapes were drawn, and the single candle flame did little to light the room. Timandra could make out nothing but shadows. Pointing to a shadowy door across the hall, Mistress Weston said, "Through there is the dining hall. I will have Cook set out a supper for you, but 'twill be cold. Cook is not apt to heat up her kitchen after her help has gone home."

"Her help is a tenant's offspring?" Timandra asked.

"Aye, not but Old John, Cook, and I live on the grounds."

"No gardener nor groom?" Timandra asked.

"Nay. Seldom need either. Mister Seldon keeps but one horse. Old John tends him. Nice big stable though. Plenty of stalls for all your horses. Old John had some hay and grain brought in, but by the looks of the number of horses you got, he will need order a sight more. Mister Seldon will not be pleased with that. He is not one for readily parting with his coin."

"Well, he need not worry," Timandra said. "I will cover any added expenses for my horses and my staff. By the by, where are my staff to sleep and eat?"

"Your coachmen and postilion can sleep in the dormitory above the stables. Footmen too, do they choose. Has not been used in many a year, but 'tis roomy. Old John had it swept out and fresh linens laid by. Most likely they will need additional linens, but there be plenty of blankets and pillows stored in a cabinet at the far end of the dormitory. Old John will show it to them. Do you want your footmen handy, there is a men's dormitory in the cellar. And there is a servants' hall off the dormitory where your staff can take their meals."

Perfidious Brambles had apparently been modernized more than Timandra might have expected, given what seemed a minimal attempt at upkeep. The addition of a dining hall for the servants told her the great hall was no longer in everyday use by Mister Seldon or his household. She was not surprised by that. At her aunt's and uncle's home, the great hall's purpose was little more than ceremonial. Guests were received in the hall, and lavish feasts and entertainments were occasionally held there, but overall, the great hall had lost its importance.

"Old John and I, and the serving girl, when she is to hand, eat in the servant's hall," Mistress Weston said. "Cook chooses to eat in the kitchen," she added with a sniff, and Timandra wondered if the cook and the housekeeper might be embroiled in a jealous rivalry.

Lifting the candle a little higher, Mistress Weston said, "Well, then, shall we proceed?"

"Indeed," Eliza answered, "I am dead to the bone and near starved. I have ne'er been in such a large house. Is there no end to it?"

"Just up these stairs, Mistress Tilbury." The housekeeper indicated the wide, oak balustrade staircase leading from the ground floor to the first floor. "Your room is next to what was once the Great Chamber. Your room was once the withdrawing chamber, so 'tis spacious. You will get the morning sun." Marching ahead, Mistress Weston entered the large room, and after clipping the wick on her candle with scissors from her pocket, she lit the candles of a brass three prong candle holder on a stand near the door. "Water for washing up is apt to be tepid. Girl carried it up hot the last thing afore she left, but that was some time back," she said, crossing the room to light another stand of candles on a small table beside the bed. The room glowed brightly, dispelling the gloom of the dark house.

Surprisingly pleased with the bedchamber allotted to Eliza, Timandra brushed a hand over the carved and inlaid paneling. Never would she have expected such beautiful decorative work in the wilds of Northumberland. The four-poster bed with carved walnut headboard had sumptuous, scarlet-velvet bedcurtains with rose-pink-satin linings and matching bed coverlet. A plush, burgundy, tufted-velvet daybed sat at the end of the bed and a tall mirror framed in intricately carved black oak was positioned over a black oak cabinet. A delft-blue patterned-china bowl and matching water pitcher sat atop the cabinet, and cream-colored toweling was laid out on the bed. A delicate walnut chair with tufted seat sat before a small, walnut, gate-leg table, and a wainscot press for linens and clothing dominated the wall opposite the bed.

What she did not see was any coal in the grate, and despite it being mid-July, the room was chill. "We will need a fire," she said.

"Mister Seldon never has fires lit in the summer," Mistress Weston said. "Says 'tis a waste of costly coal."

"All the same, must I pay for the coal myself, I want fires laid and lit in all our rooms. We are not used to the cooler air here, and we are cold." She called to Finola. "Find Old John and tell him to show Edgar and Perth where the coal is. I want fires laid before we return from our supper."

"Yes, milady," Finola said. "I will see to it. Are you after needing me to help you change? I see your trunks and portmanteaus are not yet here."

"'Tis no matter, we will but wash up, then go down to eat. Just see about getting the fires laid. Audrey can ready your cots, then you two have your supper. After that, go to bed. Eliza and I can help each other out of our gowns. We will not need you until morning. But please see Charissa and Delilah are settled. Mister Knolles can see to the boys and get them down to supper.

"Oh, and Mistress Weston," Timandra added, turning to the house-keeper, "is there no fire in the dining hall, do please have one lit."

Mistress Weston inclined her head. "As you wish, Lady Timandra, but tomorrow, I am informing Mister Seldon 'tis your doing. I am but following your orders."

Timandra hid a smile. "Please, do so. I will face whatever the consequences may be."

Mistress Weston sniffed and left to escort the others to their rooms. Timandra, after closing the door, burst into giggles. "Oh, Eliza, could you have ever imagined such a house? I am so glad I have come with you. When we first arrived, I admit I felt a tremor of shock, but now I think I would not have missed this experience for the world. I can hardly wait to meet your uncle. Mistress Weston makes him sound the worst curmudgeon."

Eliza burst into tears, crying, "Oh, Timmie, what would I do were you not here! I fear my uncle must be a curmudgeon of the worst sort, and I cannot think how I shall get on with him."

Timandra gathered Eliza into her arms and patted her back. "Here now, dear friend, let us have no tears. Your face will turn all blotchy."

Her voice muffled into Timandra's shoulder, Eliza said, "And who is here to see or care am I blotchy? I cannot think how I could be any more miserable."

Timandra laughed. "You could have a cold. Or one of the boys could be sick. Or we could still be on the road. So yes, you could be more miserable. But forgetting how miserable you are, I am here to see your face, and I would prefer it not be blotchy. More importantly, you are the eldest. Your sisters and brothers look to you for guidance. Do you show fear or misery, they will take their cue from you. Now, do dry your eyes, and let us get washed up. I want to eat and then fall into that comfy-looking bed, and I care not how late I may sleep in the morning."

Eliza snuffled and straightened, and brushing the tears from her cheeks, said, "You always have a way of getting around me, Timandra. I shall stiffen my backbone and try to make my brothers and sisters think all is well. I cannot think all is well, but I can pretend."

"Good girl. Let us get freshened up."

� � � �

Upon arriving in the dining hall, she and Eliza found Mister Knolles and Eliza's brothers seated at the table. Mister Knolles rose when they entered, but Timandra bade him resume his seat. Her head footman, Perth, had found time to wash up, change into his serving coat, and be on hand to wait on them. "My lady," he said, pulling out a chair for her at the end of the table.

"No, Perth, this seat is Mistress Tilbury's. I will sit next to her."

"As you say, my lady." He seated Eliza, then pulled out a chair for Timandra.

"I had not expected to be served this evening," Timandra said. "I would have thought you busy with numerous other duties."

"Hillock and Kearne are seeing to the fires in your rooms. Edgar got the fire going in here. He is now seeing to our beds in the dormitory in the cellar. I thought you might prefer to have us near to hand, my lady."

"Indeed, Perth, that is excellent. But you must be hungry yourself."

"The cook is a jovial soul. She gave me a hunk of cheese and a mug of ale. 'Twill keep hunger pangs at bay until I sit down to my supper." Pouring wine into amber goblets positioned in front of silver plates, he added, "I took the liberty, my lady, of procuring the key to the wine cellar from the housekeeper. She seemed reluctant to part with it, but I promised to return it to her as soon as I selected the wine for your supper. I hope 'tis to your taste."

Timandra smiled and tasted the wine. "'Tis perfect. You are a marvel, Perth. Some day when I marry, I shall insist father let me have you for my house steward. Indeed, I cannot think how I should get on without you. You have been our mainstay throughout this tedious journey."

Though his face remained a fixed mask, she believed Perth appreciated the praise but was too well trained to show it. In his late twenties, a handsome man with his dark hair and eyes, he had a good future ahead of him. He had been with their family since he was but a child. He had started out in the stables and worked his way up. Her father had been so impressed with his eagerness to learn, he had given him time off from his duties to attend the parish school. Though he had but a rudimentary education, he was not destined to spend his life as a footman.

She knew all her footmen had to be tired. They made the journey standing on footpads, and clinging to the rear of the coaches. Fortunately, they had but once been required to run ahead of the coaches with lanterns in hand to light the road. That due to a densely cloudy day. For the remainder of the journey, the summer sun shone late into the evening, and no lanterns had been necessary. The footmen were young and hardy, and she had no doubt they would quickly recover and be looking for adventure unless she found them enough work to keep them occupied.

A screech, then giggles sounded from the great hall, and Charissa and Delilah bounded into the room. "Oh, Eliza, Lady Timandra, you will ne'er guess what we have spied!" Charissa cried, and she and Delilah again burst into giggles. "'Tis there in the hall. We near ran into it."

"What! What did you near run into?" Bennet demanded, his tousled, sandy-colored curls bobbling about on his head as he bounced on his chair. He and his sixteen-year-old sister, Charissa, with their fair hair and gray eyes favored their mother. Herman and fourteen-year-old Delilah had inherited their father's dark brown hair and eyes, and Eliza had her mother's golden hair and her father's brown eyes. All well favored, they made a handsome family.

Charissa smirked at Bennet, then straightened her shoulders and raised her chin. "A knight's full suit of armor." She brushed her hand down her body. "From masked head to pointed toes. Just standing right there in the hall like he was a person. Scared us at first."

Delilah giggled. "I was talking to Charissa and near bumped right into him ... er, it. What a clanking it would have made had I knocked it over."

"I have got to go see it," Bennet said, scrambling from his chair, but Mister Knolles caught him by the coat tail. "Not right now, young man. You will finish your meal, then, when Herman and I are also finished eating, we will stop to examine the armor on our way to bed."

"Ah," Bennet complained, but Eliza sided with the young tutor. "Mister Knolles is right. We have had a long and trying day. You need your sustenance before you go to bed. Tomorrow is plenty of time for you to inspect your new home."

Bennet climbed back up on his chair and began stuffing food in his mouth as fast as he could chew and swallow. Herman watched his brother for a moment, then with a sly smile, began picking at his food. Timandra shook her head. Boys will be boys. The older brother teasing the younger one, nothing new there. Herman knew how anxious Bennet was to see the armor. He was likely anxious to see it himself, but he would gain some kind of satisfaction out of tormenting Bennet. The two boys were close, and Herman always watched out for his younger brother, but that would not stop him from being a tease.

With Charissa and Delilah seated, and their wine poured, Perth began to serve their meal, but Timandra excused him. "You have done enough. We can serve ourselves. The food is laid out nicely here on the table. Go eat. You may clean up here after you have seen to your own meal. Then go to bed. You deserve a good rest."

"Thank you, my lady," Perth said and bowed himself out.

Timandra surveyed the food spread out on the table. Incredibly thin slices of cheese, thinner slices of mutton and a bowl of mint jelly, a platter of roasted fowl of some sort, a variety of meat and dried fruit tarts, and hefty chunks of rye bread. As hungry as she was, weariness overcame her, and she had satisfied her appetite by the time the boys were finished – Herman, eventually giving way to his whining younger brother, bolted down the remainder of his supper. Charissa and Delilah dallied over their meal, but the instant Timandra suggested to Eliza she was ready to go to bed, they begged them to wait.

"'Tis so dark," Delilah said, "and the candle gives such little light. Do please wait."

Timandra laughed. "Of course, we shall wait. You need not gulp down your meal."

"Oh, I am done," Charissa said. "Come Lilah. Are you yet hungry, bring some bread and cheese with you. I am cold and tired, and I cannot wait to crawl into bed."

Timandra and Eliza escorted the younger girls to their room. It was at the opposite end of the corridor, but Charissa informed Timandra and Eliza that Mistress Weston said it was the only bedchamber on the first floor that overlooked the garden. "She also said the garden is rather overrun, Uncle Percival not wanting to spend on its upkeep, but she says the roses are beautiful right now, and that in the fall the leaves of the fruit trees are glorious."

Though not as elegantly furnished, the room appeared to be near as large as Eliza's room, and the girls seemed pleased with it. It had a closet off it where a servant could sleep should the Tilburys be able to afford an additional maid servant other than Eliza's maid, Audrey. Two doors down was the nursery, and Eliza and Timandra poked their heads in to see if the boys were settled. Mister Knolles came forward, a wide smile on his face. Not only were Herman and Bennet settled, they were fast asleep. "Asleep before their heads hit their pillows," he whispered, his gray eyes alight in the candle light.

"Your room is satisfactory?" Eliza asked.

"'Tis little more than a closet, but Mistress Weston showed me the room at the head of the servants' stairs that she will have made up for me tomorrow. 'Tis a nice size room, and the boys will have the room between my room and yours, Mistress Tilbury. And do you look down this short corridor," he pointed to his right, "you will see our school room. 'Twill be a bright sunny room with plenty of windows. However, Mistress, with your permission, I will not start the boys' lessons until they have had a chance to explore their new home. They are quite anxious to see everything in the daylight."

"As we all are," Timandra said. "So what say you, Eliza, do you declare a holiday?"

"I shall as long as you can keep them out of mischief, Mister Knolles."

He smiled, a winning youthful smile that showed all his teeth, the front two being a bit prominent. "I shall endeavor to do my best, Mistress Tilbury."

"Splendid, then we bid you a goodnight, Mister Knolles."

He bowed his head, "Goodnight, Mistress Tilbury, Lady Timandra."

In retracing their steps, Timandra noted how narrow was the corridor extending from the main staircase to the servants' staircase. She guessed, as with most houses of earlier times, before the corridor's addition, one room simply led directly into another. By cutting off one end of the bedchambers and putting up additional walls and doors, first floor rooms were provided the privacy expected in modern homes. Her aunt and uncle had enclosed a portico on the ground floor at the rear of their house and turned it into a gallery. The corridor built over it on the first floor had achieved the same objective without reducing the size of the bedchambers. Their house had no second floor except for the four rounded turret rooms. Timandra was eager to see Perfidious Brambles's second floor. She would bet anything it had a long gallery, and she hoped numerous family portraits.

Overall, she was feeling much more pleased about her friend's future. Her first glimpse of Perfidious Brambles had been disheartening. But though the grounds might appear unkempt, the inside of the house had not been neglected despite the lack of servants. Yes, she could see no reason Eliza and her siblings could not be quite comfortable in their new home.

Chapter 3

Timandra awoke with the opening of the bedchamber door. Peeking out from under her lashes, she saw Finola's pretty, pink-cheeked face peering around the door. As always, wisps of her maid's dark hair snuck out from under her cap in unruly curls, and her dark eyes danced with a merriment Timandra never failed to appreciate, though she knew she should attempt to curb. Aunt Venetia had warned her the girl was too brazen, but Timandra liked her spirit. Unable to find employment in downtrodden Ireland, Finola had left her home and family and sought work in England. From the moment Timandra first saw Finola vigorously scrubbing the kitchen flagstone floor and chirping a merry tune while she worked, she had been drawn to her. When she questioned her aunt's burley cook about the girl, he had praised her.

"Despite her being Irish," the cook said, "she works hard and ne'er complains 'bout any task I give her. And she speaks the King's English, not that silly Irish gibberish. Is she a papist, she keeps it to herself. I have ne'er seen her crossing herself nor mumbling an' fumbling with them beads. I was hesitant to hire her, but she come round on a day when Lady Tuftwick was expecting a house full of guests. Not knowing how long the guests might be staying, I thought we could use another girl to scrub the pots. I told her did she do a good job, I would give her work till the guests left."

The man who ruled his kitchen like a small kingdom shook his bald, sweaty head and smiled. "Ne'er seen pots come so clean. Had 'em shining she did. And always so cheerful. So, even though she is Irish, I kept her on."

When visiting the kitchen on an errand for her aunt, Timandra learned Finola could read. The cook had promoted Finola to pastry cook, and Timandra found her covered in flour, up to her elbows in dough, and bending over a recipe. "What do you make?" Timandra asked.

Finola looked up with her bright smile. "Apple dumplings, but 'tis not certain I am having the dough the right consistency. The recipe makes no note about it."

"Would you like me to read you the recipe?" Timandra offered.

Finola looked confused for an instant, then shook her head and grinned. "Oh, no milady, 'tis having no trouble reading the recipe, I am. I just cannot determine from the notes, do I have the dough ready for the apples. 'Tis wishing Cook would return, I am. He is after selecting the fowl for tomorrow's dinner."

Without the aid of the cook, Finola had managed, and the apple dumplings had turned out delicious. They had received Timandra's uncle's hearty approval.

Aunt Venetia's housekeeper next discovered Finola's capabilities. Two of her servant girls got sick at the same time, and despite the cook's objections, the housekeeper pressed Finola into service. "Beds must be made, chamber pots need emptying, hearths need be cleaned and laid – I need the girl," the housekeeper stated, and grasping Finola by the wrist, led her from the kitchen. Timandra witnessed the scene and saw the cook's resentment, but she had a feeling Finola would never return to kitchen duty, and she had been right.

If Finola bore resentment against the English for what they had done to her homeland, she never gave voice to it. Timandra knew by occasional comments Finola made that her life in Ireland had not been easy, but her family had once been well enough off for her to receive an education. She knew too, Finola sent most of her wages home to her family, but she never spoke of them, and Timandra decided not to pry. Finola's cheerful acceptance of any work she might be assigned, and her readiness to do that job well, had decided Timandra in her choice of Finola as her personal maid. The girl had fast learned her duties but had not learned to mind her tongue.

Shifting in the bed, Timandra beckoned to Finola, who entered on her tiptoes. "I meant not to be waking you, milady," she whispered.

"You need not whisper, Finola," Eliza said from her side of the bed. "I am awake, I just have not wanted to open my eyes."

"Have we slept dreadfully late?" Timandra asked.

"Nay, milady, I am peeping in but twice before. The scullery maid is keeping a cauldron of water hot. Are you ready to rise, I will just be popping down and tell Perth you will be needing the water brought up. Oh, and Mistress Tilbury, Audrey is after seeing to your sisters. They woke but a bit ago." Finola giggled. "Frisky as young kittens they be, all giddy and eager to be investigating their new home."

Eliza rolled over and opened her eyes. "And my brothers, what of them?"

Finola's pert grin reappeared. "Up with the birds were those two. They and Mister Knolles had their breakfast, and after examining that old knight's armor in the hall, they set off to explore the outdoors. 'Tis a glorious day." She gestured to the windows. "Shall you be wanting me to open the draperies, Lady Timandra?"

"Yes, please do. Then do have Perth bring up the water for our ablutions. And is there ought to drink, mayhap some mulled cider or peach wine, my throat is parched."

"Or a ginseng tisane," Eliza said with a sigh, a muscle flexing in her pale cheek. "I need a tonic to perk me up and give me the strength to meet my great uncle."

Smiling catlike, Finola said, "I have met the old gent, excuse me, the master, Mister Seldon. He was after having breakfast with your brothers and Mister Knolles, Mistress Tilbury. 'Tis my thinking he may bark, but I am doubting his teeth be sharp enough to do any biting."

"Finola! That is no way to refer to Mister Seldon!" Timandra chastised.

"Begging your pardon, milady." Finola bobbed a curtsy. "I will just be opening these draperies, then go see to me duties."

Timandra did her best to keep a stern look on her face while Finola drew the drapes and bright sunlight flooded the room, but as soon as her maid was out the door, she and Eliza burst into giggles. "Oh, Timandra, do you think Finola may be right. Do you think my uncle may not be so fearsome?" Eliza gasped between giggles.

"As he took his breakfast with your brothers, and not in his own chamber, he cannot be all bad. Come, let us get up. The day does look to be glorious. We should try to enjoy it."

❀ ❀ ❀ ❀

Timandra and Eliza met Mistress Weston on the staircase landing. The housekeeper, in a sober gown and neat white apron, paused and offered them a good morning, though no smile touched her lips. "I was coming to inform you that Mister Seldon, having breakfasted well over two hours ago, is in his rooms, but he says he will join you in the parlor after you have breakfasted, Mistress Tilbury."

"Thank you. We will try not to keep my uncle waiting too much longer."

Mistress Weston nodded stiffly. "Breakfast is on the table. 'Tis but the usual fare for a Thursday, bread and cheese and sausage. By the by, Mister Seldon takes his dinner at eleven."

"At eleven!" Eliza said. "What time is it now?"

"Near ten," Mistress Weston answered sweeping past them to ascend the stairs.

"Oh dear," Eliza said with a giggle. "I cannot think she approves of the hours we keep."

Timandra laughed too and drew Eliza's arm through hers. "My guess is Mistress Weston is apt to disapprove of any number of things we and your siblings may do, but she will adjust. So come, let us abate our hunger. We cannot wish to face your uncle with our stomachs growling."

As they descended the remaining steps and headed to the dining chamber, Eliza said, "I can never begin to thank you enough for coming with me, Timandra."

"Enough! You have thanked me so many times I have lost count. I am here because you are my dearest friend, and as my aunt and your mother were the dearest of friends and naught but your dear mother's death could ever have changed that, just so shall our friendship ever endure. And friends will stand by one another. Will they not?"

Eliza squeezed Timandra's hand. "I know can I ever do anything for you, I would gladly do it a hundred times over."

"Splendid. 'Tis glad I am to know I may always count on you," Timandra said, returning a squeeze to Eliza's hand as they entered the dining chamber. They found Charissa and Delilah in the midst of their breakfast.

"Oh, Eliza, Lady Timandra, do hurry and sit down. Cook has sent in a serving of hot cross buns with cinnamon and currants. Edgar said she made them special for us because she felt bad about serving us naught but a cold meal last night. He said Cook told him Uncle Percival eats naught but porridge three days a week, then naught but bread and sausage for three days, and on Sunday he fasts and reads his Bible until time for his dinner. He never varies."

"Hermie and Bennet missed the cross buns because they were up early and ate with Uncle Percival," Delilah said. "Edgar says he spoke not a word to the boys. Just nodded his head when they wished him a good morning and poked another bite of sausage in his mouth."

"What does he look like?" Eliza asked, taking her place at the end of the table.

Delilah frowned. "Perth hushed Edgar. He said he should not be discussing Mister Seldon in such a manner. But Perth said when we asked after Hermie and Bennet, that Mister Knolles told them did they wish to explore the grounds before dinner, they had best be on their way."

"So off they went," Charissa said.

Timandra was pleased to have the cross buns for breakfast, but she was not pleased with her footman, Edgar, for repeating things to the young Tilburys that the cook told him. A handsome youth, Edgar had but recently been promoted to his position as footman and was still in training. She would have to remind him not to repeat gossip and not to engage in it.

"Timandra and I are to meet Uncle Percival in the parlor after we have breakfasted. I think you two should be presented at that time," Eliza said, nodding to her sisters. "You need not stay though, do you wish to take a stroll in the garden and see some of the grounds."

"I suppose 'twould be better do we meet him before we sit down to dinner with him," Charissa said, but she looked none too pleased at the prospect, and Timandra had to hide a smile.

"I slept well last night. 'Tis a most comfortable bed, and I was so terribly tired," Delilah said, reaching for another cross bun.

"Lilah!" Charissa said, batting her sister's hand. "You have had enough. Do you get too fat for your gowns, we have no seamstress to let them out for you. You know Audrey is a poor hand with a needle, and she is the only maid we have for the three of us."

Pouting, Delilah let the bun drop back onto the platter, but she brightened when Eliza said, "I am glad you slept well, dear, and I cannot think one extra bun will hurt you. Not after our long journey. We can all use a bit of a reward."

With a snub of her nose at her sister, Delilah reclaimed the bun as Perth entered with a pitcher of steaming apple cider. He filled Timandra's and Eliza's mugs, then refilled Charissa's and Delilah's. "Will there be aught else, Lady Timandra?" he asked, his face a mask of dignity.

"Yes, Perth, are you and all the others settled in comfortably?"

"Most comfortably, my lady. The dormitory beds are satisfactory, and Cook has provided us with a filling breakfast. The coachmen, the postilion, and Tombs say the dormitory above the coach house is also satisfactory."

"What of the stable for the horses?"

"Clean and roomy, and there is room inside the coach-house for both coaches. However, Tombs says we will need far more hay and grain than what is on hand."

Tombs was the trusted outrider Timandra's father had sent to help with their journey. Well-armed and an expert marksman, and with his broad shoulders and craggy visage, he not only looked formidable, he was formidable. Timandra had felt much safer having him along. "Ask the coachmen to determine what they may need, then Tombs can ride into the village we passed south of here and place an order. I hope they will be able to accommodate us."

"Are they not able, my lady, I have no doubt Tombs will determine a way to obtain all that is needed. He is ever resourceful, if I may say so."

Timandra smiled. "Indeed, you are correct. Tombs has never failed us. And how are Mistress Tilbury's and my saddle horses? They have not suffered from the arduous journey?" After all their father's debts had been settled, the Tilburys had been left with naught but their personal clothing and belongings, and their coach and four. Eliza's horse, her brothers' ponies and her sisters' gentle mares had needed to be sold. Timandra had bought Eliza's horse at the auction and had given it back to her friend as a gift. "A lady should not be without her saddle horse," she had said while wiping away her friend's grateful tears. The two saddle horses had been tied to leads behind the coaches. Timandra had little worry for her own strong gelding, but Eliza's mare was unused to long stretches and rough roads.

"I am told both horses are well," Perth said, "although Mistress Tilbury's coachman says he means to put some ointment on the mare's hind hocks. Do you wish me to have Hardgrove report to you on the coach horses?"

"No," Timandra shook her head. "But tell Hardgrove I will stop by the stable after dinner to see him. And would you please tell Edgar I will be wanting to see him after dinner."

"Yes, my lady." He started to leave, but turned back. "My lady, I understand Old John is in the habit of serving Mister Seldon." He paused. "Would you care to have me assist him?"

Smiling, Timandra nodded. "Indeed, Perth, I do believe that would be most advisable. Thank you. Now would you find Mistress Weston and inform her Mistress Tilbury and I are near finished with breakfast, and we will attend Mister Seldon in the parlor."

"Yes, my lady," Perth answered and exited. And Timandra returned to her cross bun.

Chapter 4

Timandra and Eliza were drying their fingers after cleaning them in their finger bowls when Mistress Weston arrived to conduct them to the parlor. Their heels clicking on the oval-patterned marble floor, Timandra and the Tilburys followed the housekeeper back across the hall, past the suit of armor and the grand staircase, and into the parlor they had paused in the night before. The burgundy drapes had been drawn open and bright sunlight, cascading in through four large, diamond-pained windows, cast a warming glow over the polished hardwood flooring, helping to dispel the chill of the room. Wide window seats with gold cushions and tasseled pillows looked inviting, and Timandra envisioned herself curling up with a book on one of the seats at some future date. Two sofas and two armchairs were centered around the cold hearth as were several small tables and a couple of tufted stools. A side table and a pair of matching chairs set against one wall and on the opposite wall a lovely tapestry of a garden scene added elegance to the room. Wainscoted walls reached almost to the intricately carved ceiling, and two decorative candelabras cast delicate shadows across the floor.

Gripping each other's hands, Charissa and Delilah sat close together on one sofa, and Timandra joined Eliza on the other one. None of them spoke. In a few moments they heard a shuffling sound and Old John entered. Stepping to one side of the door, he announced, "Mister Seldon," and a tall, lean man with a shock of thick white hair entered the room. His back stiff and straight, his blue eyes piercing, he stopped inside the doorway. His gaze traveled first to Charissa and Delilah, then stopped on Eliza. His eyes widening, his lips parted, he stared at her. Then, with the slightest shake of his head, he turned to Timandra. Returning his gaze, she adopted a smile and waited for him to speak.

He fluttered his hand. "You are dismissed, John, and close the door."

"Yes, Mister Seldon," Old John said and bowed himself out, closing the door after him.

His gaze still on Timandra, Seldon said, "You must be Lady Timandra Lotterby." His voice was crisp, not feeble with age. In fact, he appeared remarkably healthy for a man Timandra knew must be in his early seventies. "I had no notion my niece was bringing a guest with her. I hope you were not greatly inconvenienced last night by our lack of preparedness."

"But Uncle Percival," Eliza spoke up, surprising Timandra with her temerity. "I wrote you that Lady Timandra would be accompanying us. She not only gave me company, she provided us with an extra coach to transport our belongings."

Seldon's gaze shifted slowly to Eliza. His voice cold, but not brusque, he said, "I feel certain you were informed all future correspondence should be directed to my steward."

Eliza squirmed under his sharp gaze. "I ... I," she stuttered and looked at Timandra, then back up at her uncle, "that is, we, Lady Timandra and I, thought 'twould be rude not to inform you personally that Lady Timandra would be visiting for an indeterminate time."

The gaze flew back to Timandra. Eyebrows raised, he said, "An indeterminate time?"

Timandra inclined her head. "'Tis a tedious journey from Warwickshire to Northumberland. I cannot believe you would think I could leave on the morrow."

She thought she saw a smile tug at his thin lips, but he suppressed it and advanced into the room. With the dignity of an aristocrat, he took an armchair and directed his gaze at Eliza's sisters. "And who are these two? I met your two brothers and their tutor at breakfast. You are all older than I expected. That is at least one good thing about this situation. No squalling babes."

"My sisters, Uncle Percival," Eliza said. "Charissa on the right is the older. She is sixteen, Delilah is fourteen. The boys are ten and seven."

"Yes, so they informed me," Seldon answered without taking his gaze from the two younger girls, who squirmed as had their elder sister. "Good morning, Uncle Percival," they said in unison. "Thank you so much for taking us into your home," Charissa added.

Seldon inhaled deeply through his long nose. "Naught else I could do. You are family. My only brother's grandchildren." His mouth twisted to one side. "Your grandfather was a fool. Married a vicar's daughter. She had nary a penny for a dowry. At least she had but the one daughter before she died. Been smarter to have had a son. However, I did think your mother did well marrying Tilbury. At your grandfather's request, I furnished her dowry." He shook his head. "Turns out your mother too made a poor choice, and now here I am saddled with the lot of you."

Timandra looked from Charissa and Delilah to Eliza as Seldon spouted his odious speech. Eliza's face blazed a bright red and tears welled in her eyes. Timandra's own face burned with heated indignation on behalf of her friend. "Mister Seldon," rising and staring down her nose at her host, she said in her haughtiest voice, "you are being most insensitive. Eliza and her sisters have but recently buried their father. They are still in mourning, yet you speak to them as though they are in some way at fault for the loss of their parents and their grandparents. They may now be dependent upon you for their home, but I can see no reason for you to so belittle them."

His eyes clear and unblinking, Seldon looked up at her. "Do resume your seat, Lady Timandra. I am in no way seeking to belittle my nieces. I am but pointing out the lairs that await those who are unwary. My brother married for love. It brought him naught financially. And despite his stewardship, he needed help from me to provide a suitable marriage settlement for his only child. What might he have done had his wife lived and borne more children? How would he have provided for them? I am not saying 'tis wrong to marry for love. I am but advising 'tis best my nieces choose wisely, that their future children will not find themselves in the same situation as they now find themselves. Dependent upon an irascible old uncle."

"To say he is irascible is an understatement, but I would ne'er have thought to hear him admit to it." A merry voice from the door drew all eyes to the intruder. Intent on Seldon's monologue, no one had heard the door open. Timandra was glad she had resumed her seat for she was not certain her legs would have continued to support her as she stared numbly at the man advancing into the room. He was the most gorgeous man she had ever seen. Like Seldon, he wore no wig and his blond hair floated about his shoulders. His vibrant blue eyes searched each surprised countenance, and Timandra's breath caught in her throat when his gaze met hers.

"What are you doing here?" Seldon demanded.

"Why, Grandfather, I have come to greet my cousins. You could not think me so uncivil as not to welcome them to Perfidious Brambles. Do please introduce me?"

Seldon shook his head. "I might have known you would be poking your nose where it was not wanted. Very well." He extended his hand toward Timandra. "Lady Timandra, my grandson, Gavin Merritt." Then in turn, he directed his hand to Eliza and her sisters. "Eliza, Charissa, Delilah, your cousin, Gavin."

Gavin bowed to Timandra, then to each of his cousins. "I am honored, Lady Timandra, and dear cousins. I hope we will all soon be well acquainted." His eyes lingered on Eliza and Timandra was not surprised. Blushing prettily, her friend, even in her black mourning, looked lovely. Her eyes aglow, her mouth smiling sweetly, she was a vision.

Seating himself in the second armchair and putting one booted foot on a tufted stool, he said, "I left my horse at the stables. I have ne'er seen such a bustle as is going on there. Two coaches being cleaned and polished, fine looking horses being curried, and a burly man by the name of Tombs asked did I think our wee Fairflex village would have enough hay and grain to feed all the beasts, or must he ride farther afield and in which direction?

"I told him Fairflex would most likely be able to accommodate his needs for a couple of days, and he could place an order with the blacksmith that should be delivered within the week. Most likely, Smithy will need send to Newcastle to supply feed for that number of horses, and 'twill be at a pretty price. More than you have paid out in many a year, would you say, Grandfather?" A teasing quality to his voice, and his lips quirked in a mischievous grin, Gavin leaned forward to peer at his grandfather. That he had no fear of angering the old man, Timandra found curious, as Seldon had not appeared pleased his grandson had joined them.

"I will cover the accounts for my horses, Mister Seldon," Timandra said. "And for my staff. Or, do you prefer, I could send my coach and some of my staff to my uncle's until I am ready to depart. My uncle, the Earl of Tyneford, has a manor near Hexham. I think little more than half a day's journey."

"I am well aware of the location of Tyneford Hall," Seldon said stiffly, "but I had not expected you would have your uncle think I am either inhospitable or so beggared I cannot afford to attend the needs of my guests."

Timandra blushed. She had been overly bold – had spoken without considering the insult to her host. Being of an older generation, he would likely not only respect traditional obligations associated with landed wealth, but he would value his reputation for dispensing hospitality. "I apologize, Mister Seldon. I spoke without thinking and meant not to offend. I believed, as you were not expecting such an increase to your household, 'twas putting an undue burden on you."

Gavin chuckled. "Grandfather could never be termed a spendthrift. Hoards his pennies, does he, but have no fear, he can easily afford your entourage and more."

"Gavin! You overstep your bounds!" Seldon snapped.

"As did you in tweaking Lady Timandra." Gavin answered his grandfather's bark with genial disregard. "No doubt Mistress Weston has been harping to her and my cousins about the cost of coal, the cost of candles, and most likely the cost of having the extra linens laundered. You cannot tell me I am wrong, for I have but to look at that cold hearth. Your guest and nieces are from the south of England. They have yet to adjust to our colder clime, yet you have made no provision for their comfort. So – that Lady Timandra should think you either inhospitable or beggared is not surprising."

To Timandra's surprise, Seldon nodded. "Yes, Mistress Weston has already reported to me that Lady Timandra ordered fires for all their rooms and for the dining parlor last night. I informed Mistress Weston to see that fires are lit in any rooms Lady Timandra wishes. But as I am unaccustomed to having guests, and feeling no chill myself, I gave no thought to having a fire laid in this room. Accept my apology for my oversight, Lady Timandra. Gavin, do you ring for John, I will have a fire laid at once.

"Why did John not announce you?" Seldon asked as Gavin rose to fetch a large hand bell from the table against the wall.

"He ne'er saw me. I came in by way of the kitchen. Had to see what nibbles Cook might have." He opened the door and rang the bell, then set the bell back on the table. "I am always hungry after my ride over here," he added, resuming his seat.

"I suppose you are planning to stay to dinner?"

"Of course. I told Cook to make sure to set a place for me."

Timandra found the relationship between Gavin and his grandfather more interesting by the minute. Obviously familiar with the house and the staff, Gavin seemed to make himself to home, and Seldon seemed to accept his presence, though he seemed not to welcome him, at least not openly. But she thought she detected a fondness in his eyes when he looked at Gavin.

"Did you ring for me, Mister Seldon?" Old John asked from the doorway.

"Yes, we need a fire in the hearth. Send the maid in to tend to it."

"She is upstairs seeing to the beds, Mister Seldon. Shall I lay the fire, sir?"

Seldon looked around at the old man, and for a moment his face softened. He shook his head. "Nay, John. Get one of Lady Timandra's footmen to lay it. I understand they saw to the fires in the hearths last night. As long as they are to be underfoot, they might as well be put to work." He turned to Timandra and inclined his head. "Do you so approve, Lady Timandra?"

"Indeed, I approve, Mister Seldon," Timandra said.

"Very good, sir, my lady," Old John said with a nod of his head. He glanced at Gavin. "Master Gavin, welcome sir, I was unaware you were here."

"Snuck in the back, John. You know me."

"Yes, sir." Again Old John nodded, then exited.

"That my staff may not get into mischief, I am hoping to keep them busy whilst here," Timandra said, "Do you have other tasks they may help with, I will gladly lend their services. With your permission, I have already asked my man, Perth, to help Old John serve dinner."

"Splendid," Seldon said. "I was wondering how John might manage. John has been with the household since my father was alive." His eyes looked thoughtful, almost wistful. "Father sent him with me when I had my tour of Europe. When we returned, he made John his house steward. Fine job John did. Always correct, polite, never overstepped his bounds, accounts kept in order, too. Now it takes two to do the job he did." Seldon sniffed and shook his head. "Weston runs the house. Colyer keeps the accounts."

"You are hardly being fair to Eustace, Grandfather. He not only keeps your house accounts, he keeps your estate accounts, monitors your coal mining and barge account and consults with your men of business, and oversees your charitable activities, not to mention ..."

"Enough!" Seldon barked. "Because you two are of an age, and you enjoy playing chess or riding out with him, you think him faultless."

"Well, hardly faultless, Grandfather. He beat me at chess recently two times in a row. To that I do take exception and mean to take him on again at the first opportunity. By the by, when does he return from Newcastle?"

"Ehhh." Seldon waved his hand at Gavin. "How should I know? He seldom bothers to inform me of his comings and goings."

"Nonsense. You know every move he makes. But never mind. We are bickering as usual and ignoring Lady Timandra and my cousins." He flashed a radiant smile, and Timandra's heart stopped, then took off at an exhilarated rate.

"Ah, here is the footman to lay the fire," Gavin said as Perth entered and moved unobtrusively to the hearth. "Grandfather, you really should hire a footman or two, especially now your household has increased. John is getting too old to do many of the jobs he feels obligated to do."

"Gavin, when I need you to tell me how to run my household, I will let you know. Until then, I will thank you to keep your thoughts to yourself."

Timandra glanced at Eliza's sisters. They had made nary a peep since Gavin Merritt had entered the room. They looked less frightened than they had before his entrance, but they still gripped each other's hands. Their eyes, darting back and forth during the vigorous exchange between their great uncle and his grandson, were unblinking. No one had remembered the two were to be excused that they might have a stroll through the garden before dinner. Timandra doubted the girls would now want to be excused.

"Lady Timandra," Seldon recalled her attention to him. "I told Mistress Weston to have a room on the second floor made up for you. 'Tis a commodious room with a good size closet for your servant as well as for your personal effects. Again, I am sorry we were not prepared for you last night. I think I recall a letter arriving from my niece, but I left it with the mail for Colyer, forgetting he would be away for more than a fortnight. I will place the blame on my advancing years and faltering memory." He looked at Gavin. "I need no comments from you."

Laughing, Gavin shook his head. "No comments, Grandfather." Sobering, he nodded toward Eliza and her sisters. "Cousins, allow me to extend my condolences for the loss of your father. My mother also sends her condolences. No doubt you will at first find Northumberland different from your leafy Warwickshire with its gently rolling hills, extensive fields, pastures, and orchards, and its mild climate. But Northumberland has its charm. To see, with the coming of spring, the verdant pastures dotted with white sheep or brown cows and their new young, to stroll under a blue summer sky beside bubbling streams or across open fields, to thrill to the sparkle of the first frost of winter, and to breathe deeply of our healthy, bracing air can do naught but delight your heart. You will see, you will come to love your new home."

Timandra, lost in Gavin's poetical descriptions, started when Seldon harrumphed. "He paints a pretty picture, but if you be cold now in midsummer, you will be a sight colder come winter. We often go from October until the end of March and ne'er see a day without frost. The wind howls down from Scotland and blows o'er the pastures. With few forests to slow the wind, it can chill you to the bone. Spring rains bring flooding, and from time to time we must endure raids by Scottish reivers, especially if they had a hard winter and lost a portion of their stock."

Wide-eyed, Delilah spoke for the first time. "What are reivers?"

"Brazen Scots who think they have the right to steal other men's cattle," Seldon snarled.

"Before James I became king of England and Scotland," Gavin said, his blue eyes alight as his gaze rested on Delilah and caused his young cousin to blush immeasurably, "we had constant strife between the two countries. Even as far south as Perfidious Brambles. Arriving late as you did yesterday, you might not have noticed, but the center house was once a fortified keep, with turrets and slats for archers; even had a moat. No drawbridge though. Naught but a small stone bridge. I never saw it. When great-great grandfather bought this manor from Baron Worndon, he tore down the bridge, filled in the moat, and used some of the stones in expanding the stables. I think he might have planned to tear down the old keep as well, but he died before he could do so. Fortunately neither Great-Grandfather nor Grandfather chose to destroy it."

He looked fondly at Seldon. "I tell you some of the best times I can remember of my boyhood revolve around the games I played in that old keep."

"I knew it had to be a keep," Timandra said. "And I am looking forward to exploring it. 'Twould seem few changes have been made to it."

"You are most astute," Gavin said. Oddly flattered by his compliment, Timandra returned his smile. "About the only change was the addition of the stone stairs leading up to what is now the keep's main door," he continued. "Originally, there were but wooden staircases that could be drawn up inside should the keep be attacked." Gavin shifted his gaze to Eliza. "As this is now your home, mayhap after dinner, you would like me to show you around it."

Flushing under her cousin's gaze, Eliza nodded. "That would be most kind of you."

"Best wear a wrap," Seldon said. "You think 'tis cold in this section, 'tis naught compared to that stone fortress."

"Will there be aught else, my lady?" Perth asked. A glowing fire burned in the hearth, and Timandra welcomed its warmth. She shook her head. "No Perth, that will be all, thank you."

"Yes, my lady," he said with a nod before exiting.

"Capable-looking fellow," Seldon said. "Do I decide I must need hire a footman or two, I cannot suppose you would be willing to part with his services."

"Never!" Timandra said with a sharp shake of her head. "I would be lost without him."

"I thought not," Seldon said, then turning to Eliza, asked, "Your siblings' and your accommodations are satisfactory?"

Eliza nodded vigorously. "Indeed, Uncle Percival. All are nice and my room is lovely."

"Yes," Seldon said. "My sister, your great aunt, liked to stay in that room when she visited. She died ten years or so ago," he stated, but he didn't look saddened by the loss. "Her two daughters married well. Both live somewhere in Cumberland, I think. I pay them small heed, and they likewise have little interest in me. 'Tis my sister's son, Dwight, I am forced to endure."

Gavin chuckled. "Ah, cousins, wait until you meet your cousin Dwight and his two ..." He scratched his head. "Oh dear, Grandfather, how shall I describe them. Hmmm." He nodded. "Grandiose! Yes, that is it, his grandiose friends, Sir Osgood Pettimill and his equally grand, widowed sister, Mistress Viola Clakenberger. Of late, Dwight is ne'er without them."

Before Gavin could impart any additional information, Herman and Bennet burst in the door, an apologetic Mister Knolles at their heels. "Boys! Herman! Bennet!" He tried to grab Bennet, but the younger boy slipped from his grasp.

"Eliza! Eliza!" both boys were crying, their eyes bright with glee. "You will never guess what a grand estate this is. Why ..."

Mister Knolles interrupted them. "Mistress Tilbury, I am sorry. I tried to control your brothers, but ..." He stopped upon noticing Seldon. "Mister Seldon, sir, I do apologize for Herman's and Bennet's behavior. They have had such an exciting morning. 'Tis the first real chance they have had in a fortnight to enjoy some freedom, being cooped up in the coach and all, and then ..."

Herman reclaimed his sister's attention by tugging at her sleeve. "Eliza, do listen. There is a maze. Right in the center of the maze there is a statute of a man on a horse. I boosted Bennet up and climbed up after him, but then Bennet could not get down and Mister Knolles had to ..."

"Herman, please, you are interrupting, and you are being rude. You know I spoke to you about your behavior. What will Uncle Percival think of you." Eliza's voice sounded both plaintive and annoyed as she tried to hush her exuberant brother.

"I remember feeling just as excited the first time I saw that maze and the statue." Gavin broke in on Eliza's plea, and her brothers turned to stare at him. A smile lurking on his lips, he returned their curious gazes. "I must admit," he added, "the first thing I did was climb up on the horse. Getting up was easy." He looked at Bennet. "Getting down did present a problem."

"Herman, Bennet," Timandra interjected. "Meet your cousin, Mister Merritt."

Slipping from his chair, Gavin squatted on his haunches. "Gavin," he said, "you must call me Gavin. We are, after all, cousins, and I have no doubt we will become good friends.

Chapter 5

Gavin made dinner a lively affair. He had a healthy appetite and seemed to relish his meal, but between bites, he entertained his awed cousins. Timandra admitted to be in awe of the man herself. Cheerful, eloquent, and indecently handsome, she doubted not he had captured all their hearts, even Eliza's brothers'. They had objected mightily to being told they must take their dinner in their school room with Mister Knolles. Gavin, though, promised they could later join his tour of the keep, and they at last acquiesced and trotted off in front of their tutor.

Timandra had feared their host would quash any gaiety Eliza or her sisters might have entered into, but with Gavin present, the old man seemed content to let his grandson hold forth on any manner of subject which ranged from the best areas on the estate to go riding, to the local gentry they could expect to meet, to the tedious sermons they would have to endure did they attend services at the parish church. "Not that the local vicar is not a fine man," Gavin said with a chuckle, "but he seems ne'er to have learned how to enthrall his parishioners."

"Nor to control that daughter of his," Seldon stated.

Gavin laughed, "Aye, young Mistress Hemphill is a lively little pixie. Grandfather has chased her out of his orchard trees more times than he can enumerate." He looked at Seldon. "Have you not, Grandfather?"

"The girl is a hoyden. 'Tis unseemly the way she roams about the parish on her own. 'Tis not that she takes an exorbitant amount of fruit, 'tis the principle. 'Tis stealing, and as the daughter of a man of the cloth, 'tis shameful. And does she take a tumble out of one of my trees, I will be the one held to blame."

"Our Vicar Hemphill is a widower," Gavin said. "He is absent-minded, and as I said, he is a man of little inspiration. How he fathered a daughter like Ebba is a curiosity to all."

"Did she not look so much like a female version of her father," Seldon put in, "her paternity would be in question."

"What do you mean?" Delilah asked.

Timandra smothered a smile as Eliza said, "Never you mind. You but need pay heed to your manners. You would not want anyone thinking you a hoyden. And wipe that surprised look off your face. I recall the way you flirted with that youth at the Cat and Pearl Inn."

Delilah blushed and Timandra pitied the girl. Her infraction had been minor and the youth had been quite handsome. Delilah, not long out of the school room, had quite naturally been drawn to her first admirer. 'Twas Seldon who should have been chastised for intimating a prospect not suitable for mixed company. To his credit he seemed to recognize his slip for he quickly changed the subject.

"In 1590, grandfather purchased Perfidious Brambles from the ninth Baron Worndon," he said. "My father was but sixteen. Having grown up in Newcastle, he found life in the country boring and unappealing. Grandfather sent him off to Oxford. When he finished his schooling, grandfather set him to work learning the coal mining, export, and marketing businesses. He spent little time here. Not until he returned one Christmas and met my mother, did he have any interest in the estate. My mother changed that. He loved her, and she loved Perfidious Brambles."

Seldon smiled for the first time, and Timandra was surprised how it lightened up his face. His eyes brightened, and the droop around his mouth and sacks under his eyes disappeared. He looked years younger. She could readily see the resemblance between Seldon and his grandson. In his youth, Seldon could easily have been as appealing as was Gavin Merritt.

"My grandfather started building this house the year he bought the manor," Seldon continued. "Took four years to complete it to his satisfaction. Gavin is correct. He meant to tear down the keep, but never found the time – or mayhap never wanted to spend the money." He shrugged. "Few realize the expense and effort involved in tearing something down, clearing the rubble, then reclaiming the sight. After Grandfather died, my father made a number of changes. First, he attached the two houses. He liked to entertain and the keep gave him rooms to house overflow guests. He had the main staircase in this house replaced with the open well balustrade stairs and cut up the rooms on the first floor to add a corridor. He removed the servants' dormitory from the second floor to the cellar and replaced the austere second floor quarters with four generous-sized bedchambers and a gallery." He sniffed. "Not that we have many portraits to fill the walls." He looked at Timandra. "I hope you will find your chamber satisfactory, Lady Timandra. I would think it readied soon, and your servant can see to settling you in."

Timandra inclined her head. "Thank you, Mister Seldon. Is it anywhere near as nice as the room you have given Eliza, I know I shall be quite comfortable. Now, may I ask, are you responsible for building the east wing which is closed off?" The instant her words were out of her mouth, she knew she had erred. Seldon's face hardened and the sparkle left his eyes.

"I had the east wing built for my wife. It is no longer needed."

The stark statement hung in the air for but a moment before Gavin filled the silence with a lavish praise of the roast saddle of mutton. "Cooked to perfection," he said. "Just the right crispness on the outside, and nicely enhanced by the roasted beets." He looked to Old John. "Do tell Cook her turbot in the cucumber sauce was superb as well."

Old John nodded. "As you say, sir. I will pass on your kind words."

Having been told of Seldon's meager breakfast habits, Timandra was surprised by the six-course dinner. It started with an oxtail soup, followed by the turbot, then a steak and kidney pie, the mutton came next, and Perth was bringing in a fruit and cheese platter which would be followed by dessert and then nuts. Not that she or the Tilburys ate much after their late breakfast.

Gavin launched into a description of the local village of Fairflex while helping himself to a serving of berries and curd, but his grandfather refrained from any further conversation until the meal ended. Leaving the two men to their port, Timandra and the Tilburys excused themselves to go freshen up. The meal had lasted long into the afternoon, but Gavin assured them he still meant to give them a tour of the keep before departing.

At a corner table in the grand hall, Mister Knolles had kept the impatiently waiting Herman and Bennet occupied with a game of backgammon, but they were growing more restive by the minute. "Why not take them out front and have them race around the drive a few times," Timandra suggested. "They could fight a few battles up and down the entrance steps. Their imaginations should carry them back to the knights of old, mayhap fight a dragon or two."

Knolles smiled and nodded. "Excellent suggestions. Herman, Bennet let us go outside. We will be summoned when 'tis time for the tour." The boys readily accepted the plan, and Timandra turned to the staircase where Eliza awaited her.

"You are so good with my brothers," Eliza said, starting up the stairs. "Far better than I."

"I have had the antics of my male cousins to observe over the years," Timandra said, chuckling and falling into step beside Eliza. "And I admit to having occasionally joined in on their larks, so 'tis easy for me to recall their fantasies."

Eliza shook her head. "No, you just have a knack I fear I will never have. I am not in the least commanding."

Timandra laughed again. "Once you have your own children, I have no doubt you will discover just how commanding you can be. Siblings are another matter. They are used to the discipline of a parent or nurse or tutor. Obeying a sister runs counter to their instincts."

"'Tis doubtful I will have any children. Who would wish to marry me? I am penniless."

Hiding a smile Timandra, wrapped an arm around Eliza's shoulders. Eliza's beauty would assure her of a husband, mayhap even her cousin, though that thought pained Timandra. She would have to examine that little twinge at a later date. Now, she needed to reassure her friend. "Worry not, Eliza. I doubt not but that your Uncle Percival will provide you and Charissa and Delilah with dowries. After all, he provided one for your mother, and despite his penurious ways, from what your cousin has intimated, he is in no way straightened. So be not so glum."

Eliza paused at the stairs' landing. "Dear Timmie, do you truly think he might be so kind as to provide dowries for my sisters and me?"

"I do. If for no other reason than to return his house to the solace he seems to enjoy."

Eliza frowned. "But how are we to meet any eligible men here at

Perfidious Brambles?"

"Well, this is but your first day, and you have already met your cousin," Timandra said, urging Eliza to continue up the stairs. "And I would think him most eligible."

Her eyes brightening, Eliza smiled. "Gavin is quite handsome, is he not? Oh, but I cannot think he would be interested in me."

"And why should he not? In fact, I did see his gaze often rest upon you throughout dinner. And did he not offer to give you a tour of the keep? So, hurry and freshen up, and I will meet you downstairs in front of the suit of armor."

Leaving Eliza in better spirits, Timandra traipsed up the additional flight of stairs to her room on the second floor. She took but a moment to glance down the wide gallery that stretched from one end of the house to the other. Seldon was right, few portraits adorned the walls, but she made note to examine them at a later time. Two long narrow tables, one with a bust on it, sat under large tapestries that added warmth and color to the barren stretch. The gallery would make a good place for Eliza and her siblings to walk and take their exercise on cold wintry days.

Timandra had no trouble finding her room. The first door to the left of the staircase was open and she could hear Finola whistling a little tune as she went about readying the chamber. "Oh, Lady Timandra, would you be looking at this lovely room," Finola said upon spotting Timandra on the threshold. "I have ne'er seen a room trimmed in gold."

The bedchamber was exquisite. The white wainscoting that reached halfway up the wall and the white ceiling molding were edged with gold. The ceiling and upper half of the walls were a swirled plaster painted a pale yellow. The furniture, too, was white and, from bedstead to clothes press to the frame around the mirror, festooned with a thin band of gold. A bright gold carpet embroidered with delicate white flowers and green stems and leaves graced the polished white pine flooring. The draperies were a heavy, dark-gold velvet, but the bed curtains were a bright yellow with embroidery that matched the carpet. The bed's counterpane was a soft yellow with a gold lace coverlet atop it. The mantle shelf over the fireplace was white marble and a gold clock in the shape of a coach between twin gold tripod candlesticks ornamented the mantle. Never had Timandra expected to find anything so grand at Perfidious Brambles.

"Mistress Weston says barons, earls, and even a marquess have stayed in this room," Finola said, shaking out a petticoat she pulled from a trunk at her feet. She nodded to a cupboard with a copper basin and ewer on it. "There is fresh water in the pitcher are you wishing to freshen up, milady, and rose-scented soap, and a close-stool in the closet, are you in need." Her bubbly voice bright with cheer, she added, "You will not be believing the size of the closet. Even with a cot for me there is room enough to store all your trunks. There is shelving with linens, and some books, and yet, space for any personal items you might be wishing to set out."

Needing to ease herself, Timandra slipped into the closet. Finola's lively chatter followed her. "Mistress Weston says Master Seldon's parents entertained a lot. But the master, not liking to give up his own chamber to his noble guests, had these bedchambers redecorated so the nobles could have the best rooms in the house. That was before the present Master Seldon built the east wing where he and his wife entertained."

Timandra, familiar with the custom of giving up one's own quarters to higher-ranking peers, remembered being forced to sleep on her maid's cot in the closet off her bedchamber when her mother and father gave up their room and moved into hers to accommodate the Duke of Bedfordshire and his entourage. She was surprised to learn Seldon had once enjoyed entertaining. She was not surprised Finola had learned so much about the room and the Seldons. Her maid had a way of gaining people's confidence. With her spritely spirit, she charmed near all she met. Apparently, Mistress Weston, despite her stiff formality, was no exception.

Timandra knew she should rebuke Finola, as she intended to rebuke young Edgar, for listening to and passing on gossip, but she would not. She wanted to find out anything and everything she could about Seldon and Perfidious Brambles, not just to satisfy her curiosity – she would be lying to herself did she not admit to her fanciful inquisitiveness – but she wanted to satisfy herself that Eliza and her siblings would be safe and happy in their new home. Besides, Finola passing on information to her in the privacy of her room was quite different than Edgar gossiping to the children. They were young and could easily misconstrue something a servant might say. In addition, his actions might be seen as being disrespectful.

Emerging from the closet to attend her ablutions, Timandra said, "I will be needing my red-woolen wrap. Mister Merritt is to give us a tour of the old keep, and I remember well how cold it was as we passed through it last night."

"Oh, Lady Timandra, might I accompany you. I can finish readying your room while you are at supper. Do, please, say yes. You will be needing someone to carry a light."

Timandra hesitated. Finola was a bright and educated girl. That she would be curious about the keep was understandable. And, they would need someone to provide light. Perth would be better, but he was not to hand. "Oh, very well, but I want to hear no mention of ghosts or the wee folk. Do you understand me?"

"Oh, yes, Lady Timandra, no mention of either – though wee folk would hardly be living in an old keep in England. But ghosts, now they might. However, I will be making nary a peep. I will just run down and find us a lantern. Should work better than candles I would think."

Finola disappeared out the door, and Timandra wondered if she had done the right thing. 'Twas too late to change her mind. She could not bring herself to disappoint Finola. She hoped the girl would be on her good behavior and would keep her mouth shut. Swinging the wrap Finola had left on the foot of the bed about her shoulders, Timandra headed downstairs.

Chapter 6

Timandra found Gavin, Mister Knolles, Herman, and Bennet in front of the suit of armor. Gavin was explaining the difficulties involved in donning the armor, then the even greater difficulties of trying to mount a horse. "And did a knight get knocked off his horse and land on his back, he was about as helpless as a turtle on his back."

Timandra joined in the laughter as Gavin flailed his arms about in imitation of a knight attempting to right himself. His smile was devastating, and his blue eyes sparkled with laughter. He was a good-looking man, and when his eyes met hers, her heartbeat accelerated. This was not good. Having observed his interest in Eliza, she must not let her own emotions get muddled. She had long ago accepted the fact she was no great beauty, yet she knew someday she must marry. She just had not been able to rid herself of the romantic notion of marrying for love. Over the years, she had met no one who stirred even the slightest flutter in her heart. Not until now.

Flushing, she dropped her gaze and turned to Bennet. "Well, young man, here come your sisters. Are you ready for the tour."

"Indeed I am," Bennet answered as Eliza, Charissa, and Delilah joined the group, and Finola appeared with a lantern.

Gavin turned his dazzling smile on the maid. "Ah, I had not thought to ask John to provide us with a light, but here you are, the answer to our unasked request."

Timandra noted Finola was no more impervious to Gavin's charm than were the rest of them. The girl, blushing under the praise, sputtered, "Mister Merritt, sir, 'tis ... 'tis most kind of you to be letting ... letting me join your tour, sir."

He chuckled. "As you bring the light, you are most welcome. So are we all ready?"

A chorus of, "Yeses," greeted him, and he set off with his group in tow. He lead them into the parlor where he extracted a large key from his pocket. "For the door at the top of the stairs," he said. The door opening off the parlor to the staircase had no lock on it. He beckoned to Finola. "Let me have that lantern. As large as this group is, I am thinking we will need more light than this." He pointed to a candle tripod on the mantle. "Fetch those candles, and we will light them off this lantern. Then you carry the candles, I will carry the lantern."

"As you say, Mister Merritt," Finola answered.

With the candles lit, they set off up the stairs. "Mind your step," he told Eliza who followed directly in his wake. He offered her his arm, and she placed her slim, trembling hand on his sleeve. Timandra felt a pang of jealousy, then chided herself. Gavin's concern for Eliza was just what her friend needed to rebuild her confidence. Still, she could not help wondering if any man would ever have as much concern for her wellbeing. Holding her skirt up to keep from stepping on the hem, she trod carefully up the dark staircase.

At the top of the stairs, Gavin handed Eliza the lantern. She held it high, and he wedged the key into the lock. A scraping noise accompanied the turning of the key and the lock snapped open. "This was originally the main entrance to the keep," Gavin said, pocketing the key.

"Not where we entered last night?" Eliza asked in some surprise.

"Nay," Gavin answered, "those doors and the stone steps leading up to them were added much later, as were these steps. As I mentioned, the former steps were wooden and could be drawn up inside in case of attack." Lifting the latch, he pushed on the door. It swung slowly open with a creak Timandra remembered from the previous night when Mistress Weston had led them from the keep to the west wing. The cold air hit them as they stepped one by one into the small chamber with the narrow, twisting staircase that she guessed lead up to one of the turrets.

"What is up the stairs?" Herman asked.

"The last refuge against invaders. When this keep was built, the rooms at the top of each turret were near invincible. They had heavy iron doors, impossible to burn or to batter down and slate stone roofs. These steps twist and turn, making it easier for the defenders in a fight. I will demonstrate later. By the time great-great-grandfather purchased

Perfidious Brambles, such defenses were no longer necessary, and great-grandfather turned the rooms into bedchambers."

"Ah, what did he want to do that for?" Herman demanded and Gavin laughed.

"I wondered the same thing when I first learned the fate of those rooms. But 'twas because great-grandfather liked to have many guests, and he needed a place to house them."

"Is there a dungeon?" Bennet asked.

Gavin tousled Bennet's hair. "Not one with chains and racks if that is what you mean, but the ground floor was not a pleasant part of the house. Come, I will show you the great hall, then what was once the only access to the ground floor or undercroft as some are oft to call it."

With the lantern casting its beam across the floor, he led them down the narrow passage into the hall. Sunlight streamed in through paned windows high above the huge oaken doors and each hand movement or head cock set shadows dancing on the thick plank flooring. The stone walls had once been plastered and white-washed, but the plaster was cracked and pealing and the white-wash had turned a dingy yellow. Timandra admired the two-story, arched, vaulted ceiling and the massive timbers supporting it. Shifting her gaze to the center of the hall, she asked, "Is there naught but the central hearth?" She pointed to the large stone slab in the floor's center. "No chimney fireplace has been added?"

Gavin shook his head. "This was not the primary residence for the Worndon barons after 1430. I think 'twas but used as a hunting lodge. Most likely they chose not to spend on comforts they would seldom need. So, no. Nary a chimney. Not even in the kitchen, though there is a large hearth and high ceiling with louvers."

"Not in the kitchen!" Eliza said in surprise. "But what of the smoke?"

"It was smoky and dirty and smelly and hot. And the poor scullions responsible for clean- up would often strip down to their bare skin or near so."

Charissa and Delilah gasped, then giggled, and Gavin laughed at their response. "Ah, ladies, in medieval days, the kitchen staff were all males. Women might have been involved in the baking. All but one of the ovens were outdoors. The bread ovens were enormous, but they have long since been torn down. Weather permitting, other cooking was done outdoors, but most meals were prepared in the keep's kitchen. We will tour the kitchen when we are done here."

Gavin swept his arm about. "Here in the great hall is where matters of import transpired. The baron or his steward would receive rents, hear grievances, hold trials, and sentence those found guilty of crimes. Most often, fines were the punishment. People were seldom locked in the so-called dungeon. It might hold enemies captured in battle. Even that was usually of short duration as they would either be ransomed or sold into slavery."

"Slavery?" Mister Knolles said, surprise in his voice.

Gavin nodded. "Serfs or villeins were tied to the land, and they owed their lord certain duties, but they could marry whom they pleased, sue in the lord's court, even improve their lot. But some household servants were slaves with no freedoms, no land. They were few in number as the church disapproved of slavery, but slavery did exist. Still does in the American colonies. At least, that is my understanding." Changing the subject, he pointed to his right. "That is where the dais used to be."

"What is the dais?" Herman asked.

Smiling, Gavin seemed happy to answer any and all questions. "The dais was a raised platform where a table was set for the lord and his guests and highest ranking servants, like his steward or bailiff. And of course, when here, his wife and her ladies also joined him. However, few women made up the keep's population." He glanced at Eliza, and she blushed under his jovial gaze. "Being higher than the household staff and retainers," he continued, turning his gaze back to Herman, "allowed the lord to see his minions and be seen by them, which was important in those days. Anyway, I know not when the dais was removed, nor does grandfather. Once the west wing was built, I suppose it no longer served a purpose. But when this hall served the generations of the Worndon barons, it no doubt was a sight to behold."

Pointing to the opposite end of the hall, he said, "There above the buttery and pantry was a musicians' gallery. They would sound their trumpets and a ceremonial procession would emerge from the kitchen with the lord's dinner."

"Indeed, I can well imagine it to be quite a fanciful sight," Timandra said. "And after dinner, did they have entertainment of any kind?"

"Most assuredly. Traveling musicians and poets, acrobats, jugglers, and soothsayers were often on hand, or the revelers might dance or play games like blind man's bluff. But come, let me show you the buttery and pantry and the opening to the ground floor, then we will finish with the kitchen, the chapel, the solar, and turret bedchambers."

Trooping after Gavin, the boys started shoving each other and pretending to fight with imaginary swords, but their antics stopped when Gavin opened a wide door and asked, "Herman, would you and Bennet like to lead the way down into the dungeon?"

Timandra choked on a chuckle as, with wide eyes, both boys shook their heads. Gavin laughed and said, "There is little of interest to see down there. I doubt there ever was. It was naught but a large storage room and that is what it is now. In its fortified days, many more supplies would have been stored there. Barrels of ale and some of wine, casks of grains for the animals and milled flour for the house inhabitants. Ropes and various tools and weapons." He waved his arm. "Any number of things.

"When great-grandfather moved the servants' quarters in the west wing from the second floor to the cellar, he lost storage space. As he enjoyed entertaining, and needed plentiful supplies, he knocked a large opening in the back wall of the keep's ground floor. He had sturdy double doors installed for easy access and gained more storage area than will ever be needed. But long before those doors were added, one of the Worndon barons had these steps installed and this entry built. Until then, the only way in or out of the ground floor was through a large trap door and by way of a ladder. Supplies were raised and lowered by a system of pulleys and ropes and tackle. At times they might even lower prized animals down to keep them safe from attack."

"Oh, that must have been smelly," Charissa said, wrinkling her nose.

Gavin laughed. "Everything was smelly then. The privies, or garderobes as they were once known, had chutes that emptied into the moat. The water in the moat being stagnate, well 'twas not water you would want drawn for your bath. I imagine the stench emitting from the moat is one reason great-great-grandfather had it immediately drained and filled in."

Everyone groaned, and Gavin, laughing again, said, "Seems we have no takers on the ground floor, let us have a quick peak at the buttery and the pantry, then on to the kitchen."

Timandra was surprised at the size of both rooms, but Gavin explained the size of the household staff, as well as the number of retainers, meant large amounts of food and drink were required on a daily basis. In the buttery the ales and wines were stored and dispensed, and the pantry held perishable foods and prized herbs. Timandra found the kitchen even more fascinating. It had a vaulted ceiling as high as the ceiling in the great hall. The smoke from the open fires would drift upward and out through louvered openings controlled by long dangling ropes. Heavy wooden tables and cabinets were still in place in the room, and stone basins with drains meant they had a ready water supply.

"There is a cistern on the roof," Gavin said. "It catches the rain. Pipes brought the water to the kitchen and to the solar, and the waste drained into the moat. Great-grandfather, though, had the pipes diverted to the kitchen in the west wing. There is also a well right outside the kitchen and another in the cellar. But the cellar well was not intended to meet kitchen needs. It was there to insure the keep had a reliable source of water during a siege. Most sieges were short lived, but some could last as much as a week before relief arrived. The door that leads outside is of as heavy an oak as the other doors to the hall. And again, the staircase was wooden and could be drawn up and secured inside the kitchen."

Finding the entire tour fascinating, Timandra asked, "Is there a staircase there now?"

"Yes, a steep stone staircase. I am guessing 'twas built at the same time as the front entrance steps were added."

"Bennet and I raced up them," Herman said. "They are steep and uneven. Bennet tripped, but I caught him. Mister Knolles says they are dangerous, and we may not play on them again."

"Good for Mister Knolles," Eliza said. "You mind what he says. Now, you interrupted Cousin Gavin." She turned to her cousin and smiled. "Please, continue."

For a moment, Timandra's joy in the tour diminished as Gavin stared in a mesmerized trance at the smiling beauty before him. He shook his head and cleared his throat, and Timandra shook herself. She must gain control of her senses. 'Twas only natural Gavin would be enamored of Eliza. And sadly, she thought, 'twas only natural she should be enamored of Gavin. But she must not let her foolish infatuation lead her to expect any kind of reciprocal ardor.

"Ah, well, yes," Gavin resumed, "we were speaking of the need to be prepared against attack. Generally, the raiders came at night. They were after cattle and sheep and horses, and did they catch a house unguarded, they might make off with whatever bounty they could carry. And possibly with one or more inhabitants they could later ransom back to the family. Winter months were the most vulnerable time when people tended to be huddled around their fires. The longer nights made for easier escape as the reivers herded the captive slow-moving animals home."

A hint of anxiety in her voice, Delilah asked, "But there are no longer reivers, are there?"

Gavin smiled, then donning a serious face, shook his head. "Nay, little cousin, not here where we live. You have naught to worry about. Near the border, some raids still take place, but they are mostly carried out by desperate men who have found no other way to feed their families. Even then, they take but a few cows and hurry back across the border as quickly as they can. Reiving is a hanging offense."

"I would have liked to be here to fight those reivers," Herman said, slashing his imaginary sword around. Bennet followed suit, stating, "Me, too."

"Enough about reiving," Timandra said, her commonsense having gained the upper hand over her emotions. "Back to the mundane. Mister Merritt, do please tell us about these vats."

Several large cauldrons in the huge hearth had drawn Timandra's attention, and Gavin explained, "Long ago these were used for soups and stews and for boiling meats. But now they are used for laundering. When the weather is inclement, the laundress, one of Grandfather's tenants, and her assistants do the wash in here. Plenty of room to spread clothes out, here and in the hall. Grandfather is a stickler for clean linens. That is one thing he will not mind spending his coin on. He wants no bugs in his bed. Every Wednesday, no matter the weather, the laundress arrives to do the wash."

"Oh, I do applaud that sentiment," Timandra said.

Gavin chuckled and said, "Shall we move on?"

"Might we see the turret rooms now?" Bennet asked.

"Why not?" Gavin said. "Follow me."

Finola, rubbing the back of her neck, whispered to Timandra, "Milady, would you not be feeling a chill in this room? Particularly next to the wall there?"

"I feel a chill in every room. No fires have been lit. What do you expect?"

"Nay, milady, I mean a chill across the back of the neck, like fingers tickling ..."

Timandra interrupted her. "Finola, that will do. Now hold that candelabra steady that we have enough light we will not trip over these rough stones."

Gavin steered them out of the kitchen into a narrow room that seemingly had no purpose other than to serve as a passage way, but he stopped before a thick door in the center of a side wall. "The privy," he said, and opened the door. "Great-grandfather had the holes covered over and made into a bench. He used the room to store his guests' extra travel trunks and such."

Charissa giggled. "I wonder did his guests know it used to be a privy."

She received a glare from Eliza, but Gavin laughed. "I rather doubt it." Closing the door, he led them back into the small chamber with the twisting staircase leading up to the turret.

"All right, Herman, Bennet, this is your chance to attack me." Gavin said. "We will sword fight our way up the steps." The boys gleefully entered into the imaginary battle, but both soon found trying to swish their swords with their right hands caused them to hit the wall as they fought their way up the staircase after Gavin. Laughing at the antics, Timandra followed after Eliza and her sisters in the combatants' wake. Mister Knolles and Finola followed her.

Huffing from their exertions, the boys finally reached the top where the battle ended. "My knuckles are banged up," Herman said, rubbing his hand.

"Ah hah," Gavin said, "now you know why the stairs are narrow, why they are spiral, and they twist in a clockwise direction. It gives the defender an advantage, most people being right-handed. The defender has full movement of his sword arm. Some men-at-arms did fight with their left hand, but most, even if they were left-handed, were trained to fight with their right."

Turning, he put his shoulder into the door, no longer iron, but a dense oak, and pushed. Holding the lantern high, he stepped aside to let everyone enter. The combination of the candles and lantern light brightened the shuttered chamber. Sheets were spread over all the furniture, but a bed, high enough to hide a trundle bed for child or servant, two chairs, and a large chest were easily distinguishable. Timandra guessed a smaller object below a mirror would be a toilet table. Several rolled woven mats and a folded screen awaited the rooms next occupant.

"How long since anyone has stayed in here?" Timandra asked.

Gavin rubbed his chin and looked upward. "I would guess this room has not been occupied in near thirty years. Not since my mother left to marry my father."

"Oh, my," Eliza said. "That seems sad. All these rooms and no one but Uncle Percival rambling about in them."

"I cannot think Grandfather does much rambling. But he does have the keep, the west wing, and the east wing thoroughly cleaned once a year. Holds down the cobwebs and such. A number of the tenant women come up, and under Mistress Weston's supervision, they scrub and polish and dust, and put clean sheets over all the furniture, then Grandfather shuts everything up again. Either Eustace, his steward, or Old John periodically check the east wing during the rest of the year to make sure there is no rodent damage. To my knowledge, that is it."

"Have you ever been in the east wing?" Timandra asked. She was curious about the newer wing of the house that Seldon had closed off.

Gavin shook his head. "Nay. I used to ask to be allowed to see it, but Grandfather never gave me permission. Eustace says it is shuttered and dark with sheets over everything, just like in this room. Mother has told me some about it. She grew up in that wing. Or at least from the time she turned ten when the construction was finished. She says it was lovely and bright and airy. She has many fond memories of her life there while her mother was still alive. Grandfather was very social then. They had lots of parties. Visitors forever coming and going. Many servants." He shook his head. "Very different than now. 'Tis hard for me to fathom. I have never known Grandfather to be gregarious."

Eliza placed her hand on his arm. "'Twas the loss of his wife that changed him, I would guess. Just as when my mother died, father was so devastated. It changed him."

How sweet she looked in the soft glow of the candlelight, Timandra thought. Gavin was looking down at her with such gentleness in his eyes. He was bound to fall in love with Eliza. And, 'twas for the best. He was just what her friend needed. He would rebuild her confidence. Yes, they would be a beautiful couple. She just had to stop her heart from rioting at the idea.

"I think," Gavin said, "my grandmother's death saddened Grand-father greatly, but that 'twas not what turned him bitter." He looked thoughtful, then thinning his lips, he cocked his head to one side and said, "You will have to learn this at some point. Better you hear it from me than through gossip. My mother and Grandfather are estranged."

Chapter 7

No one said a word. Even Herman and Bennet remained silent, though Timandra doubted they knew the meaning of estranged. Their faces, though, said they knew it was not good. She shook her head. Seldon was estranged from his daughter, his only child. No wonder he seemed an irascible, bitter old man. "Indeed, we are all sorry to hear that," she said, thinking someone needed to acknowledge his pronouncement. "But your mother is well, I trust."

Gavin nodded. "Aye, mother is lovely and cheerful and as lively as the spring wind. She and I live at Kirkworth Hall with my Uncle Phineas, my father's older brother, and his wife, Aunt Mabelle. My father died in fifty-one fighting alongside King Charles."

"I am sorry," Timandra said, grateful, due to her father's parole after he fought alongside King Charles I, he had been unable to join King Charles II when he tried to retake the throne.

Gavin shrugged, and twisting his mouth, said, "I was but five and have little memory of him, but Mother loved him dearly. She has a small sketch of him that a passing artist made. She keeps it by her bedside. You shall meet her, and my aunt and uncle, who have kindly provided us a home all these many years."

"They must be very kind people," Eliza said.

Gavin looked down at her and smiled. "Indeed they are. They are childless, and they have treated me as if I were their son. My uncle is Baron Kirkworth, and as next of kin, I will someday inherit the title and the estate plus an estate in Scotland near Edinburgh."

"You mean you are a lord?" Herman asked, awe in his voice.

Laughing, Gavin said, "Nay, not yet, and hopefully not for a good many years. My uncle is healthy. I love him dearly and hope he will live for many years to come. His father, my grandfather, lived to near eighty-five. He died not five years ago. He was a crusty old Scotsman."

"A Scotsman!" Timandra said, knowing she voiced the surprise shared by the others.

"Aye, he was born in Scotland. His father was a close friend of King James. When James inherited England's crown and moved to London, great-grandfather Merritt came with him. As did my grandfather. He was about twenty, a younger son. He became an English citizen, and to please his father, King James made him a baron, but Grandfather never lost his love for Scotland, or his Scottish accent. He made many trips back to his estate near Edinburgh which he inherited from his mother. I went with him several times.

"But here now, I ramble on. We have a tour to complete. Let me but finish by saying that due to a land dispute that has raged between the Seldons and the Merritts since the reign of King James, Grandfather Percival found my father an unacceptable husband for my mother. When my mother ran off to Scotland and married him anyway, Grandfather disowned her."

"Oh, no," Eliza said, her delicate hands going to her mouth. "How sad."

"He accepts you, though," Timandra said.

Gavin chuckled. "He does, but not particularly gracefully. That is another story for another time. Let us go now to the chapel and the solar, and then I must end this tour and head for home else I will be late for supper. Guests, close friends from Newcastle, are arriving."

Before anyone could question him further, he shepherded them out the door and back down the steps. "Both the turrets are the same," he said, "so we need not visit the other." He lowered the lantern. "Mind your step here. This board is a bit rough. Take note not to trip."

Stepping over the aged and splintered plank, they followed Gavin behind a high decorative screen into the chapel. It, more than any of the other rooms, showed its long-time neglect. The large window behind the altar was boarded over, not shuttered. The wooden altar was bare, plaster peeled in huge patches off the walls, and indentations on the floor showed where pews had once rested and had been ripped away.

"I would guess this chapel has not been used in many a year," Timandra said.

54

Gavin nodded. "I have no idea when it was last used. I am thinking not since the church was built in Fairflex Village. I do know the pews were removed to the church. Do you attend services, look for the pews with the initials, P B, for Perfidious Brambles on them. They are down front on the opposite side of the aisle from the Kirkworth pews.

"At one time this chapel would have had a mass said every morning," he continued. "Near everyone would have attended. The Worndons and their guests would have been seated in the pews, the staff would have been standing behind them with some straggling out the door. All eager to have the service over. Or so I imagine it anyway," he added with a smile, then pointed upward. "Up we go to the solar and our tour is complete."

Following on Gavin's heels, Herman asked, "What is the solar?"

"It is a bedchamber and a parlor rolled into one," Gavin answered, exiting into a spacious room. It was the opposite of the chapel below. Though sheets covered the furniture, the flooring gleamed, two large braziers were strategically placed to warm the room, and the walls were hung with tapestries though they too were concealed under sheets. Timandra, followed by Eliza, Charissa, and Delilah, could not resist peeping under some of the sheets to see the furniture – tufted stools, an intricate carpet displayed on the table, cushioned chairs positioned around the table, a day bed at the foot of the main bed, and a charming three-legged table and writing desk positioned under the large shuttered window. Two empty candelabras hung from the ceiling and four iron sconces adorned the walls. The room could easily be prepared for immediate occupancy.

"The door to the left," Gavin said, "opens into the Lord's wardrobe. It would hold his books, moneys, clothing, most likely some weaponry, and a cot for his man servant. The door on the right leads into the ladies' bower. A small room where the ladies, other than the Lady of the Manor would sleep. It was also a sitting room where the ladies could chat, sew – do whatever ladies did back then in privacy away from the men.

"So that concludes the tour, and I really must be on my way."

"Indeed, we cannot thank you enough for showing us about," Eliza said. "I cannot think I would have been brave enough to explore this part of the house without male company."

Timandra would have scoffed. What was there to fear? But when she looked at Eliza and saw how Eliza was looking at Gavin, she tightened her lips and said nothing.

"Were you really allowed to play in here, Cousin Gavin?" Herman asked as they headed back through the grand hall.

"Aye, many a time. But I was on my honor. I could only play in here, or in the chapel, or the kitchen, but I could not go in any of the bed chambers. Grandfather made it clear that if I broke my word even once, I would never be allowed to play in here again." He chuckled. "A couple of times I was tempted to go up to the gallery or to the solar, but I never did. I just knew that somehow Grandfather would know I had abused his trust. I cannot say how I knew he would know, but I never doubted he would know."

"Do you think he would let us play in here?" Bennet queried in his piping little voice.

"You will have to ask him."

"Would you not ask him for us?" Herman said.

"Herman!" Eliza gasped. "That is impolite. Do you wish to play in here, and I am not saying I think 'tis a good idea, you must ask Uncle Percival yourself."

"I do think it best you ask for yourself," Gavin said. "'Twill show your stamina. Grandfather cares not for impudence, but he admires those who show him no fear." He looked at Timandra with his last statement, and she flushed, certain he had given her a compliment. She had not been timid in her speech with Percival Seldon.

They had reached the door when Delilah asked, "Was it not terribly dark in here for play? What did you do for light?"

"The light that comes in from the windows over the main entrance doors gave me plenty of light. Plus, in no time at all, I knew my way around. I could slay dragons or fight attacking reivers back and forth across the hall, into the kitchen and back to the chapel even had I been blindfolded. I fought my way halfway up the stairs, which was as far up as I was allowed to go, and back down again, and I often had my best fights with my own shadow.

"But here we are." He tugged open the heavy door. "Down you go."

"Finola, you go first as you have the candles," Timandra said.

"Yes, milady," the girl said.

Timandra eyed her servant closely as she edged past her. Holding the candles high, Finola started down the stairs. She had been far too quiet throughout the entire tour. That was unlike her. True, she had been warned not to ask about ghosts. Timandra had not wanted Finola's fantasies to frighten the Tilburys. All the same, had Finola not questioned the chill of the kitchen, Timandra might not have known her maid even accompanied them. She hoped no repercussions would arise to make her sorry she had allowed Finola to join them. Lifting her skirts and starting down the steps, Timandra shook herself. Finola for once had been on good behavior. That was all. She should be pleased, not looking for a problem.

⚜ ⚜ ⚜ ⚜

The hour was growing late, and Timandra had yet to speak with her coachman or with Tombs. With the tour ended, she expressed her intention of visiting the stables, and Gavin offered to escort her. Alone with him in the cooling afternoon air, her heartbeat quickened. Foolish, she chided herself, so foolish. She had to curb these wayward emotions.

Not having stopped to change into her outdoor walking shoes, she was pleased to have Gavin's hand on her elbow to steady her. Her mules were hardly adequate for the rocky overgrown path leading to the stables and coach house. But she was glad of the chance to be outdoors. This was her first real opportunity to survey the grounds. They were in sad shape. Much work would be needed to set the gardens and orchard to rights.

She shook her head. "These grounds are disreputable. My footmen may not be gardeners, but they will soon find themselves gainfully employed." She looked at Gavin. "Of course, depending does Mister Seldon give me permission to set them to work. Just the weeding and pruning should keep them busy for a couple of weeks, I should think. They are apt to grouse, but they will do as they are bid. Though I doubt they would admit it, they will prefer having something to do other than loafing about."

Gavin chuckled. "I hope you may be right, Lady Timandra. I am certain, do you ask Grandfather at supper tonight, he will acquiesce to your plans. There is not much to occupy the youth around here. Those who have no land and cannot find employment go to Newcastle. They can almost always find work in the coal mines or, with luck, the shipyards.

"Hmm," he said and stopped. She paused beside him and looked up. He looked thoughtful, then he nodded his head. "Yes, am I not mistaken, the man who used to be Grandfather's gardener is one of his tenants. He is a bit too old and arthritic now to do any gardening himself, but he could direct your footmen. Do you wish, I could stop by his home and ask him to call on you tomorrow morning."

"Oh, what a splendid idea. Thank you. But I cannot ask you to go out of your way."

"Nay, 'tis but the slightest detour. Goodman Beamer will most likely be pleased he can help. I am thinking you will not want him at cock's crow. Should I tell him mid-morning?"

She laughed as they resumed their walk. "Yes, mid-morning would be perfect. I am not a particularly early riser, though I may learn to be, do I stay here for long. Seems your Grandfather keeps very early hours. I understand we will soon be sitting down to supper. Then afterwards, I am told, he retires to his rooms. I suppose Eliza and I will find something to amuse us and the girls until our bed time. Mister Knolles, thankfully, has that nice large school room he can use to keep the boys out of mischief. With all their activities today, though, they should tire early."

"Do I remember correctly from my own youth," Gavin said, "the more tired I became, the more I fought going to bed. My guess is my young cousins will be no different."

Timandra agreed, but before she could answer him, her attention was caught by a small neat stone cottage near hidden in a clump of trees far to the right of the stables. "What is that lovely little cottage?" she asked. "One would almost not know it is there."

Gavin looked in the direction she pointed. "That is the steward's cottage," he answered. "When he is here, that is where Eustace Colyer lives. Great-grandfather had it built for his steward who was married and had children." He chuckled. "Old John is one of those children."

"Oh, no, really. It is funny to envision him as a child."

"He and Grandfather shared a tutor. They rode together, went fishing together ... which reminds me, the fish pond is well stocked. Eustace and I and one of the tenants in charge of catching fish for Grandfather's meals are the only ones to fish it, officially anyway. I would not be surprised do some of Grandfather's tenants fish there just as some poach his quail and rabbits. But to my thinking, there is no harm done. Grandfather cannot eat all the fish, and the rabbits would over run the estate did the tenants not snare a goodly number of them. My guess is Grandfather knows it. He is too smart not to know. Should be fun for my young cousins to fish. Under Mister Knolles supervision of course. Mayhap tomorrow I may show them the pond."

"Indeed it will be fun for them. At least in short intervals. I cannot imagine either Herman or Bennet sitting still for very long waiting for a fish to bite," Timandra said, but her mind was on the thought of seeing Gavin again on the morrow. A pleasure she had not expected. But then, why should he not return so soon? He would want to see Eliza.

Again chuckling, Gavin said, "You may be right. They are a bit young yet, leastwise, Bennet is. They are more apt to enjoy swimming in the pond."

"Oh, I fear they have not learned to swim."

"They have not!" Gavin said, surprise in his voice and on his face. "Not even Herman?"

"No, I am certain not."

"Then I must teach them. Every boy should know how to swim." He looked at Timandra. "And what of you, Lady Timandra, do you swim?"

She blushed. "Most definitely not."

"Call me a dunderpate, but I think women should know how to swim, too. Never know when the knowledge might save your life." Then he looked her up and down. "Well, maybe not. I would guess with what you are wearing, even if you could swim, it would do you little good, your clothing would pull you right down to the bottom."

"My, you are encouraging," she said with a laugh.

He laughed, too, then sobered. "My apologies. My nurse, whom I was very fond of, drowned when I was seven. She had gone to visit her family. Coming back, when crossing the Tyne, the boat hit a rock. In moments it sank. The man rowing managed to swim to shore."

"I am sorry," Timandra said. She stopped. They had reached the stables. "'Tis hard to lose someone you love." She thought of a tenant's young son who had died shortly before his fourth birthday. He had been her playmate. She had been but six when he died. But she remembered how he had trailed around after her like Bennet trailed Herman. Thoughts of him, his baby arms lifting up to her, his sweet little piping voice, could still bring a pang to her heart.

"Milady." Timandra's thoughts were interrupted by her coachman. "I had no doubt you would be coming to see about your horse and to see how the coach horses fair. I am pleased to tell you all are well and robust. I have no doubt Pirro will be eager for a run on the morrow are you wanting a good gallop."

"Thank you Hardgrove. Do you please have Mister Merritt's horse saddled."

"Yes, milady," the coachman answered and disappeared into the stable.

"You will have me spoiled, Lady Timandra," Gavin said. "I am used to having to see to my horse myself. Oft times, did I plan but a short visit, I would not even unsaddle him. Merlin will think himself spoiled, too."

"Merlin? Is your horse a wizard then?"

"Aye, at times I think he may well be. He is a Neapolitan Courser, and I swear he flies over fences and hedges no other horse could manage."

Timandra smiled. "A fine breed. I will look forward to seeing him in action."

Grinning, Gavin said, "I will look forward to showing him off. Oh, and here is my wizard. You are familiar with his breed?"

"Aye, father has one," she answered as the postilion led a coal-black horse out from the stable. The horse had a strong neck and broad chest and long sturdy legs. His head was beautifully shaped and his large brown eyes looked at her with interest, but no fear. He swished his long silky black tail and stamped one foot as if to say, 'I am ready, let us go'.

"Oh, he is a handsome fellow," Timandra said, reaching up to rub Merlin's satiny nose.

"Ah, there you go, spoiling him even more. Next thing I know, he will be back over here without me. That is another of his tricks. He knows how to open gates."

"Does he?" She patted the horse on his neck. "Are you not the clever boy?"

"That is enough spoiling him for one day. I must need head for home. I will stop by Beamer's and tell him to present himself 'round mid-morning."

Timandra shook her head. "Nay, please do say late morning. I believe I will have a ride before I breakfast tomorrow."

Gavin nodded and swung up on his horse. "Until tomorrow, Lady Timandra," he said and setting his heels to Merlin, he rode away.

For a few moments, Timandra stared after him. The man did things to her heart. He was witty, courteous, and caring. And he would one day marry Eliza. She needed to put him from her mind. At the same time, she could hardly wait for the next day that she might see him again.

Chapter 8

"Here are your boots, milady," Finola said.

"Splendid, do please help me get them on," Timandra said.

"Yes, milady." The maid knelt at Timandra's feet and started to help her pull up the tight-fitting boots. "You will be having a care, will you not? This being a new area. You will not be trying to jump any hedges will you?"

Timandra laughed. "You sound like my mother or Aunt Venetia."

"Well, and they are not here to be looking out for you, now are they? So someone must. 'Tis not likely Mister Seldon will be giving you any such warnings."

"I should think he would not. He would not so presume. You, on the other hand ..."

"Nay, milady," Finola interrupted, "you have no need to scold. I am after knowing I am being over bold. Then I am also knowing when you get on that horse of yours, you are after thinking you can outride any gent. And mayhap you can, but I am thinking you have no need to be proving it."

Shaking her head, Timandra stood and stomped first one heel and then the other down into her boots. "Aunt Venetia warned me you were much too brazen, Finola. But I paid her no heed. No. And now I am stuck with you."

Finola grinned. "Indeed you are, milady." Rising she headed back to the closet with no indication that she knew she had been chastised, however mildly. "Will you be wearing the matching green hat or the black with the gold feather. I am liking the black better."

"I like it better, too. I shall wear it," Timandra answered, crossing to the looking glass above her toilet table. She turned sideways to study her coat. The rent she had made near the shoulder of the tight-fitting sleeve had been beautifully mended. Finola was superb with a needle.

Timandra preferred her green riding habit to the red with the gold swirls. Not only was the green a better color for her – it brought out the green of her blue-green eyes – but the habit fit her better. The coat, though close fitting to the waist, had two pleated side vents and a back slit in the tail that allowed her to move without restriction. The large, turned-back cuffs of the coat exposed the intricate folds of the sleeves of her muslin chemise, and its collarless styling showed off the lace cravat at her neck. Best of all, the skirt had no train that she had to scoop up to keep from dragging in the dirt.

Finola reappeared, hat in hand. Taking the hat, Timandra placed it on her head. She liked the cocked brim. Smiling at her reflection, she said, "What say you, Finola, did we choose the right hat?"

"Aye, Lady Timandra. Now are you certain I cannot be getting you a wee bite more to eat afore you are setting off on your ride?"

Timandra shook her head. "Nay, Finola, you know do I eat more than a crumb of toast with but a bite of cheese and some apple cider, that my stomach will revolt, do Pirro and I have a good fast gallop. Now where are my gloves?"

"Here, milady." Finola handed her a pair of short soft leather gauntlet gloves. "Mister Tombs said he would be waiting for you. I warned him he had best see you come to no harm."

Shaking her head and laughing, Timandra said, "Oh, Finola, what am I to do with you?"

Finola gave her no answer but bobbing a curtsy, she said, "Have a nice ride, milady."

Timandra had hoped Eliza might ride with her, but her coachman had said Eliza's little mare needed a couple more days of rest from their long journey. Her only companion was to be Tombs. She liked the man – ever courteous and competent – he would converse with her did she choose, or he would keep a respectful distance behind her did she want time for reflection. He awaited her at the stable door with both his horse and hers saddled. Pirro nickered and pranced about when he scented her. She laughed at her pretty chestnut gelding and offered him a carrot nub. "I do believe my spoiled beast is ready to be off."

"That he is, my lady. Might I give you a boot up?" Tombs said, cupping his hands.

"Thank you." In an instant she was up on her saddle, and Tombs handed her the reins. He untied his own horse, a sturdy, dependable Cleveland Bay, and quickly mounted. Timandra had no need to set her heels to Pirro's flanks – she but gave him his head and off they went. She loved her Irish Hobby. Swift and agile, yet sturdy and sweet tempered, his gait was smooth once they could fall into a gallop. She guided him around the stables and past the pen where the coach horses had been turned out, past an apple orchard, and out toward an open field. She put her horse over a low hedge that was meant to do no more than keep the sheep from straying, and turned him loose. Off they raced, and she laughed into the wind.

Sheep scattered, and she could hear the dull thud of hooves on the soft sod. The air smelled clean and fresh, and the sun felt warm on her face. It was a glorious day, and she reveled in its splendor. Seldon's estate was large, and Old John had told her to ride north, then east, that she might skirt the tenants' homes and fields, yet would not be hemmed in by the estate woods. On another day, she and Eliza would visit the tenants. Eliza should get to know the people who lived and worked on her uncle's estate, but this day, Timandra just wanted to ride. Pastureland stretched on and on, and the hedges were low and easy to jump. All the same, Finola would not approve, and Timandra made note not to tell her maid of her headlong dash across the meadows. She could just hear Finola scolding her in her lilting Irish brogue.

At last she began to tire and started gently pulling up on Pirro. He pranced a bit, then settled to an ambling walk. "'Twas a good ride, my lady," Tombs said, riding up beside her.

She smiled and nodded, "Aye." Tombs sat his horse well, seemed to move with the horse as if they were one. "Do we have enough feed for the horses until the grain from Newcastle can be delivered?" The evening before, he had informed her he had placed an order with the village blacksmith. The smith would see the order went out by post in the morning.

"In combination with the hay, aye, we have enough. Old John said the tenants can furnish us with more hay. He said 'twill give them a little extra coin they will be glad of."

"That is good. I told Hardgrove to hire a couple of boys to help him in the stables. With that many horses, there will be a lot of mucking and currying."

Tombs chuckled. "Aye, and neither Hardgrove, nor Mistress Tilbury's coachman, Tibbs, no, nor even your young, postilion, Putnam, are inclined to do the mucking. And 'tis for certain your footmen feel they are too superior to be doing the mucking."

"Yes, they may think so, but this afternoon, they will find themselves employed as gardeners. I have Mister Seldon's permission to set them to work. I will not have them loafing about, getting bored, and then getting into trouble."

"Have you an assignment for me, my lady?"

She looked at her trusted outrider. "Nay, I cannot think I need worry about you getting into any trouble. Do you keep the horse feed in supply, and be to hand do I need you for some errand or to ride with me. 'Tis all I ask at this time."

He nodded and said, "As you wish, my lady," but he was not looking at her. He was looking at the rider advancing toward them. "I do think 'tis Mister Merritt."

Timandra looked in the direction Tombs was looking. Tombs was right. 'Twas Gavin. He turned in his saddle and lifted his hat to wave to her. She was raising her arm to return his salute when a shot rang out. Pirro near bolted, but she jerked up on his reins. He pranced about until Tombs caught his reins.

"You all right?" Tombs asked.

"Yes, but what was that? It sounded like a shot."

"I intend to find out, my lady. You stay here."

Releasing her horse, Tombs set his horse racing across the field toward Gavin. "See to Lady Timandra," she heard him tell Gavin who had gotten his prancing horse under control. "I will see what is in them woods." Without waiting for Gavin to acknowledge him, he swerved his horse toward a thicket of trees and bushes. Gavin watched Tombs for a moment, then did as bid and rode over to join Timandra. Both horses still appeared jittery. Ears were up and swiveling, eyes were rolling, tails were swishing, but neither horse attempted to take flight.

"Are you all right, Lady Timandra?" Gavin asked, when he reached her side.

"I am fine. What of you? Was that a shot?"

Narrowing his eyes, he said, "I do think it was." He was still holding his hat in his hand, and he looked at it quizzically, then added. "I believe my hat has been shot." He poked his finger through the crown.

"Oh, my," Timandra gasped. "Why, that shot could have hit you."

"Yes, I would say a hunter has been rather careless." His eyes met hers. "I would not have this mentioned to Grandfather. First, I would not want to worry him. Second, I would not want to get some neighbor in trouble."

"But such carelessness. It should not go unpunished."

"Please, in this case, allow it to go unpunished and unmentioned."

She stared into Gavin's vibrant blue eyes and nodded. "As you wish, Mister Merritt. I am glad the hunter was not a better shot. Though I cannot think what sort of animal he took you for."

"My guess is he had been napping, woke suddenly, saw some movement and fired without thinking. But here comes your man. Do I remember correctly, his name is Tombs?"

"Yes, Tombs." Timandra nodded, but she was having trouble squelching her outrage. "Did you catch the tomfool?" she demanded when her outrider rode within hearing distance.

He did not attempt to answer until he rode up next to her and Gavin. "Mister Merritt, I was unable to catch whoever fired the shot. He must have realized what he had done, and fearing punishment, fled as swiftly as he could. I would guess him to be the son of some local neighbor. Doubtful any tenants could afford a gun. No doubt, a startled hunter mistook you for a deer."

"Oh, how could he think Mister Merritt to be a deer," Timandra stormed. The two men were being impossible. Her heart was still thudding in her chest. What if Gavin had been killed! No, she could not even contemplate such a thought.

"An old man who cannot afford glasses, my lady, or a youth startled and turning and firing without getting a clear view of his target. Has been known to happen."

Timandra frowned, but Gavin was nodding his head in agreement, and at last she said, "Well, at least you were not harmed. Are you going to Perfidious Brambles, mayhap you would ride back with me?"

Smiling, Gavin nodded and replaced his hat on his head. "I would be most delighted, Lady Timandra." He turned to Tombs. "I thank you for checking out the situation."

Tombs inclined his head. "'Twas best I should, sir. Best I know is there any danger lurking should Lady Timandra or Mistress Tilbury go riding."

"Wise," Gavin agreed, and Timandra said, "Let us head back. I have yet to breakfast and my stomach is now starting to rumble."

"By all means," Gavin said. "To breakfast we go." And he set off at a gallop.

Timandra flicked her reins and Pirro headed off after Merlin. Tombs brought up the rear.

※ ※ ※ ※

When they arrived at the stables, the coachmen and postilion came out to take their horses. Gavin, unused to such service at his grandfather's, laughed and swung down from his horse. "I thank you. I have been after Grandfather for any number of years to hire a stable hand. I could grow accustomed to having my horse tended for me." Handing his reins to the coachman, he turned to help Timandra down. He liked the feel of her hands on his shoulders, and he realized he let his hands rest on her waist a bit too long to be proper. But then, she was a fine specimen of womanhood. Tall and trim, yet shapely. He was also impressed by her horsemanship, and her keen wit. He liked that she was not faint of heart. Anger, not fear, had been her reaction to the shooting that could have caused him a severe injury – nay, though he hated to think it – could have taken his life.

"That is a fine gelding you have there," he said, hoping she had not taken offense at his forwardness. "Plenty of spirit, but I made note you had no trouble handling him. I applaud you."

"He serves me well. I think he was more than ready for a good gallop today after a fortnight trailing behind the coach." She looked toward the house. "Have you breakfasted, Mister Merritt? I care not to eat much before I ride, but now I find I am famished."

"I had a nice breakfast, but I have no doubt I could do with a mug of ale, and maybe some of Cook's honey and bread. I would be pleased could I join you at table."

He liked the smile that brightened her face when she answered, "Indeed, Mister Merritt, do please join me."

"Mister Merritt," Tombs interrupted, "might I have but a word with you. I do think I noticed but the slightest limp to your horse's left hind leg. You might want to have a look at it before you go inside."

Gavin turned to face the man. "A limp? Indeed I will have a look at Merlin." He glanced back at Timandra. "Do you please excuse me, Lady Timandra. I will see to Merlin and then join you. Do please tell Cook to set a place for me."

"I will do so. And I do hope naught is seriously wrong with your horse. Hardgrove is very capable. If aught is amiss, he will know what to do."

"Thank you," Gavin said, but before turning to see to his horse, he watched Timandra stride confidently down the path leading back to the house. Oh, indeed, she was a fine woman.

The coachman had led his horse into the stables, and Gavin started after him, but Tombs halted him. "Mister Merritt, do please excuse me for telling you a tale. Naught is wrong with your horse. I but wanted a moment alone to talk with you without alarming Lady Timandra."

Gavin looked at Tombs in surprise, but the man quickly continued. "Sir, I could be mistaken, but I am thinking I am not. I would say the person who shot at you this morning meant to shoot you. I am wondering might you suspect the same thing? The ground and surrounding area showed signs of someone lying in wait. Moss on a rock disturbed like someone had been sitting on it. Indentation of a musket stock in the dirt. Some whittling shavings, several branches bent down to give a clear view of the meadow. Have you a habit, sir, of riding the same route each time you come visiting? Are you a frequent visitor?"

Gavin slowly nodded. "Aye, I am a frequent visitor, and I usually take the same route. Even if I am but going into the village, I stop by here to see if Old John is in need of anything. Save the old fellow a trip."

"Have you call to think someone might be out to kill you, sir? 'Twould not be my business to be asking except I must see to Lady Timandra's safety."

Again Gavin nodded. "I understand your concern for Lady Timandra. I cannot say I know anyone who would want to shoot me. For now, let us say it was an accident."

Tombs nodded, but he did not look convinced. Gavin could not blame him. Tombs could be right, though he hated to admit it, even to himself. It was the second attempt on his life in less than two weeks.

The first had been outside a tavern in Newcastle. He had been set upon by three men with clubs. Had his friend not emerged from the tavern, pulled his pistol, and run the three men off, Gavin had little doubt but what he might have been bludgeoned to death. He and his friend put it off to a robbery attempt, but now he wondered if he should view the event differently.

Tombs handed Gavin a pebble. "You will want to find this in your horse's hoof," he said.

"Aye," Gavin said. He and Tombs made a show of taking a pebble from Merlin's hoof. The coachman, who was rubbing Merlin down said he had noticed no limp, but then the pebble was very tiny. Gavin agreed, then set off to join Timandra at the table. He hated lying to her, but he could see no reason to alarm her unduly. Surely the two incidents were not connected. One was a robbery, the other, an accident. He could think of no reason anyone would want to kill him.

Chapter 9

At breakfast, Timandra was not surprised that she and Gavin were joined by Eliza and her sisters. The boys, Perth informed her, amidst yowls and complaints, had been marched off to their school room for their first lessons in more than a month. "I know how they feel," Gavin proclaimed. "'Tis even harder to knuckle down to studies on such a glorious day. I often found ways to elude my tutor and make my way over here to Perfidious Brambles. Of course, Grandfather would scold me, but he never forced me to leave. I fear 'twas my truancy that eventually decided my mother she must send me off to school. She could not bear to send me far away, so I went to a grammar school in Newcastle. I could be home for a visit in but a few hours. I found I rather liked going to school. I made new friends, some who still remain close. I had some challenging teachers. One in particular who taught me not all studies need be boring."

"Really?" Timandra said. "Which subject might that be."

Gavin grinned and looked around the table. "You promise not to laugh. 'Twas Latin."

"Latin!" Timandra said in surprise. "I have had but a smattering myself. I cannot say I found it entertaining."

"Nay, nor did I when I endured it under my tutor's tutelage. But Mister Knopf, my Latin teacher, had us write short plays and then act them out. Oh, we had great fun. Many a villain did we foil, many a dragon did we slay. We students vied with each other to see who could be the most creative. And at the end of each term, the best play was performed before the faculty."

"Did one of your plays ever win?" Eliza asked.

Gavin beamed. "Aye, three years running, my plays were selected to be performed. I do think 'twas my experience here at Perfidious Brambles, and my many imaginary exploits in the keep, that helped me with my plots. Of course, the Latin had to be accurate, and I worked hard on that. So much did I want to win, 'twas worth every candle burned down to a nub as I poured over my lessons, struggled with my tenses."

"Might you still have copies of your plays?" Timandra asked. She could see he took pride in his youthful accomplishments.

Gavin turned to her. "Why, yes, I do."

"I wonder, might you loan them to Mister Knolles? They might be just the thing to stimulate the boys' interest. Especially do they know you wrote them."

Eliza clapped her hands. "What a splendid idea, Timmie. What say you, Cousin Gavin?"

His smile broadened. "Why, I would be delighted to lend them my plays. I have them tucked away in a trunk. I ne'er thought they would be of any use, yet I could not bear to part with them. I shall bring them over on my next visit." He chuckled. "That is, do I remember."

"Thank you," Eliza said with her sweet smile. "You have already been so kind to us."

"'Tis indeed my pleasure."

Timandra watched the glow in his eyes when he looked at Eliza. The special smile he seemed to reserve for her. The gentleness of his voice. 'Twould be but a matter of days, and he would be head over heels in love with Eliza. She wished she could feel the joy for her friend that she deserved, but instead, her heart plummeted every time she saw them together.

"Cousin Gavin," Charissa said. "Would you care to walk with us in the garden this morning? Show us around?"

"I would be delighted to escort you about the grounds. In fact, I came here today with that express purpose in mind." He gave Charissa a look that had her blushing. Timandra guessed Eliza's young sisters had lost their hearts to their cousin just as she had.

Excusing herself from the excursion, Timandra said "Perth has informed me the former gardener has arrived, and I must need meet with him. I suppose I will be surveying the gardens with Goodman Beamer. Mayhap I shall meet up with you."

"Do you wish, I could join you. Put off the garden tour for a day,"

Gavin said.

Timandra cast a quick look at Gavin, but fearing her heart must be in her eyes, she glanced away and looked instead at Eliza. "Nay, you must not disappoint Eliza and her sisters." How kind he was to offer to bear her company.

"Oh, dear friend, we could wait for you. After all, you are doing this for us." Eliza said, gripping Timandra's hand.

Timandra shook her head and smiled. "No, no, enjoy your tour and let me deal with the gardener. I am doing this more to keep my footmen busy than for any other reason. Now go, all of you, and leave me to the gardener."

She found Beamer and a youth awaiting her outside the kitchen. Grizzled and hunch shouldered, Beamer peered up at her out of small, dark, animated eyes. Offering a gap-tooth smile, he doffed his cap and turned to introduce his grandson. The boy had the same zestful eyes, and having no cap, he tugged at his forelock. "His name is Kipp, Kippie, I calls him," Beamer said. "He is a canny boy, a canny worker. He has done the weeding here for Cook in her vegetable and herb garden for the past three years. Ye might could ask her isin she pleased."

Timandra smiled at the old man's Northumbrian speech pattern. The burr, the dialect, and the rising intonation at the end of the sentences made him a tad difficult to understand, but she liked the challenge. Cook had but a slight accent, and Mistress Weston and Old John, having no Northumbrian accents, had either been educated in the King's English or had not been raised in Northumberland. "I will take your word that he is a canny worker," she said, assuming canny meant good. "I have three footmen to put to work on this garden. Think you we will need the boy as well?"

Beamer scratched his head. "Well, noo, milady, as ye might could see, I am not a young man. Many things me auld back and knees no longer lets me do. Some things I can point te with me cane here." He lifted a knotty stick that served as his cane. "Other things ... well, they needs more explainin'. Kippie here, he can crawl aboot on the groond and show which plants that might be in a clump are ones te save and which needs pullin' up. He can climb a tree and show your footmen which limbs needs cuttin' off, and which might not needs but a bit of trimmin'. He can run and fetch things, too."

Timandra nodded. She liked the boy's open face and snaggle-tooth grin. He might make a good playmate for Herman and Bennet. "I can see how Kippie might be useful. Now, do you show me about and tell me what plans you have to turn this overgrown acreage into a garden."

With Beamer stumping along beside her, and Kippie following in their wake, Timandra headed into the garden. She heard the Tilburys laughing at something Gavin said. Eliza and her sisters were experiencing the grounds with their handsome cousin while she was in the company of a wizened old man. She shrugged. She had brought this on herself. She needed something to keep her footmen occupied during her extended stay at Perfidious Brambles. She was responsible for them and for their behavior. Her father would not be pleased did she allow the servants under her direction to get into trouble.

She did her best to concentrate on Beamer's plans for the grounds. 'Twas the wrong time of year to trim the trees, but some desperately needed pruning and the fruit needed thinning that limbs would not break. 'Twas also too late in the season to do over much trimming on the rose bushes, but most of the other shrubbery, especially the maze's box-dwarf, could be pruned and shaped, weeds could be pulled, and paths cleared and re-pebbled. "Ah," Beamer said, "when the Mistress were alive, this were a glorious place. Mistress Seldon loved te stroll the groonds. She particular likened the rose garden, and she likened meandering the path yon be leading te the bower what is near the fish pond. No matter the weather, she were at lovin' her walks."

He grew quiet and Timandra looked down at him. A smile played across his face, then vanished. When he looked up, his eyes were misty. "The Mistress were a kind soul. I know I be speakin' oot of turn, but when she died, she taken a part of Master Seldon's soul with her. She were the light in his eyes. Noo he looks oot on the world and finds little that pleasures him."

Timandra appreciated the additional insight into Seldon. He must have loved his wife dearly. Foolish it might be, but that was the kind of love she wanted. "How many years did you work for the Seldons?" she asked.

Beamer stopped and scratched his grizzled chin. "Well, noo, let me sees. I were seven when I started in helpin' me father. He were the gardener then. I am seventy-one noo, and Master Seldon puts me on a pension comes ten years back. 'Twas right after I fallen from a tree and hurts me back. Master were kind, he were. I thinks that must have been the last anybody worked at keepin' up the groonds. Anyway, I tooked over as head gardener when me father died. I were twenty-four. So I worked here for nigh on," he counted on his fingers, "for fifty-four years, thirty-seven of them as the head gardener."

"And you liked the work?"

Beamer nodded. "Oh, aye, Lady Timandra, I loved it. Seein' the trees blossom and little plants poppin' up oot of the ground comin' spring. Seein' the trees and bushes turn color with the first nip in the air. Seein' whut me own hands could do te bring beauty te the earth and a smile te Mistress Seldon's face. Oh, aye, I loved it."

Timandra smiled. "I think you will do right by the garden. Come, let us find my head footman. Perth will introduce you to the other footmen, and you can start them to work this very morning, do we agree on your wage, of course."

"Oh, whut e'er ye say is fair, me lady."

She chuckled. "You drive a hard bargain, Goodman Beamer. Would sixpence a day and a farthing for Kippie be acceptable?"

Nodding vigorously, Beamer said, "Indeed Lady Timandra, 'tis most generous."

"Good, but I have one additional requirement."

The old man looked up at her curiously but not warily. A trusting soul, she thought, and smiling, said, "When the young Tilbury boys are finished with their lessons, I want Kippie to show them more of the grounds. They will need a playmate, and your grandson, is he willing, seems a likely lad for the assignment. Herman is ten, Bennet is seven." She looked at Kippie. "What say you, Kippie? Are you willing to show the boys about. Join them in some games."

The boy's dark eyes glowed. "Aye, me lady. Happy te show 'em aboot. I am ten meself."

"Splendid, then all is settled, let us find Perth."

She found Perth and two other footmen at the kitchen entrance helping a burly drayman unload a cart of foodstuffs. The cook was ticking

74

off the items. "The master ordered a restocking of the basics, flour, meal for porridge, vinegar, honey, lentils and peas, cheeses, nuts and currants, mustard, pepper, salt, ah, and more candles. We have more mouths te feed than we have had in o'er thirty years. Not since the Mistress died, and I were but assistant te the former cook." She chuckled. "He were a bear of a man. Could poke hunches of pork or beef onto a spit and sling them o'er the low burning coals ..." She smacked her lips. "Would they come out succulent."

Timandra liked Seldon's gray-haired cook. Big and chunky with broad shoulders, strong looking arms, and large hands, she looked as if she would have no trouble handling a hefty roast. She also had a wide grin, a robust laugh, and lively eyes. She was as cheerful as the housekeeper was dour. "Well, Beamer," the cook asked, with a chuckle, "are ye hired? Will we be setting a place for ye and the boy for dinner in the servant's hall?"

"He is hired," Timandra answered the cook, "as is Kippie. And when my footmen have finished helping you, they are to go with him so he can show them their new temporary," she stressed temporary, "employment." The men nodded their acceptance, and she smiled but added, "Not you Perth. I need you to help Old John here in the house and to be at the ready for any task I may need you to do."

"Yes, my lady," Perth said, as always, his face unreadable. Whether he was pleased to be excluded from the yard work, or whether he would have enjoyed it, he would never indicate.

Entering the kitchen, she asked, "Where is Edgar?" He was the youngest of her footmen, and the one she worried about the most.

"He is helping the serving girl redd up the bedchambers," Perth said.

Oh dear, Timandra thought. "Who set him to that task?"

"Mistress Weston," Kearne said, entering the kitchen with a bag of meal slung over his shoulder. "She asked would someone help, and he volunteered. Perth was helping Old John pick the wine for your dinner."

"Hmmm. I see." She looked at Perth. "Kearne and Hillock can finish here. Do you please find Edgar and tell him he is to ready himself for work in the garden. Does the serving girl still need help, please ask Audrey or Finola to give her a hand. Then, do you please ask Mister Seldon if I may have a word with him before dinner."

"Yes, my lady," Perth said, and hurried off to find the young footman.

"Does it ease yer mind any," Cook said, "Mister Seldon told Mistress Weston she is te hire another maid te help with the cleaning and bed making." She grinned. "And I am te have two scullions te dee the cleaning of me pots, pans, and the dishes. Lucy, me assistant, has done the cleaning but is noo te dee naught but help with the cooking. She is that pleased, I can tell ye."

Timandra glanced at the young woman who seemed barely out of her teen years. She could see Lucy's pleasure on her round, fresh face. Her bright eyes danced as she scurried about the kitchen directing the footmen where to put the various supplies.

"Mistress Weston is doon te the tenant's housing even as we speaks te see aboot hiring the girls," Cook added. "They will be canny girls, that ye cans depend on. Mistress Weston be not one te allow any dalliance or frivolity."

Timandra had little doubt of that. Poor dears, but no doubt the girls would be happy to have the work and the added income. She was pleased Seldon was making an effort to see not only to her comfort, but to his nieces' and nephews' as well. Whether such generosity would continue once she departed, she could not hazard a guess. She had not yet determined whether the old man was truly irascible, or was it all an act. She was fairly certain he had a keen sense of humor even if he kept it well hidden. And she was relatively certain he had a great fondness for his grandson.

She heard footsteps clattering on the back staircase and in a moment, Edgar appeared. "My lady," he said, skidding to a stop in front of her, "Perth said I was to see you and then ready myself to work in the garden." He looked rather sheepish, and seemed to know she was not pleased with him. She had already spoken with him about his gossiping. Still, she did not know if he had done anything untoward while upstairs with the serving girl. Too bad he was such a good-looking youth with his clean-cut features and wavy, light-brown hair. He could turn a girl's head with just his smile. For the time being, she was glad Mistress Weston would not allow any dalliances. All the same, she might have to ask Perth to keep an eye on Edgar.

She looked at Hillock and Kearne. "Are you finished unloading?"

"Aye, my lady," Kearne said.

"Very good, the three of you step outside with me and meet Good-man Beamer, the gardener. He will direct you in various jobs to put this acreage back to rights. Or as best as can be managed. We are impos-ing on Mister Seldon's hospitality for a lengthy period. 'Tis only right we contribute something to the maintenance. So you should not think yourselves abused by these extra duties, you will see an extra bonus when your wages fall due."

"Thank you, my lady," Kearne said with a slight bow of his head. "I can use the extra."

Timandra acknowledged his thanks with a smile. She knew he was the sole support of his widowed mother, so Timandra often slipped him an extra gratuity. "Well, here is Goodman Beamer," she said and introduced the footmen to the gardener and his son. She advised them to follow Beamer's instructions, then she left them and went in search of Finola. With the early hours that Seldon kept, it was near time to dress for dinner. Sniffing the air, she wondered what Cook was pre-paring. Cook had been so busy with the arrival of the supplies, Timan-dra would not be surprised was dinner a bit sparse, but she doubted it would be late.

She decided to take the servant's staircase. It was more convenient than wandering through the dining room, then the hall to the main staircase. Upon reaching the first floor, she heard giggling and recog-nized Finola's voice coming from Mister Knolles room. "That Edgar is a handsome boy, but be you wary. You would be the fool are you letting him turn your head. He will be leaving when Lady Timandra leaves, no matter what promises is he making you."

"He be not the first boy has tried te steal a kiss from me," respond-ed a voice Timandra did not recognize, but assumed belonged to the serving maid. The girl giggled. "I am guessing he will not be the last either, but I am nee fool. I may flirt, but I will be doing nee more than holding hands until I have a ring on this finger. Me mam would lay inte me good did I dee otherwise."

"That is smart," Finola said. "Now here, I am thinking these pillows are fluffed enough. Are you having more beds that need making? If not, I must be getting Lady Timandra's gown laid out. She cannot be going down to dinner in her riding habit."

Not wanting to be caught eavesdropping, Timandra did not pay heed to the maid's answer. She hastened up the next flight of stairs and down the gallery to her room. She was pleased Finola had warned the maid to be wary of Edgar's advances. The girl seemed to have good sense. All the same, she would need to ask Perth to have a talk with Edgar. She had no wish for Seldon to have any reason to resent her stay in his home.

Chapter 10

Timandra hurried her change of clothing and ablutions that she might have a word with Seldon before the others arrived in the parlor, but when she reached the door, she found her host had three additional visitors. "Oh, do come in Lady Timandra," Seldon said. "Seems we have some unexpected guests. May I present my nephew, Dwight Crenshaw, and his friends, Mistress Viola Clackenberger and her brother, Sir Osgood Pettimill." The two men bowed and Viola Clackenberger curtsied. That Seldon was not pleased with his visitors was obvious in his voice. It dripped with contempt. "They have done us the honor," the word honor on his tongue sounded more like an insult, "of stopping by on their return from Newcastle. Where I thought they were to be residing indefinitely."

Viola Clackenberger giggled. "Oh, Mister Seldon, you are always so droll. Do you not find him so, Lady Timandra." She put her hand to her cheek. "How silly of me. You have known him such a short time. You cannot yet appreciate how he will make the jest. I understand you have but recently arrived, having accompanied his nieces and nephews here."

Before Timandra could answer Viola, Sir Osgood stepped forward, and sweeping her another bow, said, "Do please disregard our travel worn clothing. We set out yesterday and would have been back to Crenshaw Manse afore nightfall, but one of the horses came up lame. We were forced to spend the night at an inn. Dreadful place." His lower lip turned down. "All the same, we made the best of it, did we not, my dear companions?" His frown turned to a bright smile as he looked to Crenshaw and then to his sister. They both nodded in agreement.

"Indeed," Viola said. "The food was revolting, the service haphazard, the bed lumpy, but am I one to complain?" She shook head, causing her multitude of dark curls to bobble about. "I have no doubt both my brother and dear Mister Crenshaw will attest to my perseverance." She smiled at Crenshaw, and he returned her smile and applauded her fortitude.

That Dwight Crenshaw was enamored of the widow Clackenberger was apparent by the way he looked at her, and the way he hurried to her side when she gave him but the slightest head movement to indicate she wanted him next to her. 'Twas obvious the woman thought herself a model of fashion, but everything from her riotous curls to her exceedingly low décolletage displaying her amply endowed bosom, to the number of furbelows and ribbons adorning her chemise, petticoats, and over gown was overdone. Still, Timandra had to admit, Viola was an attractive woman. She had a bright smile, lively gray eyes, a pert nose, and a soft round chin. Timandra guessed Viola to be in her mid-to-late thirties. She could understand Crenshaw's attraction to the widow. But not Viola's attraction to Crenshaw.

Dwight Crenshaw had to be in his late forties. A tad on the fleshy side, he had a double chin, round face, squinty eyes, and she guessed, as he wore a wig, he could well be balding. He looked nothing like his trim and fit uncle. But to Timandra, his voice was his most annoying feature – high pitched and nasal. Sir Osgood, on the other hand, had a masterful voice – deep and resonant. The kind of voice one might expect of an actor or orator. Most likely in his late thirties, to early forties, he resembled his sister in coloring, but his features were stronger, more commanding. He might have been exceedingly handsome in his youth. Now, a paunch around his middle, bags under his eyes, and advancing jowls, robbed him of his allurement. Even so, his twinkling gray eyes, thick dark hair that fell in waves to his shoulders, and his rich sonorous voice lent him a certain charm. What this colorful brother and sister were doing with Crenshaw, she could not hazard. Nor did she think it any of her business. She was disappointed she had not had time to speak privately with Seldon to tell him she had hired Beamer and had set her men to work. She had no qualms in paying Beamer from her own pocket. She was but curious as to whether Seldon would allow her to pay the gardener or whether he would accept his obligation and pay to have his grounds restored to their former beauty.

Lost in her thoughts, she realized Sir Osgood was addressing her. Hoping he had not noticed her distraction, she tried to concentrate on what he was telling her. "Being as we were so near," he said, "and being it was early in the day, my sister suggested we stop in to visit Dwight's uncle." He leaned in closer to her and whispered, "He is getting old. Could end his days at any time. I know Dwight would ne'er forgive himself did he not have a final visit with his uncle." He straightened. "Anyway, seeing as Crenshaw Manse is not but another hour down the road, we thought 'twould be best did we stop in on our way home."

Timandra, unable to see any reason anyone should think Seldon near his death bed, was saved from having to respond to Sir Osgood by Gavin's entrance. "Ah, ho, Cousin Dwight, Sir Osgood, Mistress Clackenberger, what a surprise. I had no idea you had returned from Newcastle. Thought you were sick of the country and wanted more entertainment than the locals could offer. Thought your sojourn in Newcastle was to be a long one."

The visitors greeted Gavin with ready familiarity, but Timandra thought she detected a hint of animosity in the air.

"Crenshaw would have it that he yearned for his home," Sir Osgood said. "Said summer at Crenshaw Manse should not be missed."

"And naturally upon learning from Mister Colyer, whom we chanced upon, that his cousins would be arriving, Mister Crenshaw felt he needed to be on hand to welcome them," Viola added with a bright smile and a barely discernible nudge to Crenshaw's ribs.

Crenshaw at first looked surprised, then he rapidly nodded his head, "Oh, indeed, indeed, looking forward to meeting the little dears."

"Well, here are three of them now," Seldon said, and all eyes turned to the parlor entrance. Eliza, followed by her sisters, stopped at the threshold. Despite their mourning apparel, the three young women looked radiant with the light beaming in from the windows and casting them in glowing sunshine. Timandra noted every man in the room, including their uncle, did naught but stare. Viola broke the silence.

"My, my, my," she said. "I had no idea your nieces were so grownup, Mister Seldon." She headed toward the three with her hands outstretched. "Now, are you not the beauties?" She glanced back over her shoulder. "Mister Seldon, you led us to believe they were children, not young ladies." As she reached Eliza, she gripped her hands and drew her into the room. Charissa and Delilah followed after their sister. "I would say we must throw you a grand ball and introduce you to the young men of the shire." She shook her head and her mouth drooped prettily. "But sadly, you are in mourning. All the same, we may have a few private affairs, and you will naturally meet the locals in the village and at church. You do plan to attend church on the morrow, do you not?"

Timandra guessed by the look Eliza gave her that her friend was overwhelmed by the vivacious woman who had captured her hands and was making plans for her future without even so much as an introduction. Stepping forward, Timandra said, "Eliza dear, this is Mistress Viola Clackenberger. She and her brother and your cousin have only but arrived. I will let your uncle perform the other introductions," she added, while gently extracting Eliza from Viola and turning her to face the men in the room.

Seldon harrumphed and pointed to Crenshaw, "your cousin, Dwight Crenshaw, my sister's son." He waved his hand at Sir Osgood. "His friend, Sir Osgood Pettimill, and Lady Timandra has introduced Pettimill's sister." He nodded to the group. "My nieces, Mistress Eliza Tilbury, Mistress Charissa, and Mistress Delilah. Their two young brothers are up in their school room at present. Do they finish their studies before you leave, you may have the opportunity of meeting them. But if not today, then another time. As it is now near time for dinner, I have no intention of bringing them down."

"Of course not, Uncle Percival, foolish indeed to bring them down at this time," Crenshaw said, his whine grating down Timandra's spine. Both he and Sir Osgood had bowed to the Tilburys, who had curtsied to the two men and to Viola.

Old John appeared at the door. "Sir, dinner is served."

"Splendid," Seldon said, and he extended his forearm to Timandra. Taking his arm, she noted Sir Osgood extend his arm to Eliza. She hesitated but after a moment accepted him as her escort. Crenshaw offered his arm to Viola, and Gavin offered one arm to Charissa, the other to Delilah. The sister's giggled and blushed and clung to their handsome cousin as the procession headed across the hall to the dining chamber. All stopped at the water basins just outside the door to wash their hands. Mistress Weston and a pretty maid stood by with clean towels.

Timandra pitied Cook. Not only had her meal preparations been hampered by the large food delivery, but three unexpected guests were sitting down to dinner. The table setting looked perfect, and Timandra had little doubt Perth could be thanked for that. He stood behind the chair next to Seldon's, ready to seat his mistress. Timandra smiled at him as Viola gushed, "Oh, Mister Seldon, have you hired a new footman?"

"Nay, Mistress Clackenberger." Seldon stood behind his chair, waiting for the ladies to be seated. "Perth is Lady Timandra's footman, and though I would hire him in an instant, she refuses to part with him."

At the opposite end of the table, Edgar seated Eliza while Crenshaw seated Viola and Gavin and Sir Osgood seated Charissa and Delilah. The men then took their seats. Seldon gave Old John a nod indicating they were ready to be served. Edgar exited with Old John while Perth poured the wine into silver goblets. Timandra sighed. She was to Seldon's right, Osgood was to her right. Crenshaw was directly across from her to Seldon's left, and the effusive Viola was next to Crenshaw. Hemmed in. She feared she was in for a tedious meal.

Glancing down the table, she caught Gavin's eye. He gave her a twisted smile that said he commiserated with her. She returned his smile with a half-smile and a raised eyebrow, then turned to answer Seldon's question concerning the gardens. "Indeed, sir, I was most pleased with Beamer and set him and my footmen, with the exception of Perth, to work. Perth will have called in Edgar to help with the extra guests here for dinner. As Edgar is still in training, he will benefit from observing John."

"How fortunate you are, Lady Timandra, to have well-trained footmen," spoke up Viola. "I tell you, Mister Crenshaw has just had to hire two new men. The last two were so lazy. And insolent. I cannot say what makes servants behave in such a fashion. My late husband, dear man that he was," she sniffled and put her napkin up to her eye, "he would never have imagined servants would behave as they do here in this north country."

"I take it you are not from here?" Timandra said.

"No, no," Sir Osgood said, jumping in on the conversation. "Viola and I are from just outside London. I have but a small estate left to me by my father. A delightful place." He heaved a sigh. "But when Viola's husband died, and she was in such morose straights, I knew I had to do something to bring the glow back to her eyes. I decided to lease my house to a merchant wishing easy access to London, and I took Viola on a tour of Europe. Italy will do wonders for an aching heart."

"'Twas in Rome, we met dear Mister Crenshaw." Viola patted Crenshaw's hand and smiled at him. He beamed at her and whined, "Was the brightest day of my life." Looking across the table at Timandra, he added, "I was in Rome at my physician's orders. Sunshine is what you need, he told me, bright sunshine. I was suffering the melancholy. Had been for years."

Seldon sniffed and looked at Timandra. "The physician was sick and tired of treating Dwight. So he packed him off. Poor man spent thirty years treating my sister. All she ever did was complain of one ailment or another, but she ate like a horse, downed my best wines with never a blush, then one night died peacefully in her sleep with a smile on her face. No sooner was she in the ground, and Dwight developed all her complaints."

"Uncle Percival, how can you speak so of Mother, your own sister!" Crenshaw's face had turned a bright red. "And to imply I suffer no ailments, why I ... I ..."

"There, there, dear Mister Crenshaw, you know you must not rile yourself." Viola, a worried frown on her face, patted Crenshaw's hand.

Sir Osgood, too, looked ready to protest, but at that moment, Old John and Edgar entered the room with the first course and Old John announced, "'Tis a barley broth, Mister Seldon." He and Edgar each held trays laden with bowls of soup. Perth took the bowls and distributed them around the table. Edgar exited and quickly returned with two smaller trays of dark rye bread.

Hoping to avoid a continuation of Seldon's attack on his nephew, or Sir Osgood's defensive retorts, Timandra said, "Mister Crenshaw, I understand your home is about an hour away, is that correct? Is it north or west of here?"

The man still appeared disgruntled, his lower lip stuck out, his eyes were watery, but he pulled himself up and answered. "To the north-west, near the hamlet of Wallow Wake. We have a smithy, a baker, and a carpenter, and we have a small chapel, though our vicar cannot come on a regular basis. I have a mill, and have a man and his son to see to the milling for my tenants, but do we need shoes, a scribe, an apoth-ecary, or food items we cannot grow ourselves, we must travel into Fairflex or further for such necessities.

"All the same, 'tis a glorious manor with a history to be proud of." His voice became a little less high-pitched, and his eyes lost their hurt expression and became almost dreamy. "We farm oats, rye, and bar-ley, and we raise sheep and cattle. The wool from our sheep is prized and commands top prices in Newcastle. I do think my father would be proud of how I have carried on the Crenshaw Manse traditions."

He went on telling of his cattle and his dairy products while his soup cooled. Lost in his exuberance he seemed not to notice others were eating. Timandra glanced at Seldon and noticed a change on his face and in his eyes. He seemed to be looking almost with a fondness at his nephew he had so recently disparaged. When Crenshaw said, "The Crenshaw Manse dates back to ...," Seldon interrupted him. "Do eat your soup, Dwight, that we may go on to the next course. I will recount your history." Though his words were brusque, he actually smiled at Crenshaw, who blinked, nodded, and picked up his spoon.

While Crenshaw ate, and Perth and Edgar quietly removed bowls from the table, Seldon began his tale. "Before Edward I, what is now Crenshaw Manse, and in fact most of the land around here was sparsely settled. Between the revolts against the Conqueror and his sons and the wars with the Scots, few chose to live here. But after Edward's win over the Scots in 1298, he began to fortify the region. He made land grants to his knights, and they in turn built Pele Towers or fortified manors. Sir Beverly LaGrange was granted what is now Crenshaw Manse. The LaGrange line died out during Henry IV's reign and Henry granted the manor to Sir Henry Lynley. The last of his line was Margaret Lynley. In the reign of Queen Bess, she married Malcolm Crenshaw, a woolen merchant of Newcastle. He built the present manor house, and subse-quent generations made substantial changes to it. It is a comely house. Dwight's father married my sister. Dwight took over management of the manor when his father died, and the manor has continued to prosper. So now we are brought up to date."

"Is the original fortified house still there?" Timandra asked as Perth set the next course, poached salmon and asparagus, in front of her.

"Nay," Dwight said, shaking his head, "well – but little of it. Much of the stone was used to build the stables. The original stones came from the old Picts' Wall."

"Oh, I say," Gavin interrupted, looking at the Tilburys and then at Timandra, "we should have an outing to Crenshaw Manse that all of you might see the remains of the Roman Wall built by the Emperor Hadrian in an attempt to keep the Picts out of England."

Viola clapped her hands. "What a splendid idea. After you have visited the wall, you can have dinner at the house or mayhap a picnic." She turned to Crenshaw. "What say you, Mister Crenshaw, is that not a splendid idea?"

Crenshaw looked a tad overwhelmed, but he nodded. "I suppose that would be nice."

"Let us see…, tomorrow is Sunday." She beamed. "What do you say to Wednesday of the following week?"

Rubbing his chin, Crenshaw slowly nodded. "Yes, yes, I would think Feldings could have things back to normal by then. Food ordered."

"Feldings is a good man," Seldon interposed, looking at Timandra. "When my sister's old house steward retired, I helped her select Feldings myself." He looked back at Viola. "That is why, 'tis a surprise to me he would have hired two footmen who were unsuitable."

Timandra realized he was referring back to a statement Viola had made at the beginning of the meal concerning the terminated footmen. She had thought nothing of it. She supposed the ways of servants in Northumberland could well be different from what was expected of London servants. Certainly Mistress Weston could not be termed gracious. Seldon, though, seemed puzzled, or was he offended? He was a hard man to understand. He had been surly to the Tilburys, near brought them to tears, yet he seemed intent on insuring their comfort, even asking if their rooms were satisfactory. He had set about hiring additional help, and she guessed, did they request it, he would hire a personal maid for Charissa and Delilah.

He had ridiculed Crenshaw, then had warmly recounted the history of the manor and had complimented Crenshaw's stewardship. Though Seldon was equally short with his grandson, Gavin seemed to take no offense. In fact, Gavin's speech could be as brutal as his grandfather's, even if he normally smiled when delivering his missives.

Viola's chin went up. "I cannot say why Feldings hired those two, but they were insolent."

Seldon looked to Crenshaw. "You thought them insolent."

Crenshaw looked embarrassed. "I only know what Mistress Clackenberger told me. They were rude and insulting to her, so I dismissed them."

"Well, I heard them," Sir Osgood said, his voice reverberating around the table. "'Tis not something I would repeat in the presence of ladies, but I may be more explicit at another time are you thinking the infraction minor and dismissal not merited."

Timandra looked back and forth between Seldon and Sir Osgood. Seldon sat with head cocked, eyes alert. "I have no need to hear more," he said. "I but expressed surprise. I cannot help but wonder is Feldings getting old, losing his judgment. Nothing more. Now about your planned outing." He looked down the table to Eliza. "You will be taking your brothers and their tutor, I would assume. Should be a good history lesson for them."

"Indeed, Grandfather," Gavin said, answering for Eliza, "'tis a perfect lesson. I remember when Cousin Dwight took me there for the first time." He smiled at Crenshaw. "What a day that was. Perfect weather. We can only hope 'twill be as glorious for our outing." Gavin's enthusiasm soon had the table abuzz, and as the meal progressed, and Seldon made no more prickly comments, Timandra relaxed and joined in on the plans. Still, she could not help but wonder why Seldon had taken such an interest in the dismissal of two footmen. He was a curious man.

Dinner was finished off with apple fritters. Everyone praised them. They were delicious. Timandra recognized the handy work. This fritter recipe belonged to her Aunt Venetia's cook. The only person who could have made these particular fritters here at Perfidious Brambles was Finola. So declared Old John when Seldon asked why they had never had them before.

"'Twas Lady Timandra's personal maid did prepare them. When she saw Cook was in need of help, she set right to work. Put on one of Cook's big aprons and went to chopping and cutting and mixing. Cook is full of praise for her."

Seldon looked at Timandra. "Besides your footman, seems you have another prize."

Timandra smiled. "Finola has her moments."

Chapter 11

With the dinner ended, the men were left to their port, and Mistress Weston arrived to lead the ladies to a small chamber off the hall where they could refresh themselves before returning to the parlor. Once all the women had returned to the parlor, Mistress Weston served them sherry, then left with the admonition to ring did they need her for any additional service.

Viola clucked. "That woman gives me the shivers. I cannot think how Mister Seldon abides her. She always gives me the impression she disapproves of me."

Though she guessed Mistress Weston likely did disapprove of Viola, Timandra, fearing Charissa or Delilah might join in on Viola's criticism of Seldon's housekeeper, changed the subject. "I see tables have been set up for cards and backgammon. Mayhap we may have a game or two before you must depart, Mistress Clackenberger."

Viola's gray eyes brightened. "Do you play cards, Lady Timandra?"

"I enjoy piquet or cribbage. Do you play either?"

"I prefer Ombre. Do you play that?"

Timandra did not care for Ombre. It involved playing for money, and she had a feeling, did Viola suggest the game, she was quite handy at it. "I cannot say I care for the game. And I am thinking we should wait for the gentlemen to join us before we start any games. Mayhap you would be so kind as to tell us something of Italy. None of us may ever get to travel there."

"Oh, yes," Charissa said. "I would love to hear about Italy. Once at a neighbor's gathering, we heard a troubadour from Italy sing the loveliest songs. Not that I understood the words, but his voice was magnificent." She looked at her sister. "Remember, Eliza. Was not Signore Casale wonderful? And so handsome."

"'Tis pronounced 'trovatore' in Italian, I do think, Charissa," Eliza said. "And indeed, yes. I think near every lady in the room fell in love with him that day." She looked to Viola. "So, please Mistress Clackenberger, do tell us about Italy. Did you attend any operas?"

Viola at first looked disappointed she was not to enjoy a game of cards, but she quickly brightened, and with accompanying hand gestures, she began describing an opera. She next praised the Italian countryside, and had just finished expounding on the incredible antiquities of Italian cities and was starting on the climate when the men joined them.

The next hour passed pleasantly. Viola engaged Gavin and Crenshaw in a game of Ombre, and Timandra sat down to a game of cribbage with Eliza, Seldon, and Sir Osgood. Charissa and Delilah had several rousing games of backgammon that had them threatening each other before bursting into giggles. The two sisters had a close relationship. That was good, Timandra thought. Once Eliza married, they could turn to each other for support.

"Look to the time," Crenshaw said when a clock on the hearth mantle chimed three. "We must be on our way. I want to settle in peacefully before 'tis time for supper."

"So you are right, Mister Crenshaw," Viola said, rising. "But this has been a most delightful day. And we have Wednesday of the following week to look forward to, do we not?"

"We do," Gavin answered, also rising.

Timandra wondered if he had lost much money to Viola. She could tell the widow had been winning. Her jubilant squeals gave testimony to her victories. Timandra was glad she had avoided playing with Viola.

Crenshaw's coach was ordered, and everyone but Seldon trooped out to bid the guests good-bye and safe journey. Still hoping for a private word with Seldon, Timandra, after making her farewells, slipped back into the house. Old John was not at the door, but she thought she heard voices in the parlor. Not wishing to tap tap across the tile, she moved silently on her toes. As she approached the door to the parlor, she heard Seldon ask, "What did you think of Crenshaw's new footmen, John?"

She halted when John said, "I cannot say I found them suitable, sir.

Nor do I think Nigel will be pleased with them. Their manners are, to my thinking, poor, and they were a tad free with the women, which I could not like. Nor did Lady Timandra's footmen like them. But my lady's maid, Finola, has a saucy tongue and did put the two of them in their place."

Seldon chuckled. "I will just bet she did. If you hear from your nephew on the two new footmen, let me know what he thinks of them."

So Crenshaw's steward was Old John's nephew. Timandra wondered if that influenced Seldon's concern about the terminated footmen. 'Twas curious two footmen had been dismissed for insolence, yet the two new ones seemed equally unsuitable.

"That I will do, sir," Old John said. "Will there be aught else?"

"No, but get some help putting this room back to rights. I will be in my rooms until supper."

"Yes, Mister Seldon."

Timandra gasped. For the second time in one day she found herself eavesdropping. She would chastise any servants she caught doing the same. She hurriedly backed up a couple of steps, then, wanting to be heard, she clopped her way toward the parlor door as Old John exited.

"Lady Timandra, may I be of help to you?"

"No thank you, John. 'Tis Mister Seldon I seek. Is he still in the parlor?"

"I am here, Lady Timandra," Seldon said from the doorway. "You wish to speak with me?" As he spoke, the Tilburys and Gavin entered the hall, and Timandra wondered if she had again lost her chance to tell Seldon about the plans for his gardens.

He must have seen her disgruntled look because he said, "Walk with me, Lady Timandra. I wish to see what Beamer and your footmen have accomplished this day."

She smiled and took his proffered arm. "Ah, that is precisely what I wanted to speak with you about. I wanted to tell you what is planned. You seem to know I was pleased with Goodman Beamer and did hire him to supervise my men."

"How could you not approve of him. He served me as my head gardener for over thirty-five years. You would not know it now, but these grounds were once the loveliest anywhere in the shire." Pride was in his voice and a sparkle in his eyes. Again the man surprised Timandra.

"Grandfather, do you take a turn outside, I will join you, then I must be off," Gavin said.

"You are not staying to supper?" Seldon, a question in his eyes, looked at his grandson.

Had she heard disappointment in the old man's voice, Timandra wondered?

"Nay," Gavin answered. "We have house guests, and I am promised to make a fourth at cards tonight. I hope I may do better against the Ramseys than I did against Mistress Clackenberger." He laughed, then turned to Eliza and her sisters. "Cousin Eliza, I did mean to show your brothers the fish pond, but it will have to wait for another day. I hope I may see all of you at Sunday services. My mother looks forward to meeting you."

"Oh, we do plan to attend," Eliza said, but she looked to Timandra. "We are planning to attend are we not, Timmie?"

"I cannot think why we would not. Shall I tell Hardgrove to ready both coaches for us?"

"Oh, yes, please do."

"Splendid," Gavin said. "Until tomorrow, cousins."

"Until tomorrow," Charissa said brightly, and she and Delilah headed up the stairs.

"We go to rest for a bit," Eliza said. "This has been a busy, though a lovely day."

Timandra nodded. "Indeed, it has. I mean to rest also once Mister Seldon and I have toured the grounds."

"Are you tired, Lady Timandra," Seldon said, "this could wait until the morrow."

"Oh, no, I will not let you escape now I have your attention. I want to make certain you approve of the plans we have made for your grounds."

He chuckled, not something Timandra had heard him do before. Nodding his head, he said, "Well then, let us tour the grounds."

With Gavin trailing behind them, they exited the house.

※ ※ ※ ※

Beamer greeted Seldon with near reverence. He could not help but be proud of what they had accomplished. The rose bushes had been trimmed, but enough of the blooms remained to make a good showing. The paths among the bushes and the ground under them had been cleared of weeds and grasses. "Are ye wishing the paths re-pebbled, Master Seldon, I could have some of the younger boys from amongst the tenants take a couple of days off from the fields and drag the stream bed. They would be appreciating some boon work."

Gavin laughed. "No doubt they would more enjoy splashing about in the stream to pulling weeds in the fields or picking berries or beans."

Seldon gave Gavin a sideways glance before looking back at Beamer. "Set the boys to work come Monday. But tell them I want clean pebbles, not a mush of mud."

"That I will do, Master Seldon. Now, dee ye cares te hear more of me plans?"

"Nay, I ne'er questioned you all the years you worked for me. I see no reason to question you now. Especially as you have already made a tour with Lady Timandra." He looked from Beamer to Timandra, then back to Beamer. "Whatever wage arrangement you made with Lady Timandra, know that I approve, and when all is done, you will come to me for your payment."

"Of course, Master Seldon. And thank ye, sir."

Dismissing Beamer with a nod, Seldon half-smiled at Timandra. "You would not have thought I would have you paying for the restoration of my garden?"

She returned his smile. "I asked to restore the garden to keep my footmen busy. I had not meant the activity to be an expense to you."

"I am sure I will have many more expenses with my wards here. The restored gardens should help keep them out of the house. At least for a good portion of the year."

"Grandfather, admit it," Gavin said with a chuckle. "You have had more fun in the past two days since your nieces and nephews arrived than you have had in years. Ne'er have you had so much to complain about. Or to look forward to. Perfidious Brambles can come alive again."

"What makes you think I want Perfidious Brambles to come alive?"

Seldon snapped.

"I think it because I have actually heard you laugh. You may deny it, but you laughed."

"I thought you said you had to leave." Seldon glared at his grandson.

Grinning, Gavin said, "I am on my way, even at this moment. Lady Timandra, do you walk with me to the stables to speak to your coachmen or would you have me pass on a message?"

Not wishing to pass up an opportunity for a few moments alone with Gavin, Timandra said, "I will walk with you." She looked at Seldon. "I thank you for viewing the gardens with me."

He gave her a small nod. "Until supper, Lady Timandra."

Gavin offered Timandra his arm, and she tucked her hand in the crook of his elbow. She knew she should avoid being alone with Gavin, should not be grasping at any excuse to be near him, but she could not help herself. He would someday marry her dearest friend, and she must disabuse herself of the notion she was but befriending him. Still, though knowing herself to be a fool, she reveled in his presence. "We look forward to meeting your mother on the morrow," she said, turning her thoughts in a different direction. "Will we also meet your aunt and uncle?"

"You will, and you will meet their visitors, the Ramseys. Longtime friends of my aunt and uncle. They are from Newcastle. Whenever any of our family travels to Newcastle, we stay with the Ramseys. Lovely people."

"I admire the preservation of close friendships. I would imagine Eliza and I will ever be the dearest of friends, just as my aunt and her mother were before Eliza's mother died. Her friend's death near broke my Aunt Venetia's heart."

"Cousin Eliza and her siblings have faced several loses, and yet I cannot think but that they will recover and be the stronger. They are fortunate they have each other." Gavin stopped as they reached the stables. "Do you ride again come Monday?"

Timandra's heart quickened. "I am sure I will. Do you?"

"I intend to, yes. Mayhap Cousin Eliza will join you. We could meet in the meadow where I met you today."

"Yes, that would be lovely." Timandra had a difficult time keeping her disappointment from her voice. He was hoping to go riding with Eliza. What had she expected?

"Good. Now, what of Charissa and Delilah and the boys' horses. Do they not ride?"

They were entering the stables and the coachman, Hardgrove, was hurrying up to her, but she answered Gavin, "They had to sell their horses to pay off more of their father's debts. I bought Eliza's horse and returned her to Eliza as a gift."

Gavin looked down at her, a light in his eyes she could not understand. "Cousin Eliza is most fortunate to have you as a friend," he said, his voice soft.

Gazing up into his eyes, trying to comprehend the warmth she saw in them, she cocked her head. "I do think I am the lucky one. Eliza is a dear person."

He smiled. "So she is. Now, here is your coachman. And I see your postilion is readying Merlin for me. Until the morrow, Lady Timandra." He bowed his head and turned to his horse.

Her heart had bounced back and forth so many times, she was near dizzy, but she had to focus. Hardgrove awaited her instructions. Drawing herself up, she raised her chin and told him they would be needing both coaches on the morrow. She added that he, the Tilbury's coachman, the postilion, and the footmen should all be dressed in their best. They would be going into the village to Sunday services.

Hardgrove, acknowledging her orders, asked if she would be wanting all six horses on her coach. She shook her head no as she watched Gavin exit the stables. He gave her a bright smile and a little wave, then he was gone. Heavy-hearted, she trudged back to the house to be met by Eliza's young brothers and their tutor. The boys were eager to meet Kipp. Timandra, having stopped by their schoolroom to tell them about their new playmate, was not surprised by their eagerness. Their liveliness perked up her spirits, and she took them to meet Kippie.

"Oh, do excuse Kippie from his work, Goodman Beamer," she said. "Mister Knolles has informed me the boys were ever so diligent today. They have been eager to have a bit of sport before 'tis time for their supper. Do please, let young Kipp romp with them.

Beamer nodded. "As ye wish, me lady." He looked down at his grandson's bright face. "Go ahead lad. But mind you finds me when the boys go te their supper. Then we will head home."

"Yes, Grandfather," Kippie said before turning to Bennet and Herman. "Let us go te the meadow behind the orchard. 'Tis a good place te run races, dee ye like races."

"Aye, let us go," Herman said, and the three boys took off with Kipp in the lead, Herman close on his heels, and Bennet doing his best not to fall too far behind the older boys.

�*※ ※ ※ ※

Gavin decided to take a more circuitous route home. Not that he could really believe anyone was out to kill him. All the same, better not to take his usual trek. Settling back in his saddle, his thoughts went to Timandra. She was a remarkable woman. In but two days' time she had his grandfather acting more alive and vibrant than he had seen him in years. Since his grandfather's sister's death ten years earlier, his grandfather had become more and more a recluse. For the past couple of years, other than himself and Eustace Colyer, and the vicar's effervescent daughter, Ebba, the only people his grandfather saw were his servants. Though of late, Cousin Dwight and his two friends had been occasional unwelcome guests. That was a curiosity in itself, especially as his grandfather was seldom cordial to them.

Again his thoughts turned to Timandra. He had learned she planned to stay an indeterminate time at Perfidious Brambles. He would have the long summer days to get to know her better. He had a feeling the better acquainted he became with her, the more he would find in her to like and admire. She was a strikingly handsome woman. He loved her eyes, though he had yet to determine their color. At times they appeared blue, at other times green. They had definitely been green when she had worn that green riding habit that molded itself to her figure, accentuating her shapely breasts and curving hips.

As attractive as he found the lady, 'twas her intelligence, her wit, and her humor that captivated him. He also liked her loyalty to her friend. His sweet, pretty little cousin and her engaging siblings would need Timandra's strong character to guide them as they adjusted to their new life. And life with his grandfather at Perfidious Brambles would not be an easy adjustment. His mother was eager to meet her young cousins. She had but the vaguest memory of her uncle, the Tilburys' grandfather. After leaving home, her father's brother had visited Perfidious Brambles with his wife and young daughter but once. He knew his mother planned to invite the Tilburys and Timandra to dinner sometime the following week. He looked forward to showing Timandra the home he would someday inherit.

He smiled and tilted his head back and laughed. He was exuberant. He had begun to give up hope of ever finding a woman who possessed beauty, grace, and intelligence. A woman of merit, capable of carrying on an interesting conversation, capable of assessing a problem and finding a solution without needing a man's approbation. A woman on a par with the two women who had raised him – his mother and his aunt. His Aunt Mabelle was a scholar, well read, well educated. She could read five foreign languages, including Latin and Greek, and she spoke French, German, and Italian. His mother was also well read. After his father's death, books had become her life. The more she learned, the more she wanted to learn. Yet both his aunt and his mother were gracious hostesses, matriarchs of the community, and benevolent supporters of the old, impoverished, or sickly residents of the parish. He had no desire to bring home a simpering fool to these beloved women.

He had met any number of women. He believed his well-meaning friends in Newcastle had introduced him to every maiden and widow in the city. He had been to Yorkshire a couple of times, once to Edinburgh, and had spent six months in London with his Uncle Phineas when his uncle had been called to Parliament. Some of the women he met in the various cities were pretty and sweet like his Cousin Eliza, some were merry and vivacious, a couple were heiresses, but none of the women had sparked his interest. Now, to meet a woman who seemed to be all he had been searching for, right here at Perfidious Brambles, could be naught but fate. Had he fallen in love with the lady after but two meetings? Possibly. His Uncle Phineas said he fell in love with Aunt Mabelle the first time he saw her. And his love for her had not diminished with the years.

Yet Lady Timandra Lotterby was the daughter of a wealthy Earl.

Would she consider marrying naught but the nephew of a Baron? An even bigger question, would she be willing to marry a man from Northumberland? She would be far from her family, far from London society, and certainly the climate would be harsher than what she was used to. Hurdles, certainly, but they were not insurmountable. Not if he could win her heart. That, he decided, he intended to do.

Chapter 12

Timandra was pleased to find Gavin awaiting them at the church door. When her footman, Perth, opened the door to the coach, Gavin stepped forward to assist her down the steps. His blue eyes sparkled in the bright morning sun, and his smile appeared radiant as he drew her hand into the crook of his elbow. He acknowledged Eliza, Charissa, and Delilah as Perth handed them out, then greeted the boys and their tutor when they emerged from their coach. Finola and Audrey, also in attendance, followed them inside, but the maids found seats at the rear of the church. Perfidious Brambles's other servants had attended an earlier service.

Deciding Gavin was escorting her into the church instead of Eliza because of her station, Timandra could not but feel a twinge of guilt at the pleasure she took in his nearness. Aware all eyes were upon her, she held her head high, and prayed she would not stumble on the rough stone flooring. The church was old, and its stone walls kept the interior chilled even in the summer. Timandra was glad for her wrap and could almost have wished for a coal foot warmer. Gavin stopped beside two front pews on the left of the center aisle. The letters P and B entwined in ivy were carved on the sides of the pews. Thick gold velvet cushions stretching the length of each bench seat offered comfort for a lengthy service.

Once seated, Timandra glanced across the aisle and met the welcoming smile of a dignified looking man she took to be Baron Kirkworth, Gavin's uncle. He wore no wig and his honey-brown hair was streaked with gray. By the crinkles around his eyes and the graying of his beard, she guessed him to be in his early sixties. She could not see past him to the woman at his side, but she noted the man in the second Kirkworth pew and guessed him to be the Baron's guest, Mister Ramsey. He too appeared to be in his sixties. He wore a dark wig, and his collarless coat with ornate buttons and button-holes, and his wide-legged breeches were of a rich yellow hue. Everything about him, from his perfectly trimmed beard and mustache to his ringed fingers proclaimed him a man of wealth.

The round-faced woman at his side, she took to be Mistress Ramsey. The woman wore a gown as rich as Timandra's own peach-colored damask. A popinjay brocade with frilled, full sleeves and a falling whisk collar over a milk-and-water-colored petticoat, the gown bespoke the woman's breeding. Beside her was a youth with dark curling hair and large round brown eyes. He looked bored but resigned to his present situation. No doubt the upcoming service inspired no elation in him. Timandra hid her smile and turned back to survey the altar. It was quite plain. No cloth adorned it, no cross rose above it. Gavin had told her the church was closer to Presbyterian than Anglican, but the Eucharist was celebrated once a month, the Common Book of Prayers was used, and some hymns were sung. At least the cushioned pew was comfortable, and Timandra settled back to await the vicar's arrival.

❧ ❧ ❧ ❧

When the service at length concluded, the vicar made his way down the aisle to the door that he might greet his departing parishioners. Gavin was immediately at hand to escort Timandra. He whispered in an aside, "Did I not tell you his sermons were like no others?"

Timandra controlled a giggle. "Hush you shameful rascal," she hissed. "I must now meet the man. I care not to be laughing in his face." The sermon had been wearying. If there had been a point to it, she had missed it. The vicar had rambled, digressed, and gone off on several tangents having no connection to his opening statements. That Knolles managed to keep Herman and Bennet quietly seated seemed a minor miracle. He had to have promised them something.

The other parishioners had exited the church, but they stood about the church yard, talking and waiting to meet their new neighbors. Smiling brightly as she was introduced to the vicar, Timandra took his extended hand. "Bless you child," he said. "Your presence in our humble church does us a great honor."

"Thank you, Vicar Hemphill. You are most kind, but I cannot think our Lord looks any more fondly upon my presence in his church than anyone else's."

"Well said," answered the vicar. "In God's eyes we are all equal."

"Allow me to present the Tilburys, Vicar Hemphill," Gavin said, reaching out an arm to beckon his cousins forward. "The Mistress Eliza Tilbury, Mistresses Charissa and Delilah, their young brothers, Masters Herman and Bennet, and their tutor, Mister Knolles." The introductions acknowledged, Gavin stepped to Timandra's other side and said, "Allow me to present Vicar Hemphill's daughter, Mistress Ebba Hemphill."

Timandra realized the young woman had been standing but two steps behind her father, yet she had not noticed her. That she had not noticed Ebba Hemphill was surprising – the girl was not one to be ignored. She was tiny in stature, coming up but to her father's shoulder, and he was not a tall man, but her large black eyes in her piquant face were arresting. Her father had the same dark hair and eyes, but his eyes lacked the luster emanating from Ebba's.

The girl bobbed a curtsy. Her voice clear and sweet upon the ear, she said, "Most pleased to meet you, Lady Timandra." She looked to the Tilburys. "And you Mistress Tilbury, and your family, and Mister Knolles."

More courtesies were exchanged, then Timandra felt Gavin's hand on her elbow. "I would introduce you to my mother and my aunt and uncle and their guests, Lady Timandra, do you step this way. Do excuse us, Vicar," he said. "Lady Timandra and the Tilburys have many wishing to be presented to them."

Vicar Hemphill nodded vigorously. "Of course, of course. Again, so glad all of you were able to attend. I do hope we will see you here next Sunday."

"I would expect we will be attending, Vicar." Timandra glanced at Eliza who smiled and nodded in agreement, but her smile displayed little enthusiasm for future attendance. Turning to Ebba, Timandra added, "Mistress Hemphill, I hope you will call upon us. Charissa and Delilah are eager to become acquainted with their neighbors, is that not so Eliza."

Again Eliza nodded, and her eyes brightened. "Indeed, Mistress Hemphill, do call."

Ebba's black eyes gleamed. "Thank you. Would tomorrow be too soon?"

"'Twould be perfect," Eliza said with a slight incline of her head. "Until tomorrow, then."

Taking Timandra's elbow with one hand and Eliza's with the other, Gavin steered them toward his family. Timandra saw Knolles stop for a moment before Ebba. She could not hear what he said, but the girl smiled, and Knolles colored, nodded, then hurried after his charges. Was the young tutor attracted to the vicar's daughter? She could not blame him. Ebba was a pretty little thing, and not as young as she had expected from Gavin's and Seldon's comments. She was a blossoming young woman, mayhap near in age to Eliza.

"Lady Timandra," Gavin said, "may I present my uncle, Lord Kirkworth, my aunt, Lady Kirkworth, and my mother, Mistress Merritt. Their guests, Mister and Mistress Ramsey, and their grandson, Mister Andrew Althouse, eldest son of Sir Richard Althouse." He in turn presented Timandra and the Tilburys and introductions were acknowledged all around.

Timandra realized Knolles was no longer with them. He had joined Finola and Audrey. A servant, though one of superior rank, he would not expect to be introduced as a social equal. The three stood apart from the other parishioners. They were unobtrusive, but handy if needed. For a moment she wondered what they thought of their disparate roles, then her thoughts were recalled to Gavin's mother, who, generously embracing all the Tilburys, called them, "my dear cousins."

Herman and Bennet accepted the embrace graciously, but their eyes busily searched the parishioners. No doubt looking for boys their own age. They answered questions put to them by Gavin's mother about their ages and their adjustment to their new home, but they looked decidedly relieved when their cousin turned her attention back to Eliza.

Timandra guessed Mistress Merritt to be in her mid-fifties, yet she was still a beautiful woman. She had her father's and her son's coloring, honey-blond hair and sky-blue eyes. Did she have any silver strands in her hair, they were hidden amidst the gold. Her mirthful smile was as winning as was Gavin's. That over the years no new suitor had won her hand said much about the love she had borne Gavin's father. Timandra could not believe other men had not at least attempted to breach the walls around Mistress Merritt's heart.

Gavin's Aunt Mabelle, Lady Kirkworth, was also an attractive woman. Streaks of gray shot through her dark brown hair, but few wrinkles marred her creamy complexion. Most likely in her early to mid-sixties, she was tall and trim with an attractive figure accentuated by a long, close-fitting bodice that tapered to a slim waist. Her silk red and white stripped gown appeared to be the latest fashion. It had straight, elbow length sleeves finished with the same lace that adorned the hem of the skirt. The skirt was full but gathered in small pleats at the waist. Her hazel eyes bespoke a bright intelligence, and Timandra, eager to become better acquainted with the charming Lady Kirkworth, was thrilled the lady invited her and the Tilbury sisters to come to dinner on the following Thursday.

"Thank you," Eliza said, "we would be honored. Two of the clock did you say?"

"Yes, two, is that convenient to you," Lady Kirkworth said. "No doubt 'tis a late dinner to what Mister Seldon is used to, but we seldom keep country hours. We are so often in the city, Newcastle being not a day's drive, we have become inured to the later hours kept in the city."

"Though we kept country hours at Merrywic," Eliza said, "I cannot say we ever had dinner at eleven as does Uncle Percival. All the same, I have no doubt we will adjust. After supper we are left to our own amusement at such an early hour, that last night I do believe we were all abed by nine. So we had no trouble rising this morning."

"Well, once you have met more of your neighbors, you should find things will liven up a bit. I see a number of your neighbors are desirous of meeting you, yet we are monopolizing your time." Lady Kirkworth turned to her nephew. "Gavin, you must escort Lady Timandra and your cousins around and introduce them to the good people of our parish. We will see you at home."

He agreed to his assignment, but before they made their farewells, young Andrew Althouse took Delilah's hand and said, "I will look forward to your visit, Mistress Delilah. Just knowing you are here in the parish has brightened my day immeasurably."

Delilah blushed, and Andrew's grandmother said, "Enough pretty speeches, young man. You will see Mistress Merritt's cousins soon enough. Make your bow to Lady Timandra."

The youth did as he was told, but his eyes kept turning to Delilah. That the youngest Tilbury sister had made a conquest was obvious. That she was delighted by Andrew's attention was just as obvious. A nice-looking boy, near to her in age, and a future baronet … he made a much more suitable admirer than the youth who had flirted with Delilah at the Cat and Pearl Inn. With her dimples, her innocent brown eyes, her bubbly enthusiasm, and her blossoming young figure, the fourteen-year-old Delilah did make an attractive magnet. Charissa, more sedate, was also pretty, but she lacked the vitality that exuded from Delilah. Still, Timandra had little doubt Charissa's quiet dignity would insure her a suitable share of youthful hearts.

※ ※ ※ ※

By the time they climbed into their coaches to head home to Perfidious Brambles, Eliza was rolling her eyes. "I cannot think when I have been so confused by so many names," she declared. "My head is fair swimming. What say you, Timmie? Will you be able to put names to faces when next we meet them?"

Timandra laughed. "I shall recall a couple perhaps, but most, no. No doubt some will be offended they did not impress us enough that we should remember them, but I do think most will understand we cannot remember everyone. They, of course, realize you and your sisters are still in mourning so will not be attending any grand affairs, but you can accept dinner invitations. At small functions, I should think you will have no trouble getting acquainted with the various families. You will, however, need to rely on your uncle or cousin to steer us away from any unadvisable invitations."

"Think you we will receive many invitations?" Charissa asked.

Timandra smiled. "I think you will receive so many you will be hard pressed to find time to attend them all. The locals will be eager to further their acquaintance with you."

"Nay, Timmie," Eliza said. "They will be eager to further their acquaintance with you. We are naught but penniless wards of Uncle Percival. Were you not here, we would doubtless receive nary an invitation."

Timandra shook her head. "That is foolishness. First off, how are any of these locals to know you are penniless? Second, even should they know, they would expect, as do I, that your uncle will see you have adequate dowries. Third, the Merritts, highly respected members of the parish, are your cousins. And fourth, you are all three lovely young women. The young men will be intent on courting you. Have you not noticed how young Mister Althouse is besotted by Delilah? He could not take his eyes off her."

Delilah blushed and giggled, and Charissa poked her in the ribs. "Remember that you are but fourteen and barely out of the schoolroom. In fact, were we still at home, you would still be attending Mistress Bonds' school."

Sticking out her chin, Delilah said, "Well, we are not at Merrywic. We now live at Perfidious Brambles, and you are but jealous because two boys have admired me and none have had eyes for you." She ended her remarks by sticking out the tip of her little pink tongue.

"That is not so," Charissa cried. "I would not want such boys making eyes at me. The boy at the inn was but the son of a yeoman, and Mister Althouse is but a youth. No doubt he is still in school or with a tutor."

"What does it matter is he still in school?" Delilah quipped. "He is handsome, and he likes me. And he will one day be a baronet. Besides, he …"

"Delilah, Charissa, that is enough," Eliza said. "Do you forget this is the Sabbath, and here you are bickering right after hearing the Lord's word. I want not another sound from you."

Timandra had seldom seen the two sisters bicker. They were best friends. She hoped Delilah's conquest would not come between the girls. Eliza's firm condemnation of her sisters' behavior was also out of character. Eliza was a dear, but she had but middling control over her siblings. This time, however, the girls looked abashed, and each settled into her corner of the coach. Both remained silent as Timandra and Eliza discussed what they should wear to the Kirkworth's dinner party on Thursday.

"You cannot think Uncle Percival will forbid us going can you, Timmie?" Eliza asked.

"Forbid you from going to dinner at the Kirkworth's? Why should he?"

"Cousin Gavin says they are not on speaking terms, and Uncle Percival is estranged from his only daughter. He might not like us associating with his antagonists."

Timandra twisted her mouth. "I cannot think he will forbid you." She paused. "He knows he cannot forbid me. He cannot wish to appear churlish. He is, after all, a gentleman, and he will not want to appear otherwise."

"I do hope you are right," Eliza said as the coach pulled into the drive leading to the house. She touched Timandra's hand. "Will you not bring up the subject at supper this evening?"

Smiling, Timandra nodded. "That I will do, dear friend, that I will do."

Chapter 13

Looking across the meadow, Gavin was pleased when he spotted Eliza riding beside Timandra. He wanted to introduce Eliza to some of her uncle's tenants. Goody Beamer, the gardener's wife, had expressed the desire to meet the new lady of the manor, as had Goody Sills, the laundress, Goody Morse, the wife of one of the wealthier tenants, and Goody Burke, the hayward's wife, who was known for her superior ale. They were matriarchs of the hamlet.

He was also pleased that his youthful guest, Andrew Althouse, who had pleaded to be allowed to ride with him to Perfidious Brambles, would have Eliza for company. Gavin had not wanted to share Timandra. Waving, he urged his horse into a canter, and with Andrew close behind, he breezed across the meadow.

Timandra and Eliza greeted them with cheerful salutations. His cousin looked lovely in a blue habit, but he gave her little more than a cursory glance before his gaze settled on Timandra. She wore the green habit that accentuated her figure and enhanced her eyes. She looked ravishing, and he was hard pressed to keep to his mission. After a few moments of basking in Timandra's presence, relishing her jovial quips, he forced himself to turn his attention to Eliza. She seemed leery of his proposal to meet the matriarchal tenants, but Timandra took his part.

"You need not be reticent, Eliza," Timandra said. "These good women are your uncle's tenants. They have expressed their desire to meet you. 'Tis kind of your cousin to introduce them to you. I have been thinking you must need visit the manor village and acquaint yourself with the women. Surely they can be no more intimidating than were Merrywic's tenants."

"I know you are right, Timmie. All the same, 'tis different. I grew up knowing the tenants at Merrywic. I cannot think what I may say to these women."

"You need but be pleasant, dear friend, as you always are, and they will love you." Timandra reached over and patted Eliza's hand. "Trust me. No one can help but love you."

"Lady Timandra is correct. These women are prepared to like you and your siblings. You are bringing new life to the manor, new jobs, new opportunities to better their lives. You need but offer them your lovely smile, and they will proclaim your charm to all the other tenants."

Eliza lifted her brown eyes to gaze at him, and a shy smile crept across her face. "A smile I can manage, Cousin Gavin. Let us get this over with, that I may then enjoy my ride."

Gavin glanced at Andrew. He could see the disappointment on the youth's face. The boy wanted to go to Perfidious Brambles that he might see Delilah, but he knew better than to protest. Gavin had told him of his plans ere they had set out. He would have to bide his time.

Timandra dismissed her attendant, Tombs, as he had need to consult with the blacksmith in Fairflex. "No need to frown, Tombs," she said with a laugh. "Eliza and I will be perfectly safe in Mister Merritt's and Mister Althouse's care." She turned to Gavin. "Your grandfather wishes to order new spades and hoes. The ones my footmen are presently using are in sad shape."

Gavin shook his head in disbelief. "Grandfather is a changed man." He looked at Eliza and added, "Sad though the circumstances for you and your siblings, your coming to Perfidious Brambles has been a blessing." His cousin blushed a pretty pink. She was a little beauty. He had been struck upon their first meeting with how much she resembled his mother in her youth. Not so much her coloring, but her sweet countenance and delicate features. The resemblance had at first left him spellbound. He wondered if his grandfather noted it. Eliza's gentleness and youthful innocence added to her charm. He doubted not that the youths of the shire would soon be clambering at her door.

❄ ❄ ❄ ❄

Eliza's ordeal had been brief. The women had been charmed by their pretty mistress. Why would they not, Timandra thought. Eliza had been her usual sweet and endearing self. She graciously accepted a mug of ale from the hayward's wife, and delicately sipping at it, had proclaimed it the best she ever tasted, though she cared little for ale, preferring wine or sherry. She cooed over Goody Beamer's grand-daughter and assured the laundress the bed sheets were beautifully clean, and that she had no qualms entrusting her with her personal laundry.

When they rode away, Gavin chuckled. "Not so terrifying was it?"

Eliza shook her head. "Nay, they were all very kind. I thank you for forcing me to attend my duty. Now, do I feel like strolling into the village, I will feel perfectly comfortable."

Gavin laughed again. "Dear cousin, never say I forced you. 'Twas Lady Timandra's sage advice you did heed. I would ne'er dream of forcing you to do something against your will."

"True. Had Timandra not been at my side, I could never have faced all those women, but 'twas you did arrange the meeting."

"Only at their urging."

Though happy for Eliza, Timandra's heart hung heavy in her chest. She could see how much Gavin cared for Eliza. He had outright said Eliza's coming to his grandfather's had been a blessing. And he seemed so pleased the tenant matriarchs had welcomed her, pleased she had proven herself a suitable mistress to the estate that he would surely one day inherit. What a woeful fool she was. Why had she let herself become so enamored of Gavin Merritt? Lost in her misery, she did not notice Gavin had ridden up beside her until he spoke.

"Lady Timandra, I declare your thoughts have you lost in a cloud."

Shaking her head, she said, "I beg your pardon, Mister Merritt. Did you address me?"

He chuckled. "Aye, I asked would you care for a good gallop. Andrew has convinced Cousin Eliza to return to the house. He is desirous of seeing Delilah, and I think Eliza may be pleased to encourage his admiration for her sister. He is a young man with a good future."

Timandra looked over her shoulder at Eliza. Indeed her friend was engaged in a bright conversation with the future baronet. Eliza was smart to encourage Andrew's attraction to Delilah. He was a personable youth, and a tender formed now could carry on to a marriageable age. Her own sister Vivien, now but sixteen, seemed taken with Durand Laibrook, future Baron of Blackhorn Hall. They might not wed, but at present, the prospect looked good. Of course, for Delilah, much would depend on the size of the dowry Seldon allotted her. Love would play a role, but she doubted the Althouses would favor a marriage without a suitable dowry.

Looking at Gavin, Timandra said, "I would love a good gallop." Her heart seemed to have taken wings. For a while, on this lovely morning, she would have Gavin to herself. She was foolish to be so happy, but she could not help herself. "Where shall we go?"

"To the fish pond. I promised to show it to you. And this afternoon, with Andrew's help, I hope to start teaching Herman and Bennet to swim. That is, does Eliza approve."

"I cannot think she will disapprove."

"Splendid. Shall we be off?"

With a wave to Eliza and Andrew, Gavin set off at a gallop. Timandra waved, too, and took off after Gavin. The race across the meadow was just what her horse needed. Pirro had been pulling on his bit ever since they had left the stable. Eliza sat her little mare well, but she preferred a sedate pace. She would be content to meander back to the house with Andrew and would never miss a race into the wind. Timandra shook her head and laughed as Pirro took a low fence with graceful ease. She was pleased Pirro had no trouble keeping up with Gavin's Merlin. The two horses were well matched.

She spied a silvery blue pond in the distance and gave Pirro his head. Her horse shot past Gavin's, and the race was on. She heard his laughter as he closed the distance between them, and as they neared the pond, they were racing side by side. "Turn to the right," Gavin yelled over the sound of the thudding hooves. Timandra tightened her hold on the reins, and Pirro responded to her lead, slackening his pace as he turned. Soon, both horses slowed to a trot, then a walk.

"Wonderful!" Timandra said. "I have not had such an exhilarating ride for months."

"Nor have I. 'Tis a shame, too, for Merlin does love a good run."

"So does Pirro. All I need do is give him his head and off he goes." She patted her horse's neck. "We will need give them a good rest and cool down."

"My thoughts, too. 'Tis why we turned in this direction." He pointed to a copse of trees, bordering on the pond. "There is a rock you can sit on while our horses drink their fill and munch on the tender grass at the water's edge."

"How lovely," she said, her heart singing. She could hardly believe her good fortune. Alone with Gavin. She could revel in his presence and pretend for this brief moment in time that he was falling in love with her and not Eliza. 'Twas wrong, but she could not help herself.

Upon reaching the thicket, Gavin dismounted, then lifted Timandra down. His hands lingered on her hips, and for an instant his face was inches from hers. She felt his breath on her lips. Dear God, what would she do did he kiss her? But he did not. He loosened his hold and stepped back. "Let me have your reins," he said, "and I will take the horses down to the water. Your horse is not apt to stray, is he not tied, is he?"

Regaining her composure, Timandra laughed. "Nay, not has he nice green grass to eat."

After loosening the saddle cinches, Gavin pulled several handfuls of tall grass from the water's edge and rubbed down the chest of first one horse, then the other. Satisfied with his efforts, he left the horses with their noses in the lush grass and returned to Timandra. "Come, Lady Timandra. Allow me to show you to your seat." He took her elbow and led her to a large mossy rock almost hidden by the trees. To her surprise, it was shaped like a chair.

"Did someone carve this?"

Gavin shook his head. "'Twas formed by God… or mayhap the weather o'er the years."

"It looks like a throne."

He cocked his head and eyed the rock. "Indeed you are right. It does." He held out a hand. "Do have a seat, your majesty. The moss softens the stone."

Giggling, she sat. "What of you?"

"I will sit here at your feet and lean against this tree." As he spoke he sank down onto the thick, leafy earth, stretched out one booted leg, and positioned himself against a tree trunk. "I can see the horses clearly from here. Both seem content, so we need not concern ourselves with them. As this is our first time to be truly alone, no interruptions, tell me about yourself."

Timandra was surprised he seemed to want to be alone with her. More surprised he wanted to learn more about her. Why? Was he but being polite?

"Have you any siblings?" he asked when she remained mute.

Finding her voice, she told him of her sister, Vivien, and brother, Adam. "I also have many cousins on my mother's side and several on my father's. Our families are close, and on my mother's side, the D'Arcys have large family gatherings every four years at my Uncle Kenrick's house in Oxfordshire."

"Is that the uncle who has the estate near Hexham?"

"Yes, he is my mother's oldest brother, the Earl of Tyneford. However, he resides on his principal estate on the Wirral Peninsula in Cheshire. My home is also in Cheshire but more to the north. Though I spent ten years fostered with my Aunt Venetia in Lancashire."

"Ah, yes, Eliza tells me that you and she were both fostered with this aunt of yours, who was also her mother's dearest friend."

Timandra nodded. "Yes, and Eliza and I became dear friends almost from the instant we met at my aunt's." Timandra went on to expound on Eliza's many virtues. She should have known Gavin wanted to be alone with her so she could tell him more about Eliza. She had been foolish once again, thinking he had any interest in her.

"I understand Eliza was betrothed," Gavin said.

Timandra had been staring out at the pond while talking, but she looked around sharply at Gavin's statement. "Oh, you must not think she is still in love with Ralph. That he chose not to marry her when she no longer had a dowry is to his discredit, though not surprising. But had he truly loved her, as he had sworn he did, love would have prevailed. She knows that and realizes he was not the man she had thought him. You must not think her sorrowing."

"I am glad to hear that. She is such a quiet, little thing, unassuming I would say. I thought mayhap her heart was yet broken."

"Eliza is demure, but she has lost her father and her home. Her life has taken such a drastic change. She has much to puzzle over."

Gavin nodded. "Indeed, she has." He then surprised Timandra by

112

asking, "And what of you, Lady Timandra, am I not too bold to ask – no broken heart for you?"

"For me! Why no. What would make you ask such?"

Cocking his head to one side, he looked directly into her eyes. He shrugged. "At times you seem wistful, lost in thought. I wondered were you dreaming of some lover."

She could not keep a blush from creeping up her neck to her face. Yes, she was dreaming of a lover. Dreaming of Gavin Merritt. But she could hardly tell him that. "No, Mister Merritt, I have no lover. Do I seem wistful, it must be my concern for Eliza and her siblings. I want them to be happy in their new home." Seeking to change the subject, she said, "'Tis nice young Mister Althouse seems taken with Delilah. A boost to her ego at this sad time in her life cannot but be good. You were kind to bring him with you today."

Gavin harrumphed. "Kind had nothing to do with it. The boy was insistent. Said he would ride over on his own did I not allow him to accompany me. Delilah has made a conquest."

Smiling in agreement, Timandra again changed the subject. "We are looking forward to dinner with your family. Eliza feared her uncle might forbid it, but he made no objections."

"He would not dare object. He knows I would give him no peace. My mother and aunt are both eager to become better acquainted with all of you."

They want to learn more about your future bride, Timandra thought, squiggling on her seat. Gavin was immediately on his feet. "What a lummox I am. I have left you sitting on that hard rock, probably kept you from your breakfast, when this was to be but a brief interlude. Do say you forgive me," he added, holding out his hand to assist her in rising.

"You have no need to apologize," she said, taking his hand and feeling a current sizzle through her from her fingertips to her heart. "I was paying no heed to the time. Though I may have missed my breakfast, I need not wait long for my dinner. 'Tis certain it will be served at eleven as usual. You and Mister Althouse will be joining us, will you not?"

Her heart sang, when still holding her hand, he answered, "I would not miss it."

Chapter 14

Gavin had not seen Timandra in two days, and he was stunned at how much he missed her. A commitment in Newcastle had taken him away from home, but he had returned the previous evening in time to get a good night's sleep that he might be refreshed for the dinner party. He tried to conceal his eagerness from his mother and his aunt, but both bestowed knowing smiles on him, though neither said anything.

Pacing the floor, he eagerly anticipated Timandra's arrival. She would see his home for the first time. He hoped she would like it. Like it enough that she would be willing to one day be its mistress. The house dated from the early sixteen hundreds, but his uncle had remodeled the inside of the house and had installed all the newest modern conveniences. The house was cool in the summer, warm in the winter. It was well lit and relatively smoke free, the chimneys having the newest flue systems. His mother had placed flower arrangements in the parlor and the dining hall, and the scent of geraniums and roses deposed the smell of coal.

Since his time alone with Timandra the previous Monday, he had become more confident he could win her hand. Learning she had no lover, no special man in her life, had made his heart leap with joy. Enraptured, he had ridden back to Perfidious Brambles in a fog. He and Timandra had returned to find Ebba Hemphill had called, and to his grandfather's vexation, had been invited by Eliza to stay for dinner. Ebba's addition brought a liveliness to the table. She had claimed Eliza and Charissa's attention with anecdotes about the young people of the parish. Delilah had been engrossed in Andrew, and he in her. That had left Gavin free to converse with Timandra with but occasional interruptions from his grandfather. How he enjoyed her bright wit. He prayed she would find his home and family as engaging as he found her.

He knew he had been a pain to his uncle's French cook, but he wanted the meal, from the braised rabbit in wine sauce to the blueberry posset and candied rose leaves, to be perfect. He had made certain he would be seated next to Timandra who would be to his uncle's right. His mother would be across the table from Timandra. That too was good. He wanted Timandra to have ample opportunity to converse with his mother. He had no doubt each would recognize in the other a woman of sound sense and superior wit.

Glancing at Andrew Althouse, he smiled. The youth was as eager to see Delilah as he was to see Timandra. That Delilah had enchanted the boy was evident. That his grandparents seemingly had no objection to the youthful flirtation was a blessing. They seemed amused by Andrew's infatuation with Delilah. But then they might not know the girl was penniless. Gavin made a note to himself that he needed to speak with his grandfather about providing his young cousins with suitable dowries. And in another year, two at the most, Herman would need to be sent to an appropriate school. Knolles had not the knowledge or the skill to give the boys more than an elementary education.

Gavin also determined he would speak to his grandfather about getting horses for Charissa and Delilah and ponies for the boys. Herman and Bennet must learn to ride, and ride well, were they one day to take their place as members of the gentry. He was pleased with how readily both his young cousins had taken to swimming. They had had their first lesson Monday afternoon, the same day he had learned Timandra had no lover. Still floating on air, he had been grateful he had Andrew and Kippie to help with the boys' lesson. He planned to give them a second lesson soon. He meant to take any excuse he could to spend time at Perfidious Brambles. Did he see Timandra for but a couple of hours a day, he would feel regaled.

The sound of coach wheels on the pebbled drive brought his attention back to the present. Both he and Andrew hurried out to greet their guests and hand their ladies down.

※　※　※　※

Timandra found the Kirkworth Hall grounds and drive well-maintained and appealing. An avenue of trees opened up to flowers and low shrubbery lining the drive. An abundant orchard dominated one side of the house, a verdant bowling green the other. A portico added to the Jacobean house gave the E-shaped facade a certain gracefulness.

The inside of the house was equally well maintained. Timandra admired the airiness of the rooms, the gleaming, multi-paned windows that allowed light to flood inside, and the tasteful furnishings – elegant yet not inordinately sumptuous. From the moment Gavin handed her down from the coach, he remained at her side, his nearness keeping her in a constant state of breathlessness. She had little memory of the dinner. Just that it must have been tasty, for at its conclusion, she felt satiated. Gavin, seated beside her, had been completely attentive, and from time to time their hands had brushed, their eyes had locked. She had not expected him to be seated next to her. She thought he would be next to Eliza. With a twinge of self-deprecation, she surmised her title must have dictated the seating arrangement.

She had enjoyed Gavin's mother and his uncle. She knew she had laughed and conversed with them, though she had but a vague memory of the topics – horses, the travails of traveling across England, the work on Seldon's grounds – at least so she thought. Her heart had been clamoring so loudly, she had trouble making sense of things. She hoped she had not seemed the dunce. Dinner had lasted long, and afterwards, they adjourned to the parlor for cards and backgammon. She partnered with Gavin in a game of whist against his aunt and the jovial Mister Ramsey. She managed to pull herself out of her dreamy state to make a good showing, but she and Gavin still lost to the more experienced players.

Running his fingers over his mustache, Mister Ramsey harrumphed when Timandra complimented his skill with the cards. "When you have played as many years as I have, you will be just as good, Lady Timandra. You have naught to be ashamed of in the hands you played."

"Indeed not," Gavin's aunt, Lady Kirkworth, said, her hazel eyes bright with good cheer. "You and Gavin both showed sound judgment in your plays. Neither of you fell victim to over confidence. But enough cards for the moment. Gavin tells me you enjoy reading. Come with me, and I will show you our library. You may borrow any books you might choose."

Taking Timandra's arm, Lady Kirkworth led her from the parlor to a room that housed nothing but books and comfortable chairs. To Timandra's delight, Gavin followed them. She had been certain he would seek out Eliza, but he had done nothing more than glance in Eliza's direction when she laughed, and clapping her hands, exclaimed, "Oh, a home for bees, why 'tis a hive. And the Roman numerals are IV." Involved in a game of chronogram with Gavin's mother, his uncle, Mistress Ramsey, and Charissa, Eliza seemed to be enjoying herself.

"I think you might like this," Lady Kirkworth said, carefully taking a leather-bound book from a shelf. "*The Misanthrope* by Moliere. Mayhap a bit bawdy, but the humor is so clever, I cannot think I overstep any bounds in recommending it."

"Indeed a good choice," Gavin said. "And may I recommend something by Shakespeare. Aunt Mabelle has near a complete collection. Have you not read *A Midsummer Night's Dream*, 'tis good fun, or mayhap you would prefer a tragedy like Hamlet."

"Oh, I have not read *A Midsummer Night's Dream* in many a year. Aunt Venetia had a copy, and Eliza and I loved it. I would much enjoy reading it again. I think I am in no mood during these lovely summer days for tragedies."

"*A Midsummer Night's Dream* it is," Gavin said, pulling it from a shelf.

"Thank you," Timandra said, accepting the books. "I will look forward to reading both." Then, glancing around the room, she added. "I cannot say I have ever seen such a large room devoted just to books. And you have so many books."

Lady Kirkworth laughed softly. "Ah, my books, I would be lost without them. They take me to realms all over the world. A cold rainy day, a good book, a comfy chair, and a warm fire, and I am as content as a dog with a new bone." She laughed again. "But come, I neglect my other guests. Mister Ramsey plays the lute, and we have several new broadside ballads that Gavin brought back from Newcastle. I, for one, am dying to hear them."

Mister Ramsey, only too happy to oblige his hostess, took up his lute. He played skillfully, and everyone gathered around him to sing the new songs. The songs were all of love, and Eliza's soprano voice blended beautifully with Gavin's baritone and Mister Ramsey's tenor. Gavin's mother complimented Eliza's singing, and Eliza blushed prettily, but to Timandra's surprise, Gavin seemed not to notice his lovely cousin. He was looking and smiling at her. She had no time to ponder his smiling gaze as Mister Ramsey set off on another song, and Charissa nudged her to join in the singing. When at last Mister Ramsey declared his fingers were growing weary, Lady Kirkworth announced a small supper had been laid out on the sideboard in the dining chamber. "You may help yourselves to whatever you wish."

Lady Kirkworth took Timandra's arm. "I know enough of Mister Seldon's household activities to know that little supper would await you if you arrive home after five, so I thought 'twas best you have supper here. That way, you will not go to bed hungry."

Timandra smiled and nodded. "Cook is most agreeable, but I would prefer not to put her out. She has had her hands full adjusting to this new crowd thrust upon her."

After supper the coach was brought around, and amidst numerous thanks and promises to visit again soon, Timandra, Eliza, Charissa, and Delilah settled into their seats. Before closing the door, Gavin leaned inside. "Cousin Eliza, remind your brothers I will be giving them another swimming lesson tomorrow."

"I will not forget."

"Splendid. Until tomorrow." He nodded, and before shutting the door, added, "Lady Timandra, it has been a pleasure." Gazing into the hovering summer light, Timandra basked in his words, as Eliza and her sisters chatted about their resplendent day. Clutching her two books to her chest, Timandra stared dreamily out the open window at the sliver of moon following them down the road. The footman, Edgar, ran ahead of the coach with a lantern in hand to light their way, but the glow of twilight clung to the horizon, and the lantern light was scarce needed.

Old John met them at the door. The house was quiet, but he had a candle for each of them. "Would you have me light you to your room, my lady," Perth asked from the doorway.

Timandra smiled. "That will not be necessary. You and Edgar may go on to your beds."

Perth nodded. "As you wish, my lady."

Climbing the stairs behind Delilah and Charissa, Eliza clasped Timandra's hand. "I am so relieved Uncle Seldon assigned Libby to be Lilah and Charie's personal maid. Audrey was feeling quite put upon, having to wait on all three of us, even though Finola did help her."

Timandra knew Libby, the pretty housemaid Edgar had tried to kiss, was thrilled with her promotion. She would have much to learn, but Audrey and Finola could help her. And being young, Delilah and Charissa had limited needs.

Embracing Eliza at her bedchamber door, Timandra said, "Sleep well dear friend. Many pleasant dreams."

"The same to you, Timmie," Eliza said, giving Timandra a kiss. "It has been a wonderful day, has it not?"

Timandra patted Eliza on the cheek. "Indeed, it has. A beautiful day." Turning to ascend the stairs, she tossed a goodnight over her shoulder.

"Goodnight," Eliza answered her.

Dreamily making her way up the staircase, Timandra stopped at the landing and looked out the window at the same moon that had followed them home. She knew she should not be so happy, but she could not control the lilting music that swirled about her head. It made her want to dance, to sing. Still clutching the books she had been loaned, Timandra started up the second half of the staircase. She was surprised to see light pouring out the door of her room. Finola must have every candle in the bedchamber burning, she thought in wonder.

Stopping in the doorway, she stared into the brightly glowing room. Finola sat on a tufted stool before the hearth, a poker clutched in her hand. When she saw Timandra, she jumped up, dropped the poker with a clatter, and clasping her hands together, exclaimed, "Oh, milady, I am that glad you are returned! You cannot be imagining what I have seen. A spirit! A dark spirit wandering these very corridors!"

"Finola, what kind of foolishness is this." Timandra could not keep the irritation out of her voice. She had come home, lost in a dreamy wonderment, and here was Finola with more of her reckless talk of ghosts and spirits.

"But I saw her. I am certain I did. I was coming up the stairs after a game of draughts with Cook, and I saw the spirit right outside the young masters' room. When I gasped, she turned toward me, but she had no face. Just a black veil that fell from her head to her feet."

"And just how do you know your spirit was a woman?" Timandra asked, not trying to keep her sarcastic disbelief from her voice.

Finola shook her head. "Well, now you be asking, I cannot be saying. I thought the spirit a woman because of the gown. I suppose it could have been a man."

"Oh, really Finola, I cannot believe you saw more than a shadow or some such. Did your spirit just vanish?"

"No, milady, she did glide down the corridor and up our stairs. I ran back down and made Old John come upstairs with me to be making certain the spirit was not in our room. He was after helping me to light all the candles. Then he gave me the poker to be holding before he left. I cannot be thinking when I have been so frightened."

Timandra blew a sigh out her nose. "And what good would a poker do against a spirit?"

Finola's eyes widened, and she put her hands to her cheeks. "Now I am thinking on it, no good. But when Old John did give me it to hold, it seemed to make sense."

"Well, obviously something frightened you. I am sorry for that. But you do let your imagination run wild at times. Let us just forget this incident. Enough said. You will not convince me you saw a spirit. Now, come and help me get this gown off, and I shall tell you about Kirkworth Hall. It is quite lovely."

Looking stubborn for but a moment, Finola brightened and asked, "You had a nice time, milady? That Mister Merritt is so gracious and considerate. I would guess his mother is kind."

"She is most gracious, as is Mister Merritt's aunt." Timandra liked Gavin's family. She especially liked his mother and his aunt. Both women were intelligent and able to converse on any number of subjects. With Finola helping her ready for bed, Timandra recounted her evening. She enjoyed reliving the visit from their arrival at Kirkworth Hall to their departure. She made no special mention of Gavin, but he claimed her thoughts all the same. Finola, being a good listener, murmured an appreciative 'oh' or 'ah' at appropriate times, and Timandra hoped her maid had forgotten her spirit sighting. At least she had not complained when Timandra told her to put out all but the bedside candles.

Settling back against her pillows, Timandra picked up *A Midsummer Night's Dream.* She wanted to read of love and laughter. She wanted to read the book Gavin had recommended. She knew she should not allow herself to dream of Gavin. He was but being kind and courteous to her. He was in love with Eliza. All the same, she cherished her time with him. She would see him on the morrow, and if only for a few moments, she would feel a moment's bliss.

Opening the book, she started to read. A perfect story by which to end a perfect day.

Chapter 15

With the second swimming lesson underway, Gavin was pleased with Herman's and Bennet's progress. He attributed the warm weather to making the lessons more fun. He was enjoying the cooling pond water as much as his young students. Kippie was again included in the outing. Timandra seemed adept at convincing the boy's grandfather he should excuse Kippie from his duties. "You must know he is a help to Mister Merritt," he heard her say. "Kippie, being of Hermie's and Bennet's age, does he show no fear of the water, 'twill encourage the boys."

Naturally Beamer was not going to argue with Lady Timandra, his benefactress. So to Herman's and Bennet's joy, Kippie was free to join them. Their tutor, Knolles, came along and proved to be an asset. He was not a strong swimmer, but he willingly paddled around, splashed and laughed enthusiastically, and encouraged his charges to get their faces wet. "'Twill not harm you," he told them. "Just hold your breath, go under, then come up flinging your hair from your face." Gavin had to chuckle when Knolles gave a masterful demonstration to the boys.

Knowing Timandra appreciated his efforts with her dear friend's siblings gave Gavin a sense of satisfaction. Anything he could do to win her approval was a plus. He sensed she enjoyed his company, but other times he could feel her pull away. What made her reticent, he had not determined, but he meant to delve into the mystery at the first opportunity. He decided to see if Eliza might furnish him a clue. No one would know Timandra's soul better than her friend. Putting his plan into action, when he and Andrew had met Timandra and Eliza that morning, he rode back to the house beside Eliza, and left Andrew to entertain Timandra.

When he casually questioned Eliza about her friendship with Timandra, Eliza was exuberant in her praise of Timandra. "No one could ask for a dearer or more loyal friend," Eliza declared. "She was my mainstay when my mother died. And how we would have managed without her after my father's death, I cannot even contemplate. She dealt with Father's solicitors, Mister Kenelm and Mister Severin. Mister Kenelm was rather cantankerous, and kept saying, 'You must sell that, and you still owe this amount.' He made my head ache. But Timmie never let him fluster her. 'Twas so much better when we could meet with Mister Severin."

A blush coloring her face, she added, "He is the younger partner and was always ever so kind." Cocking his head to one side, Gavin eyed Eliza. Had she formed a tender for the younger solicitor? Mayhap he had been a balm to her injured heart.

Chatting on, Eliza said, "Then Timandra made the tedious journey here to Perfidious Brambles with us. She even got her father to give us the loan of his best coach, his coachman and postilion, four footmen, and Mister Tombs. No one could be more generous. And Timandra is so brave. She is not at all afraid of Uncle Percival, and he scares me to death."

Gavin smiled. "Trust me. You have no reason to fear him. Though he tries to hide it, he has a kind heart. I will tell you a secret, do you promise not to tell anyone."

Eliza's eyes brightened. "Oh, I promise. Tell me, please."

"I meant this to be a surprise, but if 'twill help you think more kindly of your uncle, I must need tell you. Grandfather has agreed to purchase horses for Charissa and Delilah and ponies for the boys. All I did was point out the need, and he readily complied. He sent word to his steward to see to the ponies, and I am to find a couple of docile mares for your sisters."

Eliza's hand went to her cheek. "In truth?"

He chuckled. "In truth. But you must not tell the others."

"Oh, no, I shall not," she promised. "But this is a surprise. I would never have thought he would be so kind. I must rethink my opinion of him. Timmie did tell me I should not fear him."

"She gave you good advice," he said, then changed the subject. "Think you she is enjoying her stay here?"

"I do think she is, but she is like that. She looks for what is good and usually finds it. I know she is enjoying her rides, especially when she can give Pirro his head. You are very good to ride with her. You give her a challenge. I fear I am a rather lackluster companion."

"I cannot believe she thinks that, but tomorrow, I must give her a good race."

Knowing Timandra enjoyed her rides with him gave him more confidence. He was contemplating where to take her on the morrow when a screech and a giggle drew his attention back to his young cousins splashing in the pond. He chastised himself. He had been watching them with only half his attention. That was not good. Even with Knolles, Andrew, and Kippie to hand, he was the one responsible for the boys' safety. When Herman and Bennet were in the water, he should not let his mind wander. He would not let it happen again.

Glancing at Bennet's shriveled skin, Gavin called an end to the day's lesson. "Everyone dry off, don your clothes, and we will go to the hamlet and see does Goody Peale have some of her warming tarts on hand."

"Oh, yes," Kippie cried. "Just wait until ye tastes her gooseberry tarts," he excitedly told Herman and Bennet. Leading the way, with the Tilburys on his heels, Kippie raced off toward Perfidious Brambles hamlet. Gavin, with the wet towels stuffed back in their wicker basket, followed more slowly with Andrew and Knolles.

"These tarts are truly worth the walk?" Andrew asked. "They are better than what the Brambles' cook could provide us?"

Gavin chuckled. "Aye, they are very tasty." He knew the lad was wanting to go back to see Delilah. Gavin was as eager to see Timandra, but 'twas time his young cousins became acquainted with the hamlet, and he preferred to be on hand to make certain they showed the proper respect due their uncle's tenants. Best to have a good relationship with the youths of the manor as well. He would not want Herman and Bennet to be intimidated by some of the older boys. He wanted all to know they would be answering to him did his youthful cousins fall victim to any bullying. Likewise, his cousins should not put on airs.

Though his grandfather had a large cattle herd and larger sheep flocks, his land, like Gavin's uncle's, was fertile enough for the cultivation of legumes, barley, oats, and rye. The tenants of both estates, like others of the Tyne River Valley, prospered in the open field system of tillage. Gavin guessed Perfidious Brambles hamlet had some three hundred inhabitants. Many of the tenants were involved in various crafts. The women dominated the brewing, baking, and cheese and butter production; the men were engaged as tanners, carters, tinkers, thatchers, and carpenters. Gavin considered his grandfather fortunate to have Eustace Colyer, the youngest son of his coal mining and coal shipping business partner, for his steward. Eustace kept neat, succinct accounts and had a good relationship with the tenants. They liked and trusted Eustace and so did Gavin. In fact, he considered Eustace a friend.

By the time Gavin, Knolles, and Andrew reached Goody Peale's house, Herman, Bennet, and Kippie were already downing their tarts. Goody Peale had also provided them with mugs of cider, and she offered the same to the new arrivals.

"The boys say ye would be paying," she stated, her head cocked to one side.

Gavin smiled and nodded. The plump, genial woman would appreciate the added funds. Her husband had sustained an injury two years back and could no longer work his fields. He had to pay laborers to do his plowing and harvesting. He could still do light chores around the croft, but the sale of his wife's tarts supplemented their meager income.

With appetites appeased, Gavin, with Kippie's help, gave the boys and their tutor a tour of the hamlet. Whenever they encountered a resident, Kippie introduced his friends. The tenants were as pleased to meet the new young masters of Perfidious Brambles as they had been to meet the boys' older sister. The addition of the Tilburys to Seldon's household was providing them with auxiliary means of enhancing their earnings.

Five boys ranging in age, Gavin guessed, from ten to mid-teens, having delivered pebbles to Kippie's grandfather, returned to the hamlet in good cheer, obviously pleased with the remuneration for their day's toil. Tousle-haired and barefoot, their damp breeches rolled up above their knees, they grinned merrily. Once introductions were made, one of the older boys looked at Herman and said, "We means till haven us a game of windball afore we must sees till our evenin' chores. Does thee cares te joins us, thee would bein' welcome. Jonah hasen a new ball hisen father did maken him from a sow's bladder." Holding up his right hand and looking at Gavin, the youth promised, "We will no be playin' too rough."

Gavin could scarce control a chuckle when he glanced down at Herman and Bennet. His cousins had little idea what the older boy had said. The thick Northumberland dialect, though much less pronounced than that of many Northumbrians, told Gavin the lad had seldom been able to attend the petty school in Fairflex where the King's English was taught. Gavin knew a number of his uncle's tenants lacked a basic education. Some could read a little, having attended school from the ages five to seven, when reading, but not writing or ciphering, was taught. But by the age of eight, the youths were needed to help support their families. Few were able to go on to grammar school. Part of the problem with the educational deficiency stemmed from the distance of the estates to Fairflex. In the winter, when the youths were needed least about the crofts or fields, inclement weather, making long walks to the village a discomfort if not a hazard, contributed to the problem.

When Timandra and Eliza visited the hamlet, Gavin had been called upon to interpret much of the matrons' speech. Timandra had expressed her concern about the tenants' lack of education. "I dearly love their speech pattern," she said, "but I worry for their children. Across England, the enclosure of open fields on estates is increasing. Livestock rearing is replacing agriculture. Do these tenants lose their farms, what will become of them? Crafts may support some, but only do they have customers prosperous enough to need and to pay for their skills."

Agreeing with Timandra, Gavin stated, "Both Grandfather and Uncle Phineas hedged a number of fields including some of their demesne lands that were once farmed. Though none of the tenants' fields have been enclosed, fewer herders are needed and the tenants cannot earn extra pay working the demesne." Gavin could foresee a time when either his grandfather or his uncle or both might find it more cost effective to turn farm land into additional grazing land.

A youth with a modicum of education had a better chance at finding employment in the burgeoning towns and cities. Goldsmiths to mercers to grocers to wholesalers needed clerks. England's booming import export trade offered numerous opportunities to the man who could read, write, cipher, and speak intelligible English. Both estates' youths needed to be prepared for the probable changes. They needed a school closer to their homes. And he knew the perfect spot. A low hill near the stream, not more than a mile from either estate. Smack in the middle of the disputed land. The land that had caused the rift between the Seldons and the Merritts.

Convincing his uncle and his grandfather that the school would be beneficial would not be easy, but he believed he could enlist Timandra's help. That would give him another reason to spend time with her. He had little doubt but what she would like his idea. As Eliza said, Timandra had a generous heart.

Impatient to see Timandra, he explained the windball game to Herman and Bennet. Both boys professed an eagerness to participate in the game, so he left them in Knolles care, and he and Andrew headed back to the house. Having had no time alone with Timandra since their interlude at the pond, he hoped he might convince her to walk out with him to the stables, as she was often wont to do. He could then steer her to a secluded area to discuss his plan for a school. In formulating his plans, he lengthened his stride. Andrew was forced to near run to keep up with him, but the youth made no complaint, and they soon stomped into the kitchen.

❧ ❧ ❧ ❧

Her book on her lap, Timandra sat curled up on the parlor window seat. She had not been able to concentrate on the rollicking *A Midsummer Night's Dream*. Her thoughts kept returning to Gavin. Chastise herself though she might, she could not thrust the pain from her heart. She had arisen that morning still savoring the evening at the Merritts. She looked forward to telling Gavin how much she enjoyed his mother and his aunt. She had also been looking forward to a good gallop and had wondered if Gavin might again race her to the pond. Instead, Gavin devoted himself to Eliza. Why should he not? He was in love with Eliza. With yet another sigh, Timandra shook her head. She had been such a fool to think he would choose to ride with her.

Fearing her pain would show in her mien, she had excused herself from breakfast. "I am not hungry, and I must need consult with Finola about some of my clothing that was laundered Wednesday. I will be down for dinner," she told Eliza.

Eliza had looked surprised but had accepted her excuse. Unable to face Gavin, Timandra scurried up the staircase before he emerged from the kitchen where he had stopped to greet the cook. Finola looked even more surprised when Timandra returned to her room. The maid eyed her suspiciously but readily showed her the laundered shifts, stockings, and petticoats.

"Your blue gown and Mistress Tilbury's black gown are still drying in the old keep's kitchen," Finola said, "as are several other items. I will be after fetching them later today. I am thinking I will be showing Libby about ironing the young misses' gowns. She has done some ironing of sheets, but gowns are after needing a sight more care."

"Will she make an acceptable lady's maid?" Timandra asked, picking up a shift and turning it from side to side to examine it.

"Aye. Audrey is after teaching her to do various hairstyles. I am hoping she will be good at it. She is at times hard to understand does she not mind her tongue." Finola giggled. "But then, I am guessing I am not the best one to be correcting her. Audrey is working with her speech."

Timandra shook her head and chuckled. "Correct, you are not the best one to give anyone English lessons. However, no one is as good as you at mending rents. If she does not ply her needle well, do you work with her. That is important, as seamstresses may not be handy in this far north region."

"Aye, milady. From what I could make out of the laundress's garbled speech, if ladies in the area are wanting anything stylish, they are needing to go to Newcastle. Kind be the laundress and her help, but toilsome to be understanding."

After spending the remainder of the morning in her room, Finola's buoyant chatter acting as a soothing balm, Timandra mastered her emotions enough to go down to dinner. Gavin offered her a cheery greeting, and she sedately responded. She must curb her zeal when in his presence. She feared her heart might betray her did she continue giving it free rein.

Ebba again joined them for dinner, and her lively loquacity saved Timandra from having to exchange anything more than occasional trivial quips with Gavin despite the fact he was seated across from her. When dinner ended, Gavin declared he meant to give Herman and Bennet another swimming lesson. Timandra, relieved to have an excuse to busy herself, hurried off to find Mistress Weston that she might provide the swimming party with towels. She next found the gardener, Beamer, and convinced him to let Kippie join the swimmers.

To avoid any conversation with Gavin, she engaged Beamer in a series of questions concerning the garden. Pleased with the progress being made, the little wizened man eagerly showed off his crew's accomplishments. Following Beamer down a newly pebbled path, Timandra, glancing out of the corner of her eye, saw Gavin head off toward the pond, his brood in tow. She should have been pleased she had evaded him. Instead, she felt depressed. The sun no longer shone, the birds no longer chirped. Life seemed dull and gray.

Somehow she managed to make appropriate comments about the garden. She praised Beamer and her footmen, and the young boys from the hamlet who were spreading the freshly weeded paths with pebbles they had dredged from the stream. She smiled, she nodded, and at last she escaped back to the house, where she found Ebba and Eliza and her sisters preparing to take a walk. Expressing the desire to curl up with her book, Timandra bid them have a nice time, and settling on the window seat with her book, hoped to forget her pain in the tale's jocularity. Instead she found herself staring with blank eyes at the lined pages. This situation was not good, but how to rectify it she had no idea. She could but hope her heart would someday mend. In the meantime, she had to hide her misery and be happy for Eliza.

Chapter 16

Gavin found Timandra in the parlor. She appeared startled and dropped her book when she looked up at his entrance. He hastily strode across the room and picked up the book to return it to her as she uncurled from the window seat and primly placed both feet on the floor.

"Mister Merritt, I had not expected anyone. Eliza is out for a walk. I do think Ebba planned to take her and her sisters to visit a neighbor whose cat just had kittens."

Smiling, he sat beside her and handed her the book, noting it was the one he had recommended. "Yes," he said, "so Mistress Weston informed us. Andrew has set off with the hope of intercepting them on their return. But when Mistress Weston said she believed you were in the parlor, I came here."

"Why ever for?" Timandra said. The question seemed to have slipped out, for she blushed and put her hand to her mouth.

Why would she be surprised he sought her out? He laughed hesitantly. "I wanted to see you." At her questioning look, he decided to launch right into his partially conceived scheme. "I have a proposal I wish to put to you."

Her eyes widened, and she licked her lips. "A proposal?"

"Aye." He nodded. "We spoke of the tenants' need for better education. I have a plan. I would like to see a school set up close enough that tenants from Perfidious Brambles and Kirkworth Hall could attend it." Shrugging and pursing his lips, he added, "Aye, and mayhap tenants from other nearby estates."

For a moment her shoulders seemed to slump, but then she straightened, and turning more toward him, said, "That seems a fine idea, but how does it involve me?"

"I think you can help me convince Grandfather that 'tis a good idea. I can tell he likes you. Respects you, I would say. Mayhap at supper you could tell him of your visit to the hamlet. Then casually mention your concern for the youths. That would be a start. I do think if we work on this together, we can come up with more ideas."

Did he have his way, he would be working closely with her every day. Her nearness on the window seat, her sweet scent had him feeling lightheaded. Her lips looked so tempting. What would she think did he lean forward and kiss her? Dare he?

"Begging your pardon, milady." A voice from the doorway stopped him from acting upon his desire. He turned to see a youthful serving maid. Her cap on her ash-blond hair askew, she bobbed a curtsy and came further into the room.

"What is it Audrey?" Timandra asked.

"'Tis Finola, milady. I cannot find her." Her dark eyes blinking, her cheeks tinged a faint pink, the girl's voice quivered. "She was to fetch some clothing from the keep, then she was to give Libby a lesson in how to properly iron ladies' gowns. 'Tis more than an hour hence. She is not in your room, least wise she failed to answer my knock, nor is she anywhere else in this section of the house. I thought I would see if mayhap she might still be in the keep."

Timandra rose. "That is most strange. I will go with you."

"I will go too," Gavin said, then addressed the maid. "We will need a light and the key."

"Finola has the key, Mister Merritt, but I will fetch a lantern."

Audrey hurried off, and Gavin turned to Timandra. "I had not thought your maid one to shirk her duties. Fact is, I have heard not only Cook but my grandfather sing her praises."

"Finola would never shirk her duties. She may not deserve all the praise being handed her for she can be very aggravating at times, but this has me worried."

Gavin noted the crease between her brows and the concern in her lovely blue-green eyes. Hoping to ease her apprehension, he said, "I am sure naught is amiss. Likely she remembered another errand, and not thinking it would take her any time, failed to tell anyone her intention."

Timandra shook her head. "No, that is not like Finola. She…."

Her sentence went unfinished as Audrey returned with a lighted lantern. Gavin took it from her and led the way up the steep steps to the keep. He found the heavy door at the top of the steps ajar, as if deliberately left that way. Pushing it further open, he held the lantern high and stepped into the small chamber with the staircase leading up to one of the turrets. Everything seemed so quiet that his footstep on the hardwood floor sounded loud to his ears.

Timandra, following on his heels, pointed to a bright blue puddle on the floor of the corridor leading to the hall. Her voice fearful, she said, "That is my gown," and before Gavin could say anything she hollered, "Finola, Finola, are you here!"

"Look, milady." Audrey pointed to a torn patch of black cloth on the steps.

Again Timandra called, "Finola," and hiking up her skirts, headed up the twisting stairs.

Gavin caught a glimpse of a shapely calf and well-turned ankle as he followed after her. Something was amiss, and though he suspected no danger, he wished Timandra had waited and let him go first. Holding the lantern high to help light Timandra's racing steps, he heard Audrey's footsteps tap tapping at his heels. He found Audrey's concern for Finola touching, but not surprising. From what he had seen, he believed Finola to be adroit at garnering affection and at returning it in kind.

Upon reaching the top of the stairs, he heard a muffled voice coming from the other side of the door. "Saints be praised, be that you, milady?"

"Oh, aye, Finola, whatever do you do in there? Are you hurt? Can you open the door?"

Gavin heard the hefty latch being thrown, and Finola peeked out, though she looked as though she might be ready to slam the door shut again. Seeing Timandra, the maid's shoulders drooped and tears welled in her eyes. "Oh, milady, so fearful have I been. I was after thinking I might die in here ere anyone thought to look for me." She opened the door wider and slipped out and into Timandra's arms.

"Finola," Gavin said, "why were you hiding in there?" What could have made the normally sensible maid seek refuge in the turret?

Finola pulled back and looked first at him and then at Timandra. "I saw the ghost again, milady. Only this time it was a man. At least I think so. I had finished gathering up yours and Mistress Tilbury's gowns, and I heard a noise. I looked over my shoulder, and there he was."

Audrey gasped, but Timandra, shaking her head, said, "No, not the ghost again."

Finola grabbed Timandra's hand. "You must be after believing me, milady. He appeared out of nowhere. One moment no one was there – then he was there. He was all in black, and I am swearing his eyes did glow. He looked surprised to see me, but when he started coming toward me, I ran. I ran through the hall, but he cut through the privy passage and was after blocking my way out, so I ran up the steps. I could hear him panting, clomping up the stairs after me, but I was faster, and I made it inside and locked the door. I but hoped he could not come through the door. I prayed this truly was an invincible refuge as Mister Merritt told us.

"And oh, milady, I dropped your gown, and I have torn Mistress Tilbury's."

Timandra again took her maid into her arms and patted her back. "Cry no more, Finola. You are safe now, and I know you will skillfully mend the rent in Eliza's gown. But I want no more talk of ghosts. A ghost would float up the steps after you. He would not pant nor clomp. Someone frightened you, and I mean to find out who. 'Tis some kind of cruel joke, but 'tis no more than that. Now, let us go back to our room."

Turning to Audrey, Timandra said, "There will be no talk from you of ghosts either, Audrey. I will not have the Tilburys frightened. In fact, you need not mention this episode to anyone."

"Yes, milady," Audrey said, bobbing a curtsy, but Gavin could see the girl looked frightened by Finola's story. The perpetrator would need to be found and punished. He thought of all the years he had played in the keep and never once had any strange apparitions mar his joy. His grandfather would not be pleased about this.

※ ※ ※ ※

After collecting Eliza's gown, Timandra led Finola down the stairs. Audrey scooped the torn patch of fabric from the steps and gathered Timandra's gown up off the floor. "You may tell Libby her lesson is postponed," Timandra instructed Audrey when they were back in the parlor. "Tell her I required Finola's services, and do, please, run those gowns up to my room."

"Yes, milady," Audrey said and hurried off.

Timandra, an arm still around Finola's shoulders, turned to Gavin. "I believe our chat will have to wait for another day, Mister Merritt."

"Mayhap you ride tomorrow?" he said.

"I do," she answered, her heart shamelessly skipping a beat.

"Merlin is aching for another good race if your Pirro is up to it," he said. "We could race to the hilltop where I think the school should be located, are you so inclined."

Her pulse leaping, she nodded. "Yes, yes, both Pirro and I would enjoy the outing." 'Twas not truly an outing. He but wanted her help for his school. Well, she cared not what the reason might be, she but wanted to be with him. "Do we again miss our breakfast, should I pack a couple of tarts?"

Gavin chuckled. "Indeed, 'tis a splendid idea." He inclined his head. "I will see you on the morrow. Now, I think I will find Grandfather and tell him about today's occurrence."

"Thank you," Timandra said. "When Finola is more calm, I doubt not Mister Seldon may wish to question her. Now, she must needs rest. I thank you for accompanying Audrey and me in our search for Finola. 'Twas most kind."

Stepping closer, he looked deep into her eyes. "May I always be at your call have you a need, Lady Timandra." He took her hand and raised it to his lips. "Until tomorrow."

She gulped, and saying nothing, watched him stride away. Her heart was beating so fast she could hardly breathe. His hand claiming hers had been so warm, and his lips had sent a flame racing from her fingers to her midsection. She rested a hand on her stomach and dragged in an audibly deep breath.

"Oh, he does be taking one's breath away," Finola said. "And I am after thinking he rather fancies you, Lady Timandra."

"Finola!" Timandra hissed. "I thought you frightened, scared near out of your wits, and here you are making nonsensical comments." Angry she had not been able to conceal her emotions from her maid,

Timandra glared at her. At the same time, she reveled in Finola's observation. Could she possibly be right? No. Timandra gave her head a firm shake. She had been irrational enough for one day. For a brief instant, when Gavin said he had a proposal to make, she had believed he meant to propose marriage to her? Her heart had leapt into her throat. How absurd. She hoped he had not noticed the jubilation, then deflation that must have been written on her face? Oh, how foolish she had been! Foolish! Foolish!

Finola clutched her hand and regained her attention. "I have ne'er been so scared in my life, milady. Not even in that tiny boat floundering in those big waves on the crossing to England did I know such fear. I am thinking 'twas not the same ghost I saw last night. 'Twas a different one."

Timandra narrowed her eyes, and giving Finola a tug, said, "C'mon, let us go upstairs. Somehow, I must make you understand you are not seeing ghosts, but I will not discuss it here in the parlor." The last thing she needed was for one of the new impressionable maids to hear them talking. The affair would then most certainly get back to the Tilburys, and they were only now becoming comfortable in their new home. She was grateful Ebba had taken Eliza and her sisters on a walk, so they had not been present when Audrey came searching for Finola. The big question now was whether Audrey would be able to keep Finola's tale to herself.

Finola made no complaints and meekly followed Timandra up the stairs. She readily settled on her cot but then sat up. "Milady, I near forgot, there are yet several more items to be brought up from the keep."

"Later I will send Perth for them. Now, you rest," Timandra said. "I will be right here writing some letters that are long overdue. When you are more calm, we will talk."

"Yes, milady," Finola said, obediently closing her eyes.

Taking out her writing materials, Timandra pushed the day's events aside and started a letter to her mother and father. Since their arrival at Perfidious Brambles, she had written them but a brief note with the promise of a more concise letter to follow. Time she fulfilled her pledge. While concentrating on the letter, she was able to avoid thoughts of Gavin, but with the letter sanded, folded, and the wax seal stamped, the memory of his lips scorching her fingertips returned. Caressing the singed fingers, she raised them to her own lips. Closing her eyes she imagined his lips on hers. Oh, dear God, what would it be like to actually kiss him?

The pulse in her temples throbbing, she crossed her arms over her heart and hugged herself. She would ride out with Gavin on the morrow. She would have him to herself for another all too brief interlude. No Andrew, no Eliza, just Gavin. With a start, she straightened. No Eliza. Was she plotting against her dearest friend? Here she was dreaming of kissing Gavin, and Gavin was in love with Eliza. But what if he was not in love with Eliza? Might Finola be right? Could he possibly be attracted to her, not Eliza. And what of Eliza? What if Eliza had fallen in love with Gavin?

Timandra stood and started pacing. She had encouraged Eliza to think Gavin might marry her. Rubbing her temples, she tried to remember if she had noticed Eliza paying Gavin any special attention? Eliza blushed when Gavin complimented her and smiled or laughed sweetly when he teased her, but had she sought him out? If Eliza had fallen in love with Gavin, she must not again be hurt by an untrue lover. Shaking her head, Timandra wrapped her arms around her midsection. She must do nothing to interfere with Gavin's courtship of Eliza.

Oh, for heaven's sake, she was again being foolish. Gavin could not be attracted to her. Finola was mistaken. He was but being kind. A good-hearted man he was. He but wanted to help the youth of the two hamlets. She admired him for that and would do what she could to help further his cause. But she must put a stop to any thoughts of love.

Sighing, she returned to her desk and began a letter to her Aunt Venetia.

Chapter 17

Thrilled with the race across the fields and up the hill, Timandra reined in her horse and laughed exuberantly. "That was wonderful! Thank you. Pirro thanks you, too."

Gavin reined in beside her. "Let us ride down the other side to the stream, give the horses a drink and break our fast. We will come back up here later, and I will tell you of my plans."

Tightening the reins, Timandra turned her horse and followed after Gavin. A trail led through the trees down to a lovely bubbling brook. Gavin dismounted, then assisted her to alight. For a moment his hands lingered on her hips, his eyes locked with hers, and she sucked in her breath, inhaling his scent. His face inches from hers, he smiled that smile that set her head spinning and her heart cavorting.

"Sorry, but I can offer you naught but a blanket for our seating," he said, releasing her. Turning to his horse, he untied a blanket and a small leather bag from behind the saddle. He gave his horse a light swat on the rump, and Merlin, followed by Pirro, ambled down to the stream. Whipping open the blanket and placing it on the ground next to a large rock, Gavin extended his hand and offered Timandra a seat. Still feeling the effects of his nearness, she was glad to be able to sit. She needed to regain control of her emotions. She craved Gavin's company, yet she knew she must harden her heart to him.

"How is Finola?" Gavin asked. "Has she recovered from her fright? Does she still believe she saw a ghost?"

Spreading her skirt demurely about her, Timandra sighed, and shook her head. "She is but partially convinced what she saw was not a ghost, but one of your grandfather's tenants. When Finola regained her composure, Mister Seldon requested we join him in the parlor. He apologized to Finola for the fright she had been given and told her the man had been reprimanded. Apparently the tenant should not have been in that section of the house. He must have come up the stairs from the ground floor after making his delivery." Chewing her lower lip, Timandra looked up at Gavin. "I am not certain Finola believed your grandfather. She seems determined she is seeing ghosts. Ghosts dressed in black."

"Ghosts dressed in black, huh?" Chuckling, Gavin opened the leather pouch. He drew out a small jug and two delicate silver mugs. Timandra recognized the mugs as belonging to his aunt's punch bowl set that graced the sideboard in her dining chamber. She wondered if his aunt knew he had taken them. "I thought a little cider would be refreshing and would go nicely with our tarts," he said. Cocking his head, he asked, "You did bring the tarts?"

Laughing at his quizzical expression, she said, "Indeed, I brought them." Removing her gloves, she reached into the pockets of her skirt and pulled out the tarts. Each was carefully wrapped in clean linen napkins. "One apple, one pear – have you a preference?"

"Either would be fine," he answered, lowering himself to the blanket. He removed his hat, leaned back against the rock, and opened the cider jug. Filling their mugs, he handed one to Timandra. The sun glinted on his golden hair, and Timandra sighed as she accepted the mug. Oh, he was a handsome man. Too handsome. She found it hard to resist his magnetism. Blindly, she handed him a tart.

Unwrapping it and biting into it, he said, "Ah, the pear. Cook does have a way with tarts. They may not equal Goody Peale's tarts, but they are a close second."

"Who is Goody Peale?" Timandra asked, after swallowing a sip of cider. "The woman in the hamlet who fed the boys after their swim?"

Gavin nodded. "Aye. So they told you about her."

Timandra smiled. "They told me about their swim, the tarts, their new friends, and the windball game. Seems they had rather a busy afternoon. You have been so generous with your time. I hope they have thanked you."

"In a manner of speaking," he replied, grinning. "Their laughter and joyous smiles are ample thanks. I will feel better, too, when I know they are competent swimmers. As they adjust to their home here, they will venture farther and farther afield. Streams, ponds, and lakes abound,

138

and as they make friends, they will be invited to join in on numerous escapades, including ones involving water activities."

"I suppose that is true. I cannot but wonder has my brother Adam learned to swim. I think I shall write and ask my mother. Can anyone find mischief in the making, 'tis Adam."

"How old is your brother?" Gavin asked, laughing.

"He is eight. He has been fostered at my Aunt Venetia's for the past year." She tsked. "I would guess Aunt Venetia and Uncle Henry have had their hands full. Their sons, my cousins, Algernon and Doran, are fostered with my parents. I have paid little heed to their training or education. They are younger and I have had my own interests to keep me occupied. I know not whether Father includes swimming in their training. However, I cannot recall them getting into any devilment. Nor do Hermie and Bennet cause any major tribulations. Adam, on the other hand, has ever been a disruption. He is a prankster. He is rambunctious and disorderly and is curious about everything and anything. He is a trial, but I love him dearly, and I think he should learn to swim. If anyone could have a mishap around water, 'twould be Adam."

While she spoke, Gavin finished his tart. She had had naught but a nibble of hers, and her stomach was rumbling. "Here I am rambling on when you are set to tell me about your plans for the proposed school."

Wiping his hands on the napkin, he said, "No need to apologize. I enjoy hearing about your family. I look forward to someday meeting this rascal brother of yours. But yes, you would be wise to make sure he learns to swim." He took a swig of cider, crossed one booted foot over the other, and launched into his proposal for the school. "This section of my uncle's estate would be perfect," he said, nodding at the hillside rising above them. "'Tis convenient to both manors. Could I convince Uncle Phineas to donate the land, which has so long been a grievance between the Merritts and the Seldons, and could I get Grandfather to pay to build the school – his purse being more than ample, he can easily afford it – the effort might do more than benefit the tenants. It might end the feud. They would no longer have the land to fight over. At least not all of it."

"That would be wonderful. Think you, that you have a chance of convincing them?" Timandra inclined her head questioningly before taking a sip of cider. She liked watching the expressions cross Gavin's face, and she enjoyed listening to his voice, but his words about looking forward to meeting Adam kept playing through her mind. What could he mean? Why would he expect to meet her brother?

Propping up one knee, Gavin turned and leaned toward her. His blue eyes alive and vibrant, he said, "I think with your help, there might be a chance."

Unable to tear her gaze from his, she swallowed and stammered, "I...I will do what I can." Clearing her throat and straightening her shoulders, she added, "I cannot think how I can be of much help, though I will certainly try."

"I can ask for no more," he said, capturing her hand and raising it to his lips.

Searing flames raced from her fingertips up her arm to her heart to set it ablaze. The warmth of his lips, the tickle of his breath on her skin, the caress of his fingers holding hers had her near a swoon. Blinking rapidly, she gulped and managed a choked laugh. "Well, then, do tell me what you would have me do, Mister Merritt. When are we to start our assault on your uncle and your grandfather?"

Releasing her hand, he grinned and leaned back against the rock. "I think dinner today would be perfect. As we were starting to discuss when interrupted by the search for Finola, I think you could begin by talking to Grandfather about the difficulty in understanding the dialect of the tenants. Without an education, do they lose their land, they have few options but to join the ranks of the coal miners. Though the pay, at least for experienced miners, is substantive. Still, a hard life it is." He smiled wryly. "Not that the Seldons have not made their fortune through the ownership of mines and transport of coal. Grandfather and his partner, Abraham Colyer, reap immense profits off the labor of the poor. Great-great-great-grandfather was one of a group of powerful merchants who gained control of the mines in the early fifteen hundreds. Many mines were originally owned by various orders of monks. Anyway, when great-grandfather decided to become involved in the transportation of coal, he partnered with William Colyer, Abraham's grandfather, and the partnership has continued to thrive over the years."

Having finished her tart, Timandra wiped her fingers and thoughtfully folded her napkin. How might this brief history lesson help her convince Seldon his tenants needed an education? She could think of few occupations worse than working in a mine. Leaving the sun behind to work all day in a dark, dank cave, only to come out tired and aching from the long day's labor.

"Do I recall you saying Mister Seldon's steward is his partner's son?" she asked.

Gavin nodded. "The youngest of five sons. The oldest will inherit his father's land and businesses. The others, like Eustace, have to make their own way."

"Oh my, that does seem unfair."

He shook his head. "No more so than an older son of nobility being the one to inherit the title and the lands. Like property, a business continually divided, over the years, has little left of it. Of course, the other sons have all been provided with outstanding educations, and they had their choice of professions. Two went into law, one is a physician, I do believe, and Eustace chose estate management." Brows raised, Gavin said, "His remuneration has been significant, I might add. And, like his brothers, when he takes a wife, he will receive a substantial settlement."

Timandra ran her tongue over her front teeth and nodded thoughtfully. "Yes, yes, I understand. My father's father was an elder son. He inherited the Grasmere title and estates. My Great Uncle Thayne, the younger son, entered service with a very wealthy merchant in Liverpool and married his daughter." She chuckled. "He ended up wealthier than my grandfather."

Gavin joined in her laughter, then sobered, and picking up a small pebble, tossed it into the stream. "Even the tenants cannot afford to divide up their land sections. They do their best to make settlements on all their children, but there again, an education would benefit those who must seek their own fortunes."

Timandra clapped her hands. "Ah ha, now you have given me more ammunition. Not for today. But later in the week. First we must gather our information."

Straightening and again leaning closer, Gavin asked, "What is your plan?"

"We talk to the tenants. Learn which ones are or have struggled to provide for their children. We learn the fates of the children who have not inherited any land."

"Yes, yes." Gavin joined in her enthusiasm. "We sift through what we learn and choose the best, or I should say the worst, cases to prove the need for better education."

"Eustace Colyer himself will be a good example," Timandra said, shifting her legs a bit to try to change her sitting position. The ground was getting hard. "Think of the benefits a good education have given him."

"Indeed, you are right," Gavin answered, rising and reaching a hand down to her. "I fear I have kept you sitting too long again. Please accept my apology. Problem is, when we start talking, I forget the time."

Timandra took his hand, and he pulled her to her feet. Upon rising, she wobbled and swayed a little. In an instant she was in Gavin's arms. "Steady," he said, his grasp around her waist tightening. He pulled her against his chest, and she could feel his heart hammering against her breast. Her arms pinned to her side, she could do naught but wait for him to release her, but oh, she had no wish to be released. "Regained your balance?" he asked in her ear.

"I...I think so," she stammered. She did not add she was stable, unless she swooned from the scintillating thrill of his embrace.

He pulled away from her, but his hands continued to grip her under the elbows. His eyes bored into hers. "Do you feel like hiking back up the hill? There is a lovely glade amongst the trees I would like to show you. It was a favorite spot of my parents before my father died. 'Tis where they would meet in secret when they were courting."

She nodded. "Oh, yes, I would love to see it."

He grinned, and his eyes seemed to glow. "I will just get the horses. You are all right on your feet now?" He released one arm then tentatively the other.

"Yes, I am perfectly fine. Thank you for steadying me. I think my foot must have gone to sleep, but 'tis awake now." Laughing at her own quip, she added. "I am ready to face the climb."

Gavin packed up the blanket and mugs, retrieved the horses, and with bridles in hand, rejoined her. As they set off up the hill, he kept one hand on her elbow. She appreciated his support. Though normally a strong walker, her riding boots made the climb more difficult than she had anticipated. Near the top of the hill, Gavin tethered the horses to a tree and taking her hand, led her into the woodlet. The trees were not thick, but Gavin had to push aside several branches before they burst into a lovely flower strewn clearing. They surprised a deer and her fawn, and with a twitch of ears, the wary creatures bolted off into the woods.

"After my father died," Gavin said, "Mother used to sometimes bring me up here with her." Tilting his head to one side, he gazed up at the blue sky. "I suppose it must have helped in some way to ease the pain in her heart." He looked back at Timandra. "We used to picnic here. We would sit on a blanket, and after we ate, she would read to me or tell me a story. I loved the sound of her voice, but eventually I would fall asleep. When I woke, we would pack up and go back home." His gaze again distant, he said, "'Twas our private sanctuary."

Hating to disturb his reverie, Timandra questioned softly, "Are you certain you wish to build a school so near your sanctuary? Will your mother approve?"

His trance broken by her question, he lightly snorted. "I can think of nothing more delightful than the sound of children's delighted voices and laughter floating up and out of this glade. I spoke with Mother about my idea for the school last evening. She whole heartedly agrees with my plans. She has not come here in years. Fact is, I had near forgotten about it myself until our breakfast by the stream brought back the memory.

"So now, I will show you where I think the school should be built, and then I must get you back to Perfidious Brambles before your Mister Tombs comes looking for us."

Chapter 18

Upon returning to the stables, Timandra and Gavin were met by Herman and Bennet. Bubbling over with excitement, Herman cried, "Oh, Lady Timandra, Cousin Gavin, look what Mister Colyer brought us." He pointed to two ponies being saddled by the Tilbury's coachman, Tibbs. "The larger brown one is mine," Herman asserted proudly.

Timandra controlled her smile when Bennet, his little chin raised, stated just as proudly, "Mine's the black one with the white stockings. He is the prettier one. And we both have new saddles. Mister Knolles said we may take the rest of the day off from our studies, and Mister Tombs says he will take us riding."

His sentences being made in one long breath, Bennet paused to gasp for air, and Herman took over. "Uncle Percival bought them for us. I told 'Liza right from the start that Uncle was not so bad. His steward chose the ponies for us."

Interrupting, Gavin asked, "Is Mister Colyer in the house now."

"Oh, yes," Herman said with a nod. "They are all in the parlor."

Taking Timandra's arm, Gavin said, "I would like you to meet Eustace before you go up to change for dinner, does that agree with you."

"Yes, that would be nice. Has he just arrived, no doubt he is still in his travel clothes, and I will not feel I am the only disheveled person in the room."

"You hardly look disheveled, Lady Timandra," Gavin said, his eyes running up and down her figure in a way that had her blushing.

She looked back at the boys. "What of your dinner?"

Herman grinned. "Mister Knolles told Mister Tombs he may keep us out until he hears our stomachs rumbling, or when his own starts complaining. Then he is to bring us back for our dinner."

Timandra laughed and said, "Very well. Have a good ride." Turning back to Gavin, she let him lead her to the house. For once they did not enter through the kitchen which was Gavin's norm from years of visits to the Brambles. They instead entered through the garden portal, and Timandra observed how lovely the garden with its trimmed bushes and hedges was looking. She made note to commend the gardener, Beamer, and her footmen.

No sooner did she enter the parlor, than Eliza was up and rushing to her side. "Oh, Timmie, do look what Mister Severin has brought me." She held a lovely string of pearls up to her throat. "My mother's pearls." Eliza cried. "Mister Severin has returned them to me."

"Eliza! Dear friend! How wonderful!" Timandra clasped Eliza in her arms and hugged her. Looking over Eliza's head, she recognized, Bartley Severin, the young solicitor who had been so kind to the Tilburys during their humiliating reversal of fortune. From his seat beside Eliza on the couch facing the door, he had quickly risen to his feet at Timandra's entrance. Andrew, Seldon, and a man next to Seldon, she assumed was his steward, also rose. Her speculation on the new face was short lived. No sooner did she release Eliza, than Gavin introduced Eustace Colyer. She, in turn, introduced Severin to Gavin.

"How nice to see you again, Mister Severin," she said once everyone was seated, Gavin having drawn up a chair for himself and for Colyer who vacated the armchair next to Seldon for Timandra. "What a very long distance you have come. All the way from London. Surely you cannot say you came but to deliver the pearls to Eliza, though 'tis most kind of you."

A blush crept up Severin's face from his neck, and he reached a hand to his cravat to loosen it. Fashionably dressed, he wore a collarless, front-braided, gold coat reaching to just above the knees, square-toed shoes with square buckles, and a brown shoulder length wig. Timandra guessed him to be in his late twenties. A handsome man, he was clean-shaven, light-skinned, with pale-gray eyes, a straight nose, and firm lips which he tweaked into a smile before he answered.

"Due to the immense trade, particularly in coal, our firm is considering opening an office in Newcastle. As it would simplify things for a number of our clients, I volunteered to survey the area. And, as we had recovered the Tilbury pearls, and knowing how much they meant to Mistress Tilbury, I thought to bring them to her myself. 'Twas my good fortune upon arrival to meet up with Eustace at the Red Lion Inn in Newcastle."

"You knew each other previously?" Gavin questioned.

"We were classmates at Gray's Inn," Severin explained.

Colyer, as dark as Severin was fair, chuckled and took up the tale. "We had a fine reunion. Drank a couple of rounds. Then he told me of his mission, and we were both surprised to learn we were bound for the same destination." His dark eyes twinkled, and he swiped a strand of his dark hair off his forehead. "What luck, I thought. A companion to bear me company and to lead one of the ponies. We would have arrived yesterday, but the smaller pony could not keep up. We had to slow our pace. Rather than arrive after dark, we stayed the night in Fairflex. Rode in this morning and had time to wash off the dust and change before presenting ourselves."

Timandra had noted only she and Gavin were in their riding apparel, but as Eliza and her sisters were yet in their morning gowns and walking shoes, she did not feel as boorish as she would have were they all dressed for dinner. She and the Tilburys would soon need to change, though, were they to be ready in time for Seldon's early dinner hour.

"We saw the ponies," Timandra said. "Herman and Bennet could not be more excited."

"Uncle Percival says Delilah and I are to have horses, too," broke in Charissa. She looked at Gavin and added, "He said you were to find suitable mares for us."

Chuckling, Gavin said, "You are correct, Cousin Charissa. And it so happens, I do think I have found the perfect horses for you. I mean to discuss their owner's asking price with Grandfather today, and does he approve, you could get them sometime next week."

"How grand!" Charissa said, clapping her hands, and Delilah joined in her jubilation.

A wide grin spreading across his face, Andrew looked joyful. "Soon we will be able to ride out together," he said, taking Delilah's hand. Then he swallowed and glanced at Seldon. "Along with your sisters and Lady Timandra, of course."

"Of course," Delilah answered with a giggle.

Timandra was pleased at how much more at ease the Tilburys were in

146

their uncle's presence. When they had first met him, they could scarcely speak. Fear had been obvious in their stammered words and stiff movements. That he was purchasing ponies for the boys and mares for Charissa and Delilah boded well for their future. He seemed to be showing concern for their needs, even if he did it grudgingly. And she was not sure but what his gruffness was more an act, or even a defense to disguise a pain residing in his heart. When it came time for her to leave, and she would need to leave before the autumn rains started, she could leave knowing the Tilburys were content in their new home.

❀ ❀ ❀ ❀

Dinner was a merry occasion. As usual, Timandra was seated next to Seldon. When he chose to converse, though 'twas seldom, she always found him interesting. This evening, he was quiet, but Gavin, seated across from her, was in high spirits, his laughter ringing out at her slightest quips. At the end of the table, Eliza was seated with Colyer to one side and Severin to the other. The two men seemed to be vying for her attention, and she responded to their blandishments with smiles and blushes. Andrew and Delilah, attuned only to each other, ignored Charissa, seated across from them, so Timandra felt compelled to engage the girl in conversation.

During a lull in her discussion with Gavin of their likes and dislikes of London, she leaned closer to Charissa and asked, "How is your new maid doing, Charissa, dear? Is she receiving adequate help from Finola and Audrey?"

Charissa brightened, the bored look left her face, and she looked far prettier. Pretty enough that she momentarily caught Colyer's eye as she answered, "Oh, I believe Libby will do just fine. She tries hard. She knows 'tis a step up being a lady's maid. Audrey and Finola are both very helpful." She pointed to the neckline of her gown. "I had a slight tear here. Finola showed Libby how to take the tiniest of stitches and now you cannot even see it was torn.

"'Tis her speech I struggle with the most, though," Charissa said with a frown. "At times, she is quite difficult to understand. Audrey is trying to teach her to speak more intelligibly." She smiled. "Mister Knolles has also helped. He is very kind. He has told her she cannot advance in status does she not learn to speak the King's English. He has given her a book Bennet is beyond and has told her to practice reading it aloud to learn the proper manner of speaking."

Smiling, Timandra turned to Seldon. Charissa had given her the perfect opening to begin her offensive. "I suppose you have no difficulty understanding the Northumbrian dialect, Mister Seldon?" she asked.

Snorting, he finished chewing a bite of steak and kidney pie and said, "I was raised here. What would you expect? My nurse spoke the dialect, and I copied her. 'Twas being sent away to school drummed it out of me."

Timandra glanced down the table. "What of you, Mister Colyer? Have you trouble understanding the local dialect?"

Colyer looked up in surprise at hearing himself addressed from the other end of the table. "I beg your pardon, Lady Timandra, what did you ask?"

"She asked, do you have trouble understanding the locals," Gavin said. "I can answer for you." He looked back at Timandra. "He has no more trouble than do I."

Timandra nodded. "I thought not, but 'tis near like a foreign language to me." She turned back to Seldon. "When Eliza and I visited some of the matrons of your hamlet the other day, had Mister Merritt not been with us to translate, we would have been hard pressed to know what they were saying, though they were all very kind and friendly."

Raising her chin, Timandra said, "I suppose the schooling one receives is most helpful. One could not expect to carry on any business outside this area did one speak only in dialect." Hiding a smile, she again looked down the table. "Is that not correct, Mister Colyer?"

Colyer had refocused his attention on Eliza, but he jerked around when addressed anew. "Oh, indeed, Lady Timandra, my correspondence and my dealings with agents and merchants from various sections of the country require me to know the King's English."

"Are you leading somewhere with this questioning, Lady Timandra?" Seldon asked.

Had she advanced too fast? Timandra shifted in her seat so she was facing Seldon. His eyebrows raised, lips pursed, he eyed her suspiciously. He was no fool. She should not have underestimated his sagacity. Donning her sweetest smile and cocking her head ever so slightly, she said, "What can you mean, Mister Seldon? We were discussing the difficulties arising from being unable to appropriately communicate. I but wonder if 'tis a handicap." She fluttered her hand. "I mean, for those like Libby, who want to advance." She almost added but have not been able to attend school, but decided she had said enough.

Charissa rescued her by saying, "I feel certain Libby will learn all she needs to serve us, Lady Timandra. You need not worry. Lilah and I are satisfied with her."

Timandra patted Charissa's hand. "I am glad to know that." To Charissa, Timandra's concern had been for her and Delilah, not for their poorly educated maid. Seldon still looked wary, but for the time being, the discussion was ended. Gavin changed the subject by telling Charissa that his grandfather had approved his choice of horses for her and her sister, and that they should be brought round one day this week.

"Oh, thank you, Uncle Percival," Charissa said, looking past Timandra to her uncle.

"Yes, thank you, thank you," Delilah said.

Seldon but waved his hand. Was he pleased by the girls' gratitude, he made no comment.

"I wonder will they be here before we go to Cousin Dwight's on Wednesday," Charissa pondered, her gray eyes glowing.

"Even are they here, you will not ride them," Eliza said, surprising Timandra. She had not thought Eliza to be listening to the conversation. She thought her too engaged by Colyer and Severin, and for Gavin's sake, she was feeling a bit put out with her. No question about it, Eliza was flirting with the two men. "Remember," Eliza continued, "you have invited Ebba to go with us. You must ride with her in the coach."

Before Charissa could respond to her sister, Gavin said, "Until you have ridden the horses around here for a day or so and have adjusted to their gait and ways, I would not think it wise for you to take any extensive rides. Best you wait a couple of weeks before trying a long trek."

Charissa looked disappointed, but she accepted her fate. Riding in the coach on roads that were not toll roads could be extremely uncomfortable. Timandra knew that too well from her own travels and was always happiest when she could ride Pirro and not be forced to bounce around in the coach, well-padded as were the seats in her father's coach.

"What is this excursion you speak of?" Colyer asked.

Eliza explained their planned expedition to her Cousin Dwight's to see the remains of the Roman wall, and Colyer and Severin were invited to join them. Both men eagerly accepted. Severin, it would seem, would be staying for an undetermined time with Colyer in the steward's lovely little cottage that Timandra had seen nestled amongst the trees.

By the time dinner ended and Timandra and the Tilburys excused themselves, with the men's promises to soon be joining them in the parlor, Timandra was ready for a little quiet. She could well imagine Seldon must be feeling the same. She would be surprised did he join them in the parlor. Did he not, that would be a blessing. She would have time to ask Gavin's opinion on her beginning assault on Seldon. Certainly she had made her point of the importance of learning to speak the King's English. That was a start.

Chapter 19

Timandra was glad the next day was Sunday. Sitting through Hemphill's sermon would be a trial, but she would enjoy seeing Gavin's mother and aunt again. She had liked both women immensely. She hoped before 'twas time for her to leave for home, she would again be invited to their home. She believed she would enjoy a correspondence with them. They were both so witty. How lucky Eliza would be to live in a home with such lively and intelligent women.

"Oh, Timmie," Eliza broke in on her thoughts. "I never dreamed I would ever have so much fun again. I thought my life was over, but you were right. You said all would be well." She clutched the pearls at her throat. "To think I have Mother's pearls. I am so happy, I could cry."

"Well, you must not cry," Timandra said with a smile. "You would not want your eyes all red when the men join us. Come now, tell me what you wish to play. Cards or backgammon?"

"I do think cards. More people can play. And besides, Mister Althouse and Delilah so enjoy the backgammon. I do think a game of cribbage would be fun."

The men did not linger long over their port, and within short order, with the exception of Seldon, who excused himself, they had all settled down to an afternoon of games and conversing. Andrew and Delilah were at the backgammon table, Severin and Colyer joined Charissa and Eliza in a game of cribbage, and Timandra found herself engaged in a game of chess with Gavin.

She had been surprised when he suggested the game, drawing her away from the others, but then she realized he wished to discuss her initial sortie. And he would want to plan their next attack. "You were brilliant," he lauded her, and she felt her face flushing under his praise. "I think next week, we should follow your suggestion, and learn more about the problems the tenants have providing for their children. We can talk with Grandfather's tenants, and I will ask Mother to talk with Uncle Phineas's."

"Your uncle will not be offended – that you, or rather your mother, will be talking to the tenants, basically behind his back?"

Gavin made a move on the chess board. "Nay, and likely Mother will enlist Aunt Mabelle in our plan. No one could believe more strongly in the benefits of education. Her family is noted for its scholarly leanings. For generations they have been in the diplomatic service of the crown."

"I found your aunt a remarkable woman," Timandra said, advancing a pawn on the board. "Your mother, also. I thoroughly enjoyed getting to know them better."

"They enjoyed your company as well. I have no doubt they will soon be inviting you to dinner again to further the acquaintance."

Timandra raised her eyes to meet his. "I do hope so. I want very much to visit with them again before I must begin my return journey."

Gavin looked startled. "Return journey! You cannot be thinking of leaving."

Timandra shook her head. "Not immediately, but I will need to start home before the autumn rains begin. I wanted to be certain the Tilburys would adjust to their new home, and they seem to be doing better than my expectations. Your grandfather is treating them far more kindly than I might have initially expected."

Gavin chuckled. "Aye, I must say, I too am pleased with how much Grandfather is unbending. I do believe you have had much to do with his change for the better."

"Me?" Timandra could not hide her surprise.

"I keep telling you that he respects you, and I believe he enjoys your company, your wit, and, I must add, your lack of fear of him. At his age, a certain amount of deference is his due, but he has little respect for those who show fear in his presence." Gavin directed his gaze toward the window. "I was seven or eight when I first met Grandfather. Mother had told me much about him. All good things, fun things, never anything derogatory.

"When I asked why we never went to visit him, she but said she and he had a difference of opinion on a matter and had not been able to resolve it. It made no sense to me, so one day, not long after I got my first pony, I set off for Perfidious Brambles." He shook his head derisively and chuckled a little. "The poor stableman, who was supposed to bear me company wherever I went, tried valiantly to turn me back, but I was set on meeting my grandfather."

He brought his gaze back to Timandra. "I loved him and Perfidious Brambles at first sight. I think Grandfather loves me, too. If not, he would have run me off that first visit. Instead, he sent the stableman home with a note to my mother so she would not worry, and he promised to have Old John take me home at a reasonable hour. Grandfather then brought me into this very parlor, and we talked. I cannot remember what all we talked about, but I know he asked me a lot of questions about my life and about Mother. He next gave me a tour of the keep. To a boy of my age, it was the grandest sight imaginable. It was a castle.

"When finally I had to leave, I promised I would return, and I keep returning." He laughed again and looked down at the board. "Is it my move?"

Timandra wished something could be done to reunite Gavin's family. 'Twas a sad situation. Hiding a frown, she lightened her voice and said, "Yes, 'tis your move. We are making slow progress on this game, but 'tis of no merit. I enjoyed hearing of your meeting with your grandfather. I am impressed your mother made no attempt to turn you against your grandfather. 'Tis a pity they have remained estranged all these years. My intuition tells me they love each other dearly and are both pained by the estrangement."

Nodding, Gavin made his move before saying, "I am in full agreement, but neither one will discuss the other. I used to try to get them to at least talk to each other, but to no avail. My attempts but saddened Mother and angered Grandfather. So I stopped trying.

"Now, to change the subject. Do you attend church services on the morrow?"

"We do."

"Splendid, Andrew and I will see you there. Not sure about the rest of the family. Vicar Hemphill two weeks in a row is a bit much for Uncle Phineas."

That tingle she could not control whenever she knew she would again get to see Gavin raced up her spine to the nape of her neck. She decided she should stop fighting her obvious attraction to the man. Soon enough she would be starting for home. Until then, she should relax and enjoy her time with him.

The remainder of the afternoon passed more swiftly than she could have wished. The clock chimed four, and Gavin looked round at the clock on the mantel in surprise. "Ah, the time," he said. "Andrew, we must be leaving. We promised to stop by Mistress Woods' on our way home to pick up the crock of pickled beets she made as a thank you to your grandmother for bringing her that yard of yellow ribbon to trim her daughter's wedding gown."

Gazing at Delilah with such a lovesick look on his face that Timandra was hard pressed not to laugh, Andrew said, "Ah, I do wish Grandmother was not forever doing favors for people." Frowning, he looked at Delilah. "We have no choice but to leave. As Gavin says, we must stop for the pickles, or Grandmother will send me back for them." His mouth still downcast, he asked, "Will I see you, Mistress Delilah, at services tomorrow?"

"Oh, yes," Delilah eagerly replied, before a frown crossed her face. "At least I believe so." She turned to her sister. "Eliza, do we attend services on the morrow?"

"We do," Eliza answered and looked first at Severin and then Colyer. "Do you attend?"

Severin answered immediately. "If you are attending the services, most certainly I am."

"I, too," Colyer said. "I often ride in when I am staying here."

"That is wonderful," Eliza said, her sweet smile showing off her small white teeth. "And of course, you will be having dinner with us afterwards."

"Delighted. Thank you," Colyer said. "Mister Seldon has from time to time invited me to join him at dinner. He was used to take his supper in his own parlor, though."

"He oft still does," Eliza said, "but I do hope you and Mister Severin will join us for supper this evening. We have been at odds and ends, not knowing what to do after supper. Supper being served so early."

"Again, we are obliged," Colyer said with a slight nod.

"I had hopes we might join you this evening," Severin added. "I brought a book of poetry with me. I thought mayhap, after supper, you and Lady Timandra might read some poems to us."

Timandra brightened. She hated to see Gavin depart, but she was pleased they would have some form of entertainment come the evening. Most nights they did little but sit in the parlor and try to read or do needlepoint by the shared candlelight until the clock chimed nine, and they could retire to their beds.

Gavin and Andrew moved to the door after making their good-byes, but stopped when Delilah said, "Mister Althouse, why do you not join us for dinner after services?" She then looked aghast, and blushing furiously, added, "Of course, I meant you, too, Cousin Gavin."

Chuckling, Gavin said, "I assumed as much. And speaking for the both of us, I readily accept. Now, we must be off." He gave Andrew a light push on his shoulder, and with a last longing look, the boy headed toward the back of the house, Gavin at his heels.

Timandra watched them go, knowing she felt as bereft as did Andrew. Delilah had certainly charmed the youth. Did the infatuation last, 'twould be a good match. She hoped once she returned home, her own infatuation would fade, but she feared she would be a long time forgetting Gavin Merritt.

Chapter 20

Laughter rang through the hall as Timandra, the Tilburys, and their guests, scurrying in from the coaches to escape the sudden rain, shook out skirts and brushed off coats. Gavin, Andrew, Colyer, and Severin, having been on horseback, were near soaked. Old John hurried to the door. "Dear, dear," he exclaimed, "Master Gavin, Mister Althouse, Mister Colyer, and Mister Severin, look at you. Do come with me. I will get you towels, and you can dry off in the men's dormitory." He tsked. "I will have Cook make you up some hot ale and honey."

"Best do as he says," Eliza said with a giggle, and sweeping off her bonnet, added, "We will hurry upstairs and change and see you back in the parlor."

"Lead on, John," Gavin said, urging the other three to follow the old man. "And by the by, John, best have Cook make up enough of that ale and honey for the footmen and coachmen. They are easily as wet as we are."

Timandra appreciated Gavin's thoughtfulness. She found his concern for the servants admirable. She doubted few of the gentry would care whether their servants were cold or wet.

Grasping Ebba's hand, Eliza said, "Do you come with me. We must get you dried off. Your father will ne'er forgive me do we send you home with the ague."

After service, Ebba had been invited to join their party and had eagerly accepted. Laughing, she said, "'Tis not likely I will be stricken. I have oft been caught in the rain, but I will welcome a drying fire."

Heading for the stairs with Ebba in tow, Eliza looked over her shoulder. "Mister Knolles, you will see to Hermie and Bennet? Get them into dry clothes?"

"Indeed, Mistress Tilbury," the young tutor answered, a hand on each boy's shoulder.

"Oh, and Mister Knolles, you and the boys should join us for dinner today. 'Tis Sunday, and 'twas our habit at Merrywic to dine as a family."

Knolles smiled as broadly as his young charges. "Thank you, Mistress Tilbury."

"Hermie, Bennet, mind you are presentable. We have guests."

"We will, 'Liza," the boys answered in unison.

"You will be on good behavior, too, or you will be sent from the room." Not waiting for her brothers to answer, Eliza, with Ebba at her side, headed up the staircase after her sisters and the maids, Audrey and Libby.

Timandra followed in Eliza's wake, with Finola chirping at her. "We will be getting you out of that wet gown and bonnet immediately, milady. I will not be having you come down with a cold or the ague. I hope I can stir up a fire from the morning's coals."

"You are to change your own gown and bonnet, too, Finola. You are as wet as I am."

"Aye, but I am not required to go back down and entertain a party of gentlemen. I can stay by a warm fire and dry out our clothes and then go see does Cook need anything doing."

Timandra laughed. "You make it sound like you have an easier duty."

"And so I do, milady. You must smile and laugh and make idle chatter. You must be careful not to eat too much or your stays will feel too tight. You must sit erect, and mind nothing drops on your gown. You must not laugh too loud or too long."

A cough reminded Timandra that Knolles and the boys were coming up the stairs behind her and Finola. Her maid's opinion of propriety might not be what young ears needed to be hearing. "That is enough." She interrupted Finola's dialogue. "After we are changed, before you see to drying our clothing, make sure Perth and Edgar know I will be wanting them to help Old John serve the dinner. And tell Hillock and Kearne they may have the remainder of the day off."

"Yes, milady," Finola answered demurely as they headed up the second flight of stairs.

Timandra was pleased Eliza had invited her brothers and Knolles to join them for dinner. The boys needed to be exposed to proper dining experiences, but she suspected Eliza invited them because Ebba seemed to evince a fondness for the young tutor.

"The footmen and the coachmen certainly did get soaked," Finola said, resuming her chatter. "But then, they are used to it, being they went through several rainy spells on our journey here. Their wide brim hats and woolen coats do help protect them, but 'tis being a shame 'tis their best coats and breeches that got all wet and muddy."

"Yes, 'tis a shame," Timandra acknowledged.

"The laundress will have her hands full this week. Most like, she will be needing extra help," Finola said, stepping aside at the entrance to the room to let Timandra enter first. "Well, now, let us be getting these wet things off you. Come over by the fire while I stir up the coals. I think I see a wee ember smoldering."

Once Finola had a fire again glowing, Timandra let her fuss over her, but before she would allow her to help her don a fresh gown and redo her hair, she insisted Finola change and dry herself. "I will sit here by the fire and warm up. Now, do as I bid you."

"Yes, milady," Finola acquiesced. "But I am after guessing Audrey and Libby are seeing to their mistresses, not themselves."

"I cannot speak to what Audrey and Libby are doing. I but know I want you hale and hearty. I have no wish to do without a maid do you come down with the ague."

Finola giggled and threw over her shoulder as she scurried into the closet to change, "Indeed, milady, you would well be lost without me."

Shaking her head, Timandra joined in the laughter. A trial Finola might be, but yes, she would be lost without her.

※ ※ ※ ※

"I cannot think when I have had such an entertaining dining experience," Severin said. He looked very dapper in the latest style of justaucorps. The collarless, knee-length coat of blue brocade, had buttons and fancy buttonholes down the entire front and massive turned-back cuffs. His waistcoat was a lighter blue, his breeches, a dark gold, his buckle shoes, dark brown.

Hillock and Kearne had returned from the stables under a large canvas, and Colyer and Severin had appropriated it during a lull in the rain to scuttle over to Colyer's cottage to change their clothes. Gavin had also donned a fresh coat and breeches. He kept dinner clothing on hand at the house rather than appear at dinner in his riding clothes. Since he and Andrew had been joining them for dinner near every day of the week, Andrew had dinner clothing on hand as well.

Only Ebba had no fresh garments to don. She was so tiny, even the Tilburys gowns were large on her, but at Eliza's request, Finola hastily, though neatly, hemmed up a skirt and took in a bodice so Ebba had dry clothes to wear. Timandra thought the girl looked adorable in the over-size clothes. Rather like a pretty child playing grownup in her mother's gown. Knolles must have thought so, too. He had scarcely been able to take his eyes off her during the dinner. Fortunately for him, Herman and Bennet were on good behavior, and he had not needed to discipline them in any way. The boys had been so good, Eliza had given them permission to join the party in the parlor.

"You may play a game of draughts do you wish, but I will not have you thinking to join in a game of cribbage. You are not skilled enough yet," Eliza said.

"I have a better idea," Timandra said. "Instead of adjourning to the parlor, let us go up to the gallery. Perth can light the wall sconces, and we can look at the portraits. I have been curious about them, and Mister Merritt can tell us all about his ancestors."

"What a splendid idea," Eliza said, clapping her hands. The others at the table joined in the approval. As Seldon had not joined them for dinner, the men decided they had no reason to linger at the table. So the party was soon traipsing up to the gallery on the second floor. Perth had drawn open the draperies on the large windows, but the darkened day afforded the gallery little light, however he soon had the sconces lit, and the faces on the wall stared down at their viewers.

"Not a large display of ancestors," Gavin said. "Let us start here with the founding father of Perfidious Brambles, my great, great grandfather, Lucius Seldon. Not the best portrait, a bit flat, but the artist did capture the eyes. How sharp they are, and look how blue they are. Tell me those are not Grandfather's eyes."

"Oh, my," Eliza said, "you are right. Piercing blue."

"And who is this fellow?" Severin asked. "He looks a right jolly fellow."

"That is Great Grandfather, and the lovely lady with him is my great grandmother."

"Oh," Timandra said, "'tis from her you get your blond hair."

Chuckling, Gavin said, "Aye. Grandfather and my mother also favor her coloring. Dwight and his late mother, on the other hand, take after Great-Grandfather."

"So was this lady your grandfather's wife?" Ebba asked, her eyes dancing. She was standing in front of the next portrait. "She looks like she would have been a wonderful mother. Such a sweet expression on her face."

Timandra agreed with Ebba. The woman in the portrait was not the most beautiful woman Timandra had ever seen, but the artist had captured her essence in the portrait.

"Yes, that is my grandmother, but I never knew her," Gavin said. "She died long before I was born."

"I wonder your grandfather does not keep her portrait over the mantle in the parlor or some other prominent spot," Timandra said.

"I think, mayhap, he has no wish to have her on display. Once when I was allowed into his bedchamber, I saw another portrait of her hanging over his bed. I think in the evenings when he is locked in his room, she keeps him company."

"That is so sweet," Eliza said. "He must have loved her very much."

"Indeed, I think he did," Gavin said.

"Eliza, this must be your grandfather. And his sister and Mister Seldon in their youth," Timandra said, gazing up at an overly large portrait in a massive gold frame. "Your grandfather as a young man. He was quite handsome. Eliza, look, you have his brown eyes."

"Oh," Eliza breathed, and her two sisters crowded up next to her to stare up at their youthful grandfather. "Yes. That is Grandfather," Eliza said. "He visited us but once, Merrywic being so far from Lancashire, and he died but a few months before Mother took me to Lady Venetia's to be fostered with you, Timmie. Mother was so heartsick she was not able to see him at least one more time before he died."

"I have no memory of him at all," Delilah said. "I must have been too young."

"I think I remember him," Charissa said, "but I cannot be sure. I think he swung me up in the air and said I reminded him of my grandmother."

"We have no portrait of Grandfather or Grandmother," Eliza said a bit sadly, and she looked at Gavin. "It is so lovely Uncle Percival has this gallery, so we can at least see Grandfather when he was a boy." She turned to Severin. "The portrait of Mother and Father that you insisted would not be sold at auction, I have hanging in my bedchamber. 'Twas so kind of you to make sure we could keep the portrait."

"'Twas only right you should have that memory," Severin said, his eyes softly meeting hers. Timandra believed Severin had not made the long trip to Newcastle and then Perfidious Brambles just to bring Eliza the pearls. The man could well be in love with Eliza. Was that good or bad, she had yet to determine.

"I have to believe my grandfather's mother must have insisted Grandfather and his siblings sit for that portrait," Eliza said. "Grandfather's sister and Uncle Percival look happy enough, but Grandfather looks ready to bolt."

Looking at Gavin, Timandra said, "I can see the resemblance between your grandfather and his mother, and between his father and his sister and Eliza's father. And, am I remembering Dwight correctly, I can see he favors his mother. Is there a portrait of him here?"

"Nay, but there is one of him in his youth at his house. As well as one of his mother and father and a portrait of his two sisters."

"Well, that would make sense."

"I cannot think either one of Dwight's sisters ever visit," Gavin said. "To my recollection, last time they were even in the area was for their mother's funeral ten years ago."

Before anyone could comment on Dwight's absent sisters, Herman cried, "Oh, would you look at this. Uncle has a portrait of 'Liza."

"What!" Eliza said, and Gavin chuckled as everyone rushed down to the last portrait.

"Why, that does look a lot like me," Eliza said.

"Indeed. That is my mother when she was sixteen," Gavin said. "Now, you may understand why Grandfather and I kept staring at you when we first saw you. For Grandfather, it could well have been a shock. Almost like seeing my mother in her youth."

"I wonder I failed to take more notice of the resemblance when we dined with you," Timandra said.

"Well, Mother has aged. Her hair is not so blond, and a few wrinkles grace her face."

"All the same, I feel I should have seen how much Eliza looks like your mother. Mayhap 'tis because Eliza's mother also looked so much like your mother. I would think in their youth, they could well have passed for sisters if not twins. Eliza, you must show Gavin the portrait of your mother. The resemblance is remarkable."

"It truly is," Charissa said, tilting her head to one side and examining Eliza and then the portrait. "Only real difference is, Mother's eyes were more gray like mine, and her hair was not as blond as Eliza's or Cousin Gavin's mother's."

"Well, who is this man?" Herman demanded. He had moved on to the end of the gallery and was staring at a large bust.

"That is a bust of your great, great, great-grandfather. The one who made a fortune in coal. Whether it is a good likeness, I cannot say. Nor can Grandfather. Here now, I do believe we have seen all the Seldon ancestors. What say we return to the parlor for a game of blindman's bluff?"

"Oh, yes!" Bennet cried. "Might we play, too?"

Gavin chuckled. "I can see no reason why not, do your sister and Lady Timandra have no objections."

As neither Eliza nor Timandra objected, they all traipsed back downstairs to the parlor to spend a delightful afternoon in fun and games. Timandra could not remember when she had last laughed so hard, and she was happy to see all the Tilburys seemed to be thoroughly enjoying themselves. That was good. When 'twas time for her to return to her home, she believed she could leave her dear friend and her youthful siblings in a happy home.

However, the thought of leaving Perfidious Brambles and never seeing Gavin again was a heart-rending thought. Another couple of weeks, and she would have to head home. It was a long journey from Perfidious Brambles to her home in west Cheshire, a long arduous, lonely journey. Well, at least she would have Finola with her. Finola would help relieve some of the boredom. Oh, but never to see Gavin again.

"You frown. Is aught amiss?" Gavin asked.

Timandra had not noticed he had joined her at the window. "I was wishing this day would not end. It has been so enjoyable. However, I believe we must call for the coach to take Ebba home. Her father may start to worry."

Gavin snorted. "Vicar Hemphill worry about Ebba? I believe he gave that up long ago. But as you say, is she to be home at a timely hour, 'tis best you call for the coach."

"She will have to change back into her clothes as well." Timandra turned from the window to look back out at the laughing participants of a game of gossip. One person would whisper something in a person's ear, that person in turn would whisper what they heard to another person, and it would go around until all had their turn. The last person would announce what they heard, and they would all laugh at how different the original and concluding messages sounded. "I do so hate to break up this day. I suppose 'tis really Eliza should do it, but she is having such fun. I love seeing her smile again. I wish she and her sisters were not having to continue to wear mourning clothing."

"I cannot think Severin or Colyer have any complaints. Eliza is as lovely in black as she would be in any brighter color. But how about I be the one to break up the party while you order the coach."

"Thank you," Timandra said, heading for the door to ring for Perth, but all that was rushing about in her head was Gavin's words that Eliza was as lovely in black as she would be in any color. And how must he feel to see Eliza having such a gay time with the other two men? She hoped he would not think Eliza to be fickle. Or did she?

Chapter 21

"What a perfect day for our outing," Eliza said, excitement evident in her large brown eyes. "'Tis so kind of Cousin Dwight to have invited us to his home to see the old Roman wall and to have a picnic."

Timandra chuckled. "I think 'twas Mistress Clakenberger who made the invite and your cousin simply went along with her wishes."

"Well, 'tis no matter. I know we will have a lovely outing. Now, let us count heads and make certain we are all here and ready to go."

"I cannot thank you enough for inviting me to go on your outing," Ebba said. "I have long wanted to see the old Roman wall, but I could never get father to take me. He said we could not afford the expense of hiring a horse and pillion for me to ride on. Now, to think I will be traveling there in this lovely coach is near beyond any dream I might have conjured up."

Ebba had spent the night at Perfidious Brambles that she would be on hand for the early start. Everyone had been up before dawn and down to break their fast even before Seldon made his appearance. He had acted surprised at finding the crowd at the table and had even complimented them on rising with the sun for a change.

Gavin and Andrew rode up as the coach was being brought around to the front of the house. Timandra's heart did its little bounce that it normally did whenever she saw Gavin. He looked so handsome with the sun shining on his gleaming hair when he swept off his hat in greeting her. "Good morning to you, Lady Timandra. Seems we will be quite the cavalcade today. Might I help you to mount Pirro?"

Timandra looked about. "Are you ready, Eliza?" she asked.

Looking adorable in her perky, cock-brimmed hat with its pink feather, she turned her glowing smile on Timandra. "Indeed, I do think we are all here. The boys, Ebba, Mister Knolles, and Finola are now in the coach. Charissa and Delilah are mounted." She looked at Gavin. "You truly do feel they will have no trouble with their new horses, do you not, Cousin Gavin?"

"I believe they will do fine," Gavin said.

At Charissa's and Delilah's pleas, as well as Andrew's, that they be allowed to ride their horses on the outing, Gavin and Tombs and Andrew had spent the previous two days escorting Charissa and Delilah about the countryside that they might become familiar with their new mounts and saddles. The girls said they could not feel guilty they were not riding in the coach with Ebba because she had Mister Knolles to keep her company.

"And am I not mistaken," Delilah said with a sweet little smirk, "our Mister Knolles and Ebba quite enjoy each other's company."

Timandra believed Delilah was right. Plus it saved having to take the second coach as the boys also had to ride in the coach, and against her better judgement, she had given in to Finola's pleas to go on the excursion. "You will be needing someone to care for your hat, and fix your hair is it mussed," Finola said. "As will Mistress Tilbury and the young misses. I met Mistress Clackenberger's maid, and I tell you, I would not want her tending you."

"Why? What is wrong with her?" Timandra asked in surprise.

"Too much like Mister Crenshaw's new footmen. Well, 'tis not so much she has a mean look about her as do the men, but if she has been long a lady's maid, 'twould surprise me. Coarse, she is. Now, milady, you must be seeing I need go with you."

Timandra had chuckled. "Oh, very well. If nothing else, you can help Mister Knolles keep the boys out of any mischief."

And so she had watched Finola climb into the coach after Herman and Bennet.

"Well, I suppose we should mount our horses, Eliza," Timandra said. "Everyone else is ready." She looked back at Gavin, and with a nod of her head, allowed him to give her a foot up. Eliza was helped onto her horse by Severin.

Gavin, knowing the way to Dwight's manor, took the lead. Timandra was surprised he asked her and not Eliza to ride with him, but then Eliza was lost in conversation with Severin. Timandra could not help but wonder how Gavin felt about the way Severin seemed to be monopolizing Eliza's attention. Colyer had also attempted to ride with Eliza, but upon noticing Charissa had no escort, he dropped back to ride with her. Delilah and Andrew came next, followed by the coach.

Perth and Edgar were on their usual posts at the back of the coach, and because Gavin had said the road was not the best, Timandra had asked the coachman to use all six horses. That meant the postillion was also needed. And of course, she seldom went anywhere without Tombs. Ever alert, he brought up the rear.

Timandra was pleased Eliza had given in to her urging to let her sisters add some color to their black mourning clothing. "I cannot see how having a little color about the neck or head can be disrespectful," she had said. "The girls are too young to have to live their lives in black. You, too, for that matter." So Eliza had stuck a pink feather in her hat band and knotted a pink scarf at her throat, Charissa had a lavender scarf tied in a soft falling bow at her neck, and Delilah had a long blue scarf dangling down the front of her riding costume. Both girls had wrapped matching ribbons around their hat bands.

"I must tell you, Lady Timandra," Gavin said once they left Perfidious Brambles and turned onto the road leading to Crenshaw Manse, "my mother and my aunt have been working on Uncle Phineas to convince him to let a portion of the disputed land be used for the school. At first he was adamant he would not give Grandfather the satisfaction of knowing he was willing to relinquish the title to even a portion of that land, but I do think he is beginning to relent."

"That is wonderful," Timandra said, thinking she now knew why Gavin had wanted her to ride with him. He wanted to discuss their plans for the school.

"Uncle Phineas realizes how important an education can be if a man means to improve his life," Gavin continued. "For a woman, too, education can be a life changer. Libby is lucky Charissa and Delilah are not fussy about the way she speaks, or that she cannot write and can barely read. Were they older, they could well be more particular. And Libby is fortunate to have your maids, Audrey and Finola, to train her. She will have the opportunity to better her life. Be more than the wife of a tenant slaving in the fields."

"Yes, I have hopes one of the girls will keep her on as their maid when they marry and move away. Or mayhap, she might even learn enough to stay on at Perfidious Brambles as housekeeper when Mistress Weston retires. But to do either, she needs to learn to write, and keep accounts. I wonder might some adults also be allowed to attend the school?"

"Splendid idea!" Gavin said, his smile quickening Timandra's heart. She could not help but wish she would be around to see the school built and filled with students.

"I wonder," she said, "if your grandfather might be more receptive to paying to have the school built by just knowing your uncle would be giving the land over to the school."

Gavin nodded. "He just might. As the land is used to graze sheep, might be the wool from those sheep could be used to pay the school's teacher." He chuckled. "To know a portion of the profit from the land was no longer going into my uncle's pocket could please Grandfather."

"Indeed, that is something to be considered." Timandra returned Gavin's smile. "A teacher must be paid, and must have a place to live."

"I can see no reason, are we to build a school, we could not also build a cottage for the schoolmaster. And the disputed land would be like a glebe for a parsonage. The land could be worked by one of the tenants, and a portion of the proceeds would go to support the teacher and the school. The schoolmaster could even keep chickens and mayhap a cow to augment his income. He could have a little vetches garden even."

Timandra bobbed her head in happy agreement. "Oh, it all sounds so perfect. Now, can you but convince your uncle and your grandfather to support your plans."

"I will be counting on you to help convince Grandfather. He likes you. Respects you."

"I like him, too. He may be gruff, but he has been most generous to Eliza and her siblings. When I leave, I feel I can leave knowing they will be happy at Perfidious Brambles."

"Leave! Leave! Why, I had not thought of you leaving so soon. I know you mentioned it, but it seemed so distant at the time."

Did she hear disappointment in his voice? Would he miss her? "Yes, I will have to leave in a couple more weeks. As you know, soon autumn will be upon us, and the rains will make already hazardous roads worse."

He shook his head. "These past couple of weeks have flown by. Seems you have barely arrived."

"Yes, well we have certainly stayed busy."

Gavin looked at her in a way that made her pulse quicken. "Tell me what you think of Northumberland, Lady Timandra. Do you find the people friendly? The countryside pleasant, mayhap even beautiful?"

Wondering why he was asking her such questions, she tilted her head to one side. "Yes, everyone we have met from the tenants to the parishioners have been most cordial. And yes, the countryside is truly lovely. It has been a pleasant visit here. I am glad I accompanied Eliza."

Smiling broadly, Gavin said, "Good, good." He then changed the subject. "Herman and Bennet have done well with their swimming lessons. One or two more lessons, and I believe they could be trusted around any body of water. They seem to be enjoying activities with boys from the hamlet, and sooner or later, they will all decide to go swimming or fishing. Eventually, Herman and then Bennet will have to go off to school, but I trust they will remember the fun times they had with the tenant lads."

"I trust you are right. Oftentimes, friendships formed at a young age carry on through the years. One only has to look at your Grandfather and Old John. A bond exists between them. Surely, they grew up together."

"That they did. For many a year Grandfather relied on Old John." Gavin chuckled. "At one time he was Young John, his father also being named John. I will tell you something that concerns me. I could see it concerns Grandfather also. Those two footmen that my cousin recently hired, Old John said he found them bordering on rude."

Timandra blushed then admitted she had heard Gavin's grandfather and Old John discussing the pair. "I meant not to eavesdrop, but I did hear the concern in your grandfather's voice."

"Aye, well, mayhap I will keep an eye on them and report back to Grandfather do I find anything amiss."

Gavin, again changing the subject, brought the discussion around to books. They discovered they had both read and enjoyed a number of the same books. As they rode along with the summer sun beating down on them, Timandra from time to time glanced back over her shoulder at the rest of their party. Eliza was simply glowing, and she seemed completely engrossed in Severin and he in her. What might Gavin think of the relationship that seemed to be growing between Severin and Eliza. For Severin to go to the trouble to bring Eliza's pearls back to her, he must have already formed a tender for her when he was helping sell off her family assets to pay her father's debts.

Colyer, too, had seemed entranced by Eliza, but he presently seemed to be enjoying an animated conversation with Charissa. His light-hearted laughter floated out every now and then, and Charissa blushed and beamed. Quieter and shier than Delilah, she seemed to be blossoming in the lively steward's company.

And as they had been from the first moment they met, Delilah and Andrew were lost in each other. Timandra had no idea what they might be talking about, but they both continued to look dreamy eyed at each other. Young love was sweet, but not always lasting. Timandra hoped Delilah would not end up hurt. At Andrew's request, his grandparents had allowed him to stay with the Merritts when they returned home, but Andrew would be leaving when it was time for him to return to school. He could easily meet another girl and form a new passion. She knew Delilah would be devastated when Andrew had to leave, just as she would be devastated when she had to leave Gavin and return to her home.

Chapter 22

Gavin's grandfather was correct, Crenshaw Manse was a beautiful house. Built of stone, the main body of the house was three stories high and had enormous square-paned windows reaching from floor to ceiling. On either side of the main body, two square wings stretched out like the legs of a chair. They, too, had massive windows. Chimney stacks littered the roof, guaranteeing most rooms would be well heated. Crenshaw and his gregarious friends, Viola Clackenberger and her brother Sir Osgood Pettimill, greeted them at the door, and they were all welcomed into the grand hall. Viola escorted the women to a room where they might refresh themselves, and Crenshaw took charge of the men and boys. Once everyone was reassembled in the hall, Viola announced a picnic had been prepared and would be served at the wall.

"Mister Crenshaw sent the footmen ahead to set up tables and benches as well as blankets," Viola said. "It is such a perfect day, I just knew a picnic would be ideal."

"Sounds like a wonderful idea to me," Timandra said. "What say you, Eliza?"

"I agree. What could be more lovely."

"Then 'tis agreed. Mister Crenshaw has readied his coach for us, so let us head for the wall!" Viola said, flourishing her hand in the air.

The distance to the wall was not far, and soon they arrived at the site Dwight Crenshaw had selected for their picnic. Tables and benches were situated on a level section, and Crenshaw's steward, Feldings, had another table positioned near to hand. It was laden with a number of baskets and crocks and a couple of small casks.

"Shall we all admire the wall first?" Viola suggested. "Before we eat. Then if after we eat, anyone wishes to further investigate the wall, they may do so at their leisure."

"A perfect plan, my dear," Crenshaw said, beaming at the vibrant

Viola. That their romance seemed to have advanced to terms of endearment, Timandra could not find surprising. Viola seemed to have made a conquest.

After everyone had traipsed along the wall, commented on its antiquity, wondered at the time it must have taken the Romans to build it, and joked that it had prevented few Scottish reivers from crossing into England, they were all ready for their dinner. Cider and ale were the drinks offered and the meal consisted of roast chicken, thinly sliced pork and beef, venison pasties, pickled herring, boiled eggs, buttered bread, cheese, nuts, fresh strawberries, blackberry pasty, and dried figs.

"No one should go away hungry from this table," Sir Osgood jovially proclaimed.

"If they do, 'tis no one's fault but their own," Colyer said. He was seated beside Charissa and was seemingly enjoying her company. Severin was still monopolizing Eliza's attention. Gavin had chosen to sit next to Timandra, but she had seen him glance a time or two at Eliza and Severin. Was he upset by Eliza's actions? Well, if he had not made his intentions clear to Eliza, he could not blame Eliza for enjoying Severin's company. In the meantime, she was enjoying having Gavin seated next to her.

"Feldings," Colyer called over to Crenshaw's steward, "you and Mister Crenshaw's cook have outdone yourselves. Every detail from napkins to spoons to goblets to trenchers to all the foods could not have been ordered more perfectly."

"I thank you, Mister Colyer," Feldings, a middle-aged man of a nondescript height and weight, and a face that was neither handsome nor ugly, let the hint of a smile touch his lips as he gave but the slightest head bow to Colyer.

"You have a real treasure in Feldings," Colyer said, turning to Crenshaw. "You will need be careful should Mister Seldon attempt to steal him away from you. Old John is just that – old. How much longer he can continue to serve Mister Seldon is anyone's guess. But I am guessing not for all that much longer."

"I shall keep your warning in mind, Mister Colyer," Crenshaw said, ignoring the look Viola gave him. Viola had complained of the footmen Feldings had hired, might she now be finding fault with Feldings? And if so, why?

"Eliza," Herman said from his end of the table, "might Bennet and I go play on the wall? We are all done eating."

"You are finished eating," Eliza corrected, turning from Severin to look at her brothers.

"Yes, Eliza, we are finished eating. Might we go play on the wall?"

Eliza looked at Timandra. "What think you, Timmie?"

Timandra shrugged. "Do Perth or Edgar go with them, I can see no harm."

"Oh, no," Viola spoke up, "Mister Crenshaw's footmen can accompany them. Your two footmen were helping serve us. Let them eat their meal. They have earned it."

Timandra looked at Crenshaw's two footmen. They had immediately risen when Viola suggested they attend the boys. Well, Perth and Edgar had done the serving, Crenshaw proclaiming his new footmen were still learning their duties, so Timandra agreed Perth and Edgar should have the opportunity to sit and enjoy their dinner.

"Eliza, are you happy to have Mister Crenshaw's footmen watch the boys? That must be your decision."

Eliza looked at the footmen. "Just keep them out of mischief."

"Yes, Mistress Tilbury," one of the men said with what Timandra considered a leering smile. She could not think his way of looking at Eliza was at all respectful, but Eliza had turned back to Severin, and the footmen were following Herman and Bennet to the wall. What could go wrong? The boys would climb about and pretend to be Roman soldiers. No harm could come of that. Still, if appearances meant anything, she could not understand how Viola had selected the new footmen. They appeared crude and uncouth, and their speech bordered on vulgar.

She had just turned back to Gavin to continue their discussion of whether hunting with hawks was being replaced by hunting with guns when Finola dropped a quick curtsy to her left and said, "Begging your pardon, milady, but might I have a brief word with you?"

Turning to her maid, Timandra said, "Yes, Finola, what do you want?"

Leaning close to Timandra's ear, Finola whispered, "Milady, I would not be trusting those two varlets to mind the young masters. Have they ever served as footmen before, I would be willing to give up a year's wages. Something is not right about them."

Timandra pulled back from Finola and saw the sincerity in her eyes. She turned to look down the table to Knolles and Ebba who were lightly conversing. "Mister Knolles," she said, "I do think now would be the perfect time for you to be giving the boys their lesson on the wall."

"Oh, no," Viola interjected. "Do let Mister Knolles's meal settle."

But Knolles and Ebba had already risen from their seats. Timandra's instruction to Knolles was not something he would ignore. Eliza might be the boys' sister and his employer, but he well knew Timandra had been making the decisions for the Tilburys ever since their father had died. He would do as he was bid.

"Oh," Ebba said, her dark eyes dancing, "I was wanting to examine the wall more closely. I can hardly believe I am walking on the same ground that Roman soldiers once trod upon. I wonder if any battles were fought right here on this spot."

Knolles chuckled and said something to her as they headed off to the wall, and Timandra glanced over at Viola. She looked miffed. But why? And what was it Finola saw in the two footmen that made her worry about Herman and Bennet? She would have to ask her once they were back at Perfidious Brambles.

Again resuming her conversation with Gavin, she was expressing her feelings that the hawks might prefer to be free rather than do the bidding of their owners when a scream, followed by a yelp pierced the air. She and everyone else jumped. Eliza was off the bench and running to the wall with Severin right behind her before Timandra had risen. Soon everyone was headed to the wall.

"What happened here?" Gavin demanded, his voice stern and steady.

They were all looking down at Bennet cuddled in Ebba's arms, and Herman, the sleeve of his coat torn and a gash on his forehead dripping blood onto Knolles's vest. Eliza sank to the ground next to her brothers and gently dabbed her kerchief on Herman's wound. "Is he badly hurt?" she asked Knolles.

"I think not, Eliza," Ebba said before Knolles could speak. "'Twas but luck we arrived in time to catch the boys." She pointed to a portion of the wall that had collapsed. "'Twas that jagged rock that did tear Herman's coat sleeve. Had Ernest not caught him, he would have landed on that rock." She looked down at Bennet. "And Bennet is fine. Just scared. He took a bit of a tumble, but landed right in my arms." She looked down at the boy and a soft smile touched her lips.

"And where were you two?" Timandra heard Gavin ask, and she looked up to see him addressing the two footmen. "Could you not tell the wall here was unsafe? Look how lose and crumbling the dirt and rocks are here."

Both men looked surly, their eyes narrowed, but one stepped forward. "We were told to keep the boys out of mischief. Could not see how climbing on the wall could cause any harm. I be no expert on walls to be knowing whether it be like to crumble or not."

Timandra saw Viola prodding Crenshaw. He looked down at her, and she nodded toward the men. She might have said something for Crenshaw cleared his throat and said, "Here now, Gavin. These footmen cannot be expected to know what mischief boys can get into. Knolles should have been sent along with them rather than these two. You cannot be blaming them for what happened to the boys."

"Of course not," Sir Osgood said. "'Tis but an unfortunate accident, but as neither boy seems badly injured, I think all is well. And who knows, mayhap it will be a good lesson for the youngsters to be more watchful when climbing on walls."

Gavin was still eyeing the two footmen, but he turned to Timandra when she said, "I think we should not let this mar our lovely outing, and we thank Mister Crenshaw for this wonderful picnic, but I believe we need get Herman back to the house that we may tend his head and check his arm. Then we should head back to Perfidious Brambles. We want to be home in time to get Ebba back to her home before dark."

"I agree," Eliza said, rising from the ground with a hand from Severin. She looked down at Knolles. "Mister Knolles, I will talk to Uncle Percival, and I hope you will get some kind of reward for saving Herman. You, too, Ebba."

Ebba laughed as she relinquished Bennet to Gavin, and Severin took Herman from Knolles. "Does your uncle allow me to climb his apple trees and gather the apples that would go to waste, that will be all the reward I need."

"Oh, Ebba, do you really climb his trees?" Charissa said, giving Ebba a hand as she rose from the ground.

"I have and more times than not, he has caught me. I think he enjoyed catching me, but he never made me give up the apples. He always let me take them home. I suppose now, though, with all of you living at the Brambles, you will be needing more of the apples. 'Tis just the waste I could not abide."

"Knolles," Gavin said, "you take Bennet. I have something I want to check out here. Eustace, you bide with me." He nodded to Seldon's steward, Colyer, then looked at Timandra. "Lady Timandra, you go on to the house, Eustace and I will join you shortly."

She tilted her head then nodded. She had no idea what he meant to do, but she would not question him. He seemed disturbed about something. Mayhap he was as troubled by the two new footmen as she was. Especially now that they had done such a poor job of minding the boys. Indeed, they were not competent to serve the picnic, they were disrespectful in the way they ogled Eliza, and they showed no sorrow that the boys had taken a fall. Something was not right.

Eliza insisted on riding back to Crenshaw Manse in the coach with her brothers, and Finola made no complaint but popped up beside the coachman on his perch. The girl had been right about not trusting Herman and Bennet to the Crenshaw footmen. Had Knolles delayed even a moment, he and Ebba would not have been there in time to save the boys from injury. Heaven forbid, possibly even death.

※　※　※　※

"Take a look at this ground, Eustace," Gavin said. "Look at all this loose dirt."

"Aye, scattered when the wall collapsed."

"Some maybe, but look how firm the rest of this wall is. See how the turf has grown over it here." He picked up a stone and knocked it against the wall. "Solid, this wall is. So why should this one section be crumbling? It looks to me like it was loosened, then the stones put back but not by a Roman soldier."

"So what are you thinking, Gavin?" Colyer asked, his dark eyes curious.

Gavin glanced at the two Crenshaw footmen. They were involved in packing up the tables and benches and other items. He saw one of them cast a glance in his direction. Did he look worried? Gavin wished he would have a chance to talk to Feldings. Get his opinion of the two footmen, but he could not see how to manage it. The steward was too busy supervising the packing up of all the items that had been needed for the picnic.

Looking back at Eustace, Gavin said, "I am not sure what I am thinking, but I believe that wall was deliberately tampered with."

"Why would anyone do that?"

"That is what I cannot fathom, Eustace. But 'tis most curious all the same." He shook his head. "C'mon, let us join the others. I think they will all be anxious to get home before dark."

Chapter 23

Timandra had arranged to have an early ride with Gavin. Pirro needed a good run and Gavin said his Merlin also needed a run. They had arranged to meet on the edge of the Perfidious Brambles hamlet. Gavin wanted to take her back up to the spot where he thought the school should be built, but he also wanted to show her where the house for the teacher could be located. Then, mayhap, houses for a tenant or two who would work the acreage.

When Timandra went down to breakfast, she found only she and Colyer were joining Seldon. "Seems everyone sleeps late," she said taking a seat next to Seldon. "I hope I am not interrupting a discussion."

"Nay," Seldon said. "I never discuss business at the table. However, Mister Colyer will be closeted with me for most of the day. We have numerous accounts to go over."

Colyer smiled. "Since arriving here last week, I must admit to having a most entertaining time, but I have finally finished getting the household books in order. Now, 'tis time to go over business and household accounts. 'Twill easily take all day and most likely a good portion of the morrow. I hope you will make my apologies to Miss Charissa. She has been a delightful companion. Surprisingly well read for one her age."

Timandra returned Colyer's smile. "Yes, Charissa was always more studious than Delilah. Or at least, she takes things more seriously."

"But not too seriously," Colyer said. "She has a humorous side and enjoys a good laugh."

"If you are finished complimenting my niece," Seldon said, "I would have you finish your breakfast that we may begin on the accounts."

Colyer chuckled. He seemed no more perturbed by Seldon's blustering than was Gavin. "Aye, Mister Seldon, I am near finished, but would you have us leave Lady Timandra on her own here at the table?"

Seldon looked at Timandra. "Lady Timandra, I doubt you would be distressed were you left to finish your breakfast on your own."

She laughed. "No, Mister Seldon, I eat but lightly when I mean to ride in the morning. I have enjoyed one of Cook's tarts, and that will hold me until I return for dinner."

"You meet my grandson?"

"I do. Both our horses are in need of a good run."

His smile surprised Timandra. Seldon so seldom smiled.

"Have a good ride," he said, rising and beckoning to Colyer who smiled, shook his head, and after bowing to Timandra followed after his employer.

As they left the room, Timandra also rose. She realized she was growing quite fond of Seldon. He might often be irascible, but at heart, she believed him a good man.

❦ ❦ ❦ ❦

Timandra and Gavin returned from their ride in time to ready themselves for Seldon's early dinner hour. And Timandra was hungry. She and Gavin had been so busy formulating plans for the school and how to house and support a teacher, that she had not noticed her growing hunger until they had started back to the house. She had enjoyed the morning, and Pirro had enjoyed his run. At times she pushed away all thoughts of when she would be compelled to leave Perfidious Brambles. Leave Gavin. But at other times, they came hurtling back.

Giving Gavin a smile at the door, she hurried up to her room to change for dinner.

She had learned from Eliza that Severin would be leaving to return to Newcastle on the morrow. He was supposed to be finding a location for his firm to open an office. They would be expecting a report from him. Once Severin left, would Gavin again press his suit with Eliza? He had made no attempt to draw Eliza's attention away from Severin. Could it possibly be Gavin had not fallen in love with Eliza.? Nor Eliza with Gavin? Or was Eliza trying to make Gavin jealous by spending so much time with Severin? If so, her plan seemed to have failed. Gavin had not shown any signs of jealousy.

But if neither one was in love with the other, might she have a chance of winning Gavin's heart? He enjoyed her company. He often complimented her. He liked riding with her. They had good discussions of various things from books, to hunting, to horses, to the benefits of education. Oh, but could any of those things matter? She looked in the mirror at her reflection. Her chin was too prominent, her forehead too high, her lips too thin and firm, and her nose... Her father's slim aquiline nose that looked so manly on him did nothing for her. She considered her blue-green eyes her only good feature. Large and round with thick dark lashes, her eyes looked back at her with sad acceptance. No, she would never be a great beauty, but for the first time in her life, she wished she had softer, more feminine features like Eliza. For the first time in her life, she was in love, and even was Gavin not in love with Eliza, nor Eliza with him, she could not see how Gavin would ever fall in love with her. And besides that, she must surely be leaving in another couple of weeks. Two weeks would not be much time to win Gavin's love. And once she left, he would be out of her life forever. But not out of her heart or her thoughts, she feared.

"Do you go down to dinner, milady?" Finola asked. "Are you feeling well? You are not looking yourself."

Finola's face showed her concern, and Timandra turned from the mirror with a chuckle. "I am fine, my ever worrying maid. I was but thinking on when we must be heading for home. I will miss Eliza and Perfidious Brambles."

"Oh, aye, milady. I like all the people here, especially Cook. I mean to show her a sauce recipe I learned from Lady Tuftwick's cook. And Mister Seldon, though he pretends to be gruff, he is really not. I am thinking he is very happy to have Mistress Tilbury and her siblings here. And I am thinking he will miss you when we must leave."

"Do you think so, Finola? Well, I shall miss him as well."

Cocking her head to one side, Finola said, "And who knows, mayhap we will not be leaving here."

Timandra eyed Finola warily. "Now why would you say that?"

Finola shrugged. "Just being wishful, mayhap." She changed the subject. "Would you be having me brush up your riding costume, milady. Do you ride with Mister Merritt again on the morrow?"

"Yes, to both questions. But come next wash day, do have the laundress clean it. I have worn it enough now that it needs a more thorough cleaning than just dusting. Now, I will go down to dinner."

"Yes, milady," Finola said as Timandra swept out of the room.

� � � �

After dinner, Gavin, Andrew, and Severin joined the ladies in the parlor, but Colyer and Seldon returned to Seldon's chamber to continue with Seldon's estate accounts. As Herman and Bennet had experienced no serious repercussions from their fall the previous day, Gavin had promised them that after their afternoon lessons, he and Knolles would again take them to the pond for another swimming lesson. "I believe both boys have mastered enough to be safe," Gavin told Eliza, "but one more lesson will benefit them."

"You are so kind to my brothers, Gavin. And I thank you so much." Eliza looked up at Gavin with glowing eyes and her beaming smile, and Timandra's heart sank. How could Gavin not be in love with Eliza? She was so beautiful.

The rest of the afternoon, Timandra could not conceal her lowered mood. "What ails you, Lady Timandra," Charissa asked her? "You seem lost in a fog. Every card you have played has been to Mister Severin's and Eliza's benefit."

When Gavin had left with Herman and Bennet, Timandra had absently agreed to be a fourth in a game of loo. She would have preferred to take a lonely walk and chide herself and her foolish heart. She was in no mood to be sociable, but she smiled at Charissa. "I seem unable to concentrate. What a poor partner I am. To be honest, I believe I was thinking how much I will miss all of you when I must leave."

"Oh, my dear, Timmie!" Eliza hopped up from her chair to give Timandra a hug. "I cannot even bear to think of you leaving. Could you not write your mother and tell her you wish to stay with us until next spring at least?"

Timandra chuckled. "I fear I must be getting the coach to Knightswood. I did promise Mother she would have her coach back before 'twas time for the family to return to Harp's Ridge. The loan of the coach was to bring you safely here. And I can hardly ask to have the coach sent to fetch me next spring. 'Tis all the expense. And does Father go to Parliament, and Mother decide to accompany him. She must have the coach."

"Oh, yes. Now, I too am despondent. And Mister Severin must leave tomorrow. How morose I do feel."

Charissa, and Delilah, whose attention had been drawn away from Andrew, joined in a sorrowful chorus. The Tilburys' sorrow helped buoy Timandra's feelings, and she suggested they would all feel better did they take a walk in the garden. It was another lovely day, and too soon summer would end. They should check out the improvements Beamer and her footmen had made on the garden.

As a group, they agreed to Timandra's plan, and all trooped out to the garden at the same time that Knolles and Gavin were returning from the pond. Both still had wet hair, but they looked cheerful and refreshed. "We allowed the boys to go back to the hamlet with Kippie," Gavin said. He looked at Eliza. "I hope that was all right with you."

"Of course. I am glad they are making friends."

"I believe the boys sleep better, more soundly, when they have had time to run and play," Knolles said. "It wears them out, and they rarely fuss when 'tis time for them to go to bed."

With a half snort, Gavin said, "I tell you, the swimming makes me ready for bed sooner. Gives me an appetite, too. Knolles and I were headed to the kitchen to see what Cook might have to feed us."

"We were about to take a stroll in the garden to cheer us all up," Eliza said. "We are all feeling doleful because we started thinking how much we will miss Timandra when she must leave us."

Gavin whipped about from Eliza to Timandra. "When do you leave? I thought you here for several more weeks."

"Two more weeks at the most," Timandra said. What did she see in Gavin's eyes? Concern? "As I told Eliza, Mother will be needing her coach."

"I see," Gavin said. "Well, indeed, time grows short."

He looked like he meant to say something else, but Charissa exclaimed, "Oh my! Look at Herman and Bennet. They are but dragging themselves home."

Everyone turned to look at the two boys. Both were stumbling along holding their stomachs, and Herman would give Bennet a push to get him moving again anytime the younger boy stopped. Gavin and Knolles immediately ran to the boys and everyone else followed.

"What happened? What is wrong?" Gavin asked, kneeling in front of Bennet.

"My stomach. It hurts bad," Bennet said, tears streaming down his face.

"Mine, too," Herman said, tears also dotting his face.

"You get Bennet," Gavin directed Knolles. "I will get Herman. We will take them to Cook. She may know something to ease them."

Eliza was now sniffling. "Oh, Hermie, Bennie, what can be wrong?"

Severin put his arm around Eliza. "Cook will help them," he said. "Come."

Stumbling along with Severin's help, Eliza hurried her steps to race after Gavin and Knolles. Timandra followed with Charissa, and she could hear Andrew comforting Delilah. "Never fear, my sweet Delilah. Boys probably just ate something bad. Boys do that. I did when I was young. And look at me, fit as any prime horse, huh?"

"Yes, Andrew. I am certain you must be right. They just ate something on a dare, no doubt. They will be fine," Delilah agreed, though her voice sounded worried.

Gavin called to the cook as he neared the kitchen, and the chunky cook bustled out the door. She was followed by Finola. "Lordy," the cook said. "What be the trouble?"

"Their stomachs," Gavin said. "They hurt terribly bad."

Cook sat on a lower step and said, "Set them down. Let me look at them."

Gavin and Knolles did as told and gently set both boys down in front of the cook. "What was it ye be eating?" Cook asked.

"Tarts," Herman managed to answer between moans.

"Not Goody Peale's tarts?" Cook said.

Herman shook his head. "'Twas a woman…," but he could say no more. He again groaned.

"Finola," Cook said, "get me a clean spoon."

"Yes, Cook," Finola said.

Timandra was not surprised to find Finola in the kitchen. Finola was ever eager to help anyone in anyway. She had not a lazy bone in her body and in but an instant, Finola returned with a wooden spoon.

"Now," Cook said, "mix me up some milk, honey, and mustard."

Finola nodded eagerly. "Oh, aye, I will have it right up. Best thing, mustard is. Will bring the poison right out."

While Finola was doing as directed, Cook grabbed Bennet, turned him away from her, and told Knolles and Gavin to step back. In the next instant, she had shoved the handle end of the spoon in Bennet's mouth. The boy started heaving, and whatever was in his stomach was soon on the ground.

Charissa and Delilah went, "Ohhh," and turned away as Cook released Bennet and did the same thing with Herman.

"We first get out what poison we can, then the milk and honey will grab up whatever is still in their stomachs and the mustard will get them te heave up any that be sticking around in their bellies."

Both boys had dropped to the step on either side of Cook. They were still groaning, when Finola arrived with two noggins of the milk, mustard, and honey. "Now Master Herman, Master Bennet," Cook said, "ye must drink these down. 'Tis sweet with the honey. Ye will not mind it."

Both boys shook their heads.

"Do as Cook said," Eliza said, her tone firm. "This will make you stop hurting."

At their sister's admonishment, they took the noggins and downed the liquid. It had not been in their stomachs long when it came rushing back up, and everyone stepped further back as the boys wretched and heaved.

"I am guessing most of whatever poison was in their stomachs is now out," Cook said. She looked down at the boys' bowed heads. "Ye say 'twas not Goody Peale's tarts you ate, but some other woman. Would any of the other hamlet boys have also eaten the tarts?"

Herman nodded. "Aye. We shared them with Kippie and Jonah."

Cook looked up at Gavin. "Ye had best be getting over to the hamlet and see are those boys being cared for. Might need take some milk, honey, and mustard with ye." She looked back up at Finola. "There's a good girl, make up a batch for Mister Merritt te be taking with him."

Finola hurried to do as Cook bid her, and Gavin squatted before Herman, doing his best to avoid where the boys had thrown up the contents of their stomachs. "Herman, soon Mister Knolles will take you upstairs, get you cleaned up, and tuck you into bed. But if you could tell me about the woman who gave you the tarts, I would be grateful. As I am going to the hamlet, I would like to make certain she sells no more tarts."

Herman raised his eyes. "She gave us the tarts. Said they were her last ones, and she was needing to go home."

"Gave them to you. Hmmm. Can you describe her?"

"She was dressed in a ragged and patched gown. Had a shawl about her, and a large hump on her back. Her skin was pasty white, and she had a big mole on the side of her nose."

"Good boy," Gavin said, rising as Finola returned from the kitchen and handed him a jug with the prescribed ingredients. Looking up at Finola, he said, "Do knock on Mister Selden's door and apologize for interrupting him, but I want Colyer to go with me. He knows the tenants better than I do. I will start over there now. Tell Colyer to catch up with me. And tell Perth that Mister Knolles will need help with the boys."

"I am right here, Mister Merritt," Perth said. "I will help see to the boys, and I will get Edgar to clean this away from the door." He indicated the contents of the boys' stomachs muddying the ground next to the steps.

"When Perth and I have the boys settled," Knolles said, turning to Eliza, "I will send Perth for you. I know you will want to assure yourself they are well."

Eliza nodded. "Thank you, Mister Knolles."

Cook rose and said, "I have some water warming at the hearth. I will send Lucy up with a bucket to fill your pitcher."

"Thank you," Knolles said, scooping up Bennet as Perth hefted Herman.

Eliza caught Cook's hand before she could follow after Knolles and Perth. "Thank you," she said. "Thank you so much. You do think the boys will be all right now?"

"I think it be a good thing they shared those tarts with the other boys," Cook said. "Otherwise, I would not be so sure."

Eliza put her hand to her mouth and looked near ready to swoon, but Severin put his arm around her and said, "I am sure they will be fine, and Merritt and Colyer will find out who gave them the tarts."

Cook nodded. "Mister Severin be right. 'Tis my thinking they will be fine by morning and ready to break their fast with some toast and jam." She chuckled. "But I will not be putting tarts out for a day or two."

Timandra saw Colyer hurry out the garden portal and take off after Gavin at a run. She was beginning to think Gavin found the incident more than an accidental poisoning. But why would anyone want to poison two little boys? Still, two near death experiences in two days' time. That was curious.

Seeing that Severin was taking care of Eliza, she turned her attention to Charissa and Delilah. Andrew had his arm around Delilah and was holding her a bit too close, but when he saw the look Timandra gave him, he pulled away. "Well, now," he said, "'twould appear the boys will be fine, does it not Lady Timandra?"

She smiled and nodded. "I do believe they will be. But it was certainly frightening." She put an arm around Charissa. "I suggest we again stroll into the garden and let the peacefulness help calm us before 'tis time for supper."

The girls agreed, and they set off along a newly pebbled path. Soon Eliza and Severin were following after them. Their day in the sun had been spoiled, but at least the boys seemed to be all right. That was what truly mattered.

Chapter 24

Supper was a somber meal. Gavin and Colyer had returned with news that Kippie and Jonah had indeed been ill. Their mothers had followed Cook's advice, first making the boys heave up the remains of the tart and then taking the concoction Cook had sent to remove any residue in their stomachs.

"But did no one know the woman?" Timandra asked. "No one saw her?"

"Aye, a couple of the women saw her. She looked as Herman described her, they said, but those women who were not busy in the fields doing a final weeding, were busy with their sundry other chores that never end."

Taking over, Colyer said, "Goody Beamer said when she saw her, she thought she might be Goodman Bilayer's mother. His mother had gone to live with her daughter some years back. Goody Beamer thought the old woman must be visiting her son. But she was too busy to visit with her. Goody Morse, the wife of one of Mister Seldon's wealthier tenants addressed her. The woman said she had hoped to find work milking the sheep, but had no luck. Goody Morse said she felt sorry for the woman. The woman looked so ragged, so before going back to work, Goody Morse gave her a ha'penny. She said the woman acted most grateful."

"Well, I cannot but think her tarts must have been days old and full of rotten meat," Eliza said. "My poor brothers. Yesterday the fall from the wall, and today the poisoning."

"Poor dears," Charissa said.

Timandra was watching Gavin. She had a feeling he suspected something was strange about the woman. And what was she doing selling tarts if she told Goody Morse she was looking for work milking sheep? Well, mayhap she hoped to do both. But if for some reasons she had wanted to poison the boys, which in itself seemed ridiculous, how could she have known when the boys would go to the hamlet? No, it made no sense. Had to be but an accident.

"Was no one else in the hamlet made sick from the tarts? Had no one else bought her tarts?" Timandra asked.

"We learned of no one else being sick or of anyone buying any of the woman's tarts," Colyer said.

Timandra frowned. "That seems so strange."

Colyer nodded, but Gavin made no comment on her observation. He but said, "Andrew and I must be heading home after supper, but I will check in on the boys before I leave. Afterall, I was the one who gave them permission to go to the hamlet."

"Oh, Cousin Gavin, you cannot think I in any way hold you to blame," Eliza said.

"Nay. Nor do I blame myself. The boys have made friends in the hamlet and should be able to safely go there to play at any time. I but wish to tell them to never take anything again from any strangers."

"I have told them that," Eliza said. "As did Mister Knolles."

"All the same," Gavin said. "I will feel better do I visit them."

"I think they will like that," Timandra said. "After Mister Knolles and Perth cleaned them up and got them into bed, Eliza sat with them until they fell asleep, but I am guessing by now, they will again be wanting some company."

Gavin smiled at Timandra and her heart spun about in her chest. When he looked at her in that fashion, she could almost believe he had feelings for her. But no. Surely he was but being kind. He was a kind person. She knew from his earlier remark about the tenant women's work never being done, he understood what a hard life they led. He had empathy in his soul.

"Gavin," Seldon said when the meal was ended, "I would speak with you before you go up to check on the boys."

"As you wish, Grandfather," Gavin said, and though he rose when the women rose to leave the room, Timandra saw him sit back down beside his grandfather. Colyer, Severin, and Andrew followed Eliza and her sisters to the parlor, but Timandra held back. Seldon had been very quiet throughout the supper. Was he, too, curious about the strange woman who had given the boys the poisonous tarts? Well, she could not just linger in the hall. With a shrug she joined the others in the parlor.

꽃 꽃 꽃 꽃

Riding back to Kirkworth Hall with Andrew, Gavin let the youth chatter on about the lovely Delilah and how they intended to correspond when he had to return to school. Andrew seemed not to notice Gavin was paying him little heed. Gavin had learned from Herman and Bennet that they had been questioned by Viola Clackenberger about their various activities and how they were adjusting to their lives at Perfidious Brambles. How were they getting on with their uncle? Well, they assured her, he had bought them new ponies. Had they made friends? They told her about their friends in the hamlet, and how they often went back to play with their new friends after their swimming lesson. Both boys said she had been very bright and chipper.

"I think she felt bad because my head was injured," Herman said, touching his head where he had a small scab. "She was trying to cheer us up. She is kind."

Gavin had smiled at the boy. "So she does seem. Well, I but wanted to assure myself you were both well. In the future, unless you know the person or your friends know them, you stay clear of them. Do I have your promises?"

"Aye, Cousin Gavin," both boys said.

"Good." He had then risen and had gone to pull Andrew away from Delilah.

Something odd was going on. He sensed it more than he could understand it. Two attempts on his life, the attack outside the tavern in Newcastle, then the shot that had gone through his hat the first time he was to go riding with Timandra, now two attempts on Herman's and Bennet's lives. Then there was the person in black who had chased Finola in the old portion of Perfidious Brambles. He in no way believed in Finola's ghost. But someone had chased her.

He decided on the morrow he would ask Timandra if he could send Tombs to take a thank you gift to his cousin Dwight. He would instruct Tombs to search out Dwight's steward, Feldings, and learn what he could of Dwight's two new footmen. He but had to think of a thank you gift to send to Dwight. Well, his mother could help him with that. He also meant to ask his mother and aunt to again invite Timandra and his cousins to dinner. He had hopes it would be a celebratory meal. When they went riding, he meant to ask Timandra to marry him. Or to at least allow him to court her. Time was growing short. She was planning to return to her home in less than two weeks. He could not let that happen.

She had him confused. At times, he was certain she cared for him. At other times, she was aloof, almost cold. Well, he knew how he felt about her, and he had no intention of letting her slip through his fingers. She was all he had ever wanted in a wife. He chuckled to himself. His grandfather had outright asked him when he meant to propose to Lady Timandra.

"Do you let that lass get away," his grandfather said, "I will think you a bigger fool than was my brother or your mother."

Before Gavin had been able to answer, his grandfather had said, "Now what is this about the boys being injured and now poisoned? What is amiss here?"

"That I intend to discover, Grandfather," he had answered. Indeed, that was his intention. Something was amiss. But in the meantime, he liked knowing he had his grandfather's blessing to marry Timandra. He had hopes the marriage might bring his grandfather and his mother together again. He had a feeling neither would like anything more than to be reunited. And they both approved of Timandra.

※　※　※　※

Once Andrew left with Gavin, Colyer admitted to being tired and needing to be up early the next morning to continue going over the books and accounts with Seldon. Charissa and Delilah said they, too, were tired. It had been an emotional day, so they decided they would go up to their room and read a bit before going to bed. Timandra imagined they would do more chatting than reading. Delilah would want to talk about Andrew, and Charissa might well have made a conquest of Colyer. She was young to have attracted a man of his age. He had to be at least as old as Gavin. Mayhap a tad bit older. But in a little over a year, Charissa would turn eighteen. A ten-to-twelve-year difference in age was not that unusual in a marriage. Charissa was a pretty girl and a bright girl. Timandra could see how Colyer could find Charissa attractive and appreciate the young woman she would grow into.

Once the others left, Timandra debated whether she should leave Eliza and Severin alone, or should she stay and chaperone them? No one chaperoned her and Gavin when they rode out together, so mayhap she had no reason to chaperone Eliza. She thought Eliza was looking at her in such a way that she might be asking her to leave. Why not start to say goodnight and if Eliza protested, she would stay.

"I have letters I need to write," she said, rising. "I believe I will head to my chamber."

"Oh, yes, dear." Her smile bright, Eliza also rose and giving Timandra a little hug, said, "If you write your Aunt Venetia, do give her my love. And do thank Finola again for being such a help with my brothers."

"That I will do on both counts." She looked at Severin. "Goodnight Mister Severin. I understand you leave us tomorrow. I hope 'tis not too early that we may bid you safe journey."

Like Eliza, he had risen when Timandra rose, and he bowed ever so slightly. "Thank you, Lady Timandra. I hope I may see you on the morrow before I depart. I wish you pleasant dreams tonight."

Timandra nodded and left the room. By the looks passing between Severin and Eliza, she was near certain the two were in love. So where did that leave Gavin? Would he be heartbroken? She hoped not. She prayed not. And if Eliza was truly in love with Severin, and not Gavin, might Gavin come to love her? Oh, how many times had she debated that foolish question? Too many. All the same, she could not squelch that small glimmer of hope.

� � � �

Timandra was not in the least bit surprised not to find Finola in her chamber awaiting her like a good lady's maid should do. More than likely she was again in the kitchen helping Cook. Finola would never be the lady's maid that her mother's maid, Adah, was, but then Timandra could not think she would ever want Finola to be like Adah. Finola had a soft spot in her heart for everyone and everything. If Adah had ever had a soft spot for anyone except maybe Timandra's mother, Timandra had never seen it. Still, the woman served her mother well, and as long as she made her mother happy, that was all that mattered.

Having written several letters, Timandra was sitting combing out her own hair when Finola burst through the door. "Oh, milady. I saw her again. I saw the ghost, and she disappeared right through the wall." Finola pointed out the door and to her right.

Finola was panting and her eyes were huge. Something had frightened her, but Timandra was certain it was not a ghost.

Rising, Timandra said, "Calm down, Finola. I have told you before, there are no ghosts. You maybe just saw your own shadow. A flickering candle can play tricks on you."

Finola vigorously shook her head. "Nay, Lady Timandra. I was coming up from the kitchen where I had been talking with Perth and Cook when I noticed the time and thought you must be ready for bed."

"And so I am. I have been combing out my hair myself."

Finola blinked, looked behind herself, then looked back at Timandra. "I am sorry I was not here when you came up, but Perth and I were telling Cook about the grand parties Lady Tuftwick has held. Cook says before Mister Seldon's wife died, and before Mister Merritt's mother ran off and married his father, Mister Seldon used to hold grand parties here. Cook started here years ago as a scullery maid, so she knows all about Perfidious Brambles."

Shaking her head and firming her lips, Finola again looked out the door. "Lady Timandra, I was coming up the back stairs as I always do, and I saw her."

"Saw who?"

"The ghost! I saw the ghost. She was dressed all in black from head to toe, and she had a veil over her face. She was standing in front of Master Herman and Master Bennet's door, her head tilted like she was listening. I stepped back that she would not see me, but I am thinking she must have sensed I was there, for she looked toward the stairs. I was shaking so, mayhap she heard my very bones creaking. Then she turned and just glided down the corridor. I followed after her, keeping to the shadows, and I saw her glide right up the stairs to this floor. So

I followed her up, and I was just in time to see her disappear into the wall."

"Oh, Finola." Timandra frowned and shook her head.

"'Tis true, milady. I am swearing to you."

"Very well, show me where you think she disappeared."

Finola still looked frightened, but after peeping out the door, she exited into the corridor and Timandra followed. Turning to the left, Finola slowly made her way to the end of the corridor and tapped on the tapestry hanging on the wall. "She went right through here."

Cocking her head and pursing her lips, Timandra gazed at the tapestry. It was not a particularly appealing tapestry. It looked as though it had been hanging on that particular wall for ages. It was an ugly scene of hunters with crossbows killing deer and boars. Its colors were faded and the edges of the tapestry were slightly frayed. It was in sharp contrast to the rest of the well-kept gallery. Timandra also noticed no sconces were attached to the wall in this section. The area was dark and murky.

Smiling, she pushed past Finola and pulled an edge of the heavy tapestry away from the wall. Pulling it farther away from the wall, she said, "Here, hold this out." She thrust the edge of the tapestry into Finola's hands. Slowly she began feeling the edge of the wall. "We should have brought a candle."

"What do you be looking for, milady?" Finola asked.

"A door. There has to be a door here." Pushing and prodding and beginning to think either she was wrong or Finola had seen a ghost, she slid further behind the tapestry. She was near to giving up. The dark, the dust, the weight of the tapestry made the whole thing unpleasant. Giving up, she started backing out, and in the process, she leaned heavily against the wall. The wall gave way and she nearly tumbled over sideways, barely catching herself on the edge of the doorway.

A slight gasp escaped her lips, and Finola cried, "Milady, are you all right?"

Straightening herself and catching her breath, Timandra said, "Yes, Finola, and I have found the door."

Chapter 25

Dressed for her morning ride with Gavin, Timandra hurried down to breakfast. She had made Finola promise she would not breath a word about the secret door and passage they had found behind the tapestry. Timandra fully intended to investigate it before she spoke to Seldon. Someone was sneaking in and out of the house, and Timandra meant to find out how. That the woman dressed in black had been seen outside the boys' room was not a good sign. She debated whether she should mention it to Gavin, but decided to wait. She wanted to know more first.

At the breakfast table, she found Herman and Bennet both looking well and chipper. Mister Knolles decided after what they had been through, they should have a day off from their studies. He meant to take them for a ride into Fairflex on their new ponies. He was not much of a rider himself, but Mister Colyer had offered to let him use his horse with the promise that the horse was not overly spirited.

Charissa and Delilah were also up. Delilah knew Andrew would be coming with Gavin, and Delilah hoped she and Charissa might go riding with Andrew. "We thought we would ride over to visit Ebba," Charissa said.

Eliza said she believed she would ride with them. "With Mister Severin leaving today, I will be quite out of sorts."

Severin chuckled. "I have hopes that means you will miss me, Mistress Tilbury."

Tilting her head, she smiled sweetly. "How could I not?"

"Have Mister Seldon and Mister Colyer already breakfasted?" Timandra asked, drawing Eliza's and Severin's attention away from each other.

"They were just leaving when we got here," Herman said. "It sure does take a lot of time to go over the accounts. This is the second day."

"So it seems," Timandra said, and Knolles added, "I would hope it would show you the importance of learning your mathematics. Someday you may find you are a steward like Mister Colyer. Are you to prosper, you must be good at your accounts."

"Ah, that is too boring. I will never be a steward," Herman said.

"Well, you will have to do something to earn your living," Eliza said. "You cannot think Uncle Percival will pay for you to just sit around."

"Yes," Severin added. "A gentleman's professions are limited. You may be a steward, go into the law as I have done, or perhaps find work with a bank or as a clergyman, but in any of the professions, you will need to know your Latin and your mathematics."

"Good advice," Timandra said, hiding a smile as she looked at Herman's and Bennet's lowered faces. "The trick is to find the profession you can enjoy. Is that not so, Mister Severin?"

He chuckled. "It certainly helps. And speaking of tending to business, I must be getting on my way. I want to be back to Newcastle in time to look around the city a bit. I had barely settled into my abode when I encountered Eustace, and we decided to come here together." He rose as he spoke and so did Eliza.

"I have already thanked Mister Seldon and Eustace. The stableman has seen to my horse and my packs are readied." He bowed. "All I can do now is bid all of you goodbye, and tell you I will look forward to seeing you again."

Everyone at the table bid him goodbye, and Knolles rose and gave him a slight bow. Exiting with Severin, Eliza tapped Timandra on the shoulder and said, "I must see you before you go riding."

"Of course, dear," Timandra said.

Rising again, Knolles said, "Do you excuse us, Lady Timandra, the boys have finished and are eager for their ride."

She nodded to him as he and the boys left the table. Charissa and Delilah were yet picking at their food. Curious to know what Eliza wanted, Timandra told the girls not to rush, and she went to find Eliza. Her search was quickly ended, for Eliza found her and grabbed both of Timandra's hands.

"Oh, Timmie, I never imagined I would ever be so happy again," Eliza said. "Mister Severin." She blushed. "Bartley, has asked if he may

194

pay me court. He says when my mourning time is over, he means to speak to Uncle Percival. Timmie! He wants to marry me!"

"Oh, my dear," Timandra said, dropping Eliza's hands that she might give her a hug. "Did I not tell you when we arrived that all would be well?"

"You did, but I could not believe you. I thought I would die here. I thought I would never be happy again, and now I am near to burst."

Timandra laughed and drew Eliza into the parlor. "You are sure now that you are in love with Mister Severin. You are not just thinking to marry him because you think no one else will ever want to marry you?"

"No, no, Timmie. I but thought I loved Ralph. Now, I find it was a blessing I should not have married him. Bartley is everything I ever dreamed of." She again grabbed Timandra's hands. "Remember how we used to sit in bed together and talk about the men we would some-day marry. Well, Bartley is just as I described the man I wanted to marry. He is handsome, kind, considerate, loving, willing to make any sacrifice to win my love. Oh, and he has won my love."

"Yes, I can see he has. The way you two look at each other." Shaking her head, Timandra smiled. "So are you going to tell your siblings and your uncle?"

"No, not yet. Bartley has much to do in Newcastle. He must find a location for the law firm. He must interview other lawyers to see if there are enough good solicitors to man the office or must he look elsewhere. He is going to be very busy. He says he cannot say when he will be able to come for another visit. And, indeed, I am still in mourning. He has promised to write as often as he can, and I shall write him. He says Uncle Percival and Mister Colyer have given him names of men he should contact that could well be needing his firm's legal advice and wish to retain the firm's services."

"It all seems very promising, and I am so happy for you. And I will not say a thing to anyone. You have my word."

"Bartley says he plans to tell his family," Eliza said. "He has a young-er brother and two younger sisters. He says he knows his mother will love me. Oh, he is so dear."

"I have no doubt his mother will love you. Now, do you not want ev-eryone to know your news, you need to calm yourself. And are you to ride into Fairflex with your sisters, you had best go put on your riding costume."

"You are so right." Eliza gave Timandra another quick hug and hurried away. Following Eliza into the hall, Timandra heard Gavin and Andrew enter the hall from the kitchen, as was Gavin's usual mode of entrance.

"Ah, good morning, Lady Timandra," Gavin said when he spotted her at the foot of the staircase.

"Good morning, Mister Merritt," Timandra answered, her heart soaring, and a bright welcoming smile on her lips.

"I understand from Andrew that there is an expedition going in to Fairflex to visit Mistress Hemphill. I fear I have been charged with an errand for my aunt that I must attend to in Fairflex. I wonder, might you be as happy to join the expedition instead of our usual jaunt?"

Timandra felt her jaw drop, but she hastily caught herself. How could she again have been so foolish? Of course Gavin would want to ride into Fairflex. With Severin departed, he must think he now had a chance to court Eliza. Over and over again she had thought she might have a chance to win Gavin's love, and over and over again her hopes had been dashed. Fighting back tears, she managed to say, "Nay, I think Pirro needs a good run. I will ask Tombs to accompany me. But do give my regards to Ebba."

Did he look disappointed? She was quickly disabused of that thought when Gavin said, "I wonder when you are finished with your ride if I might use Tombs's services? I have a small thank you gift I would like him to take to Cousin Dwight." He moved closer to Timandra and said in a low voice. "I also want him to learn what he can about those two new footmen serving Dwight. Something seems amiss there."

Swallowing hard and hoping to hide her disappointment, Timandra said, "Of course. I have written Mister Crenshaw a thank you note, as has Eliza. We had thought to have them posted, but this way Tombs can deliver them. Have you the gift?" Trying to be calm and not betray herself, Timandra held out her hand.

Gavin coughed. "To be honest, I was so certain you would consent to my request, I have already given the parcel to Tombs. He said, with your permission, he would be happy to deliver the gift and learn what he could of the footmen. He says he too is leery of them."

Nodding, Timandra said, "Yes, something seems not quite right about the situation." She gave Gavin another small smile and turned to go up the stairs. "I will but fetch the notes and then be off on my ride so Tombs will have plenty of time to ride over to Mister Crenshaw's. Eliza is changing into her riding costume now and should be down shortly." She looked over Gavin's shoulder. "I see Mister Althouse and the girls are ready. I hope you have a nice outing."

He looked like he wanted to say something else, but fearing she would burst into tears if she stayed one more moment in his presence, she practically ran up the stairs.

※ ※ ※ ※

Gavin stared after Timandra's hastily retreating figure. She had looked so pleased to see him but then had turned distant again. He could not understand why she would not want to ride with the party to Fairflex. She liked Ebba Hemphill. Her horse had had a good run just the day before, and she seemed like she had thoroughly enjoyed their day together. Her ideas for the school and for the land needed to support the school and a teacher were inciteful. And so he had told her, and she had seemed pleased by his praise. He wished his aunt had not needed him to deliver a treasured book to a friend who was recently bedbound. She had not wanted to send the book with one of the servants. The book and the friend were too special.

"My dear Anna would be hurt did a servant but leave the book at her door with her maid. No, Gavin, you must deliver the book and have a glass of sherry with her. Poor dear."

Normally Gavin would have been only too happy to do a favor for his aunt. He owed his aunt and uncle so much. But he had planned to ask Timandra to marry him when on their outing. Now, he was not even to get to ride with her. Well, he would manage to find some way to catch her alone after dinner. But did he have to follow her all the way to Harp's Ridge to court her, then so would he do, though he hoped he was not mistaken in her feelings for him.

❁ ❁ ❁ ❁

Since she already had the notes to Crenshaw in her pocket, Timandra simply went as far as the first floor, then hurried down the corridor to the back stairs that would lead to the kitchen. She wanted to get going on her ride before she had to encounter anyone. She had no wish to have to explain why she would not join them on their jaunt to Fairflex. Knolles and the boys were riding away when she arrived at the stables. Pleased to find her horse already saddled, she told Tombs they would set out immediately that he might do his errand for Mister Merritt.

"Mister Merritt not to ride with you today?" Tombs asked.

"Nay, he has an errand in town, but I have things I want to do after my ride, so I chose not to go into Fairflex. So let us be off." She nudged her heels into Pirro's flanks. The horse needed no other encouragement. He was ready for his exercise.

As they raced across the field, Timandra decided the change in plans was for the best. She was determined to see where the secret passage led, and when she returned from her ride would be the perfect time to do it.

Chapter 26

"Oh, milady," Finola said, "are you really set on us going in there?" Finola held a lantern high and looked into the dark passage Timandra had exposed when she again found the door behind the tapestry.

"I am. Now give me the lantern. Stay close but not so close you step on the hem of my gown. And do be careful. I can see these steps are very steep."

"Yes, milady," Finola said, and the passage got even darker when the tapestry fell back into place.

Timandra had placed a heavy book against the door so it would not close on them. If the woman in black went in and out of the door, it had to have a handle, but Timandra was taking no chances that she and Finola might get stuck in the passage. Keeping one hand braced on the wall, and placing each foot carefully on the narrow steps, she started making her way down from the landing at the doorway. The passage smelled dusty, but considering the woman in black had been going up and down these stairs, she was not afraid of running into any spiders. At least not at face level. The stairs continued down and down and seemed to make no stop at the first floor. Stopping on another landing, Timandra peered into the dark. The steps continued on down and then abruptly ended at what looked like a dead end. But that could not be. The woman had to enter this passage from somewhere.

Timandra began feeling her hand around the walls on either side of her.

"Milady, what are you after doing?" Finola asked in a whisper.

"I am looking for how your ghost is getting in and out of this passage," Timandra in turn whispered. "Trust me. She is no more walking through walls than we are." Her fingers felt a small hole in the wall of one side, and she stuck her index finger inside it and pulled. Like magic a flap opened and under the flap was a latch. She lifted the latch, pushed, and the wall opened. Pushing it further, she peeped out. To her amazement, she was looking into the kitchen of the oldest portion of the house, the stone keep. She had to duck to go through the low door and Finola followed after her.

"Would you be looking at this?" Finola said. "A secret door right here in the kitchen."

"Yes, and it has been cleverly concealed behind this cabinet." The cabinet, attached to the hidden door, swung around when the door opened. "We never noticed it when we went on the tour with Mister Merritt, and my guess is as many times as the laundress has worked in this room, she has never seen it. Plus, I would not be surprised if there is a door on the opposite wall that opens into Mister Seldon's chamber. I will make you a wager. I will bet you Mister Seldon is aware of this door and may even use it from time to time."

"Why would he be doing that?"

"That we may never learn unless he chooses to tell us. But we will need to consult with him about the woman you have seen. And we need to know how she is getting in and why." Frowning, Timandra said, "Now we must make our way back up those stairs. That will not be easy, but if your ghost can do it, so can we."

"Yes, milady, but 'tis hoping I am, that we will not be needing to traipse these steps again. The dust in here has my nose sniffling."

Timandra smothered a laugh. "Aye, Finola, mine, too, mine, too."

※ ※ ※ ※

After cleaning up from their dusty trek down and up the secret passage, and with Finola in her wake, Timandra squared her shoulders and marched up to Seldon's chamber door. She could hear voices and guessed Seldon was still going over the books with Colyer, but her discovery of the passage and Finola's citing of the woman in black made Timandra feel she had to discuss the situation with Seldon. That Finola had spotted the woman outside the boys' bedchamber was of major concern. At least so it seemed to Timandra.

Taking a deep breath, she tapped on the door. She heard the scraping of a chair, and in a moment, Colyer opened the door. He looked surprised. "Why, Lady Timandra, is aught amiss?"

"Mayhap," she answered. "Finola and I need to speak in private with Mister Seldon." She peered around Colyer. "I realize you two are busy with your books, but I do think what I need to discuss must take precedence."

Colyer turned and looked at Seldon who rose from the table strewn with papers. "Of course, Lady Timandra. Do come in," he said. "You must forgive the mess of my sitting room. As you have said, we have been consumed with the accounting of my estate."

"I hope not to take up too much of your time, Mister Seldon," Timandra said, placing a hand on Finola's wrist and drawing her maid in after her.

"Colyer," Seldon said, "take a walk or some such, but check back in a wee bit. I would like to finish with this before supper tonight. I grow weary of it."

"Yes, sir, Mister Seldon. I will just stretch my legs in the garden that is coming along so wonderfully. I will return ere long."

"Good. Now, Lady Timandra, have a seat. As you have your maid with you, I hope you are not here to tell me she has again been frightened by a ghost."

"Frightened, yes, but not by a ghost. By a very real person, and I cannot but think something is very strange in this person's behavior."

His blue eyes, so much like Gavin's, met hers questioningly. "Continue," was all he said.

"Twice now, Finola has seen a woman dressed all in black and with a black veil covering her face wandering the corridors. Last night she saw the woman standing outside Herman and Bennet's chamber door. Keeping in the shadow, Finola followed the woman up to the second floor and to the end of the corridor past our bedchamber where the woman disappeared into the wall behind the tapestry."

"Oh." Seldon tilted his head. "Disappeared did she?"

"That is what Finola thought," Timandra continued. "But as I am not a believer in ghost, sir, any more than are you, I searched behind the tapestry and found a hidden door."

He sat up straighter in his chair and raised his eyebrows. "And?"

"Behind that door is a secret stairway. We have just returned from following it down to the kitchen in the old keep. My concern is that woman. How is she getting into the secret passage and why is she doing so?"

For a moment Seldon pursed his lips and narrowed his eyes. At last he said, "That is a mystery and of some concern. Why indeed would some unknown woman be wandering our corridors, but more importantly, how did she learn of the passage?"

"I believe you must have some idea, Mister Seldon, how she is entering the passage."

He nodded. "Yes. There are but four ways to gain access to the stairway. Two you have discovered. The one in the kitchen and the one behind the tapestry." He frowned then shrugged. "Another is a door here in my chamber."

Timandra nodded at Finola. "I knew it. Did I not tell you so, Finola? My guess is those steps were added when the houses were joined. And who ever joined them thought it would be fun to have a secret passage. Must have been your father. Am I not right, Mister Seldon?"

"You are partially correct. 'Twas my father had the steps added when he joined the two houses together, but 'twas not at that time any secret. Originally, the servants' quarters were on the second floor. As was the nursery and school room. The steps were a faster way for the servants to get down to the ground floor without disturbing anyone on the first floor. It was before the second staircase that empties into the kitchen had been added."

He swept his arm around his chamber. "This was not a sitting room. It was at that time the buttery which is now in the undercroft. The servants came down the stairs and went through the buttery, and the area that is now a retirement room for the ladies. Then it was a corridor with shelving holding linens, candles, and other household items. The servants ended up in the kitchen or wherever they were needed." Pointing behind him, he said, "Directly above the wainscoting is the doorway, though now it is not so obvious."

"But it is so high."

Seldon smiled. "At the time, there were steps leading down from the landing." Nodding his head toward the shelves of books, he said, "Now, do I wish to go through the door, I use the movable steps that I also use to retrieve books from the top shelves."

Narrowing her eyes, Timandra said, "And from time to time you do go through that door, do you not, Mister Seldon? And sometimes you are dressed in a black cape?"

He snorted and looked at Finola. "Yes. And I apologize for scaring you, Finola. I was not chasing you, I only wanted to tell you not to be afraid, because 'twas only me. But then, with all the fuss being made, it seemed easier just to put the blame on a worker."

"See, Finola, no ghost." Timandra patted her maid's hand.

"Oh, sir, but you did give me a big fright. You just suddenly appearing like that. Why would you be after doing such a thing?"

Timandra frowned at Finola for her tone and her question, but as was her maid's usual, she seemed not to notice she should not be addressing Mister Seldon in such a fashion. Fortunately, he seemed to take no offense.

Heaving a sigh, he shrugged and said, "From time to time I go to the east wing to just sit. I was very happy there while my wife was alive, and when Gavin's mother was a little girl. At times, I like to go back and just sit and go over some of the memories. 'Tis quick and easy to go out my door and through the keep's kitchen. Once I retire to my chambers, no one bothers me. I may come and go as I please, and no one needs know where I choose to spend my time."

Timandra's heart ached for Seldon. She wished she could do something to bring him and his daughter together again. Maybe Gavin's plan for the school might be an impetus to at least get them talking. She sighed and looked about the room before returning her gaze to Seldon. "You said there was a fourth entrance, Mister Seldon."

"It is on the ground floor and opens to the outside. It is now behind some tall bushes I had planted many years ago when the door was no longer being used. Once father moved the servants' quarters to the cellar and remodeled the second floor, there was no longer a need for the staircase. So, he hung the tapestry at the end of the corridor and locked the door. That was the end of its use, except when my siblings and I, or later Dwight and his sisters, when visiting, decided to use it for our games. But I suppose we must now go out and see if the area has been disturbed. In which case, we will know how the woman is entering the passage. Just not why." He rose. "Come let us see what we may find."

The three of them went out the garden portal, and Seldon led them along the back of the house to several tall bushes that had recently been artfully shorn and shaped. "Looks as though Beamer has had your footmen shape up these bushes. They were in dire need."

He glanced back at Timandra and huffed. "Yes, I know. The entire garden was in dire need. And with Beamer's direction, your men have done an excellent job. It has been a long time since I cared one way or another what the gardens looked like."

Her voice soft, Timandra said, "And do you care now, Mister Seldon? I do hope it pleases you."

"Yes, Lady Timandra, I will admit. It pleases me. Now let us peek behind these bushes and see what we may discover." Pushing his way behind the bushes, he looked down. "Ah, hah, footprints here in the dirt. These bushes are now so tight against the house, it is a wonder how the woman manages to get the door open, but let me see what I can do."

"Be careful, Mister Seldon," Timandra said. "You must not strain yourself."

He chuckled. "I believe if a woman can manage the door, I should be able to."

Peering in between the bushes, Timandra saw the door she had never before noticed.

"Hmmm," Seldon said, "seems the frame has been busted in order to get the inside latch undone. I doubt a woman could have done this."

"Excuse me, Lady Timandra, is there aught I might help you with?"

Timandra looked around to see Perth had joined them. "Oh, Mister Seldon," she said, "do come out from there and let Perth see to the door."

"Very well," Seldon said and squeezed his way out from between the bushes.

"It would seem, Perth," Timandra said, "that someone has broken into the house. Do please see if you can get that door open."

"Yes, my lady," Perth said, working his way behind the bushes. "Aye. The frame is busted, but when I hold the frame in place, the door opens easily enough. Still, 'tis a tight squeeze to get through the doorway, what with the bushes bumping again the door. I had no idea this door was here. What now, my lady?"

"You may come back out," Seldon said. "This is going to require some thought." He looked at Perth. "At this time, I would prefer you not mention this to anyone."

"Yes, sir," Perth said. "Would you have me mend it, sir?"

"Not yet." He turned to Timandra. "Let us go back inside and discuss this. Here comes Colyer. He can join us. Too soon all will be returning for dinner. For now, we will not mention this to anyone else." He glanced at Finola and added, "That means you, Finola. No talk of ghosts or secret passages. Now, you go on about whatever you would normally be doing."

"Yes, sir, Mister Seldon." Bobbing a curtsy, Finola followed Perth back to the kitchen as Colyer joined Seldon and Timandra.

They had just started to return to the house when Gavin, Eliza and her sisters, and Andrew returned.

"We will discuss this in my chamber after dinner," Seldon said. "Better we have Gavin in on the discussion. This is indeed a mystery."

"As you wish, Mister Seldon," Colyer said. "I will just ready myself for dinner."

"I, too," Timandra said. She had seen Gavin laughing at something Eliza said as they walked to the house. Poor man, he loved Eliza and could not have her, and Timandra knew beyond a doubt, she loved Gavin, but could not have him. Her heart aching, she could not face Gavin and her beloved friend. She hurried after Seldon and Colyer, then scurried up to her room.

Chapter 27

Dinner was a lively affair. Eliza and her sisters were full of chatter. They had enjoyed their visit with Ebba while Gavin had visited his aunt's friend, and they were just leaving to make a brief stop at Hidden Marsh Manor to call on Mistress Luella Estcott, a young lady they had met at church the previous Sunday, when Mister Knolles and Eliza's brothers arrived at the vicarage.

Ebba's dog having recently had puppies, and the boys wanting to play with them, Ebba had invited Mister Knolles and the boys to stay to dinner. "Of course, I said they could," Eliza said with a giggle. "I do believe Mister Knolles and Ebba are sweet on each other. So, while the boys went off to play with the puppies, and we returned to our horses, I saw Mister Knolles and Ebba set off on a walk around the vicarage garden."

"And how did you find Mistress Estcott," Timandra asked. She was trying to be cheery, trying to keep her thoughts off Gavin. Though he was seated across from her, and she felt his eyes on her, she had not been able to look at him. Other than a greeting, she had not addressed him. She had spoken to Seldon, to Charissa when she had prattled on about her horse and what a lovely gait it had. Anything to keep from looking at Gavin. She feared if she looked at him, she would burst into tears.

"Mistress Estcott was pleased we had called," Eliza answered, "and she said she would look forward to becoming better acquainted. She said she is hoping, come fall, when the harvests are over, but before the rains come, that her parents will commit to a ball. Seems of the nearby manors, only a couple have young people, but when her parents have a grand entertainment, they invite friends from Newcastle and other close towns."

"It sounds quite delightful," Charissa said. "And Eliza has promised that if Uncle Percival has no objections, now I am sixteen, I may attend."

Seldon huffed. "I will leave those decisions to your sister."

"Thank you, Uncle Percival," Charissa said, giving her younger sister a smug look.

Delilah just snubbed her nose at Charissa and turned to Andrew who was looking at her with adoring eyes.

"I would think by this fall," Eliza said, looking at Timandra, "that though we are not yet out of mourning, that Charissa and I might attend the ball. I should think we might not partake of the dancing, but I would think we could not be considered disrespectful to Father if we but watched the dancing."

Timandra smiled at her friend. After what their father had done to his children, that they were honoring him to the extent they were was plenty. "I can see no reason you and Charissa should not be able to attend the ball. I even think by fall, you could add a little color to your gowns or your hair and not be considered disrespectful."

"I wish you would be here to go with us," Eliza said. "I so hate it that you must soon leave. I cannot think how I am to get on without you."

"I will miss all of you." She looked at Seldon. "This has been a most delightful visit, and I thank you so very much for your generous hospitality."

Seldon frowned and looked at Gavin before looking back at Timandra. "You sound as though you are planning to leave on the morrow. Surely you are here for a couple more weeks."

"One week at the most, I fear. I must get the coach back to my mother."

Clearing his throat, Seldon said, "Why not stay on here until next spring? You could send the coach on to your mother. You have been of immense aid to Eliza and her siblings as they adjust to their home here."

Her mouth open in surprise, Timandra stared at Seldon. Had he really asked her to stay?

"Oh, yes, Timmie," Eliza said, her eyes wide and hopeful. "Why do you not stay?"

"Yes, do stay," Charissa said, and Delilah echoed her.

Before Timandra could think what to say to their pleas, Seldon said, "And I know Gavin wants you to stay. Do you not, Gavin?"

"Indeed, I do add my pleas to the others, Lady Timandra. Do consider how much you will be missed."

Timandra forced herself to look at Gavin. What did she read in his eyes?

"You are all so kind," she finally said. "So kind."

"At least say you will consider staying," Eliza pleaded.

Giving Eliza a smile, Timandra said, "All right, I will consider staying."

Everyone, including Colyer, clapped.

"Well, if dinner is concluded, I have things I must attend," Seldon said. "I will not be taking any port after dinner. Colyer, I will see you in my chamber. Lady Timandra, do give me a short time, and then do you and Gavin join us. We have some things to discuss. Gavin, if you will attend Lady Timandra for a bit. Have a walk in the garden or some such."

Mystified, Timandra looked at Seldon as he rose from his chair. What did he mean by asking Gavin to attend her?

Gavin also rose and was staring at her, but Eliza grabbed her elbow and whispered, "What does Uncle Percival want to see you about?"

Timandra shrugged. She had no intention of telling Eliza about the mysterious woman. At least not until they had worked out some kind of plan to find out what the woman was doing in Perfidious Brambles. "I would guess he has more suggestions about returning my coach to Mother without me."

"Oh, I hope so, my dear friend," Eliza said, giving Timandra a kiss on the cheek. "Now, I think I will go up and write Mister Severin. I see no reason Charissa cannot keep company with Delilah and Mister Althouse. Delilah knows her sister will report to me any untoward behavior." She glanced at Gavin who was waiting at the door. "Enjoy your walk with Cousin Gavin."

Eliza swept out of the room after her sisters, Andrew, and Colyer, and Timandra found herself alone with Gavin.

Gavin extended his arm to her, and she had no choice but to take it. "I cannot think why, Lady Timandra, but I could almost believe you have been avoiding me today. Have I in some way done something to offend you? For if I have, I sincerely apologize."

Clearing her throat, Timandra managed, "Indeed, no, Mister Merritt. How could you think so?"

"I am glad, for I have been looking for a chance to talk with you."

"You have?"

"I have, but 'twould seem one thing or another has spoiled my plans. Will you take a stroll with me in the garden?"

Timandra could do little more than nod. What was he wanting to talk to her about? Was he wondering if she thought he had a chance with Eliza? Might he still be able to win Eliza's love or had she already given her heart to Severin? Would she have to tell him that Eliza was practically promised to Severin? How she dreaded having to tell him.

"I know Grandfather has something he needs to discuss with us. Something to do with the old staircase that is no longer used, but I told him I was in need of some time with you, and he agreed to give me that time."

Timandra looked up at Gavin. "You knew about the staircase?"

"Yes, though I have never seen it. I just knew it used to be used by the servants before the house was remodeled. I learned about it one day when I came across the door behind some bushes near the steps going up to the kitchen. Grandfather said the door was kept locked because the stairs, being so steep, were a bit of a hazard and were no longer needed."

"Oh," Timandra said. Well, she would not tell him how it was currently being used. She would leave that until they joined Seldon and Colyer. Bracing herself, she asked, "What did you wish to speak to me about, Mister Merritt?"

"Let us go sit on that bench. Your footmen, under Beamer's direction, have done a wonderful job of restoring the garden. It looks vastly improved, all the way to the fish pond."

"Yes," she answered, letting him lead her to the bench sheltered under a rose arbor. "I feel certain they will all be much happier once they are through gardening and can resume their duties as footmen."

"Well, that will be soon," Gavin said, and taking out a kerchief, he brushed off the bench before inviting Timandra to sit.

Once she was seated, he sat down beside her. Before she knew what was happening, he had her hands in his. "Lady Timandra," he said. "Timandra. I know we have known each other but a short time, but in that time, as I have enjoyed your company, your companionship, your wit, and your humor, I have come to love you. I hope I am not wrong in thinking you have feelings for me as well."

Timandra could do little but stare into his eyes. What was he saying? "But do you not love Eliza?" she at last blurted out.

"Eliza?" He looked questioningly at her. "Eliza is a sweet young woman, and am I not mistaken, she will marry Severin and will be the perfect wife for him. But you, Timandra, you are the sun appearing after a storm. You are the moon and stars that light up the sky at night. You are the surf crashing on the shore. You, Timandra, are like champagne, an exciting, bubbling wine I once tasted when visiting in France. You are life itself, my beloved. Tell me, might you have feelings for me? Do I have the chance that I may win your heart and your hand?"

He had pulled her hands up to his chest as he spoke, and his eyes, never leaving hers, were pleading with her to admit her love for him.

Slowly shaking her head, Timandra said, "Mister Merritt, Gavin, yes, I love you. I just cannot believe you love me. Eliza is so lovely. I thought you in love with her. Truly I did."

Releasing Timandra's hands and clasping her to his chest, he breathed into her hair. "I cannot think how I could have given you such an idea, but more the fool am I that I should have done so." Straightening that he could again look into her eyes, he said, "I do believe I fell in love with you after our first ride together. I could hardly wait to introduce you to my mother and my aunt, for I knew they would see how wonderful and unique you are. I knew they would appreciate your wit and intellect as I do. You are the woman of my dreams. The woman I have been searching for. Do say you will marry me, for if not, then I must follow you back to Cheshire and pay you court, for I cannot let you leave my life."

Still dazed and wondering how her life could have so suddenly turned around, she said, "Yes. Yes, I will marry you, Gavin." Her eyes glued to his, she added, "I believe I fell in love with you the first time I met you and enjoyed the easy banter you had with your grandfather."

Joy written on his face, Gavin said, "You have made me the happiest of men," Bending forward, he tentatively kissed her lips.

Still in a trance, Timandra hungrily responded to his kiss, and his arms tightened around her. That this wonderful man was in love with her had to be some kind of miracle. His kisses were sending delightful shivers racing up and down her spine. She could swear the very ground was quaking, and the heavens had opened and were shedding a brilliant light down on them. Gads, but she hoped they would not have to wait long before they could be married. His touch, his kisses, his nuzzling of her neck were arousing entrancing sensations, and she believed those sensations would not be satisfied until they were sharing a bed.

When they finally pulled apart, Gavin said, "Grandfather will be waiting for us. He has known of my love for you for some time. That you have agreed to marry me will greatly please him. He holds you in high esteem."

"Does he? I have grown very fond of him. He seems to have mellowed greatly since Eliza and her siblings and I first arrived."

"You have wrought a wondrous change in him, my sweet love. But now, we had best join him and learn what it is he wishes to discuss with us."

"I know what it is, but we will explain all when we are in your grandfather's chambers. But Gavin," how wonderous it was to call him by his given name, "I think we should wait until supper before we tell anyone of our betrothal," she said, rising as Gavin rose.

"As you wish, my love. And we will have much to discuss. When we plan to marry. Where we will live. Who we will invite to the wedding. I would dearly love to hold the wedding here so Grandfather might attend. He is too old to journey to Cheshire."

Her hand on Gavin's arm, Timandra smiled. "Indeed. We must be married here. My parents are still at Knightswood Castle. Do we plan to have the wedding soon, they could come from there instead of returning to Harp's Ridge and then coming here."

A broad grin lit up Gavin's face. "The sooner we are wed, the better I will like it. So I will fall in with whatever plans you want to make."

Timandra laughed. "Oh, no, you must be a part of all our plans. However, for now, I do think we must join your grandfather."

They were halfway back to the house when they were hailed by Tombs. Still dusty from his ride, he told them he had much to relate to them.

"I think you should join us in my grandfather's chambers," Gavin said.

"Let me but freshen up and grab a bite to eat," Tombs said, "and I will join you shortly."

"Good man," Gavin said, turning with Timandra to head into the house.

Chapter 28

By the time Tombs joined them in Gavin's grandfather's chambers, Gavin, a brandy in hand, was settled back in his chair, eager to hear Tombs's report. He and Colyer had been told about the mysterious woman, her use of the staircase, the door that had been busted in order to undo its latch, and that Finola had spotted the woman outside Herman and Bennet's bedchamber the previous night.

Tombs was invited to sit, offered a brandy, which he graciously declined, saying he would not want to muddle his brain when he had much to report.

"Well, then," Gavin said, "let us hear your report." He was impressed with Tombs, had been since the day Tombs had investigated who might have taken a shot at him.

Tombs looked at Gavin's grandfather. "Mister Feldings sends his regards, sir."

Gavin's grandfather nodded, and Tombs, turning back to Gavin and Timandra, continued, "Feldings was suspicious of the new footmen from the moment they arrived at Crenshaw Manse. He says they are not footmen. He believes them to be hired rogues, mayhap even thieves. He says he can tell Mister Crenshaw has no liking for the men, but as Mistress Clackenberger chose them, he makes no complaint. Mister Crenshaw seems to be very taken with Mistress Clackenberger, according to Feldings."

"Damned if I can understand that," Gavin said. "I thought my cousin had more sense."

Ignoring Gavin's comment, Tombs continued, "Ever so often, according to Feldings, Mistress Clackenberger complains of a fierce headache and goes to bed right after supper. Sir Osgood then keeps Mister Crenshaw company in the parlor. Cards and drinking.

"In the meantime, Mistress Clackenberger slips out of the house and meets up with one or both of the footmen. The footman has a horse for her, and they ride off together."

"Oh, surely not," Timandra said. "And Mister Crenshaw nor anyone else is the wiser?"

"Mistress Clackenberger's maid is no more a lady's maid than the footmen are footmen, so Feldings said."

"Oh, that is what Finola said, too," Timandra noted.

Tombs nodded. "Feldings believes the maid would never say anything against Mistress Clackenberger, and he thinks none of the other servants, who might notice Mistress Clackenberger's actions, would dare mention them. They have seen how the previous two footmen were let go. None would want to risk losing their positions or their pensions.

"Anyway, Feldings has spied her leaving in such a fashion a couple of times. I might add, he says the lady rides astride. He noticed when she mounted her horse, she had men's breeches on under her gown."

"Well, that would help with the chafing," Colyer said, then blushed when he looked at Timandra. "Begging your pardon, Lady Timandra," he said, and she gave him a smile and a nod.

"Have you more to report?" Gavin asked, thinking he had been wise to send Tombs to check on his cousin's houseguests.

"Yes, sir. The same day as your party's visit to Mister Crenshaw's, after we left, Mistress Clackenberger told Mister Crenshaw she wanted to do some shopping in Fairflex. She asked that she might borrow the coach to take her and the maid to the village. He protested it was late, but she said she and her maid would spend the night in the village inn, then they could be up and do their shopping bright and early in the morning.

"As I mentioned," Tombs continued, "Feldings says Mister Crenshaw seems unable to deny Mistress Clackenberger any request, so the coach was readied and off went Mistress Clackenberger and her maid and the two footmen. Feldings says she was gone for two nights and had only returned shortly before I arrived." He looked to Gavin. "If you want, Mister Merritt, I can go into Fairflex and find out if, indeed, Mistress Clackenberger did stay at the inn."

"That might be wise," Gavin said. "But why would she have wanted to go to Fairflex the same day we visited?"

"So she could go to the hamlet the next day and wait around until Herman and Bennet visited their friends, as they had told her they were wont to do. She could then give them the poisoned tarts," Timandra said.

"Oh, come now, Lady Timandra," Colyer said. "The boys know Mistress Clackenberger. Besides, they described an old, shabbily-dressed woman."

"It could have been her maid," Timandra said. "We barely saw her, and I doubt the boys paid her any heed at all."

"But the maid is not old either. And why would Mistress Clackenberger want to harm Herman and Bennet?" Colyer asked.

"She did ask the boys a lot of questions about their activities and their friends," Gavin said. "When I spoke with them last night, they said they thought she was being friendly, and she felt bad because they had been hurt when the wall busted under them. But I believe that wall had been deliberately weakened and that the footmen had directed the boys to that section."

"But again. It makes no sense," Colyer said. "Why should she want to harm the boys?"

"Not to be impertinent, sir," Tombs said, looking from Colyer to Gavin's grandfather, "but who will inherit Perfidious Brambles when you die?"

For a moment Gavin's grandfather stared at Tombs, then he looked at Gavin. "My grandson."

"Did anything happen to your grandson, sir, would Herman and Bennet be next in line?"

"Now, wait a minute, Tombs!" Gavin said. "Why kill the boys and not me?"

Tombs was shaking his head. "I believe you were the first target, Mister Merritt. But once the young boys arrived here, they became the target."

"What do you mean Gavin was a target?" Gavin's grandfather demanded.

Tombs looked at Gavin. "I would guess you have not told Mister Seldon about the shot fired at you, Mister Merritt?"

"What are you saying, Tombs?" Timandra demanded. "Are you saying someone was deliberately shooting at Mister Merritt? It was not just a careless hunter?"

Tombs nodded. "That is what I am saying. From the beginning I suspected someone was intent on killing Mister Merritt."

Timandra's hands flew to her throat, and Gavin gave her a smile. "Not to worry. There have been no more attempts." Not that he knew of anyway. He again turned to Tombs. "So why switch from me to the boys?" he asked.

"My guess is, sir," Tombs said, looking from Gavin to his grandfather, "that the would-be-killer knows, or at least believes, that Perfidious Brambles is entailed. That it must go to a male heir."

"So it is," Gavin's grandfather said. "It goes through my heir, my daughter, to my grandson. But if she had not had a son, when I die it would go to the heirs of my brother."

"And Herman and Bennet are the grandsons of your brother," Gavin said, "so Herman would be next in line to inherit if I should die. And Bennet if Herman should die."

"Yes," Colyer said, "and if they should both accidentally die, and then Gavin were to die, that would leave Mister Crenshaw as the only male heir. He inheriting through your sister, correct, Mister Seldon?"

"Dwight! Good heavens!" Gavin's grandfather blanched. "Did Dwight inherit, Father would be turning over in his grave."

Rising, Gavin crossed to his grandfather. Putting a hand on his grandfather's shoulder, he said, "You should not rile yourself, sir. I have no intention of dying."

"All this talk of attempts on your life, Gavin," his grandfather said, glancing up at Gavin, "and possible attempts on the lives to those two young rapscallions is reprehensible." He looked back at Tombs. "What else do you know? Why would that obnoxious woman want to kill my nephews or my grandson?" He returned his gaze to Gavin.

Before Tombs could answer, Gavin said, "My guess is she plans to marry Cousin Dwight."

His grandfather snorted. "Dwight should have married years ago, but his mother was never satisfied with any of his choices. Now, she too will be turning over in her grave if Dwight should marry that woman.

216

But Crenshaw Manse is prosperous. I do think the estate brings in near two thousand pounds a year. What need would Mistress Clackenberger have of Perfidious Brambles? It is entailed, yes, but my coal mines and coal barges are not. They go to whatever heir I choose, and at present they go to Gavin."

"She may not know they are not part of the entailment, Grandfather," Gavin said. "But even if she does know, you must think how much better situated your manor is than is Dwight's. You are convenient to Fairflex and to the highway to Newcastle. And you have various heirlooms and art pieces, not to mention your silver pieces, which are worth a goodly fortune. Did you add Cousin Dwight's income to yours, even without your mines and barges, it would be a large enough income to allow the Mistress Clackenberger to insist they retain a house in Newcastle or even London. She hardly seems a country-loving lady."

"Gavin may be right," Colyer said. "When we were enjoying the picnic, before the boys' accident, she spoke glowingly of the theater and various other amusements to be found in the city. She prattled on about the sights she and her brother had visited while in Rome, and others they visited once they met Mister Crenshaw."

Tombs said, "I believe the two footmen were first hired to kill Mister Merritt, but upon learning of the boys, and that they would inherit rather than Dwight, should Gavin die, she decided the young masters must be killed before Gavin. And it would appear, she is trying to make it look like they were accidentally killed. I think the last thing she would want would be to have the law looking into the deaths."

"But why has she been slinking around in the house?" Timandra asked. "That is if she is the one slinking about. What can she expect to gain from it? She has to know she is at risk of being seen. And how does she know about the secret staircase?"

"I would guess Dwight must have told her," Gavin's grandfather said. "As I told you, my siblings and I used to play on those stairs, and so did Dwight and his sisters. More than likely, at some point in conversation, Dwight mentioned the staircase to her. But what her intentions are in wandering around the house, I can only guess. Mayhap she has been stealing things? I will ask Mistress Weston to make a search of the old keep and this wing and see if anything is missing. The east wing is securely locked. I doubt she could have gotten into that wing. Besides, she has been seen in this wing, which means she has some reason for being in this wing."

"When Finola last saw her, she was outside Herman and Bennet's door," Timandra said. "Could be she was attempting to determine if either or both boys had died of the poison. She may even have peeked inside and seen both sleeping peacefully in their beds."

"My guess is she sensed someone was near to hand, and she had to leave before she could do whatever it was she meant to do," Gavin said, narrowing his eyes. "She probably never expected anyone to be about that late in the evening. Finola has seen her twice, but we know not how many times she might have been here. And we have no way of knowing her plans. I would hazard she believes she is not suspected of being Finola's ghost."

"Do you wish, Mister Merritt," Tombs said, "I know of a man in London who does discreet investigation. Did you wish to write to him? And ask him if he has any information on Mistress Clackenberger and her brother, I could post the letter when I go into Fairflex to check at the inn as to whether Mistress Clackenberger stayed there or not."

Gavin looked to his grandfather. The old man narrowed his eyes, pursed his lips, and nodded. "Yes, that would be wise, I think. But what are we to do in the meantime. I cannot say I care to have this woman wandering around at night in my home."

"In the meantime," Gavin said, "we will need to keep a close eye on Herman and Bennet. I think that means we will need to bring Knolles into our confidence."

"I think Perth as well," Timandra said. "One or the other will need to be with them at all times. I hate to restrict their fun, but do they go to the hamlet to play with their friends, Knolles or Perth will have to go with them."

"Agreed," Gavin said. "Now the question is, do we tell Eliza?"

"Eliza is their older sister, but I am their guardian," Gavin's grandfather said. "I am the one responsible for their care and safety. I cannot think it will benefit anyone to worry Eliza at this point. What I do think we need do is resolve upon a plan to deal with this dilemma."

"Well, I will write a letter for Tombs to post to the investigator to learn what we can of Mistress Clackenberger and her brother when he goes to Fairflex. Though things may come to a head before we hear back from the investigator. It seems to me Mistress Clackenberger is very eager to have the boys killed. Two attempts in two days' time. She could even have something planned for this very night. I think we may need to have someone posted outside the boys' door."

"If you could do it in such a fashion so not to let the lady know we are aware of her nightly jaunts, it might be better," Tombs said. "I am thinking the only way to stop her from finding a way to kill the young masters is to catch her in the act. Is she caught just wandering around the house, she can be charged with little but trespassing."

"Tombs is right," Colyer said. "I could spend the night in the room with the boys. Then if she tries anything, I will be able to stop her."

"Not a bad idea, but how do we explain your sleeping in their room?" Gavin asked.

"I see no way without telling them the reason, and that could frighten them," Timandra said. "Best for now, we post someone outside their door once everyone has settled for the night. The guard can be gone in the morning before first light, and no one need know he was there."

"I am betting the woman has a reason she is eager to kill the boys," Tombs said. "I believe she will try again before much longer. Mayhap not tonight, but soon. And I am thinking she will have a plan. She will not want to miss a third time."

"Should we move the boys to another room?" Colyer asked.

Timandra shook her head. "No, again, we would have to give them a reason, and at the moment I cannot think of one. But it is a good idea. For now, though, mayhap the best idea is to have someone posted outside the entrance to the secret staircase."

"Yes, but you would need a reason for the guard to be there so not to raise her suspicions," Tombs said. "I would think Perth and Finola might be perfect as the guards. They could pretend to be courting on the steps near the staircase door." He smiled. "And could be, they would not be pretending."

Timandra looked at Tombs. "I think you may have made note of something I have not noticed. I know Finola has been spending a lot of time helping the cook." She tilted her head and smiled. "Has Perth also been spending time in the kitchen?"

Tombs answered her smile with one of his own. "I have seen them both there from time to time. But I would not say either has been shirking their duties. That I would not say."

Gavin chuckled. "Well, whether romance blooms between those two or not, I have no doubt they are the perfect pair for the performance. We just need them to act the lovers long enough to give us time to come up with a better plan."

"Yes," Tombs said. "And when I return from Fairflex, I will not immediately retire. If she does come tonight, I would like to learn where they are leaving their horses."

"The plans sound reasonable to me," Gavin's grandfather said. "Now, I think we had best conclude this discussion before we arouse too many questions. We will plan to meet here again after dinner tomorrow and discuss additional plans to catch Mistress Clackenberger in the act."

As they exited, Gavin told Timandra, "I will speak to Knolles and Perth."

"Good," Timandra said. "I will speak with Finola of our plan."

The glowing look she gave him before turning to the stairs made his heart expand in his chest. To think this fabulous woman had consented to be his wife. He could not wait to tell his mother and his aunt. They would be thrilled. They had been so impressed with Timandra. Determining where he and Timandra would live once they were married was the big question. He rather hoped his grandfather would let them live in the east wing that had been closed off since Gavin's mother had run away and married Gavin's father.

It was past time for the rift between his mother and his grandfather to heal.

Chapter 29

"Oh! Timmie! I am so happy for you!" Eliza jumped up from her chair and hugged Timandra before looking at Gavin and saying, "I hope you know what a lucky man you are."

Timandra started laughing. She and Gavin had just announced their betrothal, and everyone at the table seemed deliriously happy for them, even Seldon. She had never seen him grin in such a fashion.

"I told the boy, did he let you slip away, he was a fool," Seldon said. "I watched him muse about here day after day. Never saw so much of him as I have since you arrived, Lady Timandra. I cannot tell you how long I have been waiting for this announcement."

Timandra blushed. She could have saved herself a lot of heartache if she had been as sure of Gavin's love for her as Seldon had been. But now, when she looked across the table at Gavin and saw his love for her in his eyes, she wondered how she had been so foolish she had not recognized it sooner. She could hardly wait to again be alone with him. She knew he was eager to tell his mother and his aunt and uncle of their betrothal, but she hoped she and Gavin would have a few moments alone before Gavin and Andrew had to head for home. She had a feeling, though, she would have a hard time getting away from Eliza. Her friend was ecstatic.

"Dear Timmie, to think you will be staying here and not leaving," Eliza gushed. "And you are planning to have your wedding here. It is too wonderful!"

"Indeed it is," Charissa said. "I could not think how we would go on without you."

"Yes, but now we will still have you near," Delilah said. "That is so grand. But where are you going to live?"

Timandra looked at Gavin, and they both shrugged. "We have not had time to determine that yet," Timandra said. "We have only this afternoon become betrothed."

"You will live in the east wing," Seldon said, and Timandra and Gavin both turned and looked at him in surprise. "It will be my wedding gift to you. You will have your own privacy there. Your own staff. You will have to hire them, but Gavin has a small income from his father, and I will be settling five hundred pounds a year on him, more once you have children." He looked at Timandra. "I would guess your father will be making a suitable settlement on you, Lady Timandra, so you should be able to properly staff and maintain your home."

"Mister Seldon, that is so generous of you," Timandra said.

"Yes, Grandfather, I have to say I was hopeful you might let us have the east wing."

"Hopeful were you?" Seldon said. "Then you might have said something. But never mind. Tomorrow, after you and Lady Timandra have had your ride, which you seem to set such store by, I will escort you over to see your new home. I will have Mistress Weston hire a couple of women from the hamlet to get it cleaned and aired and ready for you to move in."

"Grandfather, we cannot thank you enough," Gavin said. "Not just for allowing us to move into the east wing, but for the five hundred pounds you are settling on me."

"That is nothing. Someday you will inherit everything I own. You might as well have some use of it now." He turned to Timandra. "Lady Timandra, I hope you like the idea of living in the east wing of Perfidious Brambles. I gave you no chance to raise any objections."

Smiling at Seldon, Timandra said, "I think it is lovely. I have come to love Perfidious Brambles, and as it will someday be Gavin's home, well, it seems only appropriate that we should start our lives together here."

"Good. Good." Seldon nodded his head. "You both have made an old man very happy."

"And you, us, Grandfather," Gavin said. "We will have much to do in planning our wedding. You do realize, Grandfather, that if the wedding is to be here, and Timandra and I are to live here, my mother and aunt and uncle will be coming here for the wedding and to visit us?"

Seldon frowned but nodded. "I am fully aware of that, Gavin. I cannot say no to their presence, but neither do I have to acknowledge them, nor must they acknowledge me."

Tilting her head to one side, Timandra said, "Gavin and I have a project we wish to speak to you about, Mister Seldon. I wonder if tomorrow, after the tour of the east wing, we might have a few moments of your time?" She could not think of a better time to bring up the school they wanted to build on the disputed property than now that Seldon was being more amicable.

Seldon narrowed his eyes and for a moment looked at her questioningly, but then he agreed to the meeting. "Yes, as long as we are not to delay dinner."

Timandra laughed. "No, no, we will not delay dinner. That we would never do."

The chatter turned back to plans for the wedding as Eliza, Charissa, and Delilah wondered if they might wear brighter gowns for the celebration, and Delilah wondered if mayhap Andrew might be able to return from school for the ceremony. "After all," she said, looking solemnly at Timandra and then at Andrew who was seated next to her, "he has been here near as often as Cousin Gavin. I cannot but think he must feel he is near a part of the family."

"Indeed," Andrew said, smiling first at Delilah before looking to Gavin and Timandra, "have I not watched the romance bloom and blossom? Have I not given Gavin numerous opportunities to be alone with Lady Timandra?" He chuckled. "And today, did I not keep Delilah and Charissa entertained in the parlor that you two would have time alone in the garden? Like Mister Seldon, I have not been unaware of Gavin's bemused interest in Lady Timandra."

Delilah giggled. "Indeed. We often wondered if Cousin Gavin would ever get up the courage to ask you to marry him, Lady Timandra. Just yesterday, Andrew said he expected any day now that Cousin Gavin would ask for your hand."

Timandra stared in amazement at the young couple. Was she the only one too daft to have seen Gavin was in love with her?

"Well, certainly, Andrew," Gavin said. "Do your parents agree to let you have a holiday from school to come to the wedding, you will be most welcome. Your parents and grandparents will be invited guests, so I can see no reason you should not come along with them."

Delilah and Andrew grinned at each other and Timandra asked, "Andrew, how much longer before you must leave and return to your school?"

He frowned. "I have but until the end of the week. My father is sending his coach for me. I will have a week at home, and then I will be heading back to school. Michaelmas term begins at the beginning of September. I am ever so grateful to Lord and Lady Kirkworth for letting me spend these several weeks of summer with them that I might enjoy my time here with Delilah." He looked adoringly at Delilah, and she looked starry-eyed at him.

Mutual worship, Timandra thought. And certainly that must be the way she and Gavin were now looking at each other.

"My aunt and uncle were happy to have you," Gavin said. "And you could not be considered any trouble since you were always here." He looked at his grandfather. "'Tis more Grandfather you should be thanking. He has fed you more meals than have my aunt and uncle."

Andrew pulled his gaze away from Delilah to look at Seldon. "Oh, you are indeed, correct, Gavin. And Mister Seldon, I do so thank you for allowing me day after day to visit Delilah and to partake of the many meals I have enjoyed here."

Seldon offered Andrew one of those grins he was beginning to show more often and said, "To be honest, boy, I scarcely noticed you were here. You and Delilah have always sat at the other end of the table and have always been engrossed in each other. I had no reason to make note of you."

"Uncle Percival!" Delilah said, but before she could say anything else, Colyer said, "Mister Seldon, I have also been enjoying my time here, but I have correspondence that I must finish for you to sign, as I leave day after tomorrow for Newcastle. Am I not mistaken, your new barge will be ready to set sail very soon, and I want to check it out." He glanced around the table. "I wonder if you will all excuse me. Some of these letters need be posted tomorrow."

"Oh," Timandra said, "I plan to write my parents tonight and inform them of my betrothal and marriage plans. I wonder if you will collect my letter to post along with yours."

"I will, Lady Timandra," Colyer said, rising. "Now, if you will all excuse me."

"Mister Colyer," Eliza said as Colyer rose, "I, too, have a letter that needs posting." She blushed. "'Tis to Mister Severin."

"I will be happy to post it, but the truth is, I could give it to him. As I said, I am bound for Newcastle," Colyer said.

Eliza blushed again and thanked him. With Colyer's exit, everyone but Seldon decided they, too, had finished and would be happy to adjourn to the parlor. Seldon said he had much to think on, and he would bid all goodnight and would retire to his rooms.

At the door to the parlor, Gavin drew Timandra aside. "I must head for home," he said, "but could I have but a moment alone with you, I would find the ride home much easier to take."

Leading Gavin into the shadows near the suit of armor at the rear of the hall, Timandra turned to him, and he swept her into his arms. His lips met hers, and as she found she could scarcely keep her balance, she could do naught but think the ground had to be shaking. Crushed to Gavin's chest, she could feel his heart's rapid beat against her breast. That this glorious man loved her still had her marveling at her good fortune. When she decided to accompany Eliza to her new home in Northumberland, never had she dreamed she would meet a man who would fulfill every dream she had ever dreamed. Strong, handsome, witty, kind-hearted, and a good horseman – and he loved her.

When Gavin finally pulled away from her, in the dark shadows, she could not see his eyes clearly, but she felt his breath soft on her face. "My darling, Timandra," he said. "To think you are now truly mine. I long for the day I will not have to part from you. Tomorrow, we must set a date for our wedding. I swear, I must be the happiest man in all of England."

Timandra laughed and said, "I, too, am eager to plan our wedding. Much will depend on when my parents, and other family members, who might choose to come, can arrive. Most will be coming a long distance. I come from a rather large family of many cousins, some more removed than others, but all well-loved. And we must also go ahead with our plans for the school. We must not let that go by the wayside."

"Aye. I suppose that is the project you mentioned that we are to discuss with Grandfather after we have our tour tomorrow?"

"Yes, it is. And if you could have a firm answer from your uncle when we talk to your grandfather, that might help convince him to fund the school."

"I am thinking that the news of our betrothal may be just the thing to make Uncle Phineas agree to the proposal. I know it will greatly please him."

"That is grand, but now, it grows late, and it will not be safe for you and Andrew to ride home in the dark. I think we had best say good-night and let you collect Andrew."

Gavin again took her into his arms, and again his kisses left her quivering from head to toe. When they did pull apart, Gavin groaned and said, "Gads, but leaving you is hard to do."

"Then return early tomorrow. I will be up, and we can have our ride."

"So be it," he said. "Is Finola set to play her role?"

"She is, as is Perth. And Knolles knows he is not to let the boys out of his sight."

"Good. Hopefully all will be well tonight. And mayhap Tombs will have more to report when he returns."

Timandra agreed, and together, they returned to the parlor to be greeted with gentle teasing. As was usual, Andrew was reluctant to leave Delilah. His days with her would soon draw to a close, but Timandra hoped the bond between them would continue. Sometimes young love grew cold, but other times, it ripened and became a lasting love.

After Gavin and Andrew left, Timandra joined Eliza and her sisters in the parlor for a game of cards and a discussion of wedding plans. Eliza believed the wedding should be held in the keep's grand hall, and Timandra admitted she had been thinking the same thing.

"If the chapel could be renovated without too great an expense," she said, "would it not be a lovely setting for the wedding ceremony?"

"Oh," Charissa said with a sigh. "That would be so romantic. I can just picture a brave knight marrying his lady fair in that very chapel."

Delilah clapped her hands. "Yes, yes. That would indeed be romantic! You must be married there, Lady Timandra."

"Well, we shall see. I will discuss it with Gavin. And again, much depends on the expense involved, not just in repairing the chapel, but the hall itself is in need of some work."

The discussion continued throughout the card game, but when the game ended with Timandra and Delilah the winners, they all determined they should say goodnight. Timandra needed to be up early to go for a ride with Gavin, and she yet had her letter to her parents to write. She just hoped in her excitement, she would be able to sleep. And she had to tell Finola of her betrothal. She had a feeling her maid would not be surprised.

With a shrug, Timandra admitted she seemed to be the only one surprised.

Chapter 30

Timandra thoroughly enjoyed her morning ride with Gavin. They had ridden up to the hill where they wanted to build the school and had dismounted to look the area over. After several lingering kisses, Gavin told her his uncle had given him the entire disputed section as a wedding gift. Along with the land itself, he was letting Gavin have the sheep grazing on the acreage, and the tenants' rents for their leases would now be his.

"So you see," he said, "we can easily pay the wages for a teacher. Now, we but need Grandfather to agree to pay for building the school and a house for the teacher."

"A house large enough does the teacher have a family," Timandra said.

Smiling, Gavin asked, "And have you someone in mind to be the teacher? Someone you think might be wanting to get married?"

She laughed. "You know well that Mister Knolles would be perfect for the position. And once he has a home, he can ask Ebba to marry him. She will be the perfect wife for him. Why, she could even teach some of the younger students. Of course, Mister Knolles is not qualified to teach the advanced courses that Herman and Bennet will need. They will have to be sent off to school as you were, but he can teach what will be necessary for the youths of your grandfather's and your uncle's tenants."

"I see no reason Knolles should not make a most suitable teacher. But now," Gavin said, pulling Timandra into his arms, "now, we had best head back to Perfidious Brambles. We have the east wing to view. When I told Mother that Grandfather had offered the east wing to us, she was very pleased. She thinks we will enjoy it. And, I admit, after all these years, I am eager to see it. But besides our tour, we will have but a short time to convince Grandfather to pay for the school before he is ready for his dinner." He kissed the tip of her nose. "However, I believe we have time enough for another kiss. What say you?"

Timandra smiled up into his eyes. "Yes, I do believe we have time for a kiss."

It ended up being several lingering kisses, but eventually they pulled apart, and Gavin boosted Timandra up onto her saddle. Once he was mounted, they raced down the hill. They had a busy day ahead of them.

※　※　※　※

When they arrived back at Perfidious Brambles, they found Seldon awaiting them. He had told Mistress Weston to see to having the sheets and other coverings removed from the furniture, but he reminded Timandra the house had been closed up for nearly thirty years. "However, Mistress Weston has already sent word to the hamlet that four women are needed to give the premises a thorough cleaning and airing out."

Timandra was thrilled to find every door to the east wing standing open and windows had also been opened. Mistress Weston had Libby, Finola, Audrey, Perth, and Edgar busy helping her pack sheeting and other coverings out to the Keep's kitchen where the laundress and her aide, along with some added help, would later wash them. Besides all the sheeting and other furniture coverings, all the table and bed linens would need laundering. Coverings over pictures and portraits were being removed, and draperies taken down were to be taken outside and beaten.

"The kitchen, servants' dining hall, and servants' quarters are in the cellar," Seldon told her. "Pots and pans and numerous other dishes and mugs and whatever else is in the kitchen and pantry, as well as dishes in the hutch, will need be cleaned and polished. John told me Cook gave instructions to her assistant and one of the scullions to begin on the kitchen." He frowned. "Well, let me give you the tour."

Timandra had already fallen in love with the house. Because the land on the east side of the Keep had been built up, the ground floor of the east wing was on the same level as the Keep's first floor. Instead of having to go down a set of steps to get to the east wing, as was required to go into the west wing, the heavy oak door off the Keep opened right into a short corridor with two doors, one opening into a long corridor, the other a library. Two of the library walls were lined with book shelves, a third had a large glazed window that was letting in the morning's bright sunlight, and the far wall had a hearth with two cushioned chairs in front of it.

A second library door also opened into the corridor, and Timandra could see at the end of the corridor, servants' stairs leading up to the first floor and down to the cellar. She saw that a matching corridor, with another set of servants' stairs, was at the other side of the Grand Hall. Doors could be closed off to hide the stairs, but they were presently open, and Timandra spotted Finola scurrying up the far stairs with a basket looped over her arm.

Opposite the library, on the other side of the corridor was the withdrawing chamber. It had two closets off it, and Seldon explained it could be used as a bedchamber should the need arise. The furnishings were elaborate and gilt-trimmed, as was the hearth with its carved mantle shelf. The draperies had been removed from the window, and Timandra could see out to the garden her footmen had been laboring on almost since their arrival. Fact was, she spotted Hillock and Kearne working alongside the gardener, Beamer, and his grandson, Kipp. By the time guests arrived for the wedding, the garden and grounds should all be beautiful.

Seldon led them back out into the corridor and into the Grand Hall. It was lovely. The hall was open to the first floor ceiling which was painted blue with white puffy clouds. It had marble flooring and on either side of the huge entry doors, it had marble staircases leading up to first floor balconies that overlooked the hall.

Timandra barely had time to exclaim over the hall lined with cherry-wood chairs with brocade cushions along the white-plastered walls before Seldon was leading her into the Great Parlor. It was furnished with four game tables with four cane-back chairs at each table, a couple of couches, and four wingback chairs with highly polished dropleaf tables beside them. A massive chandelier hung from the intricately carved ceiling, and, on either side of the door, sideboards, holding tripod candleholders, stood against walls of inlaid paneling. Brocade floor rugs had yet to be picked up, but Seldon assured Timandra they would be removed and thoroughly beaten or replaced if too old. Hearths were at either end of the chamber, and high windows looked out on the garden. Double doors opened onto a terrace with steps leading down to the garden. A door on one side of the Great Parlor opened into the withdrawing chamber. On the opposite side, it opened into, what Seldon termed, the little parlor with two closets off it.

"Here is where my wife and I spent much of our time in the evenings," Seldon said, a wistful look on his face. Timandra wondered if this was where he came to sit when he left his rooms in the west wing and snuck through the Keep to the east wing. "We would talk or read," he said, "or sometimes she would play the harp. Oftentimes we would eat our meals here. It was so pleasant."

The room was comfortably furnished, as opposed to the elaborate furnishings of the other rooms, and Timandra noted a harp set against the wall between the two closet doors. A hearth was on the opposite side of the room, and the windows looked out on the gardens the same as the other more elegant rooms.

"Come," Seldon said, seeming to shake off his melancholy. "I will show you the first floor. It has four bedchambers with two closets off each chamber, and with doors out to the corridor from the servants' closets so they may come and go about their duties without disturbing you or any guests. And, on the first floor is the Great Dining Chamber. While my wife was alive, we used it often for entertaining."

As they headed for the servants' staircase, Seldon pointed to another room. "That room is meant for the steward or housekeeper, but you could use it as an extra bedchamber, should you so desire, or even a small dining room. And, you will be wanting to use one of the bedchambers for a nursery, no doubt. So did we have one of the chambers furnished when Gavin's mother was young, but once she was older, and we knew we were having no more children, we turned it back into a bedchamber."

Timandra was already making plans. If her parents would release Perth from his contract, and she had no doubt they would, she would hire him as her house steward. She had already been hinting to him about the position, and he seemed to be interested. She would give him the steward's room. And if he and Finola truly did have a romance going and decided to marry, they would have their own room.

She could see little need for the withdrawing chamber. She thought she would prefer to change it into a family dining chamber. The elaborate furnishings could be used in the Keep once it was renovated. She would keep the little parlor as it was, though. She imagined she and Gavin would be spending their evenings in that room as his grandfather and grandmother had done.

The Grand Dining Chamber was all she imagined it would be. The table stretched almost the entire length of the room. Sideboards sporting candelabras were on either side of the main entrance. A hearth was at each end of the room, and the windows looked out on the garden. The four bedchambers were beautifully furnished, and Mistress Weston had already had the three maids and two footmen strip the beds, and carry the mattresses outside to be beaten and fluffed. Each bedchamber had a hearth and large windows that were presently open and letting in the fresh breeze to air out the rooms.

"Oh, Mister Seldon, it is a beautiful home," Timandra said. "We cannot thank you enough for giving us this wing of the house for our very own. Thank you."

"'Tis time this section of the house knew love and laughter again," Seldon said. "And it is also time you start calling me Grandfather."

Timandra smiled at Seldon and gave him a soft kiss on the cheek. "Thank you. I will love having you as my Grandfather, for I never knew either of my own grandfathers. And you must call me Timandra. No more Lady Timandra."

Seldon smiled the widest smile she had ever seen on his face. "I am honored." And he leaned over and gave her a kiss on the cheek. "You warm my heart, Timandra."

"Well," Gavin said, "if we are to discuss the other matter we wish to discuss with you, Grandfather, before 'tis time for dinner, we had best make our way back to your rooms."

Seldon nodded. "Yes, you can inspect the cellar where the kitchen and servants' quarters are located later on your own. I am not needed to show you that section. Let us retire to my rooms that you may discuss this new matter with me." With that, he headed for the staircase leading back down to the Grand Hall, and Timandra and Gavin followed after him.

"Kirkworth gave you the entire eight hundred acres the Kirkworth's stole from my grandfather in 1605?" Seldon said, rising from his chair behind his paper-strewn desk.

"Yes," Gavin said, a smile playing on his lips as he ignored the comment that his uncle's family had stolen the land from his grandfather's family, "'Tis his wedding gift to Timandra and me. He not only gave us the entire eight hundred acres, he included all the sheep currently grazing on the acreage. All the sheep that belong to him, not his tenants' sheep, that is. The section has four tenants with leaseholds of sixty to eighty acres each, and they have the right to graze twenty sheep apiece and their lambs on the meadows. There are two cottars who are the shepherds for my uncle, and they have four acres each, and the right to graze their cows and hogs on the meadow and in the woods."

Seldon sank slowly back onto his chair as Gavin spoke, and Timandra watched him carefully. He looked stunned. Could be this was the perfect time to ask him to help with the school. She glanced at Gavin, and he gave her a slight nod.

"Mister Seldon. Oh, I mean, Grandfather." She gave him a bright smile. "Gavin and I have come up with a wonderful idea to help the young boys, and the girls, too, in your and Lord Kirkworth's hamlets. Your tenants' children to be exact. With times changing, more and more land is being enclosed, and more of the children, as they grow up, will need to leave their homes to find other occupations. We believe they will be able to forge much better lives for themselves if they are better educated."

Seldon had given her his attention, but his face showed no curiosity. He appeared to be doing nothing more than listening. She glanced questioningly at Gavin.

Shrugging, he took over. "What Timandra and I want to do is to build a school on the knoll, mid-point between your tenants' homes and my uncle's. That way the children can go to school in the winter. 'Tis too cold for them to walk into Fairflex for school, and now, many of them can barely write their names, if they can do that. A school close to their homes will give them new options and opportunities to better themselves."

Seldon turned his attention to Gavin, but again, he said nothing. Gavin gave Timandra a smile as if to say, here goes, and after a deep breath, he said, "So, Grandfather, Timandra and I were wondering if you would pay to build the school. And a modest house for the teacher. We would see to paying the teacher by giving him acreage and paying a tenant or laborer to help him care for his farm and sheep, if he chose to have sheep. So, other than paying for the building of the school and the house, we would not ask you for any other help.

"We could pay for the furnishing of the school and the house by selling some of the sheep this fall. Plus the selling of their wool and some of the lambs should give us ample funds." He twisted his mouth to one side and stared at his grandfather who stared back at him. "Well, what say you?"

"I would think you have been formulating this plan for some time."

Gavin nodded. "Yes, Grandfather, we have. We started working on the plans before we ever knew my uncle would give us the acreage. I, and my mother and Aunt Mabelle, have been working on my uncle. Trying to convince him to donate a portion of the acreage. I was happily surprised when he gave us the entire section for our wedding gift."

"You had been formulating this plan before you asked Timandra to marry you?"

"Well, yes we were, but I had every intention of asking Timandra to marry me. I but needed to find the right time and place to speak with her."

"Yes, had I not pushed you, you might still be musing about."

Gavin vigorously shook his head. "Nay, Grandfather. You helped give me the opportunity, but that was just what I had been looking for. Time alone with Timandra."

"Does it matter, Grandfather," Timandra said, "as to when we started thinking about how grand it would be to have a school for the children?"

Seldon brought his gaze back to Timandra, and he shook his head. "No. I was but curious as to how long you two had been hatching this plan. I will think on what you have asked. Had Colyer not left for New-castle, I would consult with him. At this point, we will have to wait un-til he returns, and I can go over some figures with him. I am not saying, yes. I am not saying, no. As you will be busy planning your wedding. I suppose writing invitations, that sort of thing. And arranging the east wing to your needs and wishes, plus hiring your staff. I think you will not need to be worrying about building a school at this time.

"I would guess you are thinking of hiring Knolles as the teacher?"

Gavin chuckled. "Yes, we are. Eventually, Herman and then Bennet will have to go off to school in Newcastle as I did, but Knolles is per-fectly capable of giving a good basic education to the children of the tenants. And Herman and Bennet will most likely benefit from helping him."

Timandra decided not to mention the possibility Knolles might mar-ry Ebba Hemphill, who would also be able to help, at least with the girls.

"One other thing, Grandfather, and Timandra." Gavin looked from his grandfather to Timandra. "I know we will have Tombs join us again after dinner to discuss what to do about our night-time visitor, but I had what I think is a good idea. We want to get the boys out of harms way. No reason they and Knolles could not move up to the second floor, down the corridor from Timandra, and I will move into their room. We can say I am moving in so Timandra and I can work on our wedding plans, and it would not be appropriate for me to be housed on the same floor as Timandra. Then we will not have to keep someone posted at the entrance to the steps. We can but keep watch on the entrance, and on the corridors. What say you?"

"But that puts you in danger?" Timandra said.

"Nay, I will be alert to our mystery guest. When she opens the door, I will catch her. Tombs will be posted outside, Perth and Edgar on the servants' staircase. We will be able to catch her and her footmen."

"It might work," Seldon said. "I cannot like the idea of someone roaming around in my home. Especially not now that we have opened up the east wing. Fact is, I must see the door into the Keep from the hidden staircase is blocked so no one can go into that section." He looked at Timandra. "Until this mystery is resolved, I would request one of your footmen stand guard in the east wing. With no one yet living there, and with a number of valuable objects there, it could be tempting to thieves."

"I will have Perth assign Kearne to the east wing," Timandra said. "We will put him on night duty, at least until we have hired a staff for that wing."

Seldon nodded. "Good, good. Now, to dinner."

"Yet another thing," Timandra said. "Andrew rides back and forth with you, Gavin. He will be here for two more days. He cannot ride back to Kirkworth at night on his own. And we could not deny him and Delilah their last two days together."

Pursing his lips, Gavin rubbed his chin. "He can ride over in the mornings on his own, or Uncle Phineas can send a groomsman with him, and Tombs can see him home at night and still be back in plenty of time to take up his watch. Now, if we are in agreement, after we meet with Tombs this afternoon, I will return home and collect what I may need for staying the night and several days. I have already informed Mother that I wish to spend more time with you. I have not mentioned to Mother or my aunt and uncle about the uninvited guests."

Seldon snorted and said, "No reason you should." He looked at Timandra. "At dinner, you and Gavin may announce your plans, and then after dinner, send one of the maids to get the linens changed, and a footman to move the boys and Knolles up to the second floor. Now, may we go to dinner. Never before have I been late."

Gavin chuckled and took Timandra's arm as they followed after Seldon. Timandra was not certain she liked the idea that Gavin would be putting himself in danger, but then, it had to be better to catch their ghost in the act than to constantly be worrying when or where she might strike next. Yes, they would all have to be on the alert. She had a feeling Mistress Clackenberger was getting desperate. Why, Timandra could not know, but the woman had to have a reason.

Chapter 31

Timandra knew she and Finola were to stay safely in their bedchamber. They had no way of knowing when Mistress Clackenberger, if she was indeed their mystery ghost, would again invade the house. Tombs had learned in Fairflex that Mistress Clackenberger and her maid had indeed spent two nights at the Fairflex Inn. With the inducement of a few coins into the ostler's hand, Tombs had learned that Clackenberger and her two footmen had gone out for a late night ride. The ostler had suspected she was meeting a lover but had been paid not to mention their outing to the innkeeper.

Upon Tombs return to Perfidious Brambles, he did some additional scouting of the grounds and found where their uninvited guests were leaving their mounts. The clump of trees surrounding the estate steward's house had given them good concealment, and it was close enough to the main house that they could hurry through the garden and reach the hidden door to the steps with little chance of discovery. Broken branches and horse droppings gave testimony to the horses' former presence. Even though Colyer had been in residence for a couple of the night-time visits, once he went to his bed, his chamber being situated at the front of the small house, he would not be likely to hear any noises, even had the horses neighed or whinnied.

Timandra stayed up later than usual, but at Finola's urging, she finally agreed to change into her nightshift and ready herself for bed. No reason to think this had to be the night Clackenberger would return. Timandra decided she would leave one candle burning. With the heavy draperies closed over the windows, the light could not be seen from outside, and with the door to her bedchamber closed, the candle's dim light should not be noticeable in the corridor, or if so, she could not think it would deter the mystery ghost if she had already made her way up the steep stairs. Certainly, the candlelight from Timandra's room had not deterred the woman on other occasions. If it had been a deterrent, Finola would not have seen the ghost hovering outside Herman and Bennet's room. Indeed, one night, Timandra had been in her room with a number of candles burning while she wrote letters.

Besides the single candle, Timandra also had at her bedside a small pistol her father had long ago taught her how to use. Such a weapon had been useful to his wealthy cousin who had been subjected to abduction schemes before her marriage to Torrance Madigan. Timandra hoped her cousin Delphine, who was more like an aunt than a cousin, would come to her wedding.

Leaving her robe at the foot of the bed in easy reach, should it suddenly be needed, Timandra, succumbing to Finola's yawns, crawled into bed. Finola went to her bed in the adjoining closet, and all was quiet. Though she had not expected she would be able to sleep, Timandra found herself becoming drowsy. It had been an exhausting day. Herman and Bennet, with Knolles, had been moved to the second floor – at the opposite end of the corridor from her. She had interviewed a couple of young women from the hamlet as possible maids for her and Gavin's future home in the east wing. She had written an advertisement for a cook, and Putnam, the postillion, had been sent to Fairflex to see it posted at the inn. He was also to post a letter to Colyer in Newcastle, asking him to post handbills advertising for a cook and a housekeeper.

The Lotterby coach was being readied for the trip to Knightswood Castle, but Timandra was not willing to let the coach and footmen leave until the mystery ghost had been captured. She had decided to keep Perth with her at Perfidious Brambles. She could not think how she would get on without him. The footman, Kearne, could keep the two younger footmen, Edgar and Hillock, in line, and the coachman, Hardgrove, along with Tombs, was perfectly capable of negotiating the trip over the Pennines to Carlisle and then down to the Lake District and to Knightswood Castle at Grasmere.

Having drifted into sleep, she was enjoying a dream revolving around Gavin, when suddenly she awoke. She sat up in bed. The candle she had left burning was down to a nub and cast but a dim glow. She had no idea what had awakened her, but she rose and found a fresh candle to light off the old one. The new candle threw a brighter light over the

238

chamber, and Timandra looked at the chamber door. Had she heard something? All seemed quiet, but something had awakened her.

She jumped and nearly dropped the candle when Finola touched her arm. "Ye gads! Finola," she hissed in a whisper. "You should not be sneaking up on me."

"I wondered why you were up," Finola asked in a whisper. "Did you hear something? Has the ghost come back?"

Timandra frowned. "I keep telling you, there is no ghost. We are …" She stopped. "Did you hear something?"

"Yes, someone is yelling. And someone is coming up the stairs. Oh, milady!"

"Hold the candle," Timandra said, thrusting the holder into Finola's hand. Donning her robe, Timandra hurried to her side table, picked up her gun, and went to the chamber door. She opened the door just a crack. The yelling was louder, and she thought she smelled smoke. She sensed rather than saw two people flurry past the door, but when Finola arrived behind her with the candle, it cast enough light on the corridor for her to see two figures squeezing behind the tapestry. A third shadowy figure came up behind them, but with his hand on the tapestry, Timandra opened her door and stepped out into the corridor.

"Stop where you are," she commanded. "I have a gun, and I will use it."

The figure stopped and turned toward her. Finola held the candle up higher, and Timandra recognized the shadowy figure. "Sir Osgood!" she said in surprise. She had expected to see one of the footmen.

"Lady Timandra." He bowed awkwardly, his hand still holding the tapestry. "I am afraid I cannot stay. I bid you goodnight."

He started to duck behind the tapestry, but Timandra stepped closer to him. "I cannot miss at this range, Sir Osgood. I hope you will not force me to shoot."

"Lady Timandra, there is a fire below stairs. We need vacate the house. Come, there are stairs here. This is a safe way out." He was starting to look desperate as smoke drifted up the staircase.

"Step away from the tapestry, Sir Osgood, and put your hands behind your back."

"What are you saying? Can you not smell the smoke?"

"Do as you are told, or I will shoot you." She stressed the words will shoot. "And yes, I smell the smoke. I can also hear the shouting, and I must hope my footmen are putting out the fire I feel you must have started. Now, I need to see what is happening downstairs, and you are trying my patience. People on that floor could be in danger." Hardening her voice, she pulled back the hammer on her pistol.

Rolling his eyes, he did as commanded, turning and putting his hands to his back. Timandra said, "Finola, take the sash from my robe and bide his hands. Tightly, Finola."

Setting the candleholder on the floor, Finola did as bid. When she took the sash from Timandra's robe, the robe fell open revealing Timandra had naught but her nightshift under it, but at Finola's questioning look, Timandra just nodded and said, "Now, Finola. Bind his hands."

In a matter of moments Finola had Sir Osgood's hands secured behind his back, and Timandra said, "All right, Sir Osgood, we are going downstairs to see what mischief you have wreaked." She prayed she was correct, that Perth, Edgar, and Gavin, and Gavin's valet, he had brought back with him, were able to control whatever fire Osgood and his footmen had started. If not, she and Finola, along with Osgood, could be stumbling into a dangerous situation. All the same, she had to go. Gavin was down there and so were Eliza and her sisters and their maids.

As Sir Osgood turned, Timandra saw Knolles hurrying toward her from the other end of the corridor. He had a candle in his hand and was shielding the flame with his palm as he hurried toward her. "I smell smoke, Lady Timandra," he said.

Osgood looked surprised to see Knolles on the same floor as Timandra, but after shaking his head, he said, "That is what I have been telling her! We need to get out of here!"

"No, Sir Osgood. We need to see what is happening below." She glanced at Knolles. Not knowing whether they were in any real danger or not, she wanted the boys out of the house. "Get the boys up and take them down the stairs that are behind the tapestry. Finola, show him where the door is and be quick. Sir Osgood, you start down those stairs."

"And if I refuse?" he said, sticking out his chin.

"Then I will shoot you in the leg and leave you here." She aimed her pistol at his leg, and as Finola picked up the candle and hurriedly showed Knolles the door behind the tapestry, Sir Osgood made his way past Timandra to the stairs. Once Finola joined them with the candle, and Knolles hurried back to get Herman and Bennet up and out of the house, Timandra nudged Osgood with the barrel of her pistol, and they started down the stairs.

The smoke was denser and the yelling louder as they reached the bottom of the stairs. At the same time, Seldon, a candle wobbling in his hand, arrived at the top of the stairs leading from the ground floor. "Lady Timandra," he said, "what is happening?"

"It looks to me as though Sir Osgood, here, and his sister have set your house on fire, but it would also seem the fire has been contained and is being put out. I see Perth and Edgar, and Hillock, and even Cook are now but stomping on embers."

But where was Gavin? The maid, Libby, holding a candle high, was standing in the doorway to Charissa and Delilah's bedchamber – the two sisters peering out behind her. The fire had been started in front of the door to what would have been Herman and Bennet's room. Gavin and his valet had been in that room. Giving Osgood another nudge with her pistol, she forced him down the hall. The walls were charred, the door to the room was charred. Smoke still drifted about in the air. Panic seizing her, Timandra demanded, "Perth! Where is Mister Merritt?"

Perth looked around. His normally neat hair straggled about his head and smoke-blackened face. His clothes looked tinged with burn marks. He held a thick wet mat in his hands, but when he looked at her, he stopped beating it on the floor and said, "Mister Merritt and his valet went to see if Tombs caught the ones who set this fire." He then looked hastily away from her, and she remembered for the first time her near undress.

Pulling her robe together at the waist with one hand, but still keeping her gun pointed at Osgood, she said, "He is all right? He is not injured?"

Looking back once Timandra had covered herself, Perth said, "Has a bit of a burn to his hands, but he and his valet are both lucky these doors are sturdy oak. The fire took off hot and fast, but it did little more than char the door. Naught but smoke made it into the bedchamber."

Timandra's heart slowed, and her breath came back into her lungs, as Eliza ran up and grabbed her. "Timmie, Timmie, what is this? What has happened?"

Seldon was coughing, and Timandra turned to him in concern, but Cook, voicing Timandra's worry, said, "Mister Seldon, you need to get yourself back downstairs and away from all this. Your old lungs should not be breathing this smoke. I told Old John to stay below, and I have Lucy in the kitchen making up a bit of meal for everybody."

Seldon looked at Cook and at first shook his head, but another cough shook his body. "Mister Seldon," Mistress Weston said from the servants' staircase, "Cook is right. I have lit the candles in the dining chamber, and Old John is setting out plates. So, if Mistress Tilbury and her sisters will accompany you downstairs, we will see you all have something to drink to calm your nerves. I know I need something to calm mine. Please, do come with me, sir." She held out a hand toward him. It was the first time Timandra could remember seeing the housekeeper do anything gracious.

"Yes, Grandfather," she said, "you and Eliza, too, please go downstairs. Eliza, take your sisters and Libby and Audrey. I will be down very shortly and will explain everything to you."

"What about Hermie and Bennet?" Eliza asked.

"They are fine. Mister Knolles took them outside. I am sure once Knolles knows all is safe, he will bring them back inside."

Eliza peered at Osgood. "Is this not Sir Osgood? What is he doing here?"

"Yes, he is Sir Osgood, and why he is here will also be explained. Now, please all of you, go downstairs. As soon as Perth is sure the fire is out and can take command of Sir Osgood, I will join you." She gave Eliza a little push to the shoulder, and, with her maid Audrey following her, Eliza collected her sisters and their maid Libby and trailed after Mistress Weston and Seldon down the servants' staircase.

"Can you tell me what happened, Perth, or should I wait until we are all gathered downstairs?" Timandra asked.

"You might want to wait, milady. Suffice to say, had Edgar and I not been lying in wait on the stairs, this whole floor could have been up in flames."

Timandra's breath caught in her throat, and she looked at Osgood. Shaking her head, she said, "How could you?"

Firming his lips, he shrugged and turned his head away from her.

Perth said, "Milady, I think Edgar and Hillock can stay here and watch to make sure no sparks are left. If you would like, I will escort Sir Osgood downstairs."

"Yes," Cook said. "I had best make sure Lucy and the new scullery maid have got ale poured and a good meal ready to help us all relax before we regain our beds." She glanced at Edgar and Hillock and said, "I will send some ale and bread and cheese up to you lads, too."

"We are thanking you, Cook," Edgar said.

"Milady," Finola whispered, touching Timandra's arm. "I will be running up to get a sash to go round your robe." She nodded to Osgood's bound hands. "Your robe sash being used."

Timandra smiled. "Thank you, Finola." Still holding her robe closed, she followed down the stairs after Cook and Perth, Perth's hand on Osgood's shoulder. She wished she could see Gavin. Know that he was truly all right. What if they had not suspected Osgood and his sister meant to kill the boys? What if Finola had not seen Mistress Clackenberger roaming the corridors? Had not seen her outside the boys' room?

Timandra's heart skipped a beat. Could be the boys owed their lives to Finola. Had Finola not been spending time helping Cook or flirting with Perth when she should have been attending to things for Timandra, she would never have spotted Clackenberger, would never have thought she was seeing a ghost. And but to prove to Finola no ghost existed, Timandra would never have investigated behind the tapestry and would not have found the secret staircase.

Upon arriving at the foot of the stairs, Timandra saw Gavin entering the kitchen, and her heart leapt into her throat. Like the footmen and Cook, his face and clothing were blackened by smoke, but he looked hale and hearty, and she rushed past Cook, Perth, and Osgood to throw herself into his arms. Caring not that her display was unladylike, or that she had nothing but her flimsy nightshift between her and his damp and blackened shirt, or that her shift would soon be as blackened as his shirt, she but reveled in her joy that the man she loved was unharmed.

Gavin's arms closed around her, and he held her close for a moment before lightly kissing her forehead and saying, "Timandra, dear."

Looking over his shoulder, Timandra saw Mistress Clackenberger with Tombs right behind her. Tombs seemed to be waiting for Timandra to release Gavin before entering the bustling kitchen. "You caught her!" Timandra said.

"And you caught Osgood," Gavin said, not hiding his awe. "How did you manage that?"

Still clutching the pistol in her hand, she showed it to Gavin. "And I know how to use it, I can assure you." She looked over her shoulder at Osgood. "Sir Osgood never doubted it."

"I had no idea you had a pistol, or that you knew how to use one. Had I known, I would have felt much easier knowing you and Finola were up on the second floor alone in your room. I would have worried less."

She smiled up at Gavin. "Had I known they were going to set a fire outside your door, never would I have consented to having you stay in the boys' bedchamber. But now I can see you are not harmed, just smelly and dirty, I can rejoice. And, we have Sir Osgood and Mistress Clackenberger. But what of the two footmen? Did they escape?"

"Nay, milady," Tombs said, pushing Mistress Clackenberger into the kitchen once Gavin urged Timandra to step aside. "With the help of Hardgrove, Putnam, and Tibbs, we have them bound and secured in one of the stalls in the stable. Mister Merritt felt we should bring Mistress Clackenberger inside. At least for the present. We were watching for Osgood to come out behind Mistress Clackenberger, but Knolles and the boys appeared instead. Surprised us it did, but Knolles told us you had Osgood and were forcing him to go back downstairs. We then had Hardgrove and Putnam take the other footman to join his comrade, and we decided to bring Mistress Clackenberger here."

"Yes," Gavin said, "We have much to discuss with the woman." He glanced at Osgood. "And her brother."

Cook said, "All of you go into the dining chamber. Mister Seldon and Mistress Tilbury are awaiting you. Mistress Weston has wine poured for the ladies, and ale for you men. Lucy and I will soon be finished frying up this pork I had planned for the morning. Bread, cheese, and a couple of sweet butters are on the table. Now, give me room here in my kitchen."

Finola arrived with a sash Timandra could tie around her robe, and Mister Knolles arrived with two very excited young boys. For a few minutes no one else could say a word as the boys exclaimed over the secret staircase and proposed numerous games they could play on them.

When everyone, including Perth and Tombs and Osgood and Clackenberger, were seated at the table, Timandra squeezed in close to Gavin. Cook and Lucy brought in the rest of the hurriedly prepared meal. Lucy, with the aid of the young scullery maid, hurried off to take ale and bread, cheese, and bacon to Edgar and Hillock, who were making sure no embers were still smoldering upstairs. The girls would then take refreshments out to the stables to the coachmen and postillion standing guard over Sir Osgood's footmen. With thirsts slackened, everyone, most wearing naught but their sleep apparel, turned to Gavin.

Chapter 32

Gavin turned to his grandfather. "How are you, Grandfather? You seem to be coughing a bit." Timandra liked that Gavin's first concern was for his grandfather.

"You are not to worry about my cough," the old man said, waving his hand. "What of you? Are you burned?"

"My hands are singed a little, but I know after I eat, Cook will give me something to put on them." He glanced down to the end of the table. "Woolsey, my valet, has burns on his hands as well. Upon hearing Perth and Edgar yelling, and not knowing the cause was a fire, I opened the door to the bedchamber. That caused the flames to jump higher. The flames were licking at the door and were covering the floor."

Timandra took one of Gavin's hands and frowned. Anger filling her heart, she glared at Osgood and then Clackenberger.

With Timandra gently holding Gavin's hand, he gave her a little smile before he too looked at the culprits. "Our unwelcome guests had soaked rags in some kind of oil, placed them before the door and along the corridor, and set them on fire."

"In the dark," Perth said, when Gavin nodded at him, "Edgar and I could not see what they were doing. We could but hear them. We were waiting for them to open the door to the bedchamber, then we were set to spring upon them. Not until Sir Osgood struck a flint, and the spark caught, did we know what they had done. The scattered rags quickly burst into flames. I sent Edgar down to rouse Hillock and the others and to bring buckets of water, and I started trying to kick the rags away from the door."

"That is when I opened the door," Gavin said, resuming the tale, "and sent the flames spiraling. Woolsey and I grabbed the blankets off the beds and tried to cover the flames, but the oil soaked into the blankets and they were soon smoldering, though not blazing like the rags had been. It was when we were using another blanket to try to pat out the flames licking up the door that we burned our hands. Fortunately, Edgar and Hillock soon arrived with heavy mats Cook keeps in the kitchen to smother any fires that might start there when she is cooking. They started beating the flames, and then Cook and Lucy arrived with a couple of buckets of water, and we got the blaze under control. That is when I decided to go see if Tombs had managed to catch the perpetrators of the fire."

Gavin again looked at his grandfather. "We will not be able to assess the extent of the damage until later."

His grandfather shook his head. "That no one is severely injured, that is what matters."

"Yes," Timandra said, looking first at Gavin, and then at everyone around the table. "That all of you are safe, that is of the first importance. Perth, that you and Edgar, Hillock, and Tombs, and Cook and Mistress Weston…" she waved her hands expansively. "Oh, and all of you did so much to help put out the fire and catch these evil doers." She glanced again at Osgood and his sister before returning her gaze to the others at the table. "We are so grateful to all of you."

"How did you know they meant to do something bad?" Eliza asked, looking first at Timandra and then at Gavin. "And why did they want to?"

"That is a long story, Eliza, and I will tell you everything tomorrow, but first, I want to know from Tombs how he caught the two footmen and Mistress Clackenberger."

Eliza said she was willing to wait, and all eyes turned to Tombs.

"That was easy," Tombs said with a confident smile and a sidelong glance at Mistress Clackenberger. "I had sent Hardgrove and Tibbs to bed, but I had Putnam with me. We took up a position where we could see not only any riders arriving, but we also had a clear view of the secret-staircase door.

"I was surprised to see four riders this time, but Osgood was easily recognizable in the moonlight. I saw they were taking things from their horses, but I could not make out what they were carrying. I sent Putnam to awaken Hardgrove and Tibbs, and I stayed and watched them. They left one man with the horses, and three of them headed to the house.

"When Putnam returned with the coachmen, I sent them to keep an eye on the three slipping into the house, and Putnam and I snuck up on the footman waiting with the horses. We quickly overpowered him, and he was soon trussed up and resting easy in the stables. Putnam and I then joined Hardgrove and Tibbs and waited for the other three to come back out.

"And out they came, all but Osgood. Putnam and I bound the other footman and Mistress Clackenberger, then Tibbs took the footman back to the stable to join his friend while Putnam and Hardgrove waited for Osgood, whom you, Lady Timandra, had already apprehended. For the present, Putnam and Hardgrove are watching our prisoners. Come first light, I will ride into Fairflex for the bailiff, there being no constable in the village. But they do have a small stone gaol that we can transfer these culprits to until the constable can come from Newcastle."

"You would not put me in that gaol, would you?" Mistress Clackenberger said, the look on her face showing her dismay. She and her brother sat in seats at the center of the table with Perth on one side of them and Tombs on the other. Their hands had been freed that they might quench their thirsts, but they seemed to know they would be foolish to attempt an escape.

"I cannot think where else you could be safely kept, Mistress Clackenberger," Gavin said.

The woman looked at her brother. He but shrugged and looked away from her. She turned her gaze on Timandra. "Surely, Lady Timandra, surely you would have mercy on me."

Timandra slowly shook her head. "I think not, Mistress Clackenberger. To think what you and your brother have tried to do." With Herman and Bennet sitting at the table, their eyes wide as they watched the adults, she could not say that Clackenberger and her brother had been trying to kill the boys. That could frighten them. Better they never know how close they had come to being killed.

Rising from his seat at the end of the table, Seldon said, "I think we should all try to get some sleep. Morning will be here before we know it, and we will all have much to do. Gavin, I cannot think your room will be fit for you to sleep in."

"Nor do I think so, Grandfather."

"Have Mistress Weston give your valet some sheets and go spend the night in the east wing," Seldon said, nodding first to his housekeeper and then to Gavin's valet. "It has been aired out enough in the past couple of days that you should be comfortable there."

"Splendid idea," Gavin said, rising as both his valet, Woolsey, and Mistress Weston rose and headed out of the dining chamber. As if that was a signal, everyone started rising. Knolles was shepherding the boys out, and Eliza, after blowing Timandra a kiss, was urging her sisters and the maids, Audrey and Libby, toward the door.

"Wait," Timandra said. "Eliza, you and the girls cannot sleep on that floor with all that smoke smell. Have Audrey and Libby get sheets from Mistress Weston and make up the bed in the room across from mine for the girls, and you can sleep in my room tonight."

"Timandra is right," Gavin said. "No one can think to sleep on that floor until it has been aired out and thoroughly cleaned. We will know in the morning how bad things are."

"Thank you, Timmie," Eliza said. "We will first see Mistress Weston and then head upstairs to your room. The girls can wait there until the bedchamber can be readied."

"What of those two?" Tombs asked Gavin, nodding to Clackenberger and Osgood.

"You can make them comfortable in the stables with the two footmen. You will need to see to their horses. Best not leave them out in the woods."

"I already told Putnam to unsaddle them and turn them out in the corral."

"Good man," Gavin said.

"I will help Tombs escort this pair back to the stables, Mister Merritt," Perth said. "I would think, sir, you would need to collect a salve for your and Woolsey's hands."

"Right you are, Perth. Bind these two again, then you may take them out."

Mistress Clackenberger pleaded and groaned, but in the end, her hands were bound behind her. Osgood was bound with rope, and Timandra's robe sash was returned to her. Soon everyone had left the dining chamber but Timandra and Gavin. Gavin took the opportunity to pull Timandra into his arms. She made no protest, though knowing in her present near undress, she should be more circumspect.

"My wonderful soon-to-be-bride," Gavin said. "You are so brave. I should chastise you for so putting yourself at risk, but I find I cannot. Nor can I be surprised by your courage and quick thinking. Those are some of your attributes that won my love. Now, I will claim a quick kiss before Lucy returns to start clearing the dishes. I heard Grandfather tell Cook to let all clean up in the kitchen wait until the morrow, and everyone has been told to sleep until they wake in the morning, but if I know Tombs, he will be up and on his way to get the Fairflex bailiff. And we will need to send someone to Dwight to tell him what has happened."

"And to make certain he is all right," Timandra added, hoping she was soon going to get the kiss Gavin had promised.

"True," Gavin agreed, "Come morning, Dwight will be wondering where his guests are." Then with a sweet smile, he cupped Timandra's face with his hand and brought his lips to hers. At last, she thought, eagerly responding to his kiss. Hearing footsteps, they broke apart as Lucy and the young scullery maid entered the chamber. With a nod to the girls, Timandra and Gavin headed off in different directions; he to find Cook for some salve for his hands, and she to return to her bedchamber. Though whether she would be able to sleep was another question.

As they parted, Gavin chuckled. "No doubt Kearne will be surprised at my and Woolsey's appearance. At the distance the east wing is to this wing, Kearne cannot have any idea of all that has been happening here."

Timandra agreed, and with a candle she had taken from the dining chamber to light her way, she headed to her room. Gavin was right, Kearne would have no idea what had happened – and neither would Gavin's mother. Timandra smiled. Gavin's mother should be told about her son's injury, and her father's cough. Yes, before she went to bed, Timandra decided to write a letter to Mistress Merritt. She would tell the dear lady that her son's injuries were minor, and she should not worry about him. Timandra would add she was certain the cough Mistress Merritt's father suffered would not be long lasting.

In the morning, when the groomsmen arrived from the hamlet, she would send one to Kirkworth Hall with the letter. She guessed, in very short order, Mistress Merritt would be arriving at Perfidious Brambles's door.

Chapter 33

Timandra had not expected to be able to sleep, but she had, and had not awakened until Eliza gently prodded her, saying, "Timmie, Timmie, the sun is well up, and I think we should be getting dressed. You promised to tell me why Sir Osgood and Mistress Clackenberger wanted to set fire to the house, and how you knew about it. I must have something to tell the boys. Before Knolles could get them back to bed last night, I had to calm them and promise them that you and Cousin Gavin had fixed everything. You have fixed everything, have you not?"

Blinking and half-asleep, Timandra tried to pay heed to what Eliza was saying, but Eliza's announcement that the sun was well up had her more immediate attention. "Is Finola up yet?" she asked.

"Yes, she slipped out a little before I woke you. I hated to wake you. I know you must be exhausted after all that has happened, but ..."

Timandra broke in on Eliza's apology. "You have no need to apologize, dear friend. Indeed, I am glad you woke me. I cannot believe I slept so late. Let us rise and dress, and afterwards, I will explain everything to you."

Climbing out of bed, she found her robe and quickly drew open the draperies to let in the bright morning sun. "Trust Finola not to be here when I need her," she said, going to the armoire in the corner of the room to pull out a gown and petticoats.

"I think Finola went with Audrey to my room to get some of my clothes. I hope they are not so smoke damaged I cannot wear them."

Timandra frowned and shook out her gown before laying it on the bed. "I would guess Finola and Audrey will be bringing your clothes up here. I think we will be sharing this room for some time to come. Hopefully, just shaking your clothing out really well will give you something to wear until other things can be more properly aired, or if need be, washed. Same for Charissa and Delilah's clothes."

She no sooner finished speaking than Audrey and Finola entered the room with Eliza's clothes. "These I think are wearable," Audrey said. "The rest of your things, and mine, we will hang outside to air. Libby is seeing to Mistress Charissa and Delilah, and I promised to help her." She looked from Eliza to Finola. "Finola said she could help both you and Lady Timandra to dress."

Smiling brightly, Finola agreed to Audrey's statement, so Audrey was allowed to go assist Libby. Finola then bustled about getting Timandra and Eliza dressed and their hair done up in buns atop their heads. Chatting away, Finola described the first floor.

"Perth and Edgar have every window and door open, and that is helping clear the smoke smell out. Mistress Weston already has several women from the hamlet scrubbing and cleaning. Mister Merritt says he believes only a small portion of the floor will need be replaced, and he sent Kipp, the gardener's son, to the hamlet to bring the carpenter to have a look. Mister Merritt says he hopes a local man can repair the floor, and he will not need to send to Newcastle for someone."

Giggling, she said, "Imagine this! Mister Seldon says he is not concerned about the expense. He wants everything repaired as quickly as possible because..." she looked expectantly at Timandra. Giggling again, she added, "Because he wants all in readiness for when guests arrive for your wedding, milady. I do believe he is near as excited as Mister Merritt about your wedding plans."

Ignoring Finola's last comment, Timandra said, "Thank you for helping us dress. Now I need speak with Mistress Tilbury. But first, what of the boys? Do you know where they are?"

Stopping at the door, Finola said, "Last I saw them, they were attempting to convince Mister Knolles they should have a holiday and should be allowed to investigate the secret stairs. Oh, and the letter you wrote last night, I gave it to one of the groomsmen to take to Mistress Merritt, as you said you wanted."

Timandra glanced over at her writing desk. She had completely forgotten about the letter, but Finola had not. Troublesome as Finola sometimes was, she was a gem. "Thank you," she said, as Finola darted out of the room, off to help Audrey and Libby.

✿ ✿ ✿ ✿

Eliza was aghast upon learning Osgood and Clackenberger's real intent had been to kill Herman and Bennet. Tears filled her eyes, and she clung to Timandra, thanking her over and over for protecting her brothers. The details of the plans to catch the culprits, the suspicions, but lack of evidence that had forced them to let Osgood and Clackenberger play out their hand, Timandra patiently explained to Eliza.

"So you must see why, dear friend, that Mister Seldon thought it best, as your guardian, that the responsibility for protecting your brothers rested on his shoulders. We could well have been wrong, and then we would have worried you for no good reason. It was your uncle's decision, and Gavin and I could do naught but abide by his wishes."

Eliza slowly shook her head. "I would never have thought Uncle Percival would care so much for us. He seemed so cold when we first arrived here. But he has changed so much. I do believe he really is fond of us."

"I think he was a sad, lonely, old man, but having you and the children in the house has brought new life back to him. He has purpose in his life again. He may grump and grouch now and then, but you notice, he has never complained when the boys have been allowed to join us at the table. And he bought the new horses for the boys and for Charissa and Delilah. Yes, I think you can readily say, he is quite fond of all of you.

"But now, I think we must see what is happening in the house. My guess is your uncle will be wanting his dinner at its usual time. As we all had that repast late last night, or mayhap it was early this morning, I do think everyone will be eager for dinner, even if a few have broken their fast already."

When they arrived on the first floor, Timandra and Eliza found all was bustling. Mistress Weston advised them to take a quick look and then keep out of the way. The women who would have been working on the east wing, readying it for Timandra and Gavin, were instead employed in cleaning the west wing's first floor. Draperies and floor coverings were being taken out to be aired and beaten. All clothing had been removed and would either be aired or washed. According to Mistress Weston, the laundress had brought three assistants to help with the number of clothing items and the sheets and blankets that would need to be washed and dried. There would no doubt be some items that would need to be pressed.

Timandra's heart stood still for a moment when she saw the burned area in front of the room where Gavin had been waiting for the villains. The damage was worse in the light than it had appeared at night. Gavin could have been seriously injured, even killed. She had to put such thoughts out of her head, or she would soon be trembling and unable to stand. Best they follow Mistress Weston's advice and head down to the ground floor. She needed to see Gavin. Just being with him would ease her panic.

They had barely reached the bottom of the stairs when a loud knock sounded at the door. Old John, who had been heading to the parlor, turned to answer the door. Timandra was not surprised to see Mistress Merritt and Lord Kirkworth being bowed into the house. Andrew, looking confused, trailed in behind them. Timandra and Eliza immediately went forward to greet their guests.

"Dear Lady Timandra," Mistress Merritt said, grasping Timandra's hands. "I had to come after I received your message. You said there had been a fire, and Gavin was injured, and my father was having trouble breathing."

"Yes," Lord Kirkworth said, "what is this about a fire? Here in this wing of the house? How could it have started?"

"Indeed," Andrew said. "Is Mistress Delilah all right?"

Timandra glanced at Andrew and said, "She is fine." Redirecting her gaze to Mistress Merritt, she gave her hands a squeeze. "There is much to tell you."

"Mister Seldon is in the parlor," Old John told Timandra. "As is Mister Merritt. Shall I announce Mistress Merritt and Lord Kirkworth?"

"Oh, yes, please do." Timandra looked at the guests and said, "Do go into the parlor. Eliza and I will join you soon. Cook will be expecting Andrew to be here, but we must let her know two more will be joining us for dinner." She looked from Gavin's mother to his uncle. "You will be staying for dinner, will you not?"

Lord Kirkworth harrumphed. "You think Seldon will ask us to join you?"

Timandra nodded. "Yes, yes I do. I think you will find him greatly changed." She turned to Old John. "John, do you announce them. We will be but a moment."

Grabbing Eliza's hand, she hurried off toward the kitchen. In case she was wrong, and Seldon ended up rudely attacking his daughter and Lord Kirkworth, Timandra had not wanted Eliza caught in the middle, so she dragged her along behind her. Upon encountering Perth, she gave him the message to give to the cook, and she and Eliza arrived back at the parlor in time to see Mistress Merritt turn from embracing Gavin to embrace her father.

Their hands still locked together, Timandra and Eliza stopped in the doorway as Seldon exploded, "Now what is this!" With a lot of spluttering and fumbling, he extracted himself from his daughter's embrace.

Not being easily pushed away, Mistress Merritt said, "Oh, Father, when I received Lady Timandra's message that you might be suffering from the smoke inhalation, I was so afraid. Really, Father, I could not let you go to your grave without you knowing how much I love you."

"Well, I am not bound for my grave. At least not yet." Seldon's voice softened. "But I must admit, your concern does you credit, daughter."

"Dear Father, I am sick to death of this impasse between us. You grow old, and I have not been here to share with you the joys of my son, your grandson." She glanced at Gavin who had a smile hovering about his lips. "Things we should have laughed and cried about together, we can never reclaim. The pride we both felt as we watched Gavin grow into the fine man he has become. And now, as Gavin goes into this new phase in his life, with Lady Timandra at his side, with the babes that will join them, I want to share these things with you, Father. What say you?"

Seldon looked over his daughter's head at Timandra. "This is your doing, is it not Timandra?"

Timandra had to smile. "I did think it best to tell Mistress Merritt about the injuries Gavin suffered, though I told her they were mild. And I had to mention your coughing. But I am greatly relieved to see you seem to have recovered this morning."

"Humph." Seldon snorted then turned to Kirkworth. "I suppose I am expected to accept you into my home now also."

"I cannot see why not, Grandfather," Gavin said, entering the fray with a chuckle. "He no longer holds the land you claim was stolen by the Kirkworth's. As I told you, Uncle Phineas has given the land to Timandra and me. So you no longer have any reason to feud."

"Gavin is right, Seldon" Kirkworth said. "We have naught to feud about anymore. And as we will often be attending the same events once Gavin and Lady Timandra marry and move into your east wing, I think it would be more pleasant for all concerned if we could meet, mayhap not as friends, but without animosity."

"I will think on it, Kirkworth," Seldon said, and turning back to his daughter, he added, "I would think if we are to share all these moments with Gavin and Timandra, that we could more easily share them if you moved back home."

"Oh, Father!" Tears sprang to Mistress Merritt's eyes, and she again wrapped her arms around her father. "Yes, yes, I would love to come back home. But not until after the wedding. Gavin has told us Lady Timandra has a large family, and you may well need all the rooms here at Perfidious Brambles to house them."

"Speaking of rooms, Seldon," Lord Kirkworth said, "if your fire damage is bad, I have a man who can repair near anything, including floors. That is, if you are in need of someone."

Seldon patted his daughter on the back before releasing her and turning to Kirkworth. "Come upstairs with me, and I will show you the damage. At present, we are but cleaning and airing out the chambers and corridor, but there is one spot where the flooring is badly damaged. I have a man can repair the wall's wainscoting and plaster, but I had thought I might have to send to Newcastle to find someone who knew enough about the supports for the floor to repair it."

"Happy to have a look," Kirkworth said. "I would think even if there is an outright hole in the flooring my man can repair it."

"Let us have a look then," Seldon said. "You come along, too, Gavin." He looked at Timandra. "As you are responsible for getting my daughter here, Timandra, I believe you can entertain her until we return."

"I will, Grandfather." Timandra smiled. "And I also took the liberty of telling Cook two more besides Andrew would be joining us for dinner."

"Why does that not surprise me?" Seldon said. He shook his head. "Well, come with me, Kirkworth. We will leave the women to chat until time for dinner. Seems you will be joining us."

When the men left the parlor with Andrew following after them, Mistress Merritt embraced Timandra. "What have you done to my father, Lady Timandra? Gavin has been telling us he hardly knows him. Gavin says his grandfather has become so lighthearted. And I think you must have known, with that note you sent me, that I would have to come to see if Gavin and Father were truly unharmed."

Timandra laughed. "I admit to having hopes the note would bring you here. I thought it was high time you two stopped your feuding. After all, when Gavin and I are living here, we would expect to have you and Gavin's uncle and aunt here often. But it will be even better if you move back here to Perfidious Brambles. Having you to help direct Charissa and Delilah as they become young women, and Herman and Bennet as they grow into youths will be an immense help to your father." She extended an arm out to Eliza. "Especially as Eliza may have wedding plans once her year of mourning is over."

Mistress Merritt embraced Eliza. "I am happy for you, child. What a lot you have been through. If you have found a young man to love, nothing could be more beautiful. And I will be most happy to assume responsibility for your siblings."

"Oh, thank you, Cousin Emeline," Eliza gushed. "I was wondering how I might agree to marry Bartley, er ah, Mister Severin, when he proposes. I could hardly expect Timandra to take responsibility for my siblings, although, I have to say she has already done so much to help me with them. And I could not think Uncle Percival would be able to see to their needs."

"Well, you need stop worrying," Mistress Merritt said with a smile that was so much like Gavin's and Seldon's. "I will enjoy having the bright laughter of children ringing through the house. I always enjoyed having Gavin's friends visit. Speaking of the children, where are they?"

"Herman and Bennet will be with their tutor, and the girls slept late, what with all the flurry last night. They will be down shortly, I'm sure, as Uncle Percival is never late for his dinner hour. And as none of us have eaten since Cook fed us a late night repast after the excitement of the fire, I am sure we will all be ready for dinner."

"You must tell me about the fire," Mistress Merritt said. "How did it start?"

As they had all still been standing near the entrance, Timandra suggested they sit, and she would tell Mistress Merritt how the fire came about. "It is not a short story, but I will try to make it as uncomplicated as I can. But first, I must ask you, please, to call me Timandra. No need to be formal. You will soon be my dear mother-in-law."

"Thank you, and you must call me Emeline," Mistress Merritt said, taking the seat Timandra offered.

Timandra had barely finished recounting the events surrounding the fire to Mistress Merritt, Emeline, as she must remember to call her, when the men trooped back into the parlor. Rising, Emeline rose and went over to embrace her son. "Oh, Gavin, how could you not have told me someone was attempting to kill you? And then to put yourself at risk here. Why, you could have been badly burned or killed."

"Now, Emmie," Kirkworth said. "Gavin has explained all to me, and I find it was a most sensible plan. Had they not captured those two villains, Gavin would still be in danger, as would the two boys. What surprises me is how Dwight could have been so taken in by that woman. The one time he brought her and her brother by our house, I found both Clackenberger and her brother bordering on the vulgar side."

Withdrawing from Gavin's embrace, Emeline said, "I think mayhap Dwight might be lonely. We must invite him to visit more often. Could be what he needs is a nice respectable and sensible wife."

"Yes," Timandra said. "That is a wonderful idea. Once Gavin and I are settled in our home, we must consider having Dwight visit. And I would guess Ebba Hemphill would know all the eligible women in the parish. We could consult with her when planning a guest list."

"Listen to them, would you?" Seldon said. "Not enough we have the house to repair, the east wing to ready, the wedding to plan, and that school they want me to have built, now they are deciding to play matchmakers for my nephew."

Before anyone could answer Seldon, Old John appeared at the door and announced, "Dinner is ready to be served, Mister Seldon."

"And in the nick of time. I am near starved," Seldon said. "And I see Charissa and Delilah have finally decided to join us. Come Kirkworth, as Timandra ordered two extra plates set, and as we will be seeing each other on many occasions, let us start off this new relationship by breaking bread together."

The crinkles around Kirkworth's eyes became more pronounced as he smiled and said, "Delighted, Seldon, delighted."

Chapter 34

Sitting at her writing desk, Timandra addressed yet another invitation. Lord, but she had a huge family on her mother's side. Aunts and uncles, close cousins, less close but still dear cousins, distant cousins, and really distant cousins – those being members of the large D'Arcy clan that had bred over a couple of centuries at and around Tyneford Hall and Hexham and bordering regions. Near ten generations, all stemming from the D'Arcy stewards of Tyneford Hall. In a recent letter, her mother had told her the near proximity of those much-removed cousins made it important they be invited. Then there were all of great, great Aunt Alfreda's progeny and their children and grandchildren.

On her father's side, she had but her Aunt Venetia and her family, and her Cousin Delphine, who was like an aunt, and her family. She knew they would come to the wedding, but how many of her D'Arcy family members would come, she could not guess. All she could do was sit and write invitations until her hand wore out. Thankfully, Eliza, Charissa, and Delilah were helping her, and Gavin's mother and aunt were graciously writing the invitations for their family and friends. They also knew the locals who would need to be invited.

The wedding date was set for the second week in October. That should give everyone who wanted to come, time to make the journey, and should allow them to return home before the worst of the rains made the highways near impassable. Gavin's uncle had not only had his carpenter help with repairing the corridor and Herman and Bennet's bedchamber fire damages, he had also sent several workers to help spruce up the Perfidious Brambles Keep and rebuild the chapel, so the wedding could be held in the Keep. And if the weather was nice, as the gardens were now beautiful, guests could spill out into the garden.

Timandra and Gavin had been spending as much time together as they could. They had so much to plan. They already missed Tombs.

He was so handy to deal with so many small or large details, but he had left with the three footmen, Kearne, Hillock, and Edgar, and of course the coachman and postilion, to return Timandra's father's coach to Knightswood Castle, so her parents and siblings could use it to come to her wedding.

Colyer had returned from Newcastle, and after going over Seldon's accounts with him, Seldon had decided he would pay for the school to be built. The area for the school had been surveyed, leveled, and construction supplies ordered. They had decided not to try to build a house for the school master – Knolles had accepted the position – until the following year. With Bennet still so young, they wanted Knolles to remain in the house with him for another year. And, they would be able to pay for the house to be built with the profits from the sale of the wool and the lambs, and the rents paid by the tenants.

Putting her quill down, Timandra shook her hand. Only a few more, and she would have completed her list. She had two more interviews to conduct after dinner. They had yet to hire a cook. Timandra feared she was being picky, but she wanted someone as capable and as good-natured as Seldon's cook. Perth had been released from his contract with Timandra's parents and was now to be her house steward. Finola was to be promoted to housekeeper. Timandra hated that she would have to find a personal maid to take Finola's place. Finola would have to hold both positions until Timandra found a maid she liked.

The footman, Edgar, planned to ask to be released from his contract. He had formed an attachment to Libby, and Seldon had offered him a job as assistant to Old John, and when John finally needed to retire, Edgar would become Perfidious Brambles's house steward. Tombs, too, was asking to be released from his contract. He enjoyed working for Timandra and Gavin, and Gavin had offered him an extraordinary wage to retain his services. "He is too useful a man to let him get away from us," Gavin had said the day before Tombs left for Knightswood. "If we are going to be making long distance visits to your family and friends, I want Tombs as our outrider." Timandra had agreed. Tombs was a definite asset.

Resting her chin on her hand, Timandra dreamily hoped Gavin would soon return from Newcastle, where he had been looking at horses for the coach they had ordered. The Tilbury coach would be needed to take Charissa and Delilah, and Eliza, until she married Severin, to Fairflex or to visit friends. Timandra and Gavin needed their own coach for trips they might want to take, including long-distance visits to her parents. And of course, there was the D'Arcy family reunion at Uncle Kenrick's Walling House in Wallingford the following year. Any family members who could not make it to her wedding, she would most likely see at the reunion that was held every four years.

She picked up her quill to start another invitation when Finola came in with a message from Seldon that he wanted to see Timandra at her earliest convenience. "Did he say what he wanted?" Timandra asked.

"No, milady, but that new groomsman he hired to live above the stables and to help the coachman just returned from Fairflex. He took a letter into Mister Seldon."

Timandra nodded. "My hand is tired anyway. I shall go now to see what he wants."

"Yes, milady. If you have no special need for me, I have the rent in your riding costume you wanted repaired before you ride out again."

"Oh, thank you, Finola. I had forgotten about it. Yes, do your magic with the needle."

Leaving Finola to repair the tear in her skirt where a tree had snagged it, Timandra headed down to Seldon's rooms. She had grown to love the old man, and she loved having a grandfather for the first time in her life. Both her mother's and her father's fathers had died before Timandra was born. At least she had occasionally been able to see her mother's mother and her father's grandmother. She had fond memories of both women.

She tapped on Seldon's door, and he bade her enter. "Finola said you wanted to see me, Grandfather. As I have wearied of writing invitations, I thought I would join you at once. I hope this is a good time for you."

"It is, Timandra. Do sit down. I have some interesting news to tell you. I wish Gavin was here to share it with him, but you can tell him when he returns. You can tell Eliza as well, and she may impart however much she wants to her siblings."

Cocking her head to one side, and a slight smile touching her lips,

Timandra said, "This sounds intriguing. I am glad I came right down."

Seldon unfolded two sheets of paper and smoothed them out on his table. "This is from the Fairflex bailiff. As you recall, your man, Tombs, wrote to a person he knew in London asking for information on Sir Osgood Pettimill and Mistress Clackenberger. Knowing he would be headed back to your parents, Tombs asked his acquaintance in London to send any information he acquired to the bailiff, and the bailiff was to forward it on to me. The bailiff has had a clerk copy it and will be sending the copy on to the constable in Newcastle."

Shaking his head, Seldon chuckled. "Seems Pettimill and Clackenberger are not brother and sister. They are husband and wife."

"What! How can that be?" Shocked, Timandra stared at Seldon. "I thought she planned to marry your nephew, Mister Crenshaw."

"Apparently that became her plan when she thought Dwight was second in line after Gavin to inherent Perfidious Brambles." Seldon looked down at the paper in front of him and ran his finger down the page until he found what he wanted. "According to this fellow, Drescott, the man whom Tombs contacted to investigate Pettimill and Clackenberger..." He looked up. "Oh, and both names are made-up. They are the Bakers, and Sir Osgood is neither a knight nor a baronet. He is simply Osgood Baker.

"It seems, though Viola was married to Osgood, she also married a Hiram Bryson, a rather wealthy merchant who died rather mysteriously. Osgood and Viola disappeared with his rather large fortune when a cousin of Bryson started questioning Bryson's death."

"Oh, my. Do you think they killed the man? They were bent on killing Gavin and Herman and Bennet."

"Drescott says the sheriff of Kent, which is where they lived, near Dover, has issued a warrant for their arrest for questioning, but they escaped to Italy, which is where they met Dwight. From what Drescott learned from contacts he has in Italy, the Bakers lived rather high, and by the time they met Dwight, they had gone through most of Bryson's fortune.

"As they had done before, they decided to again be brother and sister. Whether they meant to just live off Dwight while they planned what to do next, we have no way of knowing, and they are not talking. But their two footmen are, according to the bailiff. By informing on the Bakers, they hope to avoid the rope and be transported to the colonies instead."

"Poor Mister Crenshaw," Timandra said. "He could not have been more devastated."

Seldon snorted. "Yes, he has apologized more times than needed, but his offer to pay for the repair to the fire damage, I readily accepted. I think that made him feel some better. I cannot think he is broken hearted."

Timandra nodded, "I would think it would be difficult to be broken hearted over someone who was so evil and devious. And who never loved him."

Chuckling, Seldon said, "Wait until he finds out she was already married to Osgood."

Timandra laughed, too, then covered her mouth with her hand. "Oh, we should not laugh. It is never fun to be made the fool."

"True, but Dwight brought this on himself. Should have married years ago and raised a family. I put some of the blame on my sister, his mother, but he should have stood up to her."

Looking back at the letter, Timandra asked, "Is there more?"

"Ah, yes. Seems the Bakers needed financing to put their murder plan to work. They meant to have those two footmen kill Gavin. That is where they made their biggest mistake. They knew a man in London who would make loans to anyone, but at very high interest rates. Thinking their plan was easy, they wrote to the moneylender and received a loan to cover what they thought were their needs.

"Drescott is guessing that before they knew about Herman and Bennet, the Bakers figured they could have Gavin killed, Viola would marry Dwight, have me killed, and Perfidious Brambles would be theirs. They would then be able to pay back this notorious moneylender, Andrus, and would again be living high with, no doubt, eventual plans to kill Dwight."

Seldon frowned. "Seems this moneylender wanted his money, or at least, a hefty interest payment. That is what made the Bakers panic and become desperate. Again, this is according to Drescott, Andrus is not known to be a patient man. He is known to cause physical harm when his payments are not met."

"And so they had no choice but to try to kill Herman and Bennet so they could then kill Gavin," Timandra said with a shake to her head.

"That would seem to be the case. As I said, the Fairflex bailiff has sent a copy of this letter to the constable. With this evidence brought to light along with the testimony of the two fraudulent footmen, the Bakers will probably see the rope. If not here, then in Dover where they face possible murder charges. Bryson's death being in question."

"Is that it?" Timandra asked, looking at the letter.

Seldon nodded, "Yes, I would say we are all lucky you, and your maid Finola, accompanied the Tilburys to Perfidious Brambles. Otherwise, Herman and Bennet, and Gavin and I might well be dead. We would never have suspected the Bakers."

Timandra got up and went around to the other side of the table. Squatting in a most unladylike fashion beside Seldon's chair, she put her arms around him. "Accompanying Eliza to Perfidious Brambles was the best decision I have ever made. It has given me Gavin, a wonderful home, and a grandfather. I am the lucky one."

Patting Timandra's shoulder, Seldon gave her the most loving smile she had yet to see on his face. "For the first time in more years than I care to count, I look forward to daybreak. I look forward to being alive. Thank you, my granddaughter."

Rising, Timandra placed a kiss on Seldon's forehead. "I do believe it must be time for dinner, I hear the tapping of feet in the hall. Shall we go to dinner?"

"Yes, yes, let us go to dinner." Rising, he gave Timandra his arm, and they exited his room side by side to see Colyer, Eliza, Charissa, and Delilah hurrying to the dining chamber. At Perfidious Brambles, arriving on time for dinner was a ritual.

Chapter 35

Timandra stood beside Gavin in the bedchamber they would be sharing in just over a week and stared out at the garden her father's footmen, under gardener Beamer's direction, had transformed. Finola and Audrey were busy transferring Timandra's clothing and sundry accoutrements to the east wing bedchamber. The two maids had just left to collect the last of Timandra's things, and Gavin's valet had left with his things – Gavin was returning to Kirkworth Hall until their wedding night. Finally, Timandra and Gavin were alone.

Turning from the window, Gavin gathered Timandra into his arms. "I can scarce believe I have these few moments alone with you," he said, planting a kiss on Timandra's brow.

Smiling up at Gavin, Timandra said, "It does seem like these past weeks have been whirling around like a child's spinning top." She started ticking things off on her fingers. "At least we now have our cook and scullery maid, a live-in house maid, and another for day help. We have women from the hamlet and from Fairflex scheduled to help with the wedding guests and festivities. Thank goodness for Ebba. Her knowledge of who would be dependable and honest was an immense help.

"The repairing of the corral for all the extra horses that will be pulling coaches here, as well as the new shed to shelter the horses if a rain storm happens, are completed. Our cook has worked with Grandfather's to make certain we have enough supplies to feed people, not just for the wedding, but for all the other meals. Some guests will be here for a week or even longer. Fact is, we could expect my family to arrive any day now."

Brushing a strand of hair from her brow, Timandra gazed back out the window. "I do hope Tibbs has ordered enough hay and oats. I would feel better if Hardgrove was here to do the ordering. As father's coachman, he is used to dealing with large gatherings."

"Shall I ask Uncle Phineas to have his coachman work with Tibbs," Gavin offered.

Turning back to Gavin, Timandra said, "Oh, yes, I do think that is a good idea. And I cannot believe that the D'Arcys from Hexham, other than the steward and his wife, are coming in caravans that they can sleep in. That does take the pressure off of housing them, but they must still be fed." Jumping on to another subject, Timandra said, "I am still amazed that my Uncle Kenrick is coming. And he is bringing several of his children, though his wife is not coming."

"Yes, Uncle Phineas is impressed. He is looking forward to seeing Lord Tyneford in a less formal situation than Parliament offers."

"I am sure Uncle Kenrick will use this visit to make his annual inspection of Tyneford Hall. According to Mother, Uncle Kenrick has a steward to deal with his other manors, but as Tyneford is his most productive manor, he likes to see to it himself."

Taking Timandra's hands, Gavin pulled her away from the windows. "Enough of the wedding plans for now, my dear. Do you not realize that other than our morning rides, we have not had any time alone? Just the two of us."

Nodding, Timandra withdrew her hands to place them on either side of his face. "Ye gads, but you are a gorgeous man, Gavin, and when you look at me the way you are now looking at me, my insides start turning somersaults."

"Mmmm," he said, lowering his head so his lips met hers.

His kiss was soft, and his hands reached down around to cup her buttocks and pull her against him. Pressed against him, she could feel his manhood awakening through her skirts. His desire for her stirred her own passion. She could hardly wait for their wedding night.

Gavin's mother had told her what to expect. "Though, no doubt, when your mother arrives," Emeline said, "she will give you much the same speech. Still, I but wanted you to know how such a love between a man and a woman, a love like you and Gavin share, can be the most glorious thing imaginable. There is nothing to fear."

Timandra had no fear of her wedding night. The kisses and caresses she had already enjoyed with Gavin told her she had even more to look forward to once they could share a bed. As he backed her up against the wall while nibbling her lips, she slid her hands to his shoulders and pulled him closer until his chest was firm against her breasts. She opened her lips and his tongue found hers to tantalize her even more. Her world was spinning, dancing, vibrating, and sparkling in a myriad of wondrous colors. Oh, if only the days would pass more quickly.

❦ ❦ ❦ ❦

Gavin was amazed by the constant bustle going on in all three wings of Perfidious Brambles. He had never dreamed planning a wedding could be so complicated. He could hardly wait for the wedding day to arrive so he could make Timandra his wife. He was still living on a cloud. That Timandra loved him, left him in a constant state of awe. He was eager to meet Timandra's parents but also nervous. She was an earl's daughter. He was but the son of a younger son. True, he was the heir presumptive to his uncle's barony, but the barony was only three generations old. On Timandra's mother's side, the D'Arcys had come over with the Conqueror. They were an old, highly respected family.

When Timandra had accepted his proposal, he had written to her parents, professing his love for their daughter. His mother, his uncle, and his grandfather had each also written. His uncle and grandfather included information on what they were settling on Gavin. Timandra, being of age, had not needed her parents' permission to marry Gavin, but Gavin knew she had asked their permission, and so had he. Her parents were settling one thousand pounds on Timandra and so was her Cousin Delphine, whom Timandra claimed was more like an aunt.

When Gavin had exclaimed over the large settlement from a cousin, Timandra had laughed and said, "Cousin Delphine can easily afford that and never miss it. Her grandfather had his finger in so many pies, and he made one fortune after another, and when he died, Delphine, as his only grandchild, inherited all of it. And she is the most generous person. You will love her, as I do. And she will love you, as will my parents."

Brushing aside thoughts of Timandra's family, Gavin let his thoughts linger on Timandra. She had looked so beautiful at dinner, her eyes sparkling, her cheeks still pink from their morning ride. She had re-galed Gavin's grandfather with an account of the cots that were being assembled in the undercroft below the Keep to provide beds for all the men servants, from valets to coachmen and footmen, who would be arriving with the wedding guests. The undercroft had been thoroughly cleaned and a room divider built to separate the sleeping area from the area holding the numerous supplies needed for all the guests and their servants. The fall harvests completed, men from the hamlet had been working under the carpenter's supervision for several days building the cots and then assembling them. The work would give them some extra coin for their purses before they began their grain threshing.

"I fear the mattresses will be thin," Timandra had said with a sigh. "The women in the hamlet started sewing as soon as the ticking arrived from Newcastle, but the stuffing leaves much to be desired."

"How is that?" Gavin's grandfather asked. "Is there a straw short-age?"

Laughing, Timandra said, "There is not. There is but a shortage of clean straw. Seems the sheep and cattle have been turned out in the fields after the harvesting – and, well, you can imagine what the fields are like."

"Oh, not at the table, Timmie," Eliza said. "You are spoiling my ap-petite."

"Mine, too," Delilah said, setting her spoon down next to her plate.

"Sorry," Timandra said with a giggle. "Fortunately, the women have improvised. They sent a number of the boys and girls off to the woods to collect leaves. So the mattresses have been stuffed with leaves and bits of rosemary or lavender to help sweeten them, but they will be crunchy each time someone turns over."

"Do you truly think the room across from mine will hold all the fe-male servants?" Eliza asked. The room across the corridor from Eliza's room was partially under the staircase, so with its sloping ceiling, had only ever been used for servants. It housed a couple of large beds that the women would share.

"I would think so." Timandra said. "Most maids will be sleeping in the closets off their mistresses' bedchambers. And at least, those rooms already have cots and mattresses."

And so the conversation had gone on as Timandra had covered one detail after another. Eliza and Gavin's mother and his aunt were doing what they could to help, but Gavin knew Timandra was the one who had to work out all the details. He wondered if she missed not having her mother here to help her. She had not only the wedding to arrange, but she had been busy putting together all they would need for their new home.

The nights were growing longer, the days shorter, and he knew he would soon need to start home. Just one more week and he would not be riding off to Kirkworth. He and Timandra would be making their way to their own bedchamber. He had been envisioning such a delight since before he had proposed to Timandra.

Well, all he could do for now, was hope for a kiss from his darling before he rode home. As if he had conjured her up, she slipped out of the parlor and met him in the hall. Candles burning in the sconces – a luxury Gavin's grandfather had never given in to before Timandra appeared at Perfidious Brambles – cast a dim light around the great hall.

"You look lovely in candlelight," Gavin said, gathering Timandra into his arms.

She smiled up at him. "So do you, Gavin, my love. I am still amazed that you love me."

"What nonsense. You are all I ever hoped to find in a woman. But come, give me a kiss that will keep me company on the way home."

He had no need to ask twice. She eagerly wrapped her arms around his neck and pulled him to her. Their lips met, and he felt a thrill beyond all imagination. This woman was to be his. One week. One week and he could call her his own.

When they finally pulled apart, Timandra said, "Do we ride in the morning?"

He nodded. "We do. This past month, it has seemed like the only time I get to be alone with you is when we go riding."

"Have you so quickly forgotten this afternoon in our bedchamber?" she teased.

"Nay. That is burned into my heart, but it was too brief an interlude. Your Finola returned too soon. At times, she is much too efficient."

Timandra giggled. "I will talk to her about that."

"Will you walk with me to the stables?"

"I will, let me but grab a wrap. The weather has turned chill of late."

"I will await you in the kitchen."

"Ah, I know you. You will grab a tart to snack on while riding home."

He chuckled. "You must make certain our cook gets the tart recipe."

"That is a must," Timandra said before blowing him a kiss and hurrying off to her room to grab a wrap.

Watching Timandra tripping lightly up the stairs, Gavin thought, I am one lucky man. Indeed, I am, I am.

❁ ❁ ❁ ❁

With a final wave, Timandra watched Gavin ride off before she turned back to look up at the house. She thought back to the night she and the Tilburys arrived. How frightening the dark house had appeared. It seemed to merit its name, Perfidious Brambles. Now, this house was going to be her home. And there was nothing frightening about it. She had grown to love every section of it, from its ancient keep, to its remodeled Elizabethan wing that had housed her for these past glorious and exciting months, to the modern east wing that was to be her home with the man of her dreams.

She shivered as the chill of the early October evening crept through her wrap. With a satisfied smile, she started back into the house. Perfidious Brambles, no longer a dangerous tangle of intrigue, but a protective shield, an encircling cocoon of love.

Epilogue

Early summer 1678

Timandra laughed as Gavin urged her toward the staircase. It had been a busy day, but she believed all was in readiness for their departure in the morning. "Oh, do give me another instant, Gavin, I need to speak with Finola."

"Nay, Timandra. 'Tis late, and anything you need to discuss with Finola or Perth, you can do tomorrow before we leave. I have no doubt you have all in order, and even did you not, you can be certain that between my mother and Finola, all will be well. Now, come with me, I have better things for us to be doing this last night before we take to the road."

Timandra put her hand on her husband's chest, and slanting her eyes, looked up at him. "And what might that be, my dear?"

"You continue to look at me in that manner, and I will be sweeping you off your feet and carting you up the stairs."

"Very well. Will you at least let me stop in the nursery and see that the babes are all asleep? Lucan is so excited, I fear he may have had trouble falling asleep."

"I doubt it. He was probably exhausted after bouncing all over all three wings of the house today. Toryn could not keep up with him." Toryn was the footman in charge of watching Lucan when he escaped from the nursery.

Timandra nodded in agreement. Her three-and-a-half-year-old son, who fortunately, in her opinion, favored his handsome father in looks and in coloring, from his golden hair to his brilliant blue eyes, was beyond excited. On the morrow they were headed on the long trip to Timandra's Uncle Kenrick's Walling House near Wallingford, Oxfordshire. Every four years, the D'Arcy family met for a gigantic family reunion. Kenrick D'Arcy, the Earl of Tyneford, like his father, grandfather, and great-grandfather, Oswin, who was the first to have a family gathering, continued the family reunion tradition. Timandra had no doubt it would be a huge gathering. It always was.

She was looking forward to seeing her parents and her siblings, and her new nephew. Her sister, Vivien, would be bringing her four-month-old son. At the previous reunion, four years ago, Timandra had been pregnant with Lucan. Gavin had wondered if traveling such a distance was safe for Timandra in her condition, but she would not miss seeing all her close and extended family members. Only a limited number of family members had made it to her and Gavin's wedding, and she had wanted to show off her new husband. So Gavin had given in, and they had gone to the reunion.

At this upcoming reunion, she would be showing off her son, and her one-year-old daughter, Valora. Climbing the stairs beside her husband, she wondered if she had packed enough toys to keep the children entertained on their long journey. They would be staying most nights with various friends of her father or her uncles, and would need stay only a few nights at inns. They would make a longer stay in Leicester at her Uncle Nathaniel's to rest up, then the two families would travel the remainder of the journey together.

At the top of the stairs, Timandra turned to her left to go to the nursery, but Gavin caught her wrist. "You do naught but see that the babes are sleeping. That is all. No more last minute instructions to Libby. She will have the children up and dressed in plenty time come morning."

Timandra smiled and nodded. "Yes, I just mean to check on them."

When Gavin released her wrist, she headed down the corridor to the nursery. The nurse, Libby, would be accompanying them to help take care of the children. Libby had been Charissa and Delilah's maid, but when Timandra got with child, Finola had suggested that Libby would be the perfect nurse. "Libby has had the care of her young siblings left to her for a number of years," Finola had stated. "And no matter how hard she tries, Libby is not good with hair, and her stitches, I fear, will never be more than adequate. But I have seen her with children, and they love her, and she loves them."

"Well, I will consider it" Timandra had said. "But that will mean I need to find not just a new maid for me, for you cannot continue forever as my maid and the housekeeper, Finola, but I must then find a maid to serve Charissa and Delilah."

"Well, now, milady. I am after having an idea about that."

Timandra looked up from her writing desk to study Finola. Still acting as Timandra's maid, Finola had just brought up one of Timandra's newly washed and pressed gowns and was putting it into the armoire. "So what is your idea?" Timandra asked.

Straightening and meeting Timandra's gaze, Finola said, "Well, milady, you may have noticed that Perth is sweet on me."

Chuckling at Finola's phrasing, Timandra nodded. "Yes, I think he has been for a long time. I thought you might also be sweet on him."

"Oh, yes, milady, I am."

"Yet, you have not decided to get married?"

"Well, that is part of the solution I am after having. Mistresses Charissa and Delilah are old enough now, they should each be having their own maids. And your coachman is still in need of another groomsman to train as his postillion, since the previous postillion left, him thinking it is too lonely here and wanting to be back in the city. So Hawkins needs someone good with horses. Not afraid of them. And you could be doing with another footman, too, milady."

Timandra tilted her head to the side. "I suppose you have a solution to all these needs?"

"Indeed, I have, milady." Finola fairly danced on her toes. "And if you are agreeing to it, then Perth and I can be getting married. He is a good man."

"Yes, I know Perth is a good man. But how does filling all the positions make it possible for you to marry Perth?"

Finola looked pleadingly at Timandra. "All the positions could be filled by my siblings, milady. When they have work, good work, I will no longer be needing to send my wages home. Then Perth and I can be getting married."

Timandra put her hands together and shook her head sympathetically. "I knew you always sent your wages home, but I never gave it any real thought. Have you a large family? Do they need help financially? You could have asked me to help."

"Nay, milady, 'twould not be right to be asking you for more than I earn. 'Twas Cromwell who did us in. My father was a merchant, but he sided with the King, and like many other Irishmen, Father lost everything. We were forced out of Waterford and made to move to Galway with naught but our clothes and a few furnishings." She shook her head. "But now, about my siblings."

Obviously, Finola had no wish to continue discussing the woes of her family. Fact was, Finola had never talked about her family, and Timandra had never questioned her, so she was surprised to learn of Finola's siblings.

Before Timandra could say anything, Finola launched into a description of her siblings. "First there is Toryn. He is twenty-one, and tall and handsome. He would be making a good footman. Then comes Crevan. He is eighteen, near to nineteen. And he has a way with the horses. Loves them he does. He is smaller. Not big like Toryn. But strong. He can handle the horses. Then come my twin sisters, Brighid and Moyna. The twins are just turned sixteen, but they are bright girls. And mother taught them to sew as she taught me. I know them to be fast learners. 'Twould be taking Libby and me no time to be teaching them what they need be doing to help the young mistresses.

"And could you but be advancing the fare to bring them here, they would be working for but their room and board until they had paid back their fare."

Timandra had agreed to Finola's plans, and after a couple of months, Finola's siblings had arrived in Newcastle, where Tombs met them and brought them to Perfidious Brambles. Timandra had hoped all would go smoothly, and that the new arrivals would be as Finola had promised, but she had determined, were they not, she would find some kind of employment for Finola's siblings. However, the four siblings could not have been more perfect. And shortly after their arrival, Finola and Perth were married.

Peeking into the nursery, Timandra saw her two cherubs were sleeping soundly. But Finola's two-year-old, who now shared the nursery, was lying on her cot, her eyes wide open. Alma was a miniature of her pretty, dark-haired, dark-eyed mother. And just as full of energy. "Oh, milady," Libby said. "I thought you might pop by. I think all is ready for tomorrow." She looked over at Alma and frowned. "Only, I cannot

276

get that one to go to sleep. She keeps saying she wants to go with us."

"Let me talk to her for a moment," Timandra said. "Has her mother been up to say goodnight to her yet?"

"She has, and she promised Alma she would let her go play with Mistress Colyer's little girl tomorrow if she went to sleep like a good girl. So Alma obediently closed her eyes, but the moment Finola left, those eyes popped back open."

Charissa had now been married to Eustace Colyer for three years. They lived in the cottage tucked in amongst the trees behind the manor house. They had married shortly after Charissa's eighteenth birthday, and a year later, Charissa had presented Seldon's estate steward with a beautiful little girl but a couple of months before Finola had Alma. Sitting on the edge of Alma's cot, Timandra caught the little girl's hands in hers.

"Alma, dear, you are such a sweet, dear girl, do you really wish to make your dear mother cry?"

Alma's eyes widened, though Timandra wondered how they could get any larger. "Mother cries?"

"She would if you were to go with us and leave her."

"She goes, too."

Timandra shook her head. "Then your dear father would cry. He loves you and your mother so much. And you know he cannot go because he must take care of the house."

Alma frowned. Timandra could almost see the thoughts rampaging around in the little girl's head. Shaking her head, Alma said in a low sad tone, "I no go."

Timandra patted her hands. "You are a wise and loving little girl. And just think, while Lucan and Valora are gone, you will be staying on the trundle bed in your mother and father's room. And I think your mother will be very pleased to let you play with Accalia every day. Now, do you think you might go to sleep so Libby can go to her bed?"

Nodding solemnly, Alma said, "I sleep now."

"Good girl," Timandra said, and rising, she looked over at Libby who mouthed a thank you. Hopefully the little night owl would soon be asleep.

With that settled, Timandra headed back to her bedchamber. She loved living in the east wing of Perfidious Brambles. It was like having their own house, but they were close enough to the west wing to visit with Gavin's grandfather and mother whenever they wished. Seldon was now seventy-eight years old, and, though still straight-shouldered, he moved more slowly. Timandra knew he adored Lucan and would miss his great-grandson while they were gone. Gavin's mother had been a great help to Timandra when she gave birth to her children. Emeline had also helped with Finola's and Charissa's deliveries.

With Herman home from the school he was attending in Newcastle, the house was again ringing with boyish laughter. Herman had attended the school Seldon had paid to be built on the disputed property that had for so many generations caused conflict with the Kirkworths for but one year before he turned twelve and was sent off to boarding school. Bennet had then been left on his own. However, he had many friends in the hamlet, so his school days, with Knolles as the teacher, had given him plenty of companionship. Knolles and Ebba Hemphill had married once a house was built near the school. Ebba helped teach the younger children and the girls. The Knolles had no babies yet. Ebba had lost their first babe, but she was expecting again, and Gavin's mother seemed to think she would carry the child to term this time.

The following autumn would be much quieter in the west wing as Bennet would be joining his brother at the Newcastle school. Herman had one more year there, and he would be off to Cambridge. Delilah would be the only one of Eliza's siblings still living full time at the manor. She was nineteen, and she and Andrew Althouse were still enamored of each other. They carried on a constant correspondence, and Andrew visited at every opportunity. As Seldon was providing Delilah with a sizable dowry, as he had done with Eliza and Charissa, the Althouses found no fault with their son's choice of a future mate. Andrew had one year left to finish at Cambridge, and then he was expected to spend at least one year at one of the inn's of court in London, but everyone expected Andrew and Delilah to become betrothed before the young future baronet left for London.

Eliza, having married Bartley Severin a month after her year of mourning ended, was happily ensconced in a small house in Newcastle, but she and her two-year-old son visited often, and whenever Severin had to go to London to consult with the main office, she always came to stay at Perfidious Brambles. And whenever Timandra and Gavin went to Newcastle for shopping or just to enjoy the entertainments offered in the city, they stayed with the Severins.

Upon entering her bedchamber, Timandra found her maid, Stella, had laid out her nightshift and robe and had turned back the bed coverings. "Mister Merritt is in his closet, milady," Stella said. "Would you have me help you ready for bed?"

"Yes, Stella, thank you." Timandra was pleased with her maid. The young woman had been with her for four years now, and they were comfortable with each other. Timandra knew she had to thank Ebba for finding her the maid. Ebba, who knew everyone in Fairflex, had recommended Stella. Stella had been serving as maid to an elderly woman who had taken to her bed and needed a different type of help than Stella could provide, so Stella had needed the job. Not beautiful, Stella would be considered plain by many, but she had a bright smile and was handy with her needle and always at the ready. Timandra considered her a treasure.

Timandra had just settled into bed, and Stella had entered her closet when Gavin emerged from his. His eyes lit up when he saw Timandra. "Ah, you kept your word. Here you are, my love. I had feared I might have to go in search of you."

Timandra laughed. "Nay, my dear husband. You promised me certain delights here in our bedchamber, and I was not about to miss them. Shed your robe and join me."

"I thought you would never ask," he said with a chuckle and blew out the candle on his side of the bed. The draperies were open to let in the moonlight, so the room was not in absolute darkness. When he stripped off his robe and pulled his nightshirt off over his head, Timandra was able to admire her husband's fine figure before he crawled into bed with her.

In a matter of moments, Gavin had Timandra's nightshift pulled off over her head, and the two of them were wrapped in each other's arms. Five years of marriage had not dimmed their desires. If anything, their love had grown more intense. They had each learned how to pleasure one another, and both wanted nothing so much as to bring continual joy to their lovemaking. With whispered words of endearment, they joined, and, becoming as one, they rose to the heights of heaven, sharing a blissful love found and forged at Perfidious Brambles.

The End

Look for my Next Novel!

An Unexpected Treasure
By Celia Martin

Prologue

Derbyshire, England 1681

Lady Flavia D'Arcy groaned as the coach hit yet another rut in the poorly maintained road. Her traveling companion, the dove-like Carola Mead, echoed her groan. Across from Flavia, her personal maid, Gertrude, widened her large blue eyes, crinkled her perky nose, and clamped her prominent front teeth down over her lower lip. The ride was not only rough, it was boring. They had little they could do but sleep, yet sleep was made near impossible by all the bumps. If her parents had sent the better coach to retrieve her from Tuftwick Hall, she would not be suffering as much. Brushing a curl of her light brown hair off her cheek, she could well imagine she would be black and blue by the time she arrived at her home, Whimbrel Hall.

The muslin shades were drawn to keep the dust out, but Flavia still felt her face, eyes, and tongue were coated in grit. She envied her brother, Ewen, and his friends. Riding their horses, they were out in the fresh air, not cooped up in a moving box. Ewen, his brown eyes, so like her own, had glistened with mirth when he joked she could be like her cousin, Selena, and ride astride. That had set his friends to laughing. The memory of that quip brought her thoughts back around to Selena. Pooh! She had worked so hard to rid herself, at least temporarily, of thoughts of her annoying cousin. Thinking of Selena made her even more miserable.

Why her mother believed she would be able to have any influence on Selena was beyond Flavia's comprehension. No one had any influence on Selena. Selena had influence on everyone else. Flavia had not a doubt in the world that Selena would lead her into some kind of trouble. Oh, why, oh, why could her mother not have let her go to London with her Aunt Phillida and her cousin, Elizabeth, to find a husband? But no, her mother said she was too young. Well, she was eighteen, after all. Plenty old enough to marry. Her mother had married her first husband when she was but fifteen and had her first child by the time she was sixteen.

Gads, but she would be glad when they reached their evening's destination. Her father had arranged for them to stay each night with a friend or acquaintance of his. But for their noon meals, they were forced to stop at village inns. The food was seldom appealing, but at least sitting down to the table was a respite from the pounding she was receiving in the coach.

She felt sorry for Carola Mead. Carola had traveled in this hideous coach all the way from Whimbrel Hall to collect Flavia, and now the poor, unassuming dear was having to travel back over the same bumpy road. Carola was a distant cousin of her mother. As Carola had no immediate family or means of support, Flavia's mother had taken her in, given her a home, and treated her as a member of the family. Flavia believed Carola, in order to show her gratitude, often volunteered for egregious tasks no one else wanted to do. This had to be one of those tasks. And Carola was no younger than Flavia's mother who was now in her mid-fifties.

Flavia was grateful she was at least to be allowed a week's visit with her two half-brothers who had estates outside the town of Derby. Their wives would coddle her and make over her and understand all she had endured on this wretched journey. When Aunt Phillida and Elizabeth left for London, Flavia had been sent to stay with Aunt Phillida's sister-in-law, Lady Tuftwick. That dear lady had also coddled her, and Flavia had loved her time at Tuftwick Hall. She had enjoyed flirting with Lady Tuftwick's two sons, Algernon, and Doran, when he was home from school on holiday, and she had treated Lady Tuftwick's thirteen-year-old daughter, Lexina, like a sister.

Then came the letter from her mother telling her she was being sent for so she could help turn Selena from a hoyden into a lady. Impossible!

Ewen knew it was impossible, but he admitted, he liked Selena the way she was.

"Not that anyone with any sense would want to marry her," he proclaimed to his friends.

"I found her a regular pixie, I did," Ansel Yardley said. He had met Selena four weeks earlier at Crossly Oaks, Flavia's half-brother's manor in Derbyshire. "Right pretty, too," he added.

"True enough. A bright spirit, she is," Ewen agreed, "but would you want your wife riding astride? Would you want her ignoring her duties because she is off riding or walking or bringing home stray animals or people from who knows where. She does that and a lot more. Animals and children love her. They follow her about like she was some kind of Pied Piper."

Algernon LaBree chuckled. "I look forward to meeting her. She sounds amusing."

"Amusing, yes. One of the fellows, but not wife material, I swear to you," Ewen said.

"She has a good portion coming to her," Yardley said. "A manor in Lincolnshire, am I not mistaken."

"Aye, that she has. But I will say no more on the subject. Are any of you foolish enough to fall in love with Selena, 'tis your misfortune. You have all been warned."

Ewen's companions had laughed at his sally, but Flavia could find nothing humorous about the subject. Her mother had asked Ewen to bring a couple of his friends to Rotherby that Selena could practice being more genteel around gentlemen. Flavia guessed her mother might also have hopes Selena might find a mate. But here was Ewen, warning them off. Not that she could blame him. They were his friends, and he could not wish them tied to Selena.

Flavia liked all three of the Ewen's friends. Ansel Yardley was the funniest. When he laughed, which was often, his dark eyes fairly twinkled. He had a strong chin and firm mouth, but his grin was so infectious, she doubted he could ever seem stern. Algernon LaBree was the most handsome of her brother's new friends with his bright blue eyes, dark hair, and Greek god facial features. Though ever courteous, he was a flirt, and Flavia was drawn to him. She could see herself falling in love with him did she not ever so often conjure up the fleeting image of Ewen's childhood friend and their neighbor, Orland Darnell. She wondered if Orland might also be invited to Rotherby to help with Selena's civilizing lessons. She hoped he would be.

Silvester Preston, Yardley's cousin, was intriguing in that he seemed always to be studying everyone from under his lowered eyelids. His eyes were a light-colored hazel, almost a pale green, and his dark hair was incredibly thick. His thin, aquiline nose gave him an aristocratic appearance though he was but the son of a baronet. While Carola rested for a week after her arrival at Tuftwick Hall, Yardley and Ewen rode to Nantwich in Cheshire to collect Preston because Yardley was certain his cousin would be delighted to join them.

"He is ever bored," Yardley proclaimed, "and eager to escape his mother, my Aunt Arcadia. She wants him to marry and produce a son, an heir to the baronetcy. If she thinks he is going to meet a potential mate, she will pack him off herself." And so Preston, the future Baronet of Britteridge, had joined them, but Flavia was not certain Preston was at all interested in finding a mate. Fact was, from snippets of conversation she had overheard, but should not have, she believed he fancied himself a dallier, in no hurry to limit himself to one woman.

Another bump, another pair of groans. Wretched road. None of the counties maintained their highways as they should, though her father swore they were far superior to what they used to be, especially the new toll roads that had been built. Settling back against the cushioned seat, Flavia wished it was plusher. Was she ever to ride in this coach again, she would be certain to provide herself with more cushions.

Closing her eyes, she tried to sleep, but again, Selena swam through her mind. She wondered what Selena would do that would get her into trouble and prove to her mother that she was not as grown up as she considered herself. She wished she was stronger willed. Wished she could say no to Selena, but Selena had a way of making everything sound or appear reasonable. Oh, well, she might as well just face up to it, Selena meant trouble.

Chapter 1

Leicestershire, England – Whimbrel Hall

Rowena D'Arcy, Lady Rotherby, lightly drummed her fingers on the small table beside her cushioned chair. Her drumming caught her husband's attention.

Next to her in a matching armchair, Nathaniel D'Arcy, Lord Rotherby, asked, "All right, Row, what is troubling you?"

"Look at her, Nate," she said, nodding to the young woman sitting in the window seat across the parlor. A book rested in the girl's lap, yet she did naught but stare out the window at the fading night sky. "She has done nothing but mope since she arrived here. Again this evening, she barely touched her supper, nor her dinner earlier today. And that is not like Selena. In all the years I have known the child, she has always had a more than hardy appetite. But now, in the three weeks she has been here, she is losing weight. The maid who is seeing to her says does she lose more weight, she will have to take in some of her gowns."

"I would say our Selena is a very unhappy young woman," Nate answered.

Frowning, Rowena turned to him. "I can see that, Nate. 'Tis what I am to do about it that puzzles me. Her dear mother sends Selena to me, trusting me to turn her into a lady, and all I have done is make her sick. How will it look to Angelica if I must send her daughter back to her ill and looking like a rail?"

"Selena cares not for her lessons?"

"She says, could she but understand the need to learn the things I am attempting to teach her, she might be better able to apply herself, but she can see no reason to learn what she needs to learn about how to run a home. She cannot understand why she cannot have a competent housekeeper or steward manage the running of her house."

"And is there a reason she cannot?"

Rowena rolled her eyes sideways at her husband. "We have a wonderful housekeeper as well as a butler and a steward, but which one should I allow to do the seating arrangement for a formal dinner? Which one would you like to choose the fabrics for your next breeches or coats? Which one should have chosen the furnishings for our bedchambers? Or for any of the rooms in the house? Yes, the butler keeps order and gives the footmen their duties. He sees we are appropriately served at our meals. But he informs me," she stressed the me, "when your wine supply is running low and it must be replenished by ordering from France. Sugar, spices, salt, pepper, any number of items must be ordered in a timely fashion, and the correct amount must be ordered or we will run out of the items."

Her husband tried to interrupt her by agreeing she had a point, but Rowena would not be stopped. "Yes, our steward sees our meat is cured and stored, he works with the gamekeeper who supplies our game and fish. And he works with the head of our dairy and our brew-house and insures we have the wood or coal we need for fires in our rooms and for the kitchen. And he keeps the books, but I go over them with him on a weekly basis. You see them but once a month. I know when we can afford special treats, a new gown for Flavia or coat for Ewen.

"And though our housekeeper is in charge of directing the maids ..."

"Enough!" Nate said, his voice raised to a measure Selena turned to look at him. He lowered his voice. "Enough, my dear. You have convinced me."

"I have not told you the half of it."

His blue-green eyes danced, and the smile Rowena loved spread across his face. "Of that I have no doubt. But I think, do you believe you can teach these things to Selena, you will be sadly disappointed. The question to ask is, do these things that matter to us, matter to Selena."

Rowena returned her gaze to her niece. With her dark hair and blue-green eyes, Selena looked more like Rowena's husband than his own children did. Both their children looked like her with their brown hair and brown eyes. Selena, on the other hand, had the typical D'Arcy coloring, and a straight nose, high cheekbones, and a firm chin. The golden tan of her skin was fading slightly as Rowena had the girl spending most of her time indoors with various training activities. Slowly shaking her head, Rowena wondered if her husband could be right. Was any attempt to convince Selena of the importance of learning to care for a house and home useless.

Just this morning she had been trying to teach Selena how to properly make a bed. "But why must I know how to make a bed?" Selena asked. "The maid will do it as she does now."

"You need to know how so that you may show a new maid how to do it."

"Why would not the housekeeper or another of the maids show her?"

"Mayhap the housekeeper is ill, and you have guests coming. All your maids are busy cleaning, and the new maid is to make the beds."

"I would simply tell the new maid to do the cleaning. Surely I would not have hired a maid who had no knowledge of cleaning, and the old maid could then make the beds. Mother never has to show maids how to make beds. Of course, she cannot. So if a new maid needs training, the housekeeper or Mother's maid, Esmeralda, trains them."

Selena was right about that. Due to a terrible accident when her coach overturned, Angelica D'Arcy, Lady Rygate, was left paralyzed from the waist down. Confined to a chair or her bed, the lovely woman had been unable to give Selena the guidance she needed in her early years. Consequently, Selena's father, doting on his daughter, spoiled her and allowed her to run wild with her four brothers. Selena had even shared her brothers' tutors. Lord Rygate had kept all his children at home in their youth. He had not sent any away to foster homes or to schools until the boys were old enough to be sent to Oxford.

What training Selena did receive in proper decorum came primarily from her father or her mother's devoted personal maid. Selena could dress appropriately when forced to do so, she could dance, could sit at a table and not embarrass herself with unladylike behavior, but that was about it. She could not sew a stitch, she could not plan a meal or a social gathering. Oh, she could curry a horse or train a dog to hunt, but she had no idea how to insure a table was properly set or in what order the dishes or wines should be served.

"Mayhap you could work out a compromise with our unhappy lass," Nate said, interrupting his wife's thoughts.

Rowena turned to him. "What might you suggest?"

"Well, at present, Selena is allowed to go riding in the morning before she breaks her fast. That means, if she wants that treat, she must rise early, which our girl hates doing. She does it, though, because she loves her horse and loves to ride. Then the remainder of the day, she is locked into activities with you that to her seem senseless."

Nodding, Rowena admitted all her husband said was correct.

"Suppose you limit her lessons to just the mornings. Then, after dinner, the afternoons can be hers to use as she pleases. To take walks, to read, maybe take her rides does she choose not to get up so early in the morning." He held up a hand as Rowena started to interrupt him. "These new privileges would be contingent upon her willingness to learn the lessons you are attempting to teach her. Does she work hard and cooperate in learning her lessons, she has her freedom in the afternoons."

Rowena eyed her husband from under lowered lids. "Nate, my love, that might just work. I know you think does a man love Selena, he should love her as she is, but that would not be fair to either of them. A man needs his wife to properly run his home."

"That may be true, but Selena need not marry. She will someday inherit a very nice estate, so she will never be destitute. Her brothers love her. She will always be welcome in their homes. Does she not find a mate, would it be so terrible?"

Picking up her husband's hand from the armrest of his chair, she placed it on her cheek. "Would you have her miss the joy that we experience every day? For Selena not to know love?" Rowena shook her head. "That would be sad. That is why her mother asked me to train her to be a lady. Angelica and Ranulf know the kind of love we know. Can you wonder Angelica wants that for her daughter?"

"Not to know a true love would be sad. But I am not certain it is worth changing Selena. She has a way about her that delights children. And the way animals take to her is uncanny. Should she lose that luster, that joy of living that has always encompassed her ..." He shrugged.

"Well, I shall think about your suggestion. Could be it would produce results. It could well be worth trying, anyway."

Biography

Celia Martin is a former Social Studies/English teacher. Her love of history dates back to her earliest memories when she sat enthralled as her grandparents recounted tales of their past. As a child, she delighted in the make-believe games that she played with her siblings and friends, but as she grew up and had to put aside the games, she found she could not set aside her imagination. So, Celia took up writing stories for her own entertainment.

She is an avid reader. She loves getting lost in a romance, but also enjoys good mysteries, exciting adventure stories, and fact-loaded historical documentaries. When her husband retired and they moved from California to the glorious Kitsap Peninsula in the state of Washington, she was able to begin a full-fledged writing career. And has never been happier.

When not engaged in writing, Celia enjoys travel, keeping fit, and listening to a variety of different music styles.

Visit my web site at:
cmartinbooks.kitsappublishing.com